THE PECOS UNDERTAKER

Stark & Buchanan Book 1

MEL ODOM

WOLFPACK PUBLISHING
— EST 2013 —

WOLFPACK
PUBLISHING
— EST 2013 —

Copyright © 2020 (as revised) Mel Odom
Paperback Edition

Published in the United States by Wolfpack Publishing, Las Vegas

Wolfpack Publishing
6032 Wheat Penny Avenue
Las Vegas, NV 89122

wolfpackpublishing.com

Paperback ISBN: 978-1-64734-030-8
eBook ISBN: 978-1-64734-029-2

THE PECOS
UNDERTAKER

1

"There comes trouble."

I remember Mister Henson saying that clearly because it was one of the last things he ever said.

He was talking about Angel Blunt and his gang. They were riding up the hill to where we were digging a grave in the Sunflower Cemetery. The grave was for Missus Louise Mead, who had been the organ player down at the First Baptist Church. The heat was still enough that the riders looked blurry, like a mirage out on the desert.

I didn't recognize any of the men, but I tensed up because Mister Henson seemed on edge pretty quick when he saw them. I looked around, wondering if there was anyone else there at the cemetery, because folks visited their loved ones, but it was just me and Mister Henson among the tombstones and grave markers.

"What's wrong, Mister Henson?" I gripped the shovel handle I was holding a little tighter. I was nineteen, raw-boned, and carried a chip on my shoulder so I was always ready for a fight. I got into scrapes with local toughs over my undertaking apprenticeship with Mister Henson, and sometimes I fought over a girl. Mostly the girls were just teases, though, using me to make their boyfriends jealous. None of them wanted me, not knowing I handled dead folks pretty regularly.

Mister Henson had been a father to me for the last five

years even though he had no blood invested. I'd just been an orphan he'd taken in when no one else would. I'd have probably died shortly after my parents had because I had no family. Or maybe I'd have been sent to an orphanage, if Marshal Buchanan could have gotten a church to donate the price of a train ticket. Instead, Mister Henson had buried my folks, taken me in, and taught me a trade.

It was 1884 then, and I was over twenty years too late to ride for the Pony Express, which I had dreamed about doing after I'd learned about it as a child.

Mister Henson was a slight built man. He'd looked bigger when I was twelve, but I'd grown bigger than him pretty quickly. He wore his iron gray hair long and a big, thick beard that he cut himself. Normally he dressed in what we were wearing then, a shirt and overalls that we'd mended ourselves. He had a black suit for when he was selling caskets in his funeral home. I had one too.

An old knife scar split Mister Henson's right eyebrow and trailed down his right cheek almost to his earlobe. He never once mentioned how or where he'd gotten that scar, but it was old when I went to live with him. He was sixty when he'd taken me in nine years ago, a man living alone and comfortable with himself.

I'd made his life challenging even though I hadn't meant to. I'd wanted to grow up fast, and he'd wanted me to grow up right. We'd argued and fought, but he'd remained steadfast and I'd loved him more than I ever had my father who had been a mean drunk.

Seeing those men coming, I started to climb up out of that grave.

"Just you sit tight, Charlie," Mister Henson told me in that calm voice he used when folks came to look at the caskets we built after a loved one had passed on. He'd used that voice with me while we were burying my folks. "Let me handle this."

"Yes sir." I went back to shoveling because I knew the sooner we finished up, the sooner we'd get to supper. Miss Abbie, Mister Henson's lady friend of the past few weeks, was bringing over fried chicken and fixings when we got back. I was looking forward to that because Miss Abbie could fry chicken something fierce.

Mister Henson stood beside the grave and took out his makings from his shirt pocket. Blunt and his men were riding slow, so Mister Henson had time to tap a line of tobacco into a rolling paper, twist it up, and flick a thumbnail to a match to light up. He breathed out a cloud of smoke as Blunt and his men reined up.

"Evening," Mister Henson said.

"Evenin', undertaker." Angel Blunt crossed his hands on his pommel and leaned forward in the saddle. Leather creaked.

He was a dapper man, dressed nice with a black suit coat, not a jacket, and a dark red bow tie over a shirt that had once been white. But he was covered in road dust, like he'd come a far ways and had traveled hard. His blond hair was a little long but I could tell he kept it groomed. The same went for the Van Dyke beard he wore. He had a nice smile, the kind a lot of women would like, and blue eyes that burned like cold fire. Even with the threat of violence clinging to him, he looked like a man who would like a good joke.

My attention went instantly to the holster he wore. It was a thing of beauty, Spanish leather with inlaid silver. A man who favored such things would never forget it. He carried a blued pistol like nothing I'd ever seen. It was smaller than the Single Action Army .45s, Smith & Wesson Model 3s, and .36 Navy Colts I'd seen. It was sleek and deadly, and the grips were polished ivory with an Ace of Diamonds engraved on them.

"My name," the blond man said, "is Angel Blunt. I think you know me."

"I've heard of you," Mister Henson said. "Lots of folks around here have heard of you."

"You're a hard man to find," Blunt said.

I was a little scared. I'd heard of Angelo Blunt. All of Reeves County knew the name. As far as I knew, Blunt had never come to Pecos. The Texas and Pacific railroad passed there on its way to somewhere else, but no one had ever robbed the train in Pecos.

Of course, the talk in town was that Jay Gould, one of the rich robber barons out of New York and the man who had leased the railroad, was going to change things. So I was thinking maybe there was something about the railroad that would bring Blunt to Pecos. Even so, there wasn't much in all of Reeves County that would interest a career criminal, which was what I'd heard Blunt called in the newspapers.

I had no idea what Blunt wanted with Mister Henson, but I could tell there was an edge between them the same way there was between a fox and a coon, only I didn't know which was which.

"It's been a long time, Terry," Blunt said. "It took me a minute to recognize you. Salsa Jack said you'd changed. Got old."

Terry hadn't ever been a name I'd heard Mister Henson called. He was John Peter Henson to everyone who called him by his right name.

2

Mister Henson didn't correct Blunt about his name. Instead, Mister Henson breathed out another stream of smoke and said, "It's not been long enough from where I'm sitting."

Blunt laughed a little. "I can see how you might think that."

"The last I heard, you were in prison out in Jefferson City for killing that bank guard," Mister Henson said, getting right to it and surprising me.

Blunt shrugged, like mentioning that he was a criminal and a murderer was all no big deal. "I was for a little while, but the amenities there aren't what I found acceptable. So I took my leave. I've done a few things that haven't shown up in the papers yet. Or maybe they never will. If nobody finds the bodies." He smiled again, and those blue eyes sparkled. "You're not the only one that's gotten good at burying folks, Terry."

His men laughed.

"The work is steady," Mister Henson said. "Folks ain't found a way out of dying."

Blunt laughed at that. "I suppose they haven't."

I was still shoveling, but I'd definitely slowed down production. I couldn't help myself.

"Did you know that the prison in Jefferson City was the first one built that is west of the Mississippi?" Blunt asked.

"I did not," Mister Henson said.

"It was, and you'd think they would have done a better job of it."

"You might mention that in a letter to them."

"Is this your boy?" Blunt glanced at me for the first time.

Sickness twisted in my guts the way it had when I'd been helping dig out a well that we hadn't known was infested with cottonmouth snakes until they were in the water with me. I'd barely gotten out of there ahead of the snakes, and I still dreamed about that sometimes.

"No," Mister Henson said. "He's just a local boy I hired to help me with this grave."

I have to admit, his answer hurt me some. We hadn't talked about exactly where things stood between us, but I'd always felt Mister Henson cared about me a lot. As far as I knew, he hadn't had any children and I figured I was about as close as he had come to having one.

Mister Henson turned to me. "Charlie, why don't you go on home? I'll pay you tomorrow for the work you've done today."

I stood and stared at Mister Henson for a moment. First of all because I had no home other than his house, and second because the job wasn't done. We still had two feet to dig and Mister Henson might have done it himself, but it was a lot of work for one man. Besides, I was there to do most of the digging.

"No," Blunt said in a quiet manner that suddenly seemed even more threatening. "You stay right where you are, Charlie. Right there in that grave."

Fear went into Mister Henson then, tightened him up and made him look small. I had to look twice to recognize it because I had never seen it in him before, though I had seen it in a lot of other people when they came to buy a casket for a loved one. Funerals made folks think about things they normally didn't give much concern to, about losing someone and about the fact they would one day die too.

I didn't know what to do, so I stood there and waited for Mister Henson to tell me.

"The boy doesn't have anything to do with what's between us," Mister Henson said. "Leave him be."

Blunt just smiled again, and there wasn't anything pleasant about his expression.

"Charlie," Mister Henson said, "you go on and do what I told you."

I started to climb out of the grave and had just about cleared it when Blunt drew that pistol of his so fast if I'd blinked I would have missed it. He fired twice just by pulling the trigger, something I'd never seen before except when one of the Pinkerton detectives who had come through had killed a rattler when he was getting off the train. The detective carried a Beaumont-Adams double-action revolver. All of the pistols I'd shot were single-action and you had to pull the hammer back each time before firing.

Whatever that pistol was that Blunt carried, it was double-action too.

His first shot broke the shovel handle I had hold of and the second took my hat off my head.

I froze where I was, and I'd never felt so scared in a grave before. None of them I'd dug had ever before felt so permanent.

"The boy stays," Blunt declared, "until we've finished our conversation." He didn't put the pistol away, just left it hanging there.

"You're wasting your time, Angelo," Mister Henson said.

The rumor was that Blunt had some Mex blood in him. I couldn't see it, but the name was something you'd usually hear only among Mexicans.

"Nobody calls me by that name," Blunt said.

Mister Henson moved slowly and kept his hands out from his body. He didn't carry any weapons, but I guessed maybe I was the only one certain of that. "I told you the last time you found me that there wasn't no gold. You're chasing a lie."

Blunt shook his head. "You know, the last time you told me that, I believed you. That's why I left you alone. Then, while I was in prison, I met a man who rode with you and my father down in Mexico. He said El Presidente Benito Juárez loaded up gold he intended to feather his nest with before he got ousted from Mexico City when the French invaded. You and my father masterminded the robbery of the gold shipment and made off with it. Are you going to tell me that's a lie?"

Mister Henson hesitated, and I thought for a minute Blunt was going to kill him.

Instead, Blunt pointed his pistol at me and fired.

3

My left leg went out from under me like it had been struck with an ax handle. I toppled into the grave and fell on my back. Somebody was screaming in the grave, and it took a minute for me to realize it was me doing the screaming.

Blunt looked down at me over the pistol barrel. "Shut it," he ordered.

Mister Henson stepped toward the grave and I was hoping he was coming to help me. I felt the blood pumping out of me and my hand came away covered with it.

"If you let that boy distract you," Blunt said, "I'll put a bullet through his head so you can focus on me."

Fear and hurt filled Mister Henson's face as he looked at me. "I'm sorry, Charlie."

"Now you," Blunt said, addressing me again, "shut it."

I quieted, but it was hard. It felt like somebody had set my leg on fire. Blood spread over the denim material of my overalls at my thigh. Shaking, trying hard to think even though it felt like somebody had stuffed my head full of cotton, I took my neckerchief off. It was still damp with sweat from around my neck, but I tied it around my leg to stanch the blood.

I was scared then, more scared than when my pa used to come back from the saloon and beat on me and my ma. More scared than I'd been when I heard Ma scream in pain that last night and the gunshot ring out only a short time later.

"I don't have a lot of time, Terry," Blunt said. "We stuck up a bank in El Paso and didn't do a good job of it. We got some money, but we also have a posse on our trail. The banker we took the money from doesn't care if he gets it back now. He wants my head on a pike."

Even as hurting and as scared as I was, I wanted to laugh at the idea of Blunt's head on a fish. That didn't make sense to me at all. Then I remembered that a pike was also a spear. I guessed getting shot interfered with me thinking straight.

"I ran across Salsa Jack over in Las Cruces in the New Mexico Territory last year," Blunt went on. "He was living with the Mescalero Apache when I found him. He was some kind of healer or doctor, but he'd gone native."

"I should made sure he was dead when I had the chance," Mister Henson said, and I'd never heard him say a bad thing about anybody.

Blunt laughed at that. "You probably should have."

I held on tight to the neckerchief and kept pressure on. The blood seemed like it was slowing, but I still had no idea how I was going to get out of that grave.

"I was a Regulator then, fighting in the Lincoln County War." Blunt looked proud of himself. "John Chisum himself hired me, and I swapped lead with the Seven Rivers Warriors before the smoke settled on that imbroglio." He shook his head. "But, like I said, while I was out there, I crossed paths with Salsa Jack. You know what he told me?"

"He lied, Angelo. There's no gold. It was just a story your pa liked to tell when he was drunk. And he was drunk quite often, as I recall."

"Salsa Jack told me he was with you and my pa when you took the gold off that train. He said you couldn't get it out of the country at the time because of all the confusion going on between the French and the Mexicans, but that the gold was still there."

Mister Henson didn't say anything.

"The last time you and I talked," Blunt said, "I believed you when you said there was no gold. But Salsa

Jack seemed pretty adamant about it. He ended up blinded in that shootout you had getting out of Mexico, you know. And he lost a leg after you shot him and it turned septic. Still, he was lucky. The Mescalero Apache believe a blind man has special powers. That he can see things most normal people can't. I don't hold with any of that myself." He paused. "But I do believe Salsa Jack knows about the gold. I told him if I found the gold, I'd cut him in for a share. He's the one that told me you were an undertaker here, and had been for years. You didn't leave any friends behind in New Mexico Territory when you quit it."

Calm as he could, Mister Henson turned to me and looked sorrowful. "I'm sorry I got you caught up in this, Charlie. You're a good boy. You don't deserve any of this."

I wanted to cry. It sounded like he was giving up, and I didn't understand why. I couldn't understand how I could know him for as long as I did, work with him every day, and somehow not know him at all.

"The problem is," Mister Henson said calmly, "Angelo is going to kill us whether I tell him or not. So I'm not going to tell him. I want you to know I'll die with you."

I didn't want to die, but I couldn't open my mouth and tell him that because I couldn't speak, and before I had a chance anyway, Blunt was firing again.

Two bullets shattered Mister Henson's knees and he fell beside the grave. Fresh-turned dirt slid into the hole over me and formed a cloud of dust that choked me down for a minute. I was crying and dirt got in my eyes. Mister Henson screamed in pain above me and I watched him trying to pull himself up.

"You're going to talk," Blunt said. He motioned to his men and two of them got down.

One of them was Indian, or at least a half-breed. He was grim and solemn as he slid a Bowie knife from a sheath at his belt. He had shoulder-length black hair, dark eyes, and bronze skin. His cheekbones looked like they could have cut stone. He was young, though, probably only a handful of years older than me. He wore dungarees and a fringed buckskin jacket with the sleeves hacked off.

"This is Cornelius Crying Bear," Blunt said as he reloaded the spent cartridges in his pistol. "He tells me, when he's drinking and bothers to talk, that he's the illegitimate son of General Stand Watie. I don't know how true that is, but he likes the story. He's also got a love of torture. I've seen him keep a man alive for three days and in constant pain."

Mister Henson tried to crawl away, but with his busted knees, he couldn't. The big man grabbed hold of Mister Henson and sat him up. The man was six and a half feet tall if he was an inch, and though he wasn't fat, he was large and had a big belly. He wore a bowler hat with a turquoise and silver hatband. The walrus mustache under his big nose was red and matched his eyebrows, but he was bald as an egg.

"My other associate is Daniel Asbury," Blunt said. "Since we don't have three days, Crying Bear is going to hurry this along, but I can tell you right now he's disappointed at the rush."

Crying Bear started in with that knife and blood flew. Mister Henson screamed in pain, and I screamed with him because I didn't want to look and I couldn't turn away. It was the most horrible thing I'd ever seen, and some of the corpses we got in at the funeral home came looking pretty bad.

I managed to get myself to a standing position in the grave, but Asbury slammed me back down with a big fist. I lay there gasping, my mind spinning, and my body hurting all over. Then I tried to get up again, but Asbury rammed the other shovel we'd brought into my stomach and took my breath away.

I don't know how much time passed, but I don't think it was much. All I can remember is the yelling and the smell of the blood. There was a lot of that, and some of both was mine.

Things ended pretty quickly after Mister Henson mentioned the map to find the gold was at his house. He told them where they could find it.

Then Blunt fired again and Asbury picked up Mister Henson's body and dropped it into the grave on top of me. I tried to scramble out from under, but Blunt rode his horse over to the grave, pointed his pistol at me, and fired. Something slammed into my head.

After that, I don't remember anything.

4

"Charlie! Charlie!"

I heard my name being called, but I couldn't quite wake up. There was too much pain waiting on me and I didn't want to get to it. It wasn't just from my leg and my head. I knew I was going to be hurting over Mister Henson's death too.

And I was going to be confused over who Mister Henson really was.

I didn't want any part of any of that.

"Charlie Stark, can you hear me? You're not dead. I can see you breathing."

I blinked my eyes and looked up to see Maggie Buchanan leaning over me. I thought I'd died and gone to Heaven at first, because she was so pretty and I didn't remember who she was for a minute. The sky was full dark and shot full of stars behind her. I knew then that me and Mister Henson had been in that hole for a spell.

"Is he alive?" a woman's voice asked.

"Charlie's alive," Maggie answered. "Mister Henson is dead."

"Oh my God," the woman said. A soft cry came from her.

The woman stood holding a lantern to one side of the grave and shining the light down inside. Maggie was in the grave with me and Mister Henson, and it was a tight fit.

It was hard to see her at first. I was lying under Mister Henson, who was dead and bloody and I guess somewhat covered in dirt because I heard later that Blunt and his men had shoveled in dirt a bit. I don't think it was out of respect for the dead. More likely, they were just trying to hide what they'd done a little longer, but they hadn't wanted to wait on getting that map.

"How'd you know me and Mister Henson were out here?"

"I asked her to come look for you when you and Mister Henson missed supper," the woman said. She leaned down and I saw that she was Miss Abbie. She was a handsome woman, a lot younger than Mister Henson, and wore proper dresses. She had manners and Mister Henson took pride in that. The thing I noticed most about her was her eyes. She was always watching people's faces. "I was worried about the two of you. She knew you were out digging a grave. I didn't."

It didn't surprise me that Maggie knew me and Mister Henson were digging the grave. She took her job as a deputy seriously and kept up with a lot of things that went on in Pecos.

She was a town deputy, more or less. Pecos was small, and her father the marshal could only afford two men at full wages to keep the peace. Maggie helped her father run the marshal's office regarding paperwork, but she also worked shifts at night, rattling doors and walking drunks over to the jail.

That day Marshal Buchanan was working the murder of a ranch hand on the Bob-A-Loo spread that had started over a card game. Instead of going after him, which was a longer ride in the dark, Maggie had decided to come looking for me and Mister Henson on her own.

Like I said, I thought I was dead because Maggie looked like an angel. Her heart shaped face and brown eyes always captured my attention whenever our paths crossed, but she never gave me the time of day. She was about five feet six, much shorter than my six feet four, and built slim. Her dark brown hair and dark skin made people think she was half-Mexican or half-Indian, and I'd actually heard it both ways because her ma was supposed to have been a saloon girl from Fort Worth that Marshal Buchanan met in his younger days.

Light gleamed on the deputy's badge on her flannel shirt. Her gun belt was a nice piece of work, with loops for extra cartridges, and a place for handcuffs, and it supported two Colt .45s, the new ones. Neither the marshal nor the other two deputies carried handcuffs, but Maggie used them on occasion with drunken prisoners who insisted they weren't going to be arrested by a girl. That had been their mistake. Her Stetson hung by its chinstrap against her back.

Nobody in Pecos knew for certain what happened to her ma, because the marshal didn't have her in tow when he took the job, but there was a lot of talk about other men and killings.

Naturally, all of that idle, mean speculation was hurtful to a young girl, so Maggie didn't cotton to most people, and she was a no-nonsense deputy. Her pa might have put some weight into the issue of her position at first, but during the last year, Maggie had proven herself. She could fight as good as any man, and she would cheat more. She'd kick, bite, scratch, and gouge eyes. Whatever it took to get the job done. She didn't go looking for a fight, but when pressed into one, she'd get on top of it from the get-go. She was also quick with a pistol, something no one expected from her.

"Charlie," she said again, and this time I knew her.

"Mister Henson," I said. I tried to push myself up so I could help him and couldn't quite get there.

Her face softened as she helped pull me up. "I'm sorry, Charlie, he's gone. Can you tell me what happened? I can't find the gun."

"What gun?" I asked.

"You were both shot. There has to be a gun here somewhere."

It took me a minute to figure out what she was talking

about because my head was throbbing so much. And when I did, I couldn't believe what I was hearing.

"You think Mister Henson shot me?" I asked.

"You could have shot him," she replied.

"Then how did both of us wind up shot and in the grave?" I tried desperately to understand her logic because it was all my pain-fuzzed mind had to focus onto.

"You could have been fighting over the gun, and whoever shot first got shot second."

"While we were in the grave?"

"That's the way it looks."

I decided then and there that being a deputy had purely turned her too suspicious.

"You know," I said, "it could also look like both me and Mister Henson got shot by somebody else."

"I was wondering about all the hoofprints I found in the new dirt," she admitted. "But Pa always told me to start with the most obvious suspects. You're the only two here, and Mister Henson's not talking. So I'm asking you."

"I didn't shoot Mister Henson. He didn't shoot me. We both got shot by Angel Blunt."

"Blunt?" Maggie frowned. "He escaped the Missouri prison only a few weeks ago."

"I know. He was here."

"Why was he here?"

I wasn't sure I wanted to answer that, so I ignored the question and looked at Mister Henson. He had died hard. Crying Bear had butchered him something awful. I guess some of that showed on my face, because Maggie gave up on solving the murder and attempted murder for the minute and helped me.

Together, we slid Mister Henson over and she pushed me up over the side of the grave.

Full dark had fallen now, and only the lantern held by Miss Abbie pushed back the night.

"Are you all right, Charlie?" Miss Abbie asked me as she slipped a shoulder under one of my arms to help support me.

I'd always thought she was a fragile thing, but she was

taking in everything at the graveyard in stride. And she was strong enough to manhandle me as I limped toward her buggy. Maggie's paint horse was tied behind the buggy.

"Where's Blunt now?" Maggie wanted to know. She helped Miss Abbie get me into the back of the buggy, and neither one of them were as gentle as I would have liked.

"I kind of lost track," I said, "after Blunt shot me. You'd be surprised how quick things get blurry."

"Maybe it would be better if we questioned him later," Miss Abbie suggested. "Let's let Doctor Gilbride look at him first."

Maggie was still looking at me suspiciously, and when she headed back to the grave, I thought for certain she was going to keep searching for the pistol she thought me and Mister Henson had fought over.

Instead, she climbed down into that grave and brought up Mister Henson's body. He was smaller than me, but so was she. I was surprised to learn that she was that strong. Miss Abbie took a minute to straighten Mister Henson's clothes, and I was surprised to see she wasn't crying or showing much emotion. She seemed more mad than anything. Finally satisfied, she climbed into the buggy seat and shook out the reins to get her horses moving.

I sat there in the back of the buggy beside Mister Henson, not knowing for sure how I was supposed to feel. I kept thinking about Angel Blunt, the story about the Mexican gold, and Mister Henson turning out to be somebody completely different than I thought he was.

Somewhere in there, as Miss Abbie drove the buggy toward Pecos with the lantern swinging from the hook and Maggie Buchanan riding to one side, my head kept spinning and I went out again.

5

When I woke up again, I was in Doctor Gilbride's office on a bed. Morning light burned bright against the eastern window. I'd been in those offices three times before, twice to get stitches after cutting myself, and once to have a broken arm set.

The stitches came from working with the saws in Mister Henson's shop. People didn't realize how dangerous making caskets could be. I sure didn't when I took the trade on, but I learned after getting sewed up the second time. I'd figured the first time was bad luck, but the second time I knew I wasn't as watchful as I could be. I'd learned.

The broken arm came from a fight in the Ugly Toad Saloon, which was named for a porcelain carving of a toad that Dewey Spradlin, the owner, supposedly got all the way from China. Other people say it was something he picked up in San Francisco.

I couldn't remember what the fight in the saloon was about that night, but I did remember getting arrested by Maggie Buchanan. She hadn't been happy with me, told me she'd expected better from me. I didn't know why she did. She hardly talked to me, which was how everybody else treated me too.

To most people I was just the undertaker's assistant, and the unfortunate orphan whose parents had died.

"Mister Stark, how are you feeling?"

I glanced over to the other side of the room to see Doctor Gilbride working on what was left of Mister Henson. He was doing an autopsy, which I could have told him was wasted because I had witnessed Mister Henson's murder. But maybe Marshal Buchanan had asked for the work to be done.

There was a lot of paperwork in law enforcement. I knew because Mister Henson had sometimes had to fill out papers for Marshal Buchanan when folks died, and there was even more paperwork when they killed one another.

The doctor had two beds in his office, and me and Mister Henson had filled them both.

Gilbride was in his early forties and got around well. Mister Henson had called him spry and feisty, and he had liked the doc a lot. That seemed to make sense, because a lot of the business we did came through Gilbride first. Old folks whose time was up, folks who'd been in bad accidents or had gotten real sick, they came to me and Mister Henson when medicine couldn't fix them.

He had dark brown hair with a little curl that the women, even Miss Abbie, would comment on, and a small mustache that was always neatly kept. He always wore a suit, and today he had on a vest and had rolled up his shirt sleeves to almost his elbows.

"My head's hurting," I said in answer to his question. "So's my leg."

"That's understandable," Gilbride said. "You were shot."

Sometimes Gilbride and Mister Henson had some pretty strange notions about what was funny. Miss Abbie said it was because both of them worked with life and death every day and a man had to learn to be light-hearted. Otherwise all there would be for him was a bottle to hold off the nightmares.

I'd seen nights where Gilbride and Mister Henson, after a particularly sorrowful situation, such as the passing of a child at the hands of a parent or a sickness, would spend an evening in the Ugly Toad getting "comfortably numb" as the doc put it.

Gilbride came over to me and pulled the dressing off my head. I reached up and found it was still swollen. The stitches felt rough under my fingertips.

"You were very lucky, Mister Stark," Gilbride said. "Unlike my dear colleague."

"You don't have to do an autopsy. Angel Blunt killed Mister Henson." I didn't like the idea of Mister Henson getting cut up any more than Crying Bear had already done

Gilbride nodded. "That's what Deputy Buchanan told me last night when she interrupted my supper, but the marshal wanted it done for the court. He believes it will help bring murder charges against Angel Blunt when he goes before a magistrate."

The doc was one of the few citizens in Pecos that used Maggie's deputy title. I wasn't sure if he cottoned to the idea of a female deputy or was just being polite. He was from New Jersey and had trained in England for his medical practice, and I knew they did things differently in both places than in Texas.

"A man named Cornelius Crying Bear tortured him," I said.

"She did not mention that." Gilbride frowned. "Mister Henson was hard used. I was sorry to see that."

I started crying then, and it surprised me, but it didn't seem to surprise Gilbride. He pulled up a chair and sat as I told him what had happened the day before.

Well, I didn't tell him everything. I didn't tell him Mister Henson wasn't Mister Henson, and I didn't mention that Angel Blunt was there to find out about stolen Mexican gold that was still south of the Rio Grande.

But I told him enough to satisfy his curiosity. Mostly. He still had some questions about why Mister Henson was tortured, but I told him I was in the grave Missus Louise Mead was supposed to be going in this morning when that happened and that I didn't hear anything.

I wondered if that grave had ever been dug, and if the

funeral had taken place, or was going to take place, but I didn't ask. After being in one myself and almost needing one, I thought I might be out of the grave digging business. I just couldn't see digging another one.

There were two other undertakers in Pecos, which wasn't something that was needed except to give folks choices, and for when sickness swept through a small area. Or there was a big problem at a family reunion.

When I was finished, Gilbride put his hand on my shoulder and smiled at me gently the way he had after he'd set my arm and both times he'd stitched me up. "You're going to be all right, Mister Stark. In time. Time takes care of all things."

I knew that. I'd helped bury a lot of people time had taken care of.

I asked about my wounds.

"Like I said, you were lucky," Gilbride told me. He touched my head. "The bullet caught you a glancing blow here along your temple. If it had been even a sixteenth of an inch over, it would have cracked your skull and probably have killed you."

I didn't point out that if it had been a sixteenth of an inch over the other way that it would have missed me entirely because I knew that probably wouldn't have been so fortunate. Angel Blunt would have shot me again.

"The wound is messy," Gilbride went on, "but it will heal fine and there will be no permanent damage."

"What about my leg?" I patted my thigh, which didn't hurt as much as I'd thought it was going to, but I still wasn't going to be dancing anytime soon.

"Again, you were lucky. The bullet went through the muscles without hitting bone. You're young, Mister Stark. You'll have to work at it, but I'm confident you'll recover the full use of your leg in a few weeks with some rest and exercise."

I nodded and thought I was a little lucky. Angel Blunt didn't seem like a man who made many mistakes.

"Did the marshal pick up Blunt's trail?" I asked.

"He and his deputies, and some of the local trackers,

are endeavoring to do that this morning. Blunt evidently didn't stop with just killing Mister Henson. He came on into town last night afterward."

"What do you mean?" I didn't want him knowing I'd heard anything about the map Blunt was looking for because that would have led to questions I didn't want to answer about Mister Henson. I had too many of my own to start answering those of other people.

"After Blunt killed your mentor and thought he'd killed you, he and his men broke into Mister Henson's building and burned it down when they left. There's hardly a stick left standing."

I was stunned, not knowing what to think except that I was glad Missus Louise Mead had already been tucked into her casket at the church, even if she didn't have a grave to go into immediately. Otherwise she'd have been burned up in that fire.

I struggled with the bed and edged to the side.

"What are you doing?" Gilbride asked.

"I need to see," I explained.

He acted like he was going to argue with me about it for a moment, but he didn't. I guess he figured if I fell on my face, I'd know I'd done something foolish.

I got my feet under me, rested for just a moment as I waited for my head to stop spinning, then limped over to the window, which was open. The doctor's office was over shops that specialized in women's clothing, window glass, and furniture. They were all places families would come to, so Gilbride got plenty of advertising just being there.

I leaned out the window and looked down Main Street. Like I said, Pecos wasn't very big. Gilbride's office and Mister Henson's undertaking building had only been separated by a few buildings.

There, situated between a saddle shop and Dawson's hardware store, Henson's Caskets was nothing more than a burned-out hollow of what it had been. Mister Henson and I had lived on the second floor. It was all gone.

Not only had I lost my mentor, but I'd lost my job and my home as well.

6

After I complained enough about being hungry and insisted that I was well enough to walk, Gilbride finally agreed that I could walk on down to Wick's Diner to get something to eat. I was glad to get out of there. I like open spaces and not being closed in. I enjoyed the hard work of building caskets, but I preferred outside work.

It was almost ten in the morning, so I had the place pretty much to myself because the business people, what few of them there were, were off conducting trade in their stores and shops.

Wick's Diner was one of those places were folks gathered for the food and the ambience. Missus Wick made the curtains and the tablecloths, and they were all festive pieces that featured bright colors, chickens, and fruit, some of which I'd never seen.

Missus Wick and her daughter insisted on waiting on me, so I got good service and my coffee was always full, but they kept asking questions that I didn't know the answers to or didn't want to talk about. They wanted all the details and the gossip, of course, and tongues were already wagging about why Blunt had come to Pecos to kill Mister Henson.

After a while, Missus Wick and her daughter got frustrated with my lack of knowledge, and maybe my barely concealed rudeness, and went to take care of baking and preparing for the lunch rush. Thankfully, I was pretty full of breakfast by then, so I was content to drink my coffee and try to figure out what I was going to do.

I wondered what Blunt had learned from Mister Henson, and why he'd gone to the shop and then burned it. Something had drawn him there, and he'd wanted to cover up what he was doing.

Unless he'd just burned the place out of meanness, which I wouldn't have put past him after being shot by him. Twice. I knew Blunt had a mean streak in him.

I couldn't imagine Mister Henson having any gold in that building. The rooms we'd lived in had been small, and there hadn't been anything on the first floor that didn't have to do with making caskets and embalming folks. We also helped build houses and raised barns when folks hired out for those things. And I'd learned to do finish carpentry inside homes from Mister Henson. He'd said I was gonna be better than him one day because I had a natural touch for such things.

Missus Wick had been surprised I could eat after losing Mister Henson. She told me that after her ma passed, she hadn't been able to eat for a week. I couldn't imagine Missus Wick being less than plump, so I figured that was an exaggeration. Or that maybe as big as she was going without a meal for a week was something she could do. Kind of like a camel and water.

I ate because I was hungry, and because after working with Mister Henson for five years building caskets and digging graves, I knew people died. And if you didn't eat, you'd die too.

Besides, eating gave me something to do that I understood. I didn't understand much else that was going on in my life at the moment. When I finished my coffee, I felt a little steadier on my feet and the coffee wasn't flowing as quickly as it had, so I decided to walk on down to the funeral home and see what was what.

***

The strong scent of burned wood hung over everything and filled my nose. And it burned my eyes. I blamed that for the tears that came when I'd thought I didn't have any left.

I could still see where the two floors had been, there was a little shelf of charcoaled wood at the back that was all that was left of the second floor. The place had never looked so small. It was hard to imagine that building had held all the dead folks that had come through there, and all the sadness that followed them with their families and surviving friends.

Mister Henson had a showroom up front where he kept a half-dozen different caskets made of different woods and in different styles. We'd made one out of Purpleheart wood that had been so hard to work with we'd given up on it three times before we'd finished. We'd blunted saws and chisels enough so that we were both cursing it before it was over.

Purpleheart was also called violetwood, tananeo and saka, and it grew in Central and South America, which made me wonder how Mister Henson had come to know of it. He'd had the Purpleheart shipped from Mexico. I'd never even thought about his knowledge of the wood before. He'd always known a lot of things.

Nobody ever bought that Purpleheart casket, though a few had come close. The wood was a rich, dark purplish color, not the color the Phoenicians made popular for royalty, but a more somber hue. Because Purpleheart was so durable, it was often used as flooring, on boats, and as veneer.

As of this morning and thinking of Mister Henson, who wasn't really Mister Henson, I was getting as suspicious as Maggie Buchanan. I was maybe a little more understanding of her attitude last night when she'd found me sharing a grave with Mister Henson. But I hadn't liked her suspicions, and I didn't much care for mine this morning either.

I liked thinking of Mister Henson the way I'd known him to be up until yesterday.

I walked through the charred wood and ash, from the showroom to the private room where we'd prepared the bodies, to the little office Mister Henson had kept in the back. It had all burned. There were some bones of the building that had been there before, some timbers that hadn't burned completely, and some metal door hinges here and there. Even some scattered broken glass from the small windows in the doors to the office and knick-knacks Mister Henson had collected had survived.

"This place went up like a matchstick," a man said.

I about jumped out of my skin because I hadn't heard him walk in behind me. I turned around, but not without looking for something to use as a weapon as I did. A couple chunks of wood came to mind, but I knew if the man had a gun, having a length of timber wasn't going to matter much.

I stumbled when my leg almost gave out from under me, and my head spun a little as I focused on the man.

Mister Dawson stood at the open mouth of the funeral home and looked around like he didn't believe what he was seeing. Since he owned the hardware store next door, I was willing to bet this wasn't the first time he'd seen the results of the fire.

7

Mister Dawson was a portly man in his forties and wore a hardware apron. His pockets were usually filled with odds and ends, bolts and screws and nails. And he carried peppermint candies that he said were for the children that came into his store, but I'd noticed he ate a lot of them himself.

"It looks like it did," I agreed.

"For a while last night, I thought it was going to take out my place too," he said. "I have to tell you, it was mighty scary."

"I bet it was." I wished I'd seen the fire. Couldn't help myself. I was curious by nature, which was why Mister Henson kept me reading books.

Whenever I asked him too many questions, I'd always know. He'd send away for a book and tell me to read it when it came in on the train. Then I'd have to tell him what I'd read, which got tedious at times, so I was more careful about the questions I'd asked. The Punic Wars between Rome and Carthage were probably exciting to the men who fought in them, but the history was mighty dry reading.

I preferred Beadle's Dime Novels and Frank Starr's American Novels, especially anything to do with Kit Carson and other mountain men who did business with John Jacob Astor's fur trading companies. I'd been in the middle of Female Trapper, or Lone-Star Lizzie, but that DeWitt's Ten Cent Novel had gotten burned up with everything else, so I wasn't sure if I'd ever find out if she got out of her troubles alive.

I wasn't quite as invested as I'd been, I have to admit. When you crawled out of your own grave, even someone else's, everything you read on the printed page just paled by comparison.

Then I realized what Mister Dawson was saying, about him being here last night.

"Did you see who set the fire?" I asked.

He shook his head and popped a peppermint candy into his mouth. "No. I didn't know there was a fire until men across the street in the Ugly Toad came out yelling about it. I was taking inventory."

On occasion, I'd hired on to help Mister Dawson with his inventory and I knew for a fact that was a time-consuming ordeal. It wasn't an easy task, though I felt certain if he just kept things organized he'd have a better idea of what he had from month to month when the salesmen came through offering goods.

"If we hadn't had all those ranch hands in from the Double Diamond last night," Mister Dawson went on, "probably two or three other buildings might have burned out too. But those hands were here, and they were mostly sober. I helped with the bucket brigade and we got the fire put out as quick as we could." He looked guilty then. "Wish we could have done more."

"You did what you could, Mister Dawson."

He looked at me. "The way I hear it, Angel Blunt killed Henson."

I nodded.

"You saw Blunt?"

"Blunt shot me a couple of times." I pointed at my head and my leg.

"You're lucky to be alive, boy."

"I know."

"Did Aiken find you?"

Eugene Aiken owned a small printing press and was

the town's only reporter. He'd come to Pecos three years ago and bought The Pecos Pioneer from Delbert Wells, who Mister Henson and I had buried just last year. His widow had almost bought the Purpleheart casket, but she decided to save her money and get on back to Richmond, Virginia, where they were from and she still had family.

The Pioneer was more bulletin than newspaper. It usually came out the second and fourth Tuesdays of the month and covered what was going on in town. Aiken usually discussed the national news a little, but only what pertained to us, which was not a lot.

"No, sir," I said, "he did not."

"Well, he's been by bothering me this morning, getting what I knew about the fire and such, and he's looking to bother you too. He said he wants an eyewitness to Henson's murder. I know he went by Doc Gilbride's this morning, but Doc chased him and wouldn't let him talk to you."

I appreciated that because I wasn't feeling like going over all the details again. I knew I'd still have to talk to the marshal.

Then I realized maybe I could ask Aiken some questions about Angel Blunt and Mister Henson too. As I looked back on it, there was a lot I didn't know.

So I excused myself from Mister Dawson and figured I'd go see Aiken and ask some of those questions. Before I left, Mister Dawson gave me a peppermint from his apron pocket like he had all those times when I was a kid.

Truth to tell, it made me kind of sad. The peppermint just didn't taste the same, but maybe that was because of all the wood smoke I'd inhaled.

8

The office of The Pecos Pioneer was at the top of the Chinese laundry that had come into town with the railroad. If tracks started getting laid in California and headed east, Chinese laborers followed them in, pounding stakes into ties and laying steel.

The Goose King Laundry did business with Mister Kuáng and his family because they washed out the surgical sheets we used, and they washed the bolts of material we used to line the inside of the caskets. Missus Kuáng and her daughters sewed the small pillows for the deceased's head. The hanging sign out front showed a goose with a knob over its beak and its wings spread like it was proud of something.

Missus Kuáng and her daughters also managed the Fine Noodle Bowl, a noodle shop on one side of the laundry. They took up most of the floor space at the front of the building. Mister Kuáng just maintained a front office where folks could drop off their dirty clothes without seeing other people's dirty clothes.

Me and Jimmy Hadley found out that the saloon girls at the Ugly Toad also had their clothes cleaned there, so one night three years ago, we snuck over to the laundry to see if we could spot those clothes drying on the line out back. We figured it was as close as we'd get to knowing what that was all about. Jimmy and I had gotten hold of some beer. His uncle was a bootlegger who ran 'shine up to the Indians in the Territories, so it was there to be had. We hadn't exactly been at our best.

Maggie Buchanan caught us that night, and she'd threatened to run us in for trespassing. It was her first night on the job as a deputy and she had been pretty hardnosed about enforcing the law. We'd talked her out of arresting us. And probably the fight that night at the Ugly Toad had been more serious. She'd told me she'd expected more of me then too.

Funny thing was, after Maggie had told me that a second time, I'd been kind of disappointed with myself too. And she'd told Mister Henson about catching us, which made for a rough couple days.

So maybe that whole business of who shot who at the cemetery wasn't something I should have been so contrary about. Maggie probably didn't have the best view of me.

I headed for the narrow wooden stairs beside the laundry that led up to the Pecos Pioneer. Mister Kuáng had had the second story fixed up so he could sublet the rooms and turn a quicker profit on the building. In addition to the newspaper, Noel Ekarius, the barber, kept shop up there. Aiken and Ekarius were both young bachelors, so they saved money on renting another place by living on the premises.

Mister Kuáng must have heard me tromping up those stairs, which I was regretting on account of my leg, because he came out of the alley door with a huge wooden laundry ladle in his hands and looked up at me.

"Hello, Charlie." Mister Kuáng's English was good, better than mine most days. He'd been educated in British school systems over in Hong Kong when he'd been a boy. He was at least as old as Mister Henson and he was a skinny guy

I stopped for a minute and didn't mind because I got to rest my leg, which was throbbing pretty fierce. "Hello, Mister Kuáng."

"I am sorry to hear about your loss. Mister Henson was a fine man."

I hesitated. Mister Kuáng probably thought I was feeling emotional, but I was also thinking that fine men didn't go around robbing Mexican presidents, not even if they were getting ousted. In fact, maybe especially not then because I was pretty sure Benito Juárez needed his gold if he was losing his country to the French.

"Thank you, Mister Kuáng," I said, not wanting to get into any of that.

"When it comes time to bury Mister Henson, Charlie, please let me know. I know all of his clothes and yours were burned in the unfortunate fire. I have a suit you can use, and some other clothing too."

Well, that choked me up. I hadn't even thought about burying Mister Henson, but that would have to be seen to as well.

Not only that, I realized that the only set of clothes I had to my name I was standing in, and they were bloodstained and dirty.

Life was getting harder faster than I was prepared for, and for a moment I felt overwhelmed. Then I focused on what I was there to do.

"Yes sir, I'll do that."

"When you finish up with Mister Aiken," Mister Kuáng said, "come see me. I have some garments I think will fit you."

I nodded, thanked him, and went on up to see Aiken.

At the top of the stairs, I knocked on the door and waited, and I realized how powerful the stink of bleach and cleaning chemicals were. The smell was almost enough to sting my eyes.

I stared at the simple sign that announced: The Pecos Pioneer and wondered if it had always hung there. I hadn't ever seen Delbert Wells in his office even though I had helped prepare his body and assisted in dressing him for his last appearance.

In fact, there were a lot of people Mister Henson and I never saw outside of the churches before they arrived at the mortuary. Or we went to fetch them. Mister Henson insisted that we go to all the churches in town because prospective clients were everywhere.

At the end, a lot of them got embalmed on that table in the back of Mister Henson's shop.

"Coming," a mild voice called from inside.

Standing there waiting, I suddenly felt vulnerable, and that sensation was a lot like the one I'd had while I was up to my armpits in Missus Louise Mead's grave. If she'd gotten buried there.

My heart beat something fierce and I broke out into a cold sweat. All I wanted to do was hide. I glanced down into the alley, but it was empty at the entrance and the only things moving behind the laundry was the wash drying in the breeze and Missus Kuáng and her daughters hanging clothes. They didn't appear disturbed. White sheets and folks' clothing rustled a little bit.

I watched that for just a minute and convinced myself that it was just the clothing that had unnerved me. I felt pretty foolish, and even more so when Aiken opened his door and found me standing there looking around like a chick who couldn't find his mother hen.

9

"Can I help you?" Eugene Aiken was a short, thin man in his late twenties or early thirties. He was built like a fencepost and looked like a scarecrow with pince-nez glasses resting on his blade of a nose under a mop of wild brown hair. He wore suit pants and a white shirt with sleeve garters. He'd shrugged out of his suspenders and they hung at his hips. Ink stained the fingers of both hands.

I'd seen him a few times at Wick's Diner and at the funeral home. Aiken had always pestered Mister Henson the first of every month about taking out advertisements in his paper. Mister Henson had always insisted that folks would get to know him when they needed him, and when they needed him, they would find him.

It was a solid business plan if you ask me, because that's how it happened.

"Mister Aiken," I said, still feeling a little scared and foolish at the same time. "I'm Charlie Stark."

He studied me for a minute like he didn't know if he was supposed to recognize the name, then he did and he reached for me.

"Charlie," he said, catching hold of my elbow. "Charlie Stark. Mister Henson's assistant."

"That's right," I said.

"I'd like to speak to you."

"Yes sir, that's what I'd heard. So I thought I'd come

by." We'd get to my reasons for that soon enough.

"Please," he said, stepping back and pulling me into his office. "Come in."

I followed him in. Otherwise I would have had to fight him for my arm.

The biggest thing in the small room was the printing press. I'd never seen one before and didn't know exactly what I was looking at, but the boxes of ink-stained cubes of letters gave me a big clue. As did the box of blank paper sitting beside it. Evidently Atkin had been working on the press because it looked like he'd used some of the letters to lay out one of the two pages that would be the newest issue in a few days.

A desk occupied one corner by a window that overlooked Second Street which was a block off Main Street. The laundry was right behind Latham's Mercantile, which I'd heard women say was a good idea because they could do their shopping and have their clothes worked on in nearly the same place.

A small bookshelf sat next to that and I spotted several dime novels from various publishers on the shelves with a few books on writing, including How to Write Letters, by J. Willis Westlake. I also spotted worn copies of The Adventures of Tom Sawyer by Mark Twain, Twenty Thousand Leagues and The Mysterious Island both by Jules Verne, and The Narrative of Arthur Gordon Pym of Nantucket by Edgar Allan Poe.

There were others I couldn't quite make out and I wished I could look through them. Evidently Mister Henson's forced reading had marked me deeper than I had thought.

In a corner sat a pile of newspapers and magazines, all of it covered in dust, which told me that the newspaperman didn't like throwing things away and didn't have a lady friend who looked after him. Not even a cleaning lady, it seemed. A small fireplace was built into the central wall that split the top floor of the laundry into two units. Gray ash was piled deep enough to be a hazard.

The whole room smelled of Middleton's Cherry Blend

tobacco and a gray haze drifted up from the briar wood pipe sitting on the desk next to a sheaf of newspapers and a softbound pocket notebook like one Mister Henson had used to keep track of burials.

That made me wonder if Doc Gilbride had found Mister Henson's notebook in his clothes when he'd undressed the body. I figured I would ask about that later. I was getting tired of asking questions about this whole thing because it seemed like one question led to ten.

"Please," Aiken said, dragging a straight-backed chair from the wall and putting it in front of the desk, "sit."

I did.

"You have a very exciting story to tell, Mister Stark," he told me. "Our readers will be thrilled to hear it. I want to be the one who helps you share it."

I stared at him and tried to swallow my sudden anger, but I was pistol-hot. "An exciting story? Mister Aiken, I lost a man who was like a father to me. Angel Blunt had Mister Henson tortured and killed."

He hesitated a moment. "I suppose that was rather insensitive of me."

I silently agreed, but I bit back harsh words doing it.

"But you must admit, having a bad man like Angel Blunt show up in Pecos and commit the horrendous deeds he did is well off the beaten path for a town like Pecos."

I just looked at him, and if it weren't for the fact I wanted information from him as badly as he wanted it from me, I'd have got up and left.

But I'd come here to find out what I could about Angelo Blunt and I meant to see that done.

"I apologize for my transgressions, Mister Stark," Aiken said. "I blame my inexperience in handling such big stories. Please forgive me. I would very much like to talk to you."

"All right," I said.

"Good." Aiken smiled at me. "I usually have a pot of tea brought round about this time of day. Would you join me in a cup?"

"I'm not much of a tea drinker." When I drank tea, I

wanted it dark and sweet, not the way Easterners seemed to prefer it. That was something Mister Henson had taught me.

"I think Missus Kuáng makes coffee as well. I'll check." Aiken went out to the second floor landing and hollered down to one of Missus Kuáng's daughters and asked that a pot of tea and coffee be brought up.

Once he had that squared away, he returned to his desk and flipped to a new page in his notebook. He dipped his pen in ink. "Okay, let's begin, shall we?"

10

"I've got some of the basic story down," Aiken continued. "Talk spreads quickly in this town. If it weren't for the fact that folks like to read news they already know a lot about, I wouldn't have much of a readership. And sometimes they like to mail copies to relatives in other parts of Texas and to states beyond."

He seemed a little proud of that.

"What I'd like, Mister Stark, is the story in your own words."

So I gave it to him like I'd given it to Gilbride, leaving out the parts about Mister Henson probably not being Mister Henson and any mention of the gold. I just put it out there that Angel Blunt and his gang had come out there to rob us and Mister Henson had put up a fight.

In the middle of all that, the tea and coffee were delivered and I poured myself a cup. It smelled like the bleach Mister Kuáng used to wash the laundry, and I thought I understood why Aiken preferred smoking a pipe.

Aiken wrote quickly, and I couldn't read a lot of the words. I suspected that was because everything he wrote was upside down to me, but he was using characters like I'd never before seen.

I couldn't stop myself, and before I knew it, I'd asked him if he was using shorthand.

A look of surprise crossed Aiken's face. "Indeed it is.

Do you know it?"

"No, but I know the ancient Greeks used it." That knowledge had come from one of the books I'd read.

"So did the Chinese. May we get back to your story now? We left off where you were in the grave, thinking you were dead."

I gave him the rest of it, about Miss Abbie and Maggie Buchanan and waking up in the doc's office. And when I finished, Aiken looked a little dissatisfied.

"Not to be indelicate, Mister Stark," he said when I'd finished, "but Blunt just showing up out of nowhere and unleashing violence on Mister Henson and yourself doesn't make much sense."

"No," I agreed. See, that's the way it is with lying. People know the truth of a story when they hear one. Even if it's whopper, if has its own sense and all the parts are there, they'll believe it. Or they'll at least enjoy the telling of it.

"Of course, there are a lot of other questions in matters of violence that people never get to know the whole truth of," Aiken said. "Take for instance the murder of Wild Bill Hickok. He was shot by a man named John McCall in Nuttal & Mann's Saloon in Deadwood in the Dakota Territory three years ago. Did you know McCall was living under the alias of Bill Sutherland at the time?"

"I did not." I also didn't see what one thing had to do with the other and I was confused, but I was glad Aiken wasn't asking any more questions.

"He was," Aiken went on. "No one ever found out why he was using the Sutherland name. Nor did they know why McCall felt so beholden to kill Wild Bill in cold blood. Pardon me for talking so much about that. I've just shipped a manuscript about Wild Bill to Beadle's Dime Novels in New York. My research is still fresh on my mind." He looked at the notes he'd taken. "Such are the vagaries of the human heart. We don't always get to know these things."

I was thinking that, too, only I was thinking about Mister Henson. And I was hoping that wasn't true. I'd lost what I'd thought I'd known of Mister Henson, and I was hoping that somewhere in here I would get back something that would allow me to hang onto memory of the man I believed I'd known.

"Mister Henson was a long-time resident of Pecos," Aiken said, "but everybody agrees he arrived in town about eighteen years ago. They said he swung down off the coach—we didn't have a train then—and went into business as an undertaker."

I nodded. "He built the funeral home himself, raised it from the ground up. It took him a while."

Aiken consulted notes he'd written on another page. "That's what people say. They also say he was 'quiet, mannered, and reserved.'"

"He was."

"Well, who was he before he showed up eighteen years ago? No one seems to know that."

That question caught me flat-footed. I just sat there for a minute, and that was a minute too long.

"What are you not telling me, Mister Stark?" Aiken asked softly.

I looked at him and made myself as guileless as I could. I wasn't going to let him tear down Mister Henson's good name. "I'm telling you everything I know, Mister Aiken."

Aiken leaned back in his chair and sipped his tea. "Do you know why men come out West?"

"A lot of us are born out here." I wanted me and him to be separate at that moment, so I pointed out we'd grown up in different parts of this nation.

He gave me a thin smile. "Yes, some of you are. But Mister Henson wasn't. He came from somewhere else, and a lot of men who come West are doing it so they can leave somewhere else. Somewhere that isn't so hospitable to them, if you catch my drift."

What he meant was how a lot of folks had run off on problems they'd had in the East.

I got mad about that and I narrowed my eyes so Aiken would know I wasn't taking his questions well. "Mister Henson was a good man."

"Everybody says that."

"Because that's what he was."

Aiken leaned forward again. "There's something I know, Mister Stark. Good men don't get savaged the way Mister Henson did. And I don't believe for a minute that Angel Blunt just happened onto that gravesite and decided he needed to perform a couple murders and arson before he went to bed last night."

I didn't say anything because I was trying to figure out what to do.

"Another thing I'd like more information on," Aiken continued, "is Mister Henson's adoption of you."

I felt like I'd been slapped and I didn't know whether to run or fight back. I hadn't been expecting that. "Mister Henson didn't adopt me," I said. "He took me in and he gave me a home."

Aiken sorted through the newspapers he had lying on the desk, found the one he wanted, and spread it on his desk in front of him. It was an edition Delbert Wells had put out seven years ago.

Part of the headline was: WIFE KILLS HUSBAND...

I didn't read the rest. I knew the story.

"I'd like to talk about you now," Aiken said. "About all the sadness you've already gone through once in losing parents."

"No," I said, and I stood up. Right then and there, I forgot all about getting information on Angel Blunt from Aiken and got out of that office.

I had enough bad memories from last night. I didn't need to dredge up all those events from seven years ago. My hands were shaking when I let myself out.

Aiken got up from his desk and called after me, trying to excuse himself and his bluntness, but I ignored him.

I almost missed the flash of somebody moving out of the alley because I was so mad. But I saw him, a man dressed in dungarees, a dark blue shirt, and a light jacket against the wind. His Stetson dipped too quick for me to see his face, and he was gone by the time I limped down to the bottom of the stairs on shaking knees.

But he'd been there watching Aiken's door.

Watching me.

11

I took Mister Kuáng up on his offer of clothes and he outfitted me in a simple black suit, a starched white shirt, and some underclothes. It all reminded me of the black suits Mister Henson had instructed me to wear during funerals.

I offered to pay Mister Kuáng for the clothes, but he wouldn't accept my money. He said it was his gift to me during unfortunate times because he considered us friends and because he could afford to be generous.

I had to shift the bandages on my thigh a lot to get into the clothes, but at least the stitches were holding and I wasn't bleeding through the compress.

After I picked out the suit for Mister Henson, another black one that I knew he would look as normal in as was possible under the circumstances, I walked on down to Sowers Bank & Trust and got some cash money from my account there.

Mister Henson had paid me a modest wage for helping at the undertaking business because he hadn't wanted me working for him for free even though he was giving me room and board and a whole lot more than that. I'd gotten paid separate from the side work we did in carpentry and well digging, so it had all added up.

I wasn't exactly flush with cash, but I had enough to do

what I needed to do and I wouldn't have to worry about eating or having a house over my head for a few days. I would have to find work, though, and soon.

The first thing I did was walk on into the Kearney Arms gun shop because I hadn't liked the way I'd felt on Mister Kuáng's stairway. Feeling naked and alone was something I couldn't abide. Not anymore.

The gun shop was owned and operated by Jacob Kearney, an ex-artillery officer who'd served in the Texas Brigade and had fought for the Confederacy. He was proud of his service, but he had gotten on with his life after the war like a lot of other folks in the area still hadn't. Losing didn't fit Kearney, but he had been a professional soldier. He'd accepted his loss and moved forward.

Still, every now and again when I was in his shop, I heard him whistling "Dixie" or singing "Nearer My God to Thee" which he'd said had been sung by survivors of Pickett's Charge. He had a good baritone voice and they were proud to have him down at the First Baptist Church where he was sometimes featured in solo songs.

His shop was, like I said, small and neat, and it was perfectly organized. He also had a big selection of weapons, from long guns to revolvers to hideout pistols favored by gamblers.

"Good afternoon, Charlie," Kearney greeted me when I walked through the door and set the little bell mounted overhead to tinkling.

He was a medium-sized man in his forties with ramrod posture. He could sit a horse like he was born to it or he could march all day. The Texas Brigade was known as an infantry unit and they marched everywhere, all the way out to Virginia to fight in the war. Well, they took trains out there, but there was still a lot of marching.

A Sharps buffalo rifle lay in pieces on the counter in front of him, but he looked up at me and gave me his full attention. I could see the sorrow in his eyes. He and Mister Henson hadn't been close, no more than nodding acquaintances, but we had built the casket for Kearney's father three years ago and dug him a nice grave. He had spoken to me like grieving folks sometimes did, and we'd remained friendly afterward.

"Good afternoon, Kearney." I reached up to take my hat off and realized I still wasn't wearing one. That would have to be fixed too.

"That's a good-looking suit," he said.

"Thank you. I was hoping you'd have something that would go good with it." After talking with Aiken, after being addressed like I was that newly orphaned kid again, I was feeling like somebody had rubbed salt into my wounds and I was pretty sore about things. So I talked brave, like nothing bothered me.

Kearney saw right through all that. He'd seen men on the battlefield and knew false faces when he saw them. He looked a little undecided.

"I want a revolver, Kearney," I said, putting it to him plain.

"Why?"

That made me pause. When I went into the mercantile to buy canned peaches, nobody in there asked me why I wanted them. They had them and they sold them to me. I figured Kearney was in the business of selling goods too and there wouldn't be any questions other than if I could pay for it.

"Because I need one," I said.

"To do what?" Kearney folded his arms over his chest.

He wore a Colt Single Action Army .45 with the four and three-fourths inch barrel on his hip. I knew because me and Jimmy Hadley had made it a point to find out after the shooting in the gun shop.

A couple years ago, two men had made the mistake of trying to rob Kearney. He'd killed them both and me and Mister Henson had buried them. Kearney had paid for the burying and had stood at the graveside when we put them in the ground.

Eugene Aiken had sold lots of papers that week because two people had been in the gun shop when the robbery took place. As I recall, there was no one quote from Kearney. He didn't talk about the war much, and he didn't talk about killing those two men.

"I want to be able to protect myself," I answered.

"You're sure about that?"

"I am."

"Because if you're planning on riding out after Angel Blunt and his gang, I'm not selling you a gun."

"No sir." I swallowed because I knew I wanted to do that, but I also knew I'd just get myself killed if I did. "I was out there yesterday evening, Mister Kearney. Me and Mister Henson. Neither one of us had a weapon. I can't help but think maybe if that wasn't how it was, maybe Mister Henson would be alive."

Kearney looked at me for a minute, then he shook his head. "It wouldn't have made any difference, son. Mister Henson would still be dead, and you're lucky you're not."

"I know. I don't ever want to be in that position again, but if I am, I don't ever again want to feel that helpless." I looked at him. "Do you understand that?"

"Yes." He sighed.

"And I'm afraid Blunt might come looking for me." I didn't want to explain about the man I'd seen. Or thought I'd seen. Now that I was getting away from that moment, things didn't seem so sinister, but I was still cautious.

"Why would he do that?"

I'd been wondering that too, and I'd only reached one answer. "I was a witness to Mister Henson's murder. Blunt might not want me to testify in front of a judge."

"Have you ever shot before?" Kearney asked.

"Squirrel guns and shotguns when I was hunting with some friends. A Winchester and Henry occasionally when we hunted deer to make meat." I was a good shot with a rifle, from a .22 to a .44 to a Spencer rifle .56-56 we'd borrowed once. I could hit what I aimed at. It was as much skill as it was a knack.

"I've got some targets around back," Kearney said. "Let's see if we can set you up with something that works for you."

12

Behind the shop, gunny sacks thick with straw hung from posts at five, ten, and twenty feet. They fronted a short hill where the spent bullets would end up.

"That seems close," I said. I could almost reach out and touch the bag that stood five feet away.

"This is for pistol shooting," Kearney said as he loaded a .36 Navy Colt with cartridges. "You get much farther apart in a shootout with pistols, it takes a steady hand to connect with a target. And most pistol work is done up close and sudden. A man who wants to kill you will step up on you close enough to grab you and make sure of his kill."

He didn't bother to explain how he knew that, but I remembered Aiken's story about how quick Kearney had pulled his sidearm that day and stopped the robbers in their tracks. They'd only been standing across that counter.

His words scared me too. It had been bad enough facing Blunt while he sat on his horse from twenty feet away. I couldn't imagine having somebody in my face and pulling the trigger on a pistol aimed at my belly.

"Okay," I said. I took the pistol, turned sideways to the target, and rolled the hammer back with my thumb like I'd been doing it all my life. I wanted to impress Kearney.

"Charlie, if I can offer a suggestion," Kearney said.

"Sure."

"Aiming like that is fine if you're shooting in a competition at something that doesn't shoot back, but that's not how it's going to happen if you're using a pistol in self-defense. Lower the hammer on that weapon and step aside."

I did what he said and watched him step into where I'd been.

Kearney stood facing the gunny sack like he was going to reach out and shake hands with it. In the next instant, he pulled that Single Action Army from his holster and started firing, fanning the hammer back with the palm of his left hand. The detonations rolled like thunder. The gunny sack jerked every time he hit it, which was every time. When he'd shot all six rounds, he opened the loading gate and punched out the spent shells.

"One of the things you have to know," Kearney said, "is to fire all your shots. Make every round count, and don't think a man who's tried to kill you is dead. Know it. You don't want him getting back up when you least expect it."

"And if there's more than one man?" I asked.

"Well, for starters, you're someplace where you're not supposed to be and you should get out of there." Kearney's eyes went dark for a minute and I knew he was peering through gun smoke on a distant battlefield for a minute. "But if you're up against more than one opponent, you have to put the first one down and spread the bullets around. Reloading takes time. You want to shoot for the center of a man when you have to shoot. Even if he's moving, you're bound to hit something." He pushed new cartridges into his pistol from his gun belt and holstered it. "Now you."

I took the spot and tried to do what he'd done. At five feet, I hit the gunny sack every time, but I wasn't nearly as fast as Kearney. I couldn't get the fanning down and I kept knocking the pistol off target, but every bullet hit what it was supposed to hit. Firing just took time. If the gunny sack had been shooting back, I'd probably have been a dead man and I knew it.

***

I shot pistols for the better part of two hours, trying to find one that I liked and felt comfortable in my hand. I never did get the knack of fanning the hammer the way Kearney did. So I told him about Angel Blunt's pistol and how he didn't have to pull the hammer back each time before he fired.

That surprised Kearney and we returned to his shop.

"There are not many pistols that do that," he told me. "None of them are made by Colt or Smith & Wesson. But there are some that are made by the British and the French. The Confederacy bought a lot of those weapons because we didn't have any munitions manufacturing shops in the South."

He showed me Beaumont-Adams revolvers and Tranters that didn't look as elegant as Samuel Colt's products or Smith & Wesson's, but he said they were accurate, reliable pistols that just hadn't caught on overmuch in the United States.

When he showed me a French revolver he called the MAS Modéle 1873, I recognized it as the same weapon that Blunt had carried.

"It's a good revolver," Kearney said. "But Blunt's going to have trouble getting ammunition for it. Those are chambered in eleven millimeter, a European cartridge you don't see over here much."

"So he'll have to special order cartridges," I said.

"Yes."

I filed that away. I knew that special orders could be tracked. Mister Henson and I had to send away for special hardware folks wanted on caskets for their loved ones. You could get something like that, but you had to look for it and there weren't many people you could get it from.

In the end, I settled on one of the Tranter pistols, a .50-caliber beast that only held five rounds in the cylinder. It bucked like a wild thing in my hand when I squeezed the trigger, but I was big enough and strong enough that I handled it just fine, which surprised the gunsmith.

"That thing is a hand cannon," Kearney said.

I agreed that it was.

"Not many men could hold onto something like that or would want to."

I took a little pride in that, and it felt partly like a foolish thing, but I didn't care.

"With that fifty-cal load," he said, "you'll only have to hit a man once. Even if you don't hit him square, he's going down."

That was what I was hoping. I could hit what I was aiming at with the first shot, but I wasn't fast with that second shot. Or the third or the fourth.

I paid for the pistol, a gun belt, and five hundred rounds of .50-caliber ammunition, all that was in the gun shop. Kearney told me I needed to practice every day if I was going to be any good with the Tranter. I looked forward to the practice because I'd surprised myself by having some skill with it.

And that big Tranter felt right at home in my hand.

I also picked up a Winchester Model 1876 chambered in a .50-95 cartridge meant for big game hunting. According to Kearney, the Model 1876 was just a step down from a Sharps buffalo rifle but it was a repeater. I didn't know what I was going to do with the rifle, but I saw it and I wanted it.

Buying those guns meant I was going to have to find work sooner than I'd planned on.

"A word of advice," Kearney said before I left. "Hang onto your brass when you can. If you get to a gunsmith that doesn't carry that cartridge, chances are good that he can reload the brass that you have."

I nodded and thanked him. I don't think he truly believed I just wanted to be armed for self-protection.

Truth to tell, after getting in that first day of practice, I was feeling more vengeful than I had. Or maybe it was because I wasn't hurting as much and I was hungry.

Or it could have been because Aiken's questions had me thinking about things I didn't want to think about. Things that I thought I had stopped thinking about years ago. I hadn't had any control over my circumstances back then, but I was different now.

13

I bought a new Stetson at Latham's Mercantile, and I hated it. Not the hat, because it was a dun color that I thought looked good. I hated buying the hat. Nothing ever stayed new after I got it.

The boots I had on now were a fairly recent addition, and I'd paid a good price for them because my feet had finally stopped growing. I hoped. Keeping me in boots had been pure misery there for a while. I still loved my boots, but they didn't shine the way they had when Mister Stuart had first handed them to me.

Walking down the boardwalks along Main Street, I felt conspicuous. The Tranter rode high on my hip, which Kearney had told me was the best position to wear it, not hanging low like the gunfighters were supposed to favor. It was also heavier than I'd thought it would be. My limp had smoothed out some, but walking felt different again.

I was glad the suit coat I wore was cut to thigh-length because it concealed the Tranter. Mostly.

It was getting on toward supper time and I realized I hadn't eaten anything since that big breakfast at Wick's Diner. I was feeling hollow about then, so I headed down to the Trail's End Restaurant.

Before Pecos was a town, before the railroad came through, a permanent camp had been set up there for cattle drives to cross the Pecos River. Trail's End Restaurant had started out of the back of a chuck wagon and had grown into a small tent and into a circus tent and finally into the two-story building it now was at the west end of Main Street not far from the gun shop.

Mister Henson and I had replaced some of the chairs and tables in the place because cow hands still came through and still got rowdy now and again. Missus Griffin, herself the daughter of Abraham Todd, who had started with the chuck wagon, had taken over the restaurant and run it after her pa had passed. Her husband had been a drunkard and had run off with the proceeds one night, and she hadn't missed a step.

The inside of the Trail's End was roomy, but simple. Tables and chairs were arranged so folks had elbow room but could still be packed in. A long painting of a stagecoach crossing a desert with buzzards circling overhead hung behind the front counter.

There was also a portrait of Abraham Todd at one end. He looked like a fine old gentleman who'd seen some hard years. He had died before I was born, but I had seen his grave out in the Sunflower Cemetery. Missus Griffin visited there regularly and brought flowers even though she had her hands full with the day-to-day business of running the restaurant.

A lot of folks kind of forgot the people they buried.

I felt a little guilty then because I hadn't thought about Mister Henson much all day. I mean, I had, but only in memories. Not anything much about how I was going to deal with his funeral. And that had to be done soon.

So I wasn't really happy when I took a table to myself and ordered a steak and a baked potato. I started with a bowl of chili because Trail's End was hard to beat when it came to chili. I drank buttermilk Missus Griffin kept chilled in the well out back.

I knew I couldn't eat high on the hog like this every night without burning through my savings. Right now I had no prospects, though everyone in town knew I had a strong back, once my leg healed up, and I was willing to do pretty near anything when it came to work. Most of those folks wouldn't have handled the dead.

But for the minute, I had nothing, and I had to admit, that scared me. I didn't even have a place to sleep tonight. That realization hit me like a sledgehammer and almost put me off my supper, but I was hungry and I'd always had an appetite.

The first few days after starting work with Mister Henson on dead folks had put a dent in my hunger, but I'd recovered quickly enough.

So I worked my way through the chili and the steak and potato, and even a slice of apple pie and blackberry cobbler with ice cream on the side. I ordered another glass of buttermilk and sat there trying to figure out what to do about a bed for the night.

There were three hotels in town, but I didn't feel right about staying in one of those. I'd only ever stayed in whatever cheap rooms my parents had been living in, and then in the funeral home. I hadn't ever been inside a hotel. They delivered folks unlucky enough to die in them to the back alleys once a doctor had pronounced them dead.

Then that uncomfortable sensation of being watched again settled into the pit of my stomach.

I glanced around the room. Some folks had recognized me, of course, even with me sitting in a back corner of the restaurant, because they knew me from what had happened with my parents, and now with what had happened to Mister Henson.

Most of them were polite and offered condolences, and a few had questions, but I'd quickly let them know I wasn't in the mood to answer those questions. Anyway, Aiken had already hit the streets with an extra edition of the paper so a lot of folks knew everything I knew.

Well, except for what had brought Blunt to Pecos and who Mister Henson had really been. I only knew one and not the other.

Mister Hunziker, who owned the general store, had stopped by and offered work to replace some shingles on his building once I was back on my feet. It was hot, hard work, but it was work, so I accepted and told him we'd work out the details once I knew when I'd be getting around better.

But I knew someone was watching me. In fact, it was two someones.

The two men sat over in the corner of the restaurant across from me. They wore dusty clothing and were big, rough men with hard eyes.

Just looking at them formed a knot of ice in my belly, and that made me mad. I didn't want to be afraid then. I was sick of being afraid.

Not only that, but now that I got a better look at them, I would have sworn one of them was a man from Blunt's gang who had been in the Sunflower Cemetery.

For a long minute, I looked at them, trying to work out how I was going to handle the situation. The man I thought looked familiar gave me a slow grin, and a gold tooth gleamed at the front of his mouth. That tooth sealed the deal. I was sure I remembered that.

I got up from my table and headed over, threading through a bunch of ranch hands that had just arrived.

14

If my approach bothered either of the two men, they didn't show it. In fact, Gold Tooth grinned at me and sipped his beer.

"Careful what you do, boy," he sneered when I stood next to their table. His right hand rested on the butt of his Colt .44. "Buyin' that pistol ain't made you no gunslick. You were lucky yesterday. Angel thought he'd killed you."

A few times during the day, I'd entertained thoughts about what I would say to Blunt, or any of his men, if we ever crossed paths again. In fact, a couple of those thoughts were wishful thinking on my part. I hadn't liked feeling helpless. It was the most onerous feeling in the world, and when I'd been twelve, I'd sworn I'd never feel that way again.

"I'll make sure you're dead if you try somethin' on me," Gold Tooth said.

"What are you doing here?" My voice came out squeakier than I'd intended, and it was like I had to force air out through my throat.

"Angel thinks you know where the map is."

"What map?" I demanded.

"That old man said there was a map to the gold, but he wasn't speakin' clear at the end, so we don't know what he was sayin'." Gold Tooth shifted his boots like he was bored. "Angel was sure he'd killed you last night. That's why we didn't take you with us. Me an' Possum were stakin' out Ellie Deno's house when we found out you were still alive."

I looked at them. "I don't know anybody named Ellie Deno."

Gold Tooth shook his head and looked at his partner. "I told you this was a waste of time. He don't even know Ellie."

Possum kept looking at me with those hard eyes. "It doesn't matter. Angel wanted us to find out what this boy knows about the map, so here's where we'll be until he gives it to us."

Gold Tooth shook his head and cursed. "If you know where the map is, you'd best hand it over an' save yourself some more pain." He stood and pulled a short jackknife from his pocket. Then he reached for my arm. "We've been followin' you all day, boy, so now we're gonna go out into the alley an' finish this. You'll tell us what you know soon enough, an' be glad of it."

I didn't think. All I could see was that knife, and I remembered what Crying Bear had done to Mister Henson with his. I balled up a fist and hammered Gold Tooth right in the face. Like I said, I was strong from digging ditches and wells, and lifting wood and bodies. When I hit a man, he usually knew he was hit.

Gold Tooth stumbled backward, blood leaking from his nose and his mouth. He bounced off the wall behind him.

I was getting set, ready to hit Gold Tooth again when Possum kicked their table forward and hit me in my wounded thigh. Pain swept over me and the leg wouldn't hold my weight for a minute. I fell backward and struggled to keep my balance. Instead, I ran straight into those drovers.

I found out right quick that they'd already stopped in for a few beers at the Ugly Toad. And they were in a mood. The man I bumped into tried to catch me, but he barely got me on my feet when Gold Tooth came at me with that knife, aiming to take my head off at the neck.

I ducked under the swipe and the blade cut across the cheek of the man trying to hold me. That got everybody's attention, and the fight started in earnest. I unloaded a left jab into Gold Tooth's face. Before I could congratulate myself, and I would have because I'd wanted to break his face, he swiped again, missing me and cutting another cowboy who cursed in pain.

I planted a solid punch into Gold Tooth's stomach that let the air out of him in a sour rush. Before I could take advantage of that, one of the cowboys behind me roared a curse and punched me in the ear, which set my head to spinning and fresh blood leaking down the side of my face.

I tried to find Gold Tooth in the sudden rush of double vision that hit me, but I swung and I missed. I got caught by the chair Possum came up swinging. I didn't think it was one of the chairs Mister Henson and I had made because this one shattered pretty quickly. Then again, Possum was a big man and could probably swing a chair pretty hard.

I went down and struggled to get up on my throbbing leg and with my head spinning. By then, though, the drovers were obviously thinking me and Gold Tooth and Possum were there only to make all their lives miserable.

Somebody kicked me, and somebody else after that. The kicking picked up speed and there was a lot of cursing. I covered up as best as I could, but I still took some pretty good shots. I thought I saw Gold Tooth and Possum pulling guns and backing the drovers off so they could get away, but I couldn't be certain because I was hoping to keep my ribs intact.

I don't know how long the beating went on, but those drovers took it on as their life's work for the few minutes it lasted before I heard someone say, "Stand down! Stand down now or I'll run you all in for the night!"

I recognized Maggie's voice immediately and was thankful because the kicking stopped.

15

"It's the girl deputy," a man said in the sudden silence that followed.

"She's a deputy?" another man else asked.

"She is," a woman replied. "That's Maggie Buchanan. She's a deputy, and you'd better mind your tone."

Cautiously, I lifted my head and watched Maggie step into the Trail's End.

Her face was cold and hard, and I knew she meant business.

"Somebody here tell me what's going on," she demanded.

A chorus of accusations against me followed the question. I noticed not much was said about Gold Tooth or Possum. They were just referred to as two guys with guns who were with me. Maggie was most interested in that, but when she found out they'd quit the premises and someone had seen them ride off, she dropped it.

Everyone, it seemed, agreed that I had thrown the first punch. No one had seen Gold Tooth's knife till he'd come up swinging it.

"I need you men to move away from that man," Maggie said, nodding at me. "Give me some room to deal with my prisoner."

Prisoner? I didn't care for the sound of that at all, but if it would get me out of Trail's End more or less in one piece, I thought maybe I was okay with that. I suspected that if Maggie left me there, the beating and kicking would recommence.

I started to get up, but one of the cowboys dropped a boot in the middle of my back and knocked me back down. My chin hit the hardwood floor and the metallic taste of blood filled my mouth. My head spun again. Even as bad as I felt, it was just one man this time and I thought I could fight my way up him. But I held still out of respect for Maggie, and because there was a good chance that I'd make things worse.

"Where's the marshal?" the belligerent cowboy who'd stomped me asked.

"The marshal's out of town," Maggie said. "Get your foot off my prisoner." She stated the order calmly, like they were discussing the weather. "I won't tell you again."

"Look," the cowboy said, "I ain't gonna listen to some slip of a—"

That was as far as he got. Maggie kicked him right in the crotch before he knew what was coming. If the effort wasn't the hardest she could deliver, it was at least administered with considerable force.

The cowboy gave a high-pitched yelp and grabbed himself like he was trying to keep everything together. Before he could recover, Maggie reached up, grabbed him by the hair of the head, and drove his face into a nearby table. When she released him, he fell over and curled up like newborn. Nobody leaned down to help him.

Like I said, everybody in school learned quick that Maggie fought to win, and it didn't matter how dirty she had to get to do it.

"Anybody else want to interfere with me carrying out the law?" Maggie asked. She talked almost normal, like she kicked a full-grown man in the crotch every day and twice on Sunday.

She'd always been matter of fact since I'd known her. I'd never seen her mad or happy or excited or scared. She just was Maggie every day. The boys at school had learned to leave her alone because she'd fought every one of them who had tried to give her trouble. Even the fights she hadn't won outright had proved bad for the winners. They'd worn bruises and black eyes, and other girls would ignore them from then on.

The cowboys backed away immediately. A couple of them helped their friend to his feet, but he wasn't in any particular hurry to get there. The one Gold Tooth had cut with the jackknife had a hand wrapped around his wound and it was obvious he was going to need some stitches. At least after the visit to the Ugly Toad, he wasn't hurting as much as he could have been.

"Can you stand?" Maggie asked me.

"Yeah," I answered.

"Good, because I'm not carrying you. The best you could hope for without walking is to be dragged to jail."

"Jail?"

"That's where you're going," she told me. "I'm taking you in for disturbing the peace." She leaned down and cuffed my hands behind my back. The iron manacles bit into my wrists. "Now get up."

I didn't see how I was going to accomplish that with my hands cuffed behind my back, but she grabbed me by one arm and got me started up. I managed to make it the rest of the way under my own power and stood there feeling foolish.

Maggie pulled that Tranter pistol from its holster and held it in her other hand as she walked me out of the Trail's End.

"You need to be careful," I told her as she marched me across the street toward the jail.

"I do?"

"You do," I said. "Those men in there, one of them was a gold-toothed outlaw that was with Angel Blunt yesterday at the cemetery. He's partnered up with a man he called Possum."

Maggie looked around the street, but it was dark and most of the light came from the Ugly Toad and a couple other eating establishments still open for business.

"What were they doing there?" she asked.

"Following me, as it turns out." I negotiated a deep wagon wheel rut that cut the street.

"Why?"

I hesitated over that one, and I knew Maggie noticed. She stayed quiet and waited on me to answer.

"I don't know," I said.

"I don't believe you," she said.

And that was all we said to one another all the way to the jail.

At least the matter of where I was going to be sleeping tonight had been resolved.

16

After she put me in one of the empty jail cells, Maggie went to fetch Gilbride. I sat on that thin cot that was bolted to the wall and tried not to think about Gold Tooth or Possum stopping by the marshal's office long enough to kill me. It wouldn't have taken them but a minute to accomplish, and inside that cell, there was nowhere for me to run.

I sat back in the corner of the cot as much against the wall as I could so no one could stick a gun through the bars covering the window and shoot me from there either.

The last two days had spurred my imagination up something fierce.

Finally, Maggie returned with Gilbride. He told me to strip to my underwear so he could examine me, and I wasn't comfortable doing that in front of Maggie. She didn't say anything, and she leaned against the stone wall with her arms crossed and a look on her face that let me know she wasn't leaving.

So I stripped, and it was an embarrassing thing to do, but not so much in some ways. I had seen a lot of naked folks while I'd worked with Mister Henson. People worried about how they looked and how fat they were, but I'd noticed people generally looked the same in a lot of respects.

Gilbride poked and prodded my ribs, which were

considerably sore and promised to get even more so in the coming hours. He checked my eyes, then checked the stitches in my thigh and head and changed the compresses on both when he pronounced them still holding.

Then he told me to get dressed and I did. I noticed the suit Mister Kuáng had given me had suffered some damage from the fight, but it wasn't anything that a good cleaning and a little mending wouldn't put to rights.

"You're going to be good and sore tomorrow," Gilbride said as he put his supplies back in the black bag he'd brought with him.

"He's well enough to stay the night in the jail?" Maggie asked.

"He is." Gilbride frowned and looked at me. "I kept hoping you'd come back by the office today, Charlie. We need to talk about some things."

Guilt stung me, but I didn't want to deal with it, so I kept my mouth shut.

"I sure didn't expect this." Gilbride looked disappointed. "We need to talk about Mister Henson's body. And about the funeral."

"I know," I said.

"I've finished my autopsy and written up my report for Marshal Buchanan," Gilbride said. "We're ready to bury Mister Henson, and it needs doing."

"Yes sir, I know."

"Do you know what Mister Henson would want?"

I couldn't believe I was having that conversation while I was in jail after I'd almost gotten murdered a second time. Of course, all Gilbride knew was that I'd been in a fight.

"No," I answered.

Gilbride nodded. "Actually it's not a matter of what he would want, Charlie. It's what you want."

I wanted Mister Henson back. I wanted him to be alive and the funeral home to still be standing and for Mister Henson to have never been anyone but Mister Henson. That was what I wanted.

But that wasn't going to happen.

I blinked away tears. "We need to see to it he gets buried proper."

"That sounds like a good idea. How do you want to do that?"

"Mister Henson bought some plots out in Sunflower Cemetery," I said. "He worked out a deal with Mister Parks, the man who owns the cemetery. Sometimes folks come to us and they don't have the money for more than a casket. Mister Henson would give them one of the plots and never mention a price. Mister Parks wasn't so generous."

"Mister Henson was a good man, Charlie."

I nodded even though my thoughts were bouncing around all over inside my head. There were so many things no one else knew about Mister Henson.

So many things I still didn't know.

"He'll have a plot then," Gilbride said.

"Yes." I took a breath. "Mister Kuáng down at the laundry has a suit we can bury Mister Henson in."

"That's good," Gilbride said. "We can get a casket from one of the other funeral homes. So we should be all set."

That was when I remembered the casket Mister Henson had built for himself. When I'd helped him do it, I'd thought the idea of building your own casket was pretty morbid, like something out of a Poe story.

That casket hadn't been in the funeral home. Mister Henson had moved it into storage. He'd told me that it was to keep him from selling it. I'd always thought that was strange, but now, sitting in the cell, I thought maybe I knew why he'd had that casket put someplace else.

"Charlie?"

Realizing Gilbride had called my name more than once, I glanced over at him.

"We can bury Mister Henson the day after tomorrow," Gilbride said. "If that's all right."

"All right," I said. The thought of Mister Henson being buried bothered me because it meant I'd never see him again. Not that I wanted to see what was left of him after what Crying Bear and Gilbride had done to him. Everything just seemed so...final.

"I'll contact Mister Parks and find out which plot we can use," Gilbride said. "If you want, you can pick it out."

I nodded.

"I'll arrange for some grave diggers," Gilbride said.

"I can do it," I said.

Gilbride stood with his medical bag in one hand. "You're not going to be able to do that, Charlie. Even if you weren't banged up and stitched up, that would be more than you need to be doing."

"But—" My voice broke and it took me a bit to get it back. "I need to do something for Mister Henson, Doctor Gilbride."

"Charlie," he put a hand on my shoulder and looked at me with a small smile, "you've already done so much for Mister Henson. You respected him and took care of him."

"We took care of each other," I said.

Gilbride nodded. "That you did, and that's all a father can ask of a son. Let me, as your friend and his, take care of this. Please."

I nodded, because I didn't trust my voice.

After he told me and Maggie goodnight, Gilbride left us.

Maggie continued leaning against the wall and said, "You've had yourself a busy day. Poked around in the wreck left of the funeral home, got new clothes, saw Aiken at the Pioneer, bought a new pistol and rifle, and went by the bank. And then you got arrested."

I looked at her and let her know I wasn't any too happy about her locking me up.

"Were you following me around?" I asked. "If so, you missed Gold Tooth and Possum." But I was pretty sure she hadn't been following me around all day because I would have noticed Maggie Buchanan. I always did.

So I was wondering how she knew so much.

17

"I wasn't following you," Maggie said. "You had soot on your bandages and on your face that I figured came from the fire because it wasn't on you last night. You're wearing new clothes. New underwear too."

My face got hot at that, but I didn't look away from her.

"I ran into Aiken later and he wanted information about you," she went on. "I didn't give it to him. It's not my job to do his job. When I brought you in, you were wearing that hand cannon, and Missus Griffin had one of her kitchen help run over your rifle and your new hat. I assume you got the weapons at Mister Kearney's."

I didn't answer.

"It doesn't matter," she said. "I knew you went by the bank because you had cash money on you when I brought you in, and you didn't have it last night."

"You know all that?"

"I do. It's called being observant."

I glared at her. Maggie had always done really well in school too.

"If you're so observant, then you know I didn't start the trouble at the Trail's End," I said.

She sighed and shook her head. "Of course I know that. Why would you pick a fight with seven cowboys you didn't even know?"

I didn't know how many of them there were. I hadn't

been paying attention.

"Then why did you arrest me?"

She looked at me. "Where else were you going to sleep, Charlie?"

I didn't have an answer for that because I hadn't known.

"At least this way you can get a good night's sleep and be protected from Blunt's men."

"You believe me about that too?"

"I do." Maggie studied me. "I've been a deputy for three years, Charlie. My pa wouldn't let me do it before that. I'd been wanting to do it sooner, but I understood his arguments. I was too young. Most folks think I'm still too young, but I get the job done."

I remembered how she'd kicked that cowboy in the crotch and knew she was good at being a deputy.

Evidently she knew what I was thinking because she frowned at me. "This job requires more than just the ability to shut down a handful of rowdies."

"You've got to be observant," I said sarcastically.

"You do. And you've got to be logical. Blunt didn't ride up to Sunflower Cemetery and kill Mister Henson for no reason. Logic says that Blunt had a reason." Maggie's dark eyes locked with mine. "Last night, I almost believed you when you said you didn't know why that happened."

I sat quiet and still.

"Just for the record," Maggie said, "I no longer believe you. Especially not with two of Blunt's men still hanging around town watching over you." She paused. "What are they hoping to learn?"

I thought about lying to her, but I didn't. I had the feeling she would sniff out a fib in the blink of an eye.

"Blunt had a reason for killing Mister Henson, didn't he?" Maggie asked.

"I don't want to talk about this," I said.

"Sure you do," she replied. "That's why you went to see Aiken."

I shifted on the bed and wondered how I could escape the inquisition now taking place.

Maggie proved relentless. "It didn't take me long to figure out that you didn't go to Aiken just to get your name in the paper. You went there to get information about Blunt, something beyond the fact that Blunt is an outlaw and a murderer. Am I right?"

I didn't answer.

"Keeping secrets is going to get you killed, Charlie," she said, "and I'd really not like to see that happen."

Me neither. "What did Aiken want to know about me?"

I figured I'd be observant and learn some things too.

Maggie didn't pull any punches. That wasn't her way. "He wanted to know about the deaths of your parents," she said. "I know some of the story, but I'd like to know more."

She might as well have kicked me in the groin too.

18

When I was twelve, my pa, as I have said, had been a drunkard. He was a man who had no trade, no skills, and he couldn't read or write. Ma had told me he'd been a cowboy for a time, and that he'd been on several longhorn cattle drives up to Kansas and to Colorado.

Ma had met him up in Kansas and she'd been swept off her feet by this young cowboy. On his second trip up to Baxter Springs, Kansas, to see her after eating dust following a herd, he'd married her in a fever and brought her back to Texas. She'd been sixteen years old and he'd been twenty.

They'd lived on whatever dirt-poor acreage he could find. During the whole time I was growing up, Ma never mentioned what she'd dreamed would come from the marriage. I was sure she'd thought there would be a small house with a picket fence somewhere.

Or maybe she would have just been content with Pa.

I don't know. Then Pa went off to fight in the Civil War. He was with the Texas Brigade, like Kearney had been. Only when Pa came back from the war, he wasn't the man Ma had married.

He'd gone from being that bright-eyed young cowboy she'd met in Baxter Springs to a shell of a man haunted by the war. He'd turned to drink on his way home, and he'd stayed with it once he got there. I was born the year the war ended, but I don't think either of them wanted me.

Over the next twelve years, they pulled up stakes and moved one step ahead of creditors, ducking out just far enough away that folks wouldn't know who my pa was or the troubles we'd seen.

Pa would get a job, any kind of job he could do with a strong back, that didn't pay much, and he'd work for a time. He was always filled with regret when the drinking got bad. Ma would get him sobered up, or maybe it was just the sheer lack of money to buy beer or whiskey, and they would find a new town to move to.

Ma helped out when she could. She'd take in laundry and do mending and housecleaning for folks, and she wouldn't make any friends, not even at the church, because she didn't know how long we would be staying in town.

As I recall, Ma loved church. She'd take me every Sunday when I was growing up. Then, when Pa just kept drinking more and more, she finally quit going.

Looking back now, I realized that was when she started giving up too. She didn't turn to drink like Pa did. She gave in to laudanum, which she took "to help her sleep." By the time I was ten, she was matching Pa in binges, both of them unable to work or take care of me.

They started fighting then, and I remember the screaming and crying, the bruises, the blood, and the broken bones. Some of that was mine, because even when I stopped trying to keep them from fighting, sometimes I would get roped in.

I learned to fend for myself and help them out where I could, but even the odd jobs I got didn't make enough money to touch what we needed for rent or food.

I'd learned to go outside and sometimes sleep on the roof so rattlers couldn't get at me while they went at it. The town marshals came by, the church folks, but Ma and Pa would just pick up and move on.

Everybody reached rock bottom in Pecos.

In Pecos, Pa's horse took sick and died, and he sold our wagon, so when the time came, even if we could have gotten another horse, we were stuck and had no way of fleeing town. So, feeling it was all over for them, Ma waited up for Pa to come home from the saloon and started the fight. They gave it to each other pretty good, both of them I guess using up their last reserves of hate and unhappiness.

Then, when Pa got the upper hand, and told her he'd had enough and was leaving us, Ma took out his old .44 and shot him. She kept on shooting him too.

I can still remember the shots cracking thunder while I was lying on the roof of that room they'd been able to afford. Ma emptied the pistol into Pa, but she'd saved one final bullet. She put that pistol into her mouth and pulled the trigger.

Maggie's pa, Marshal Buchanan, had climbed up on that roof and brought me down. I didn't speak for four days.

19

I felt even more worked over after telling the story than I had when I'd started it. I sat there on that jail cot and felt chilled and alone and exhausted.

The only thing that kept me going was the idea of checking Mister Henson's casket quick as I could come morning.

For a time, silence lingered in the space between me and Maggie. Her face hadn't changed a lick during the whole time I was talking. If what I'd said had touched her in any way, I didn't know it.

In a way, I was glad she had no response. I didn't want her feeling sorry for me. I'd already been all through that and I knew sympathy didn't help. Lots of people had felt sorry for me when I was living with my ma and pa, but nobody had stepped in and done anything about it.

Not like Mister Henson had after I thought there was nothing in the world left for me.

"I already knew some of that story," Maggie said. "I guess I'd heard some of it, and I read Pa's notes about you this afternoon while I was looking up history on Blunt and his gang."

"Well, tell me about Blunt," I said. "That was the deal."

She shot me a small frown, and I think that was just to let me know what she was thinking because I couldn't detect any real emotion. "What you just told me hasn't helped me understand why Blunt killed Mister Henson."

"You wanted to know about my parents."

"Only because that's what Aiken was asking about." Maggie thought for a minute. "You went to Aiken to find out more about Blunt. He put you off by asking you about your parents. That's easy to figure."

Actually I was surprised by all that she was able to guess at. I'd known before that Maggie Buchanan was smart, but she was going beyond all my expectations. Now she was actually a threat to the secrets I was trying to keep.

"I've got information that Aiken probably doesn't have because I'm a better investigator than he is," Maggie said. "When Pa needs details on criminal activity, he asks me to get it."

"And you pull that out of thin air?" I was a little salty over having told her the story of my parents. That was never an experience I wanted to relive. So I was a little sarcastic toward her.

"No," she said, not acting offended. "I'm friends with one of the Pinkerton detectives that works the train. The Pinkerton Detective Agency keeps files on lots of outlaws, especially the ones who rob trains, and what he didn't know, the man at the other end of the telegraph line did."

That soured me a little because I knew most folks thought the Pinkertons were dashing lawmen. Except for the Confederate flag wavers in town who hated them because Allan Pinkerton had started his business up as a private detective agency and ended up protecting President Abraham Lincoln during the war. The Pinkertons had also done a lot of spying and sabotage against Confederate forces.

Some of those Pinkertons were young men who would probably fancy Maggie. That idea bothered me.

"Friends, huh?" I asked, and I sounded even more accusing than I'd intended.

She gave me a sharp look. "If you don't want to hear the story, Charlie, I can leave you in that cell and let you out in the morning."

Well, I was mad enough after getting locked up and being forced to get undressed in front of her, and still hurting over the beating, getting shot, and losing Mister Henson that I almost called her on her threat.

Except I knew she wasn't bluffing. She'd leave me locked up without batting an eye.

I wanted to know what she knew, but I wanted to learn it in a way that didn't tip my hand.

"No," I said. "I want to hear."

"Then we have a deal? I tell you what you want to know and you'll tell me?"

I nodded.

She took a big ring of keys from the wall and opened my cell.

"C'mon," she said as she swung the door open. "I've got coffee and my notes in the front office. We can talk there."

***

The marshal's office hadn't changed much since I'd last been there when I was twelve. Marshal Buchanan had brought me there after he'd gotten me that night when my parents died. I was surprised by how much I remembered, because I'd been pretty traumatized.

There was a desk, a potbellied stove with a pipe that ran up through the ceiling, and a gun cabinet that had a chain running through the trigger guards of the various rifles and shotguns racked there. I noticed my new rifle was there and thought it looked fine beside all the other Winchesters and Henrys and Greeners. My new dun-colored hat sat on the hat rack by the door.

Maggie sat behind the big, scarred desk and looked totally at home in the swivel chair. She took a pocket notebook from her dungarees that reminded me of the one Aiken used.

I sat across from her and drank warmed-up coffee that wasn't too bad from a tin cup that let me warm my hands.

She read through her notes for a minute and I watched

her, thinking I'd never noticed how pretty her eyes were. Well, I had, but I never thought I'd be talking to her as much as I was or sitting this close so I could see them so clearly.

Of course, she had arrested me and I was now part of an investigation, so I guessed we would be talking.

She had a fine, elegant hand for writing and I watched her turn through the pages with interest.

"Angelo Blunt is a murderer, a bank robber, and has held up trains," Maggie said. "Most of that you knew already."

I nodded.

"He's thirty-two years old and has served five years in prison, off and on, over the last fourteen years. So he's spent a third of his adult life behind bars at one institution or another. That's not counting drunk and disorderly charges and disturbing the peace charges he might have incurred." Maggie glanced up at me. "In all the records I've read, not one of them has mentioned Mister Henson."

"What about people who are known to work with Blunt?" I asked. "What do you know about them?"

She opened a desk drawer and pulled out a small stack of wanted posters. She pushed them over in front of me. "These are the men who have, at one time or another, ridden with Blunt. I looked for a dodger on Mister Henson. I didn't find one."

Anger stirred in me at that. "Why would you look for a wanted poster on Mister Henson?"

"For the same reason you're asking me about Angel Blunt. Something tied those two men together, and whatever it was, that was the thing that brought Blunt here to kill Mister Henson and almost kill you." Maggie paused. "It's also what's keeping two of Blunt's men in Pecos watching you. Mister Henson is dead. Unless they're hanging around to kill you, they'd be gone. And they had their chance in the Trail's End."

I resisted the impulse to look out the window that faced Main Street, but I did.

"Where is your pa?" I asked.

"Still out tracking Blunt and his gang, I suppose."

"So it's just you in town."

"Yes."

I wished we had more firepower as I looked through those dodgers. Blunt had fourteen known associates, and all of them were killers.

20

I found Gold Tooth five posters in. The drawing showed him with more beard growth than I'd seen, but that gold tooth was distinctive even in the sketch.

His name was Elroy Courbet and he was a wanted man from over in Louisiana. He'd robbed a bank in New Orleans where he had killed a guard and a woman teller and roughed up a handful of bank patrons. After that, fleeing a posse, he'd jumped through Texas and gone into holding up stages in Arizona and New Mexico Territories. He'd pulled his first train robbery working with Blunt.

I pushed the dodger over to Maggie. "This is one of the men I ran into at the Trail's End."

She nodded and studied Courbet's poster.

Possum was the eighth dodger down. His name was Oscar Jack Lavery and he was an Irishman from Chicago where he'd been a strikebreaker at the meatpacking plants until he'd gotten too zealous about his job and killed a man. Evidently killing folks got to be an easy thing for him because he'd killed nine of them that were known of since he'd headed out West. Most of them were in California, so Texas was new territory to him.

I pushed his dodger over as well. I told her about Cornelius Crying Bear and the man named Asbury. Neither of them had a dodger in the pile.

"Can you identify any of the others as being with Blunt that day?" Maggie asked.

She was thorough.

"No," I said. "I knew Blunt right off when Mister Henson called his name, and I watched him most of the time. Then…everything else just happened so quickly. The faces I saw yesterday, they look a lot like the rest of these faces." I waved at the pile of dodgers.

Maggie took a minute to go get us more coffee. When she sat down and slid my cup over, she asked, "Why was Blunt out there after Mister Henson?"

I sipped my coffee and wondered about lying to her and instead settled for shading the truth. A deal was a deal, although I thought she was holding back as much as I was.

"Blunt thought Mister Henson had gold," I said. "That's what he came there for."

"How much gold?"

"A lot."

"Did Blunt say how much?"

"No." At least, not that I knew of, so that was the truth as far as I was concerned. I'd never seen any of it.

"Why did Blunt think Mister Henson had gold?" Maggie asked.

"Did Blunt ever go down to Mexico?" I tried to ask that casually, but it was hard because I really wanted to know the answer.

Maggie didn't have to check her notes. "He robbed a bank down in Ciudad de Durango in the state of Durango, a train in Hermosillo, and killed three men in Chihuahua City."

I knew Chihuahua City was where Benito Juarez had holed up when the French Invasion had happened. I'd learned that in one of the history books Mister Henson had made me read. Now that I thought on it, Mister Henson had talked to me about the French Invasion and Emperor Maximillian I while I was reading that book.

Of course, he'd talked to me about a lot of things, but I hadn't really paid that much attention at the time. I'd just figured it was his way of checking up on whether I was doing the reading.

But thinking back on it now, I thought maybe Mister Henson knew a whole lot about that conflict between the French and the Mexicans. The problem was that looking back on a memory didn't mean that was what really happened. Sometimes a man could remember more than what actually happened at the time.

"Did your Pinkerton friend happen to tell you the dates of those crimes in Mexico?" I tried not to be spiteful about her having a friend, but I didn't think I succeeded. The idea of it rankled me.

Instead of being mad, though, Maggie looked at me with renewed interest. She checked her notes.

"Blunt and his gang robbed the bank in Ciudad de Durango in early April five years ago. The three men killed in Chihuahua City were murdered in the middle of April that same year, and the train was robbed in Hermosillo on April 28. The Pinkertons are much more detail oriented when it comes to anything that happens to trains. Again, that same year." Maggie tapped her notebook. "What does this have to do with what happened here?"

"I don't know about here," I said, "but those locations probably mean Blunt robbed the bank in Juarez to get enough funds to finance his trip into Chihuahua and robbed the train in Hermosillo while getting out of Mexico. Who were the three men Blunt killed in Chihuahua City?"

Maggie had to leaf through her notes, but she frowned. "I didn't write all of that down because I wouldn't have guessed anything that happened in Mexico would have any bearing on what happened in Pecos."

"Do you remember anything?" I knew from school that Maggie had an incredible memory.

"One of them was an historian, I think, another might have been an architect, and the third had something to do with President Benito Juárez's political cabinet."

"Is Juárez still president?" I asked. The book on Mexican history had been at least twenty years out of date.

"Juárez died in office in 1872," Maggie said. "We learned that in history class in school."

She'd learned that. I had evidently not paid attention or forgotten. Like I said, Maggie had an incredible memory. She hadn't even cared that much about history.

I felt like I'd learned something, though. Blunt had been down in Mexico looking for that gold he believed was still there.

"What does Mexico have to do with what happened yesterday?" Maggie asked.

I ignored the question for a moment. "Do you have anything in your notes about Angelo Blunt's father?"

Maggie fixed me with her gaze. "Charlie, I'm not going to follow you around in circles. What's the point here?"

"I need to know about Blunt's pa," I said. "Then I can tell you more."

"There's some information on the father," she told me grudgingly. "The Pinkertons don't have much on him. Just a first name, Simon. Blunt was Angelo Blunt's mother's maiden name. She never married. According to what we do have on Blunt's father, he was Mexican, maybe from Chihuahua, and was supposed to be a highway bandit who robbed people along the Rio Grande. He died robbing a train outside of El Paso."

"If they didn't know his last name, how do they know he's dead?"

"Because the Pinkertons make it a point to kill train robbers who don't surrender immediately." Maggie tapped her fingers on the desk, drawing me out of the thoughts I was trying to put together.

It sounded like Blunt had gone down to Chihuahua City to find the gold his father and Mister Henson had supposedly stashed somewhere, had failed, and ended up in Missouri where he'd found another breadcrumb that had eventually led him back to Mister Henson.

"Charlie," Maggie said.

I looked at her.

"What does any of this have to do with the murder of Mister Henson?" she asked.

"Some gold went missing in Chihuahua City during the French Invasion in 1861," I said. "When Benito Juárez decided he was going to welsh on the money he owed France, Great Britain, and Spain, he prepared a war fund to fight off any attempt those countries made to come and take over. Supposedly, Angelo Blunt's father helped steal that gold and told Angelo about it."

"So Blunt believes this Mexican gold is still somewhere he can get at it?"

"Yes."

"And Blunt thought Mister Henson would know where that gold is?"

"That's what he said."

"Did Mister Henson know?"

21

"No," I said, and I pulled it off pretty well, considering the fact I was pretty certain I was lying through my teeth.

Maggie searched my face with her eyes and I forced myself to not blink or back off an inch. "You're sure?"

I almost cursed at her because I hated being put in a hard place. Also, I was passing out from sheer exhaustion while I was sitting there, and I was hurting badly from the beating I'd taken.

"Maggie," I said in exasperation, "you saw what Blunt and his men did to Mister Henson. If he had known anything about what Blunt was talking about, do you think he would have kept it to himself?"

"You don't know that he didn't. You said yourself that you didn't hear everything that went on between them while you were lying in that grave."

That particular lie was going to come back to haunt me. I could see that.

But it also meant I could lie to Maggie in a roundabout way.

"Mister Henson told Blunt he wasn't the man Blunt was looking for," I said. "He repeated that over and over, even when Crying Bear tortured him." I took a sip of coffee to give myself a temporary respite, but my hand was shaking when I did.

Maggie glanced at my hand, then back to my eyes. I

think she relented a little then, but her face didn't change.

"It was a case of mistaken identity," she said.

"Had to be."

"I saw what they did to Mister Henson." Maggie leaned back in the swivel chair. "It would have taken a strong man to hold back anything during that."

I nodded. "That's what I'm telling you. Mister Henson wasn't whoever Blunt thought he was."

"Or Mister Henson was a lot stronger than Blunt thought he was. Maybe Blunt saw he'd never break Mister Henson, so he killed him. Otherwise Courbet and Lavery would have shaken the dust of this town off their boots too. They probably hung around to see if anything fell out of hiding after Mister Henson's death. Then they found you, so they're fixated on that."

Her summation made my skin crawl a little, and it added an edge that lifted me out of my exhaustion.

"If that was the case, it seems like we'd know if there was anything," I said. And I was thinking about Mister Henson's casket locked up in storage. I kept my face as blank as I could.

"You'd think so," Maggie agreed, but she was looking at me pretty hard.

I wanted to distract her, and I wanted some more information myself. Courbet had mentioned a name and I couldn't get it out of my head.

"Have you ever heard of Ellie Deno?" I asked.

Maggie tilted her head to the side, but that was the only reaction I got out of her. "Why are you asking about her?"

"Courbet mentioned her tonight."

"What did he say about her?"

I shook my head. "I want to know who she is before we talk."

She tried to stare me down for a moment. I didn't know if she quit on it because she figured she couldn't get the job done, or if she felt a little sorry for me.

Or that maybe giving me what I wanted would be just enough for me to blab whatever I was hiding anyway.

I was learning she was a lot cleverer than even I had thought.

She surprised me, too. I hadn't ever heard of Ellie Deno, or any Denos for that matter. Maggie got right up, walked over to the filing cabinet where she'd gotten the wanted posters, sorted through them quickly, and returned with a dodger. She laid the paper in front of me as she sat down.

I looked at the sketch but I didn't see anything at first. Eleanor "Ellie" Deno was wanted ALIVE for some kind of con job she did in Denver. Her bounty was fifty dollars.

I examined her face but only saw a woman in her thirties or forties. She had dark hair that curled around her shoulders and a wide, generous mouth. Her eyes were intense, though, and there was something about them that seemed familiar.

"You know her." Maggie made the statement an accusation.

"No," I said, being truthful. But I also had the impression that maybe I did.

"What does she have to do with Blunt?"

I got irritated at that. "I'm not the one with friends in the Pinkertons," I said. "Seems like you would be the one who would know about any relationship between Blunt and Ellie Deno."

Maggie shot me a hard look and I almost broke down and fessed up. I hung onto my silence because I knew that if I pursued the course I was on—and I was going to do exactly that because maybe I was feeling more vengeful—things were going to get dangerous.

Even more dangerous than they already had been.

I didn't want Maggie to get twisted up in that.

Thinking like that was kind of stupid on my part. She'd faced down a group of unruly drovers who had been waling the tar out of me.

Except Angel Blunt and his gang weren't a group of drovers. They were, to a man, killers. I didn't know what I was going to do with what I was learning, but I knew it was going to involve a lot of risk.

"Eleanor Deno," Maggie said in a crisp, no-nonsense tone, "is a con woman and a bunco artist. She's got charges against her in San Francisco to Denver to Kansas City and up to Minneapolis and Chicago."

Oscar Jack Lavery had been from Chicago too, I remembered. But I didn't point that out.

"The fifty-dollar bounty was posted by a man in David Moffat's circle after Deno bilked him out of a few thousand dollars."

I nodded at the poster. "I don't see any of that on the dodger."

"That's courtesy of my Pinkerton friend," Maggie said.

I bridled at that, but I refused to say anything.

"Detective Castor and I have discussions from time to time over dodgers," Maggie went on. "I try to stay current on any outlaws that might be passing through."

"Something special about Ellie Deno?" I asked.

"She caught my eye. You don't see wanted posters on many women. Fifty dollars isn't much to a bounty hunter, which is probably why she's stayed on the loose so long. The offer was probably made to get her sketch out there and make her life uncomfortable to keep her looking over her shoulder all the time. It's a shame the sketch is so bad."

It was bad, but it had gotten me thinking. There was also the issue that women could do things with their looks that men wouldn't think of.

"Why would the Pinkertons be so interested in a bunco artist?" I was also wondering what had brought Ellie Deno to Pecos, Texas.

"Because the man who posted the reward is one of David Moffat's people."

She'd mentioned the name earlier. I shrugged. "I don't know that name."

"David Moffat is an important financier in Denver. He helped bring the railroad to Denver when the decision was made to run the Transcontinental Railway through Cheyenne, Wyoming. So that makes him important to the Pinkertons."

"And your friend?"

She nodded. "Him too." She focused on me. "Who is Eleanor Deno to you, Charlie?"

"I don't know her." I drained my coffee cup. "And I'm tired."

"We had a deal. You were going to tell me what you were holding back."

"I did. That's all I'm going to say about it. Now, if that offer of the cot in the cell is still good, I'm going to bed."

"It is."

Trying to hide all the hurt going on inside me, I walked to the back of the marshal's office and lay down on the cot. Maggie followed me back and swung the door shut after I stretched out. The clang of metal on metal echoed in the stone-walled room.

I didn't mind.

I knew I'd be getting out in the morning.

I was going to check on Mister Henson's casket in storage, and then I was going to talk to Ellie Deno.

22

Ellie Deno found me first the next morning.

I was coming out of the Goose King Laundry after leaving my suit for repairs and after buying another. Mister Kuáng had another black suit similar to the one he'd given me yesterday and I took it because I'd liked the other one so much. I also liked the look it gave me.

I paid for this one, thanked Mister Kuáng again for the gift of the first, and made arrangements to pick up that suit in a couple days.

Outside, I put my new hat on gingerly. Some of the swelling around the stitches had gone down, so the fit was better, but the wound was still tender. The sunlight that morning seemed especially bright too, but Gilbride had told me to expect that for a few days because of the concussion I'd suffered from the impact of the bullet.

I looked the street over for any sign of Courbet or Lavery but saw nothing. It was just shy of eight o'clock and I figured that was too early for criminals who'd been out late the night before.

I wasn't feeling too good myself, but excitement pushed me on even though it felt like I was running on fumes. I wore the Tranter on my hip under the long coat, but I'd left the Winchester and spare rounds for both weapons with Mister Kuáng for safekeeping.

His wife was checking with one of the boardinghouses

where her sister cleaned to see if there was a room to let. She promised if I came by after one, after all the boardinghouse rooms were cleaned, she'd let me know about room availability.

Missus Kuáng assured me that she could find me a good room I could afford, and I believed her. Mister Kuáng was going to put the word out for me that I would be looking for carpentry jobs and well digging jobs, and pretty much nearly anything that paid in a few days.

I intended to go have a look at Mister Hunziker's roof and see how much work there would be on that. Knowing that would give me an idea of how much money was in it for me. The last two days, I had done nothing but drain my savings, and that worried me.

I was walking toward Wick's Diner, intending to get breakfast and wait for Mister Malpert to open his warehouse so I could check on Mister Henson's casket when someone reached out and caught my forearm.

After the last couple days I'd had, I spun, made my injured leg hold up under me, and shook my arm to break the hold. To my surprise, I'd reached down for the Tranter too. In fact, I had hold of the revolver and had half-cleared the holster when I realized who had grabbed me.

"Charlie!" she screamed and stepped back. "It's me!"

"Miss Abbie?"

She stood against one side of the alley, out of sight from the street for the most part. Fatigue had tightened her features and made her look older than I'd ever seen. She wore a brown dress that, honestly, made her look frumpy instead of well put together as she usually did. A veil dropping from her small hat covered her eyes and nose, so it was mostly the mouth that identified her for me.

"Yes," she said. "We need to talk."

"We do," I agreed.

"But not here." Miss Abbie linked her arm in mine and tugged me along after her as she walked down the alley. A small buggy and horse waited near the other end. "I don't want to be out on the street. And you shouldn't be there either. They'll find you."

I didn't bother to ask her who would find me because I figured I had a pretty good idea already.

*

"I have this room to do business in," Miss Abbie said when she opened the door to a small suite at the Shannsey Hotel.

With my new hat in my hand, I followed her in and looked around in surprise. Although the Shannsey was located at the east end of Pecos and not a place where there was a lot of foot traffic, it was well appointed and clean. The hotel also had a bad reputation for shady business dealings. Soiled doves who worked independent of brothels and madams were said to do business there.

There had been a couple of murders there that I knew of. Both times the victims had been out-of-towners, not citizens, and as far as I knew, those murders were still unsolved.

The room was nicer than anything I'd ever been in. There were French doors at the back of the room. I recognized them only because Mister Henson and I had put some in for a couple of the businesses on Main Street. These led to a short balcony with a small table and two chairs I could see through the sheer curtains.

A rectangular mirror hung over the stone fireplace on one wall, and gilded columns ran from the mantel to the ceiling. A sofa, a settee, and an armchair were arranged around the room, but a small table and four chairs occupied the middle of the room under a chandelier.

"What business?" I tried to figure out what Miss Abbie might do there.

I also wondered if Mister Henson had known about this room. All we'd ever seen was the modest house Miss Abbie had rented on the outskirts of town.

It was like she was two different women, which I guess shouldn't have surprised me given what I suspected about her. But it did. The difference between this suite of rooms and that little ramshackle house where Mister Henson and I had repaired the roof, both porches, and a couple spots in the flooring was night and day.

"Investments," Miss Abbie answered.

"Investments?" I repeated.

"Mining and land ventures in Texas and in neighboring states," Miss Abbie said. "When I was younger, I traveled a lot. I got to know a lot of businessmen in a lot of places. I'm a good person to connect one person with another these days. I get paid a small fee for those introductions." She waved a hand to one of the chairs at the table. "Please sit, Charlie. You're so tall looking up at you makes my neck hurt. And I know you've got to be in pain from your wounds."

I ducked my head away when she reached up to touch my face. I'd already seen the shiner and other bruising I'd collected from the Trail's End fiasco.

She drew her hand back and looked hurt. I almost felt bad about her, but I just remembered she'd been lying to Mister Henson—and me—for months.

I waved my hat at the room. "Did Mister Henson know about this?"

She folded her arms, walked over to the little table, and sat. She didn't speak and just stared at me.

Finally, feeling guilty for ignoring her hospitality and because I knew she wouldn't talk unless I gave in a little, I went over and sat across from her.

"No," she said. "John Peter didn't know about this place." She frowned as she looked around. "He wouldn't have liked this side of me. He liked a woman who was simple and needy." She lifted her head a little. "I could be that for him."

"From what I hear, you've been a lot of things for a lot of people, Miss Deno."

Her hand came up quick to slap me.

23

I wasn't thinking when I reached out and caught her hand only inches from striking me. I just knew I didn't want to get hit anymore. I held her there for a minute and looked into her green eyes as they clouded up.

Instead of crying like I thought she was going to do, Ellie Deno laughed as though at a joke.

"So you know who I am, Charlie?" she asked as she tugged her hand gently.

I released her hand and leaned back out of her reach because I wasn't going to completely relax my guard. The last couple of days had offered some harsh lessons and I'd always been a quick study on those kind.

"I do," I told her.

"For how long?"

"Since last night."

"How did you find out?"

"Courbet mentioned you when we were talking at the Trail's End."

"I'd heard about the fight." Ellie bit her bottom lip a little.

I didn't know if that was for show or if she was really nervous or contrite. I didn't trust anything about her, and I was going to keep it that way. But I could see how if I didn't know what I knew about her I'd be feeling a little sorry for her about now.

I wasn't going to think of her as Miss Ellie anymore. In fact, I wasn't going to think of her as Miss at all. She was Ellie Deno from that moment on, and she was a criminal.

"Then John Peter didn't know who I was," she said, and nodded to herself.

"Not as far as I know," I told her.

"Well, that's something then." Ellie took a breath and let it out. "And you know about Courbet being in town?"

"Yeah. Him and Lavery." I looked at her, knowing I had questions and being afraid to ask them. "Do you know who Mister Henson really was?"

Her eyes shuttered a little now and I knew we were playing a game for stakes I didn't quite understand.

"Don't you?" she asked.

"No. I always knew him as Mister Henson."

"Did he ever talk to you about the gold?"

At that point, I knew I had to start bluffing if I wanted a peek at Ellie's cards.

"The Mexican gold that was stolen from Benito Juárez," I said. "Sure. Mister Henson and I talked about it some."

"Did he tell you where it was?"

I smiled at her and I knew this was the part where we figured out who wanted what the most. "In Chihuahua City."

She frowned at me and cursed, and it was one of the most unladylike things I'd ever heard. She had nothing on the swampers that worked the slaughterhouse killing floors after the butchering was done for the day. I'd tried my hand at that for a couple days, thinking all the blood wouldn't bother me after working in the mortuary, but it did.

"Do you know where in Chihuahua City?" Her green eyes were bright with interest now and I didn't know how I'd ever thought she was a kind and gentle soul who made the best fried chicken I'd ever tasted.

"I'm going to ask some questions before we go any further," I said.

She laughed at me. "You ain't big enough to take a seat

at the table, kid."

Her voice, just like the softness I'd seen in her face, had turned coarse and rough. I knew she was trying to scare me, but I didn't have much scare left in me after the last couple days.

There was enough to keep me cautious, though.

"I already have a seat," I told her. "I know about the gold. I'm the only one Mister Henson trusted with the secret."

In that moment, I realized Mister Henson hadn't trusted me with any such a thing, and I felt pretty miserable that he hadn't. I couldn't help wondering why he didn't.

Ellie regarded me for a minute, then she reached back toward the mantel and took a machine rolled cigarette from an ivory box. Using a match she scratched to life with a red thumbnail, she lit the cigarette and blew out the flame with her first breath of smoke. She waved away the gray-white cloud that hung in her face.

"That gold will get you killed," Ellie said, "and Angel Blunt will be the one to do it."

"Not if I kill him first." That was when I first knew what I was going to do. Try to do, at least. Saying it out loud like that, I heard the need and drive in my own words.

Ellie laughed at me, then had a hacking, coughing spell.

I waited on her.

"Boy," she said when she recovered, "you escaped death once. Maybe twice if you count that run-in with Courbet and Lavery, and you should count that. You taking a run at Blunt is just stupidity."

"Maybe," I said, "but that's how it's got to be. Unless Blunt gives himself up to Marshal Buchanan."

"Fat chance." Ellie said some other stuff that was pure evil.

"Tell me who Mister Henson was."

"Are you going to tell me where that gold is?"

"No." I knew she wouldn't believe me if I told her anything else.

"Then I'm not going to tell you anything. You're so

smart, you figure it out."

"You're going to tell me," I said patiently.

She snorted.

"I'm going to tell you why," I continued.

"Are you going to threaten me, Charlie? Is that what you're thinking?"

"No, ma'am," I replied. "I'm going to make a deal with you. I'm going to let you in on an investment opportunity. That's what you do, right? Get people to sign onto business ventures."

She took a draw on her cigarette and the ember crawled more deeply in among the minced tobacco. She squinted at me through the smoke.

"I'm not interested in buying into a dry well or a piece of property that's more swamp than land," she told me.

"You hung around Mister Henson for months," I told her, "hoping to find out about that gold. I'm making a deal with you now. When I get that gold, I'm going to give you a ten percent finder's fee."

"How do I know I can trust you?"

"You don't," I replied honestly. "You won't know it until the day I lay that gold in your hand. And if it's possible, I will."

"You know I don't know where the gold is. What can I tell you that will help you find that gold?"

"I already know where the gold is," I lied, but I was thinking about Mister Henson's casket and the secret I hoped it contained. "What I don't know is who Mister Henson really was."

"Why do you even care about that?"

"Because I do." I did. More than I thought I would. But the answer was right here. Who he really was mattered to me.

Unless Ellie Deno was lying as much as I was.

She smoked in silence.

"Here's the deal," I pressed. "If I get up and walk out that door, you get nothing. But if we to go in partners, if you see me as an investment, you get a piece of that gold. Is anyone else going to make you that offer?"

Tension filled my belly as I waited on her to reply.

24

"Until he decided to start a new life as John Peter Henson, his name was Terrence Leopold Petway," Ellie said. "Before he was an undertaker, he was a shipbuilder out in San Francisco. That's where he learned all his woodworking skills. After that, he was a gold prospector. He never made a strike, but he got enough trace to keep at it for a few years."

My head filled up with images of a young Mister Henson—no, a young Leopold Petway, I had to stay focused on that—working on the fine details of a merchant ship's gingerbread coaming and out in the gold fields with a mule and a pick. I thought about all those stories he had and could have told me.

Now they were lost forever.

"When his gold fever finally cooled, Petway tried the military for a while," Ellie continued. "He served as an enlisted man in the Mexican-American War and killed an officer in Mexico City over a woman when the United States Army occupied that place. Facing a court-martial and a hanging, Petway broke out of the military garrison and ran."

My stomach dropped at that, and Ellie must have seen some of my feelings.

She grinned at me, and I saw the evil in her again. I hated the fact that I had to deal with her.

"It's a shame when your heroes turn out to be not so heroic, ain't it?"

"Get on with it," I said.

"While he was in Mexico, Petway signed on with the French as a mercenary," Ellie said. "France was hoping the United States would jump into the fight too because the US was already grabbing land from the Mexicans everywhere it could."

"Only the United States couldn't get involved," I said, "because of the Civil War."

Ellie nodded. "That's right. When Petway was down there, the French ran Juárez out of Chihuahua City. Petway was an enlisted man in the Mexican army, a sergeant, but his squad of soldiers of fortune was loaded with Mexicans. Angelo Blunt's father was part of that group."

I nodded. "Simon," I said.

"That's right." Ellie nodded and her eyes were bright again. She was enjoying telling the story. "Petway found out that Juárez or one of his men was planning on taking off with a shipment of gold. Petway and his unit stole it away, but they couldn't get it out of Chihuahua City because the Mexican army was searching for it, so they hid it somewhere there. Most of them died getting that far. Only three of the men who had taken that gold got out of Mexico alive."

I measured greedy and violent Petway against the Mister Henson I knew and I just couldn't make the two men fit together. What had changed? How had Mister Henson become the kind and gentle man I had known? The man who had taken in an orphan boy and given him a good life?

"While Mexico was in an uproar," Ellie said, "Petway returned to the United States with a wounded man named John Morganfield. Simon, Angelo Blunt's father, made his own way out. For a while, Petway stayed with Morganfield and helped him get settled among the Mescalero Apache."

"Salsa Jack," I whispered, remembering the story Blunt had told Mister Henson about how he had found the man and putting it together then.

"That's him. How do you know Jack?" Ellie stubbed out her cigarette in a ceramic ashtray.

"Blunt mentioned him. Keep on with the story."

Ellie looked put out, but she kept the tale flowing. "I knew Jack before I knew Petway. Jack is the one who told me the story of the stolen gold, and part of it he told was about the necklace Petway wore."

"What necklace?" I asked before I could stop myself.

Ellie laughed at me. "You're supposed to be my investment? And you know so little?"

"I didn't know about Mister Henson. He hid that part of his life from me. That's the part I want to know. And I know about the gold, which is what you want to know."

A dark look smoldered on Ellie's face. "The necklace is how I identified Petway." She touched the hollow of her throat. "It has a black stone that has a jaguar carved on it so that it stands out from the stone."

"Bas-relief," I said automatically. Me and Mister Henson had done that on some of the special-order caskets. It was tedious and tiring, but I loved the detail work more than Mister Henson ever had.

"If you say so." Ellie waved her hand dismissively. "I saw the necklace and I knew it from Jack's story."

"There could be other necklaces like it."

"If there are, I've never seen one."

For the moment, I conceded the point. "You never told Mister Henson you knew who he really was?"

"No. I had to gain his confidence first. That's the only way you can get a man to tell you all this secrets. But sooner or later, men confide to the women in their lives. But only if they trust them." She frowned. "I worked on building Petway's trust for weeks, but he never did believe in me enough to tell me about the gold." She looked at me. "You were the only one I ever knew him to trust with that."

And he hadn't, not really.

"He never even told Salsa Jack who he'd become after he left Las Cruces," Ellie said. "I was the one to tell Jack when I went back out there and told him about seeing the necklace he'd said belonged to Petway. When he'd told me that story about the gold, the necklace had stuck in my mind."

"Salsa Jack told Angel Blunt about Petway being Mister Henson." I felt sick when I put it all together. It was as final as screwing down the lid of a casket before putting it into the ground, never to be seen again.

Right then and there, I buried my memories of Mister Henson as the man I'd known him as. I was going to have to make peace with who I now knew he was and had been. That was what was left.

"And now," Ellie said, "here we are."

I sat there for a minute and felt tired and hurt and lost. It was a pretty miserable experience.

"Angel Blunt wants the map," Ellie said. "The one that shows where the treasure is. The one that Petway gave to you. Now that he knows you're alive, he'll come after you."

"Because he thinks I have the map."

"That's right." She grinned malevolently. "Not only that, I'm going to tell him you have it."

"Why would you do that?" I couldn't believe she was so callous about it.

"Because Angel Blunt is an investment for me too. I'm the one who told him, for a percentage, that I'd confirm that you had the map. Now I've done that."

I stood up.

"It doesn't make any difference to me which of you finds the gold," Ellie said. "I'm getting a ten percent cut from either one of you that brings it out of Mexico. I'm working with both of you, so telling Blunt that you have the map will hurry things along nicely, I think." She drummed the fingers of her left hand on the tabletop. "Frankly, I think Blunt stands a better chance of bringing that gold out. And I think if I delivered you to him, I might better my bargaining position."

Something flashed in her right hand when she raised it and an instant later I saw the small Derringer pop out of her right sleeve on a telescoping rail. Her thumb caught the hammer and eared it back as she pointed it at me.

From where I was sitting, that muzzle looked enormous.

25

I didn't consider the possibility of Ellie Deno shooting me. I just reacted to what was in front of me and I didn't want to be shot. Running wasn't an option because I knew she'd put a bullet in me before I made it to the door. I'd made a point of backing out of her reach, but she'd forgotten I had longer arms than she did.

I swung my hand toward her at the same time she was taking aim. I slapped her hand aside and the gun went off. The detonation inside the room was loud. The bullet smashed into the wall behind me and shattered the rectangular mirror above the fireplace. Shards of silvered glass spilled across the wooden mantle.

Ignoring all that because I was focused on survival, which I didn't know if I'd ever truly forgotten about these past two days, I closed my hand around Ellie's hand and the gun. Like I said, I was strong from hard work and because of my size. Bones inside her hand broke with sharp snaps and she cried out in pain.

I kept hold of her hand and used my other hand to pull the small pocket gun from her broken fingers. The Derringer was one of the over-and-under models I'd seen in Kearney's gun shop, but I couldn't recall what it was.

I dropped the hideout gun in my jacket pocket and stepped back from her. I was so scared and so mad that I wanted to hit her, but I didn't.

"You hurt me!" she squalled.

Guilt ate at me for what I'd done, but I remembered the lies she'd told me and Mister Henson and I forced myself to be cold. I squashed those feelings down and headed for the door. Whatever pain she was suffering, she'd earned. I left without saying a word, but she gave me an earful even after I was out in the hall. We didn't have anything more to discuss and I knew I was running out of time.

Angel Blunt's men would hunt me even harder after Ellie Deno talked to them.

***

It was a long walk back to Main Street from the Shannsey Hotel. I went as quickly as I could, and it felt like my wounded leg and my ribs were on fire from all the hurrying. I realized then that I needed a horse. Mister Henson kept a team at the livery with the funeral coach. All four of them were broke for riding in addition to pulling the coach.

My stomach growled when I passed Wick's Diner and smelled the food from inside, but I stayed on task and headed directly to Mister Malpert's warehouse. If I was still alive later, I'd eat then. Maybe I'd even celebrate the fact that I had Mister Henson's map showing where that gold was down in Chihuahua City.

Of course, I'd make sure that was a quiet celebration.

But thinking about celebrating made me wonder what I was going to do if I did find the map. Mexico wasn't so far off from where Pecos was located, but it was a long distance to me, who had never gone very far even though I'd moved around often when my parents were dodging creditors.

I got the shakes along the way too, something that came after all the fear and looking down that barrel, and that made me angry. When I was grabbing Ellie Deno's pistol from her hand, I hadn't been afraid. Honestly I hadn't been thinking at all.

Now, though, I kept wondered what would have happened if that bullet had smashed through my head instead of breaking that mirror. Me and Mister Henson hadn't built a casket for me. A time or two in there, I thought I might be sick. I was even glad I hadn't had breakfast.

***

MALPERT'S STORAGE was painted in white paint against the second-floor level of the warehouse. I thought it could have looked better, because I'd painted the words on there with Mister Henson holding the ladder, but it was straight and the letters were all the same size.

Winston Malpert hadn't put much money into the place since he'd built it. He was tight-fisted with a nickel, and he'd squeeze a dollar till it screamed. Mister Henson and Malpert would often have long arguments over the pay we got for the repair work we did on the building, but we got paid and they'd go have a beer. I'd always trailed along and got something to eat. Malpert would buy my meal and he'd always joke that feeding me was hitting his bottom line something fierce.

The warehouse sat across from Folsom's Livery, and both businesses had fairly close access to the train station and constantly moved goods and livestock. Goods were offloaded there and brought to the warehouse by wagon. Malpert stored dry goods and sundries that traveling merchants would pick up, and he stored goods that local farmers shipped down the railroad line to other markets.

Malpert turned a pretty penny storing other folks' stuff while shipping was worked out in one direction or another. He liked to sit in Wick's in the morning and dicker with folks needing storage space. He also liked catching up on the gossip, which Mister Henson had told me Missus Malpert insisted on.

He was standing in the middle of the sliding double doors that allowed access to the warehouse when I arrived. A teamster was calling out names and items, and Malpert was checking things off in his notebook. Every bit of business Malpert did was kept in his notebooks.

While Malpert was otherwise occupied, I took the opportunity to look around. I didn't see Courbet or Lavery, and Ellie Deno hadn't followed me from the hotel either. I'd thought she might. Now that I'd seen her real face, she didn't seem to be the type of woman who'd quit on a treasure map even if she'd gotten some broken fingers.

Short and narrow shouldered but broad through the backside, Malpert looked like a successful man in his suit. He wore glasses and a bowler hat and a pointed gray beard that touched his collar in front.

"That's everything, Mister Malpert," the teamster called down.

"Very well, Dudley." Malpert waved the man into the warehouse. "Drive on in. Mister Taylor and his stalwarts will get you squared away."

The teamster touched his hat and shook his reins to get the mules moving. They flicked their ears and plodded on, but didn't have much heart for it.

Malpert's gold watch chain caught the morning sun as he checked the time. He put his train conductor's watch back in his vest pocket, made a notation in his notebook, and looked over to me.

"Charlie," he greeted, and he smiled gently at me.

"Good morning, Mister Malpert," I replied, and I took the hand he offered.

"The suit caught me by surprise," Malpert said. "I usually only see you dressed like that when there's a funeral." A worried look crossed his face. "Mister Henson's funeral isn't today, is it? I was told it would be tomorrow morning at ten."

Gilbride had gotten the news out quickly.

"No," I said. "The funeral's tomorrow."

The words hit me pretty hard when I realized how I'd just said them without giving them really any thought. Mister Henson's death and the coming funeral were just facts in my life now. I didn't want to accept them, but I guessed I was starting to.

Then I felt guilty on top of that, especially when I

knew I'd come there seeking an ill-gotten fortune instead of just to make sure Mister Henson's casket was ready for tomorrow. I felt disloyal and I didn't like that.

I almost hoped the map wouldn't be there after all, but that would mean Crying Bear would get his turn at me if I was caught by Angel Blunt and his gang.

"Good, good." Malpert clapped me on the shoulder. "My wife and I will be there. Sometimes you can't trust Mister Aiken's impromptu notices because they coincide with a sale at one of the big shops instead of the event. If you ask me, there's too much advertising in newspapers these days, even the small newspaper we have here."

"Yes sir. I've come to check on Mister Henson's casket, if I may."

Malpert's eyes softened and glistened a little. He had a reputation as a tough man, a fair man, but I knew he cared about things and people. "We haven't moved it, and it's been in good care since we received it. I'd thought about having one of the crews uncrate it and get it ready."

"I'll take care of that, sir." I took a breath. "It's something I can do for Mister Henson." And, when I said it, I realized that was the biggest reason I was there. This was something I was doing for Mister Henson. I needed to do it, no matter what else might be in there.

"You know where it is, Charlie. Go on in and let us know if you need anything."

"Thank you." I touched the brim of my new hat and headed inside. Then a thought crossed my mind.

Malpert hired Otis Wilson and his brother and their cousin to watch over the warehouse at nights. The railroad people, the Pinkertons, Maggie's friends, had insisted on that to make sure all the cargos were protected.

"There's one other thing, Mister Malpert," I said, turning back to him.

"Yes?"

"There haven't been any—" I hesitated, searching for something to say that wouldn't draw too much attention. But there was nothing. This would be a sensitive matter for the warehouse owner. "There haven't been any disturbances lately, have there?"

Malpert frowned. "What kind of disturbances?"

"Like if the warehouse got broken into," I said. "Anything gone missing? That kind of thing."

"Charlie." Malpert smiled reassuringly. "Malpert's Storage has never been broken into, and we've never lost a single thing." He tapped his notebook meaningfully. "I keep track of everything that comes and goes through here."

"I didn't think so." I continued on inside.

"Charlie?" Malpert looked nervous. "Is that a pistol you're wearing?"

I ignored him because I didn't want to get into a discussion and there was obviously a pistol on my hip. He turned away to deal with the newest wagon that rolled up.

I headed back to the far northeast corner where me and Mister Henson had delivered that casket after we'd built it.

26

The casket sat just where we'd left it. At least, I thought it did. It didn't look like it had moved an inch. The pine crate we'd built to store it in sat there partially cloaked in gloom. The unfinished wood had aged, dried out, and lost its luster. Covered in dust, the crate didn't look like anyone had touched it in years.

I borrowed one of the lanterns hanging on the wall on that side of the storehouse, lit the candle with a match, and lowered the glass when the flame took. In a couple seconds, a soft yellow glow pushed back the shadows and I studied the crate, dreading unboxing it and hating the need for it.

PROPERTY OF HENSON'S FUNERAL HOME was stamped in black on the top and both of the long sides. The crate was slightly larger than the casket's eighty-four inches in length, twenty-eight inches in width, and twenty-three inches in height.

Those dimensions had been drilled into my head and I'd never been comfortable with them. The seven feet in length was comfortable, even to me, and I was six feet four inches tall.

It was the width and the height that always made me feel claustrophobic. When I was younger, and smaller, I'd crawled into one of the caskets at the funeral home just to try one on. It had taken years to work up the nerve to do that, so it hadn't been all that long ago. I hadn't liked the feeling and had almost panicked. I still didn't like tight places.

For a moment, I just looked at that crate and remembered the night me and Mister Henson had built it around his casket. I still wasn't happy with the idea we'd made it, and I told Mister Henson that.

He'd just laughed at me and told me it didn't bother him so much because I'd be the only one who'd ever see it again, and maybe not even me.

Now...here I was.

I made myself get moving. In the background, Malpert's warehouse crew unloaded the wagons arriving with goods from this morning's train. Evidently there had been a big load, then I realized it was the first of the month and there would be a lot of supplies for businesses and the big ranches outside of town.

I borrowed a crowbar from one of the crews, took off my jacket and draped it over a nearby crate, and set to work. I pried the top off gently, not wanting to damage the casket within.

The nails screeched as they stubbornly pulled free, and some of the warehouse workers stopped working to watch what I was doing. I ignored them and concentrated on the task, but thoughts of me and Mister Henson building this casket, taking time with it, and somehow not dealing with the fact that we were constructing his final resting place kept stumbling through my head.

I'd gotten up before Mister Henson did the morning after we'd built the casket because I hadn't been able to sleep well. Thoughts of my parents' deaths and the surety of Mister Henson's death at some later date kept howling through my dreams, turning them all into nightmares.

I'd stood and stared at the casket in the workroom, hating what it stood for. Mister Henson had found me there when he got up. He'd asked me what was bothering me and I'd told him. He'd told me that he understood; that he didn't know if he'd have the strength to build a casket for me if the need ever came up, and he was glad I was there with him.

Then he'd taken me and fed me breakfast, and we didn't talk about the casket anymore except when we'd built the protective crate and stored it at Malpert's warehouse.

I'd never wanted to see it again. Now I was the one getting it ready.

We'd used Purpleheart wood as a veneer for the oak substructure, and the casket, under coats of varnish, gleamed a deep, royal purple. Looking at it now, with the gold-plated hardware, I couldn't help thinking a thing of beauty like that should never be used for such a horrible occurrence.

When I had the crate stripped off, lying in pieces around me, and the casket just sitting there, I ran my hands over it. I felt small imperfections in the wood, saw the two places where I had burned the wood working with a hand plane, and I wanted to strip it down and refinish it.

Except there was no time.

I put those things out of my mind and felt the hardware, looking for any indication that Mister Henson had hidden a map or anything else inside those bits.

There was nothing.

Then I opened both halves of the top of the casket and searched through the lining, then moved on to the bottom and walls. When I didn't find anything in the bottom, I started feeling disappointed, that maybe there was nothing there for me to find.

Angel Blunt and his men were going to come after me for a map they thought I had, and I didn't have it. They'd kill me and I'd die in horrible pain because Angel Blunt wouldn't believe that I didn't know where it was.

I cursed myself for trying to be so clever with Ellie Deno. I'd only made my circumstances worse.

It took some time to notice the extra headboard at the top of the casket, and in the end I just got lucky because the lantern light happened to catch the irregularity just right when I was doing a close inspection. The additional thickness was lost behind the pillow Missus Kuáng had made for Mister Henson's casket.

But there it was.

To anyone else, it might have looked like a blemish, just a small irregularity in the finish. But I knew it wasn't. Me and Mister Henson would never have accepted such a thing in any casket, and especially not that one.

Mister Henson had added that piece after we'd finished, when I wasn't around.

I used my fingers to try to shift the section, and finally got it to slide away at the bottom, where the head wall met the base. A leaf half the size of my palm popped out of place and revealed the hiding place within.

With trembling fingers, I coaxed the thick sheet of paper from the hiding spot. I was kneeling beside the casket then, barely able to tolerate the throbbing pain in my thigh and ribs, but I was so caught up in my discovery that I wasn't feeling any of those things.

The paper was heavy bond and cream colored. It was good stationary, made from cotton rag, like the stationary Mister Latham kept behind his counter at the general store for folks who wanted to send out special family announcements or letters lawyers wrote when they wanted to impress the reader.

And it was the same kind of paper we used at the funeral home.

I opened the trifold and turned the page so the lantern light fell across it. A carefully drawn map of buildings and streets had been rendered on the page. There were no names of buildings, no names of streets, and there were only three points of interest that I could find, all of them were symbols.

An angel, a pistol, an eagle, and a Spanish word some distance from those three.

The few words were listed in Spanish and I couldn't understand what they said. I could speak some Spanish. Most folks in Texas could. But I couldn't read much of it.

The only word I recognized for certain was oro. A lot of folks knew that one.

It was Spanish for gold. It was marked under another word, and my heart beat a little faster.

That was why I didn't hear Courbet and Lavery walk

up on me until they were only a few feet away. The Spanish rowels on Lavery's boots jangled and drew my attention.

"Is that the map, boy?" Courbet asked me gruffly.

I dropped my hand down for the Tranter as I turned around, but Courbet already had his pistol drawn. So did Lavery and the two men that had come with them.

Courbet pulled the trigger on his pistol and it barked and blasted out a foot-long muzzle flash visible in the semi-darkness of the warehouse around them. The bullet struck Mister Henson's casket with a hollow thump. Bright white oak showed around the edges of the hole in the casket's side. The echo of the detonation rolled around the warehouse and sounded even louder because it was trapped inside the building

Shocked, I looked at the hole and thought about how the casket and Mister Henson had both worn veneer to hide what was truly inside.

Malpert had been headed for us, probably to find out what the four men were doing inside his warehouse, but when Courbet had fired his pistol, the warehouse owner turned around and ran for the big doors.

All of the warehouse workers ran for cover when they realized they'd heard a gunshot. None of them wanted any part of what was about to happen.

27

I stood there frozen, looking at the guns pointed at me.

"I asked you," Courbet said calmly, like he had all day, "if that was Petway's map to the gold." He grinned at me, totally confident that he held every card in the game.

My mouth had gone dry and I was sure I'd be dead the minute I gave that map to the man. They wouldn't need to leave me alive.

Seeing them standing there so calmly, I was surprised at how brazen they were, until I realized Marshal Buchanan and his posse hadn't yet returned from tracking Angel Blunt. All the town had in the way of peace officers was Maggie Buchanan, and she was nowhere—

Another gunshot rang out, this one heavier and sounding like it came from a rifle, not a revolver.

Snarling an oath, Courbet jerked back and looked down in surprise at his left shoulder where blood was spreading across his shirt. He clapped his free hand over the wound.

"Town marshal!" Maggie yelled out from somewhere amid the crates piled high in orderly rows. The lever action on a rifle ratcheted and sounded loud. "Drop your guns now!"

"It's that girl!" Courbet shouted. "Kill her!"

The two unknown gunmen sprinted for cover among the stacks of goods. They fired shots in Maggie's general direction, then her rifle cracked once more and one of the men fell, rolling, and got back to his feet as the rifle action worked again.

Unfrozen now, watching Lavery bring his pistol to bear on me, I pulled that Tranter from its holster and fired from the hip like Kearney showed me even though I figured the outlaw had me dead to rights. I couldn't let Maggie go up against the four of them by herself. Inside the warehouse, that pistol sounded like an artillery piece when it went off. It bucked it my hand, but I held it steady and fired again.

Surprisingly, I had a second round into Lavery's broad chest before I realized I'd hit him with the first. I didn't know if it was luck or instinct or proximity or that little bit of training that allowed me to be so accurate, and I didn't care. Lavery fell backward into a loose sprawl.

By that time, Courbet realized I had a pistol in my hand and took aim at me again. He was grimacing against the pain in his shoulder and I could tell he wasn't as steady on his feet as he had been. Or as quick.

The third shot Maggie put into the man she'd targeted did the trick. He sprawled into a loose bundle as I dodged to the side to avoid Courbet's line of fire.

Courbet's second shot split the air where I'd been standing before I hunkered down and dove behind Mister Henson's casket. The outlaw emptied his pistol at me and the bullets ripped into the wooden sides but didn't reach me. Me and Mister Henson had made those oak panels strong and thick.

I rose and pointed the Tranter at Courbet, aiming for the center of his body just as Kearney had instructed. When he saw me, Courbet blanched and turned to run. As a result, my bullet caught him in the side and knocked him down. He lay there when he hit and his pistol slid from his hand.

Ducking behind the casket again, listening to the last man swapping shots with Maggie, I broke the Tranter open and replaced the three spent cartridges. Since I was leaving the chamber under the hammer empty to prevent an accidental discharge, I only had one shot left. I fed new cartridges into the pistol, filling all chambers now, and slipped the hot brass into my shirt pocket.

I picked up the map from where I'd dropped it, refolded it, and tucked it inside my shirt up against my undershirt for safekeeping. Then I sprinted over to Courbet.

He was still breathing, but he looked out of it, his eyes wide and his mouth slack. I thought maybe he'd never been shot before and was in shock. If that was the case, I'd had a lot more experience with it than he had.

On some level, that made me feel good about myself. Not everyone who got shot survived the experience. Lavery was among those on the other list. He lay on his back and stared blindly up at the top of the warehouse.

For a moment, a wave of guilt passed over me. Although I'd seen a lot of dead folks, I'd never made one that way.

I picked up Courbet's dropped pistol and tucked it into my holster in case he decided maybe he wasn't so hurt after all and wanted to get back into the gunfight. I also took Lavery's abandoned weapon.

Then I followed the gunshots and worried about Maggie because those reports were coming pretty fast and furious. I also wondered what she was doing at the warehouse. She'd stayed at the jail all night. She should have been at home catching up on sleep.

I held the Tranter in both hands before me and checked the narrow alleys between crates and barrels and sacks of grain and flour as I went through them and searched for Maggie and the surviving outlaw. My heart was beating fast, and I was scared, but I was in control of myself despite all the memories of I had of getting shot two days ago.

I was also suddenly aware of the silence that filled the warehouse. I stood still and listened, wondering what had changed. Something moved on top of the crates twenty feet away and I glanced up to see the man I was looking for pointing his pistol at me.

I ducked to the side and a bullet chewed splinters from

a crate only a few inches above my head. I slipped in behind the crate and lifted the Tranter as Maggie's rifle fired again.

The man on top of the crates fell and thudded against the hardwood floor in front of me. After he hit, he didn't move. When I went over to check on him and take his pistol, I saw that a bullet had punched through his heart.

"Are you okay?" Maggie asked as she stepped out from between two rows of crates only a few feet away. She was pushing fresh cartridges into the rifle she carried. Her hands were calm and steady while mine had small tremors coursing through them.

"Yeah," I said. I waved the Tranter toward the dead man. "He's dead."

"I hope so," Maggie said. "I shot him in the heart. He had you in his sights."

"Thanks," I said.

She nodded and laid her rifle in her elbow. She looked at the man with no emotion. "I made a mistake with Courbet and the first guy I shot. I hesitated a little over killing them."

"Hesitated?" I repeated.

"Yeah. I shouldn't have done that. I shot to wound Courbet instead of kill him, and I knew they were going to kill you." Her voice was a monotone.

My voice cracked and I couldn't quite seem to catch my breath. I knew I was going to need to sit down soon.

"I'd never killed a man before," Maggie said. "That was why I hesitated. It was a lot easier than I'd thought it would be." She looked at me. "The next time I have to kill a man, I won't falter."

"Courbet's still alive," I said, and I didn't know if I meant that to make her feel better or what. Her reaction to all the violence was confusing to me.

She nodded. "Well, we'll need to arrest him for attempted murder. But first, give me your pistol."

After a brief pause, I handed it over.

Without a word, she took the Tranter, looked it over real quick, then pointed it at the dead man at our feet, and fired.

The bullet struck the same spot she'd shot him.

She handed me the pistol and looked me in the eyes. "I'll take credit for the other man over there. I didn't recognize him from the dodgers associated with Angel Blunt. But I know this man was one of Blunt's gang. When I file my report, that's how I'm going to write it up."

Before I could ask her why she would do that, she turned and walked back toward the cries for help that I only then realized were coming from Courbet.

28

Malpert readily agreed to allow Maggie the use of one of his wagons and a couple of men to help load her prisoner and the dead men. He was paler than I'd ever seen and looked a bit sick, but he had his notebook open in no time and was walking around to assess the damage created by the gunfight.

Maggie took charge of Courbet. She put him in handcuffs despite his protests of being injured and in pain. There was no sympathy in her.

She squared up at him, shoved him back against the wagon, and dropped that rifle muzzle on his chest so that the barrel pointed up at Courbet's chin. He tilted his head back to try to get it out of the way, but with the wagon behind him, he couldn't go anywhere.

Looking up at him, she stared at his vulnerable throat and I thought for a minute she was going to blow his head off. I couldn't move, could only wait and see what happened. It was like watching a snake take a baby chick.

"You killed a good man two days ago," Maggie said softly. "You were going to kill Charlie. You probably would have if I hadn't shot you when I did. And you've killed other folks. If you ask me, you don't deserve to live. Since I didn't kill you when I had the chance, I'll watch you hang, Mister Courbet, and I'll be glad when you're dead."

Probably being in front of the crowd of teamsters and warehouse men gathered around us, as well as passersby on the boardwalks and in the street, spurred Courbet on. I guessed he had his outlaw image to uphold. He swore at Maggie, calling her all manner of filthy things.

I stepped toward him, but before I could do anything, Maggie busted him in the face with the Winchester's barrel. That gold tooth in the center of his foul mouth disappeared, and I still don't know if he swallowed it or somebody found it later on the ground and took it.

Courbet stopped swearing and started moaning. I grabbed hold of him and slung him into the back of the wagon like he was a sack of feed. I wasn't gentle in putting him down either. He bounced pretty good and couldn't get back up.

Then I helped Malpert's men with the dead bodies.

Maggie climbed into the driver's seat and took the reins, shaking them out to get the team moving. I asked Douglas, the warehouse supervisor, to convey our appreciation to Malpert and pulled myself onto the wagon bed. The rough ride jarred me and made me hurt all over.

Across the street, I caught sight of Ellie Deno's buggy. She sat in the seat and watched me for a time, then slapped her team into motion and rode out of town trailing a cloud of dust behind her.

I thought I knew where she was headed, and I guessed that if Marshal Buchanan could follow her, they'd know right where Angel Blunt was.

***

"No new injuries?" Gilbride peered at me from head to toe while I stood outside his office.

I shook my head, not knowing what to say. I'd gone with Maggie and we'd delivered the dead men to one of Mister Henson's competitors, Baskins Funeral Home.

While we were unloading bodies, Joe Baskins asked me if I'd like to work for him now that Mister Henson was gone. I'd told him I was likely through with the mortician business until I knew I couldn't find any other work. He'd told me to keep him in mind if things didn't work out, and he'd made his condolences about Mister Henson.

Then I'd ridden with Maggie to put Courbet in jail. I'd told her I had to get on to Gilbride's to see to Mister Henson and she'd nodded. When I'd asked, she'd said she was fine. And she'd acted it, too. She'd put on a fresh pot of coffee and sent one of the lookie-loos crowding the marshal's office door over to Trail's End to arrange for her lunch because she hadn't had breakfast.

Her calm demeanor seemed strange to me, but I hadn't said anything about it. I'd killed a man, too, and I wasn't sure how I was supposed to think or feel. I couldn't forget the way she'd dealt with Courbet afterward either. She was a whole lot colder and harder than I'd ever known her to be.

She'd asked me if I'd wanted to join her because she'd been following me all morning and knew neither one of us had had anything to eat. I decided then and there that Maggie was really good at following folks, because I'd been keeping watch and hadn't seen her anywhere.

I wasn't sure how she'd known Ellie Deno had taken me to the Shannsey Hotel that morning, and I realized Maggie had to have been keeping tabs on everyone. Or maybe she'd tripped to Miss Abbie really being Ellie Deno when I did and had just chosen to say nothing.

After I turned down her offer of joining her for a meal, I'd told her I had to get on to the doc's.

"Charlie?" Gilbride said, looking at me more closely. "Are you all right?"

"I'm fine. Just really tired, I guess."

"By the time I heard about the gunfight down at Malpert's Storage, it was all over." Gilbride waved me in and the strong scent of chemicals overwhelmed me.

Before I knew it, I got sick. My stomach turned over and I headed to the small bucket Gilbride kept on hand for used bandages and other trash. I threw up plenty and thought my head was going to explode, but the sickness finally passed.

The whole time, Gilbride steadied me and told me in a soft voice that everything was going to be all right, and that the reaction I was having was perfectly normal under the circumstances.

When we were both convinced I was empty and once more under control, he guided me over to a chair. I looked around and saw that, except for Mister Henson's body, we were alone. I was thankful for that because I felt embarrassed.

"Sorry," I whispered. I blinked tears from my eyes. "I don't know what happened."

"You went through a traumatic experience, Charlie." Gilbride sat in his swivel chair across from me, almost close enough for our knees to touch. "In fact, you've been through a lot of traumatic experiences lately. In this case, I think what you just went through was the aftereffects of nearly being killed."

"That's happening with an astonishing regularity these days," I said.

"It is. Being sick after a battle isn't anything to be ashamed of, Charlie. While I was working in the medical corps at the end of the Civil War, a totally ghastly experience, I assure you, I saw many men react exactly the way you just did. You've done nothing to apologize for."

I looked at him. "I killed a man in that warehouse."

Gilbride nodded. "Mister Aiken says he has it on good authority that you killed two of them."

I didn't bother to argue the point. Maggie had spread that story since we'd walked out of the warehouse. And I was surprised at feeling a little better after telling him what I'd done.

"What you did," Gilbride said, "was to protect yourself and Deputy Buchanan. I take it, since she's not shown up here, she's doing well?"

"Maggie's fine. She ordered lunch from Trail's End. I'm over here puking my guts up, and she's having lunch like nothing happened." I shook my head, hoping that the anger I felt about that didn't show. "I don't understand that. It's like none of what we did has touched her."

Gilbride was silent for a moment, then he took in a deep breath and let it out. He looked unsettled. "Deputy Buchanan is…different."

And that was all he would say about the matter.

I got the feeling he didn't want me to press, so I didn't.

29

I'd been dreading helping prepare Mister Henson's body for the funeral, but once I got to it, the work helped settle my nerves. Everything came natural. Except for the fact that Mister Henson was there with me in an altogether different way.

I only teared up for the first half hour or so. I think I was too drained from everything else, and from killing Lavery back in Mister Malpert's warehouse, to shed any more tears after that. I was pretty dried up.

Gilbride had done a good job of putting Mister Henson back together after the horrors Crying Bear had committed on him. The stitches were nice and tight, and I felt certain they would have won Missus Kuáng's approval. There were just a lot of them and not all of them could be hidden.

Mister Henson almost looked like himself, except for being dead. I'd borrowed a cosmetic kit from Baskins to put some color back in Mister Henson's cheeks.

When I was finished, Mister Henson didn't look like he was going to sit up and talk to us, but he looked as good as most folks we'd prepared for burial who'd died hard, and a whole lot better than some. You couldn't put a man or a woman back together in any real fashion after feral pigs had been at them.

During the time I was working on Mister Henson on

the other side of a curtained-off section of the room, Gil-bride had gone to the marshal's office to work on Courbet, who wasn't as near death as I'd feared, then continued to see patients. Some of them, when they found out I was behind the curtain, asked questions about the shootout at the warehouse, but I politely declined to answer.

I think a few of them complaining of a cough only came by to see me and maybe ask questions. Gilbride charged them anyway, and some of them, particularly Hamilton Bingham, weren't happy about it.

Eugene Aiken came by and wanted to ask questions when he learned where I'd gone after I'd left the marshal's office. He told me he wanted an interview for his latest edition. I told him I wasn't interested and Gilbride got testy with him, forcing him to leave. After that, when patients wanted to talk to me, Gilbride told them they could read the Pioneer and learn everything they needed to know.

I sat there for a while and looked at Mister Henson in that black suit Mister Kuáng had sent over for the funeral.

Gilbride locked his office door and sat beside me. I thought maybe he was waiting for me to leave and didn't want to just rush me out the door.

But I'd been thinking about other things, too.

"Do you have the personal effects Mister Henson had with him when he...died?" I asked. I couldn't believe I hadn't thought to ask.

"I do." Gilbride got up from his chair and went to a cabinet. He took out a small cloth bag with a drawstring and handed it to me.

It wasn't much.

I spilled the contents out onto the bed where Mister Henson lay quietly with his hands folded. Him being still like that bothered me, because he was always up doing something when he was awake. Unless he was drinking coffee. Then he'd sit still and enjoy the quiet.

There among the wallet and small change and a few nails Mister Henson carried to mark dimensions on lum-ber, hold measuring tape, and a thousand other things it seemed like he could do with them, was the necklace Ellie Deno had mentioned.

I couldn't help wondering under what circumstances she'd had a chance to see the stone with the jaguar raised in bas-relief, and once I thought I figured it out, my mind shied away from even considering any more.

The stone was slightly bigger than the ball of my thumb and about as thick as two quarters mashed together. I had to turn it so the light would catch the carved jaguar, but once I saw it, it was always there. The big cat stood on a rock and had its mouth open and one paw lifted. Its tail curled behind it like a whip. Silver bits marked its eyes and claws and it was framed by a thick silver ring.

It hung from a knotted rawhide cord, not a chain. The rawhide had been cut near the knot.

"I couldn't cut untie the knot," Gilbride said. "I tried, but he must have worn that for a long time because that leather had shrunk and expanded so much it was almost like it had grown back together."

I nodded and let the obsidian stone rest on my palm. Small burrs on the outside of the silver ring around it caught at my skin but never pierced.

"It's a pretty piece," Gilbride said. "A lot of work and skill went into it."

"Yeah."

"Do you know where he got it?"

I shook my head and closed my hand over it. "I've never seen it before."

Gilbride looked surprised, but he didn't ask any questions.

"Can I have this?" I asked.

"Charlie," Gilbride said, "as far as I know, you're the only family Mister Henson had. Take it."

I thanked him. Then I tied that rawhide around my neck in a knot just like the one I figured had held it together. It was one of the sailor's knots Mister Henson had taught me, only now I knew that he'd probably learned it out in San Francisco while he was building ships.

That snarling jaguar hung in the hollow of my throat

and it felt like that was where it was supposed to be.

"I'm going to eat supper at Wick's, Charlie," Gilbride announced. "You're welcome to join me." He smiled at me. "In fact, as your physician, and as your friend, I insist on it."

I hesitated, but at the mention of food, my stomach rumbled and I thought maybe I was getting back to being myself.

***

Wick's featured meatloaf that night, and it came smothered in gravy. There were also peas, carrots, and mashed potatoes to keep the meatloaf company. Wick's also had some of the best buttermilk biscuits I'd ever had.

I surprised myself with how much I ate, and I surprised Gilbride too. I caught him staring at me as I was working my way through a second plate.

"Sorry," I said. "I don't mean to make a pig of myself. I'll pay." He'd offered to buy my supper.

Gilbride laughed at me and said, "No you will not, Charlie Stark. You'll eat every bite you want, and have pie afterward if you have room."

Everybody else in the diner kept to themselves. They'd gotten quiet when we'd come in, and I supposed that was because of the gunfight. Pecos usually didn't have much going on, and to have a murder and men getting shot dead two days later was definitely out of the ordinary.

After we finished eating, I had room for pie, but I didn't tell Doctor Gilbride that. We said our goodbyes at the door. I told him I was going to the room Missus Kuáng had arranged for me, but as soon as he was down the street, I went back into Wick's and bought a piece each of cherry cobbler and peach cobbler and asked them to wrap it up for me.

30

With the package from Wick's Diner under my arm, I walked down to the marshal's office, wondering if I should have just gone off to my room. I was tired, and I definitely could have used the sleep, but honestly I was afraid of what I'd find waiting in my dreams after killing Lavery and working on Mister Henson.

And, honestly, I was worried about Maggie. She wasn't acting like I thought she should be. The cold-blooded way she'd used my pistol to shoot the dead man had stuck with me all day. I didn't know why she'd done that.

The candle lantern inside the marshal's office threw a crosshatch pattern of yellow light onto the boardwalk out front. Through the curtains, I could barely make out Maggie sitting behind the desk with her rifle across her thighs and her boots resting on the desk. A tin cup of coffee sat on the desk and a curl of steam crawled toward the ceiling.

I smelled the coffee standing there on the street, and that was what decided me to go on in. At Wick's I'd had buttermilk and coffee sounded good to me then.

I stepped on the boardwalk and Maggie's head came up. So did the Winchester.

I realized then she'd been prepared for Angel Blunt or one of his men to come bust Courbet out of jail.

"It's just me," I called out to her. I made sure I was

standing in front of the window so the light fell onto me and she could see me clearly. "Charlie Stark."

"What are you doing here, Charlie?" she asked.

"I had an extra piece of cobbler," I told her. "I thought I'd bring it by."

"Come on in."

After I walked in, I took off my hat and hung it on the rack in the corner by the door. Then I crossed to the desk and took out the two pieces of cobbler, placing them in the middle.

"An extra piece?" Maggie cocked an eyebrow at me. "What you have here are two different pieces of cobbler. Not an extra piece."

"Do you want a piece of cobbler or not?" I was feeling a little frustrated with her.

"Are you sure you're not here to bring me cobbler and ask for a cell to stay the night in?"

"I've got a rented room," I said, "where I can take both pieces of cobbler."

Her lips twitched a little and her eyes sparkled. She looked pretty sitting there, but she also looked tired.

"Are you planning on joining me?" she asked.

"If I may."

She nodded to the chair in the corner. "Help yourself to coffee. It's fresh."

I poured coffee into a tin cup, juggled it a bit on the way back to the desk because it was so hot, and sat. When I did, I noticed the peach cobbler was on her side of the desk. She reached into one of the drawers and took out a fork and a spoon.

"Do you have a preference?" she asked. "These are my silverware and I only need one of each."

"Do you have a preference?" I asked.

She handed me the fork. I reached over and took the spoon just to push things back at her a little. She frowned at me but didn't object.

I sat back in my chair with my cherry cobbler and spooned up my first bite. "Your pa isn't back?"

"Nope." She forked up a bite and ate.

"You worried about him?"

"Nope. He'll be back when he runs Angel Blunt down, or when the trail goes cold and he can't find him."

I ate and sipped coffee, and she did the same.

"How's Courbet?" I asked.

"Breathing, which is more than he deserves."

I was surprised at how cold and efficient she sounded. I tried to think of something to say and couldn't.

Maggie looked at me then, and I got the feeling that she realized she'd said something wrong. "Did I say something that bothered you?"

"No. I agree that Courbet deserves to be hung for what he took part in with Mister Henson."

"Would you hang him?"

I didn't know where that question came from, and I was puzzled and cautious at the same time. "You mean me? Would I hang him?"

She nodded. "If you had the chance, would you pull the lever and drop him through the gallows hole?"

Well, that almost put me off my feed, but I stuck with it because one of the other things Wick's does well besides breakfast and meatloaf was cobbler. Didn't matter what kind.

"No," I said. "That's not my job."

"A lot of people wouldn't work in a funeral home the way you do." She forked up another bite and I noticed that cobbler was disappearing pretty quickly. "But you do."

"I do," I agreed, and I suddenly realized I'd talked to Maggie Buchanan more than I ever had in my whole life up to that point.

"So if you were to have a job as a hangman, you wouldn't have a problem hanging Courbet?"

I thought about that for a minute and answered honestly. "I don't think I'd ever have that job, Maggie."

"Somebody has to do it."

"That's true."

"I keep thinking that maybe I should have killed him this morning and saved everybody the trouble of a trial and a hanging." She forked up more cobbler and ate it.

Her eyes gazed out over my shoulder, looking at what I didn't know. "Except that a lot of folks seem to like the hangings we've had. They bring picnics and such."

I supposed that was true, but I had no idea why she was thinking about such a thing.

"Are you doing okay, Maggie?"

She looked back at me. "I'm fine, Charlie. How are you doing?"

"I'm good."

She nodded. "That's nice. Pa says sometimes when a good man kills another man, or a woman too, I suppose, even if that man or woman is bad and has a killing coming, that his head can get all twisted up with guilt and regret."

I remembered the sick spell I'd taken in Gilbride's office, but I didn't mention it.

"You don't have any guilt or regret, Maggie?"

She shook her head. "Not even a bit. Those were bad men, Charlie, and they would have killed you. I like to prevent crimes when I can. In this line of work, you don't often get to do that. I'm glad I could do that today. And I would have missed you." She forked up the last bite of the cobbler. "I'm just thinking I should have killed Courbet. That was a missed opportunity. But maybe it will come around again."

31

The next morning, I stood at the gravesite Gilbride had arranged for when I wasn't available to do that yesterday. I wore one of the black suits and held my hat in my hands. Tears came and I let them fall and I wasn't ashamed because saying goodbye to Mister Henson that way hurt something awful.

Gilbride was there, and Maggie. Aiken stood apart from the group and wrote furiously in his notebook, sometimes stopping folks going to and from. Mister and Missus Kuáng came with their three daughters. Malpert and his wife came, and the Wicks. Missus Griffin showed up and told us the Trail's End would be catering a meal after the funeral over at the First Baptist because Mister Henson had been such a fine and upstanding citizen for so long.

I looked for Ellie Deno, but I saw no sign of her.

A few dozen other townsfolk showed up as well, but I think most of them just came to see what would happen. Or maybe they came for the free meal Missus Griffin was providing. And then there was the attraction of that bullet-riddled casket. I'd patched it as best as I'd been able, but it wasn't like it had been. Nothing was.

The service was over a lot quicker than it had any right to be for something that was going to leave such a big hole. Which, I realized, was a strange thought considering we'd come to fill a hole.

I stayed after because I needed to. I dismissed the gravediggers and started filling in Mister Henson's grave myself. I felt like it was my job, and it was something I could do.

Gilbride took off his coat, rolled up his sleeves, and found a shovel. Maggie took up a shovel as well. She was still wearing dungarees and hadn't worn a dress, but I supposed she was there as the town deputy.

Together, we put Mister Henson in the ground good and proper.

***

I stayed busy the next six days, even though the day after the funeral was a Sunday. There were things to do, arrangements to be made, because there were still bills that had to be paid, including the one at Folsom's Livery for storing the funeral coach and the horses.

I got one of the mares and purchased a good saddle from Calvin Folsom. I carried my Tranter and my Winchester with me every day now because the idea of going unarmed with Angel Blunt still out there just didn't make sense.

Then I set to work doing what I could to keep myself employed. The first couple of days, going up and down the ladder to replace the shingles on Hunziker's General Store were difficult, but I managed. I worked as quickly as I could, but I did it right, and I was glad to have the work. It wasn't just about the money, which was good, but I was thankful for the sheer need to do something other than grieve and be afraid and confused.

My thoughts wouldn't leave me any peace. Mister Henson's murder lingered, and the smell of gun powder that had filled my nostrils in the warehouse would show up at strange times and stay with me for a bit. Every now and again I'd get so that I felt like there was a hive of bees buzzing inside me. But I worked through those spells and they got better.

During the shingling, Missus Hunziker made sure I had a plate at noon and supper, and in the afternoons she brought by lemonade and fresh-baked cookies. She said it was to keep my strength up. I thought she was trying to mother me because her own two sons were gone from the house. One of them was a lawyer in Fort Worth and the other worked as a conductor on a Kansas Pacific train in Kansas. Neither of them came around much.

Truth to tell, I appreciated the attention. Missus Hunziker was a welcome diversion to my thoughts and the food was always good. Eating at the restaurants chipped away at my savings. I didn't know how Mister Henson had afforded my upkeep.

In the evenings, I'd cleared out the burned wreckage that was left of the funeral home. That was hard, back-breaking labor and I was glad of it. The lifting and carrying made me realize how weak my wounded leg was, but I was surprised at how quickly strength came back too.

Mostly it kept my mind occupied and not circling things it had no business thinking about. And I began to have some plans.

Gilbride checked in on me, though he claimed to just be passing by, and he was happy with my healing progress as well. I also saw Maggie several times, but she was always busy with marshal business and didn't seem inclined to stop and talk.

I probably should have gone by and talked to her, but she was always so quiet that I felt like I was a bother most of the time. I was talking when she could have been catnapping in the chair behind the desk. Plus, I was tired when I went to bed in my rented room at night and didn't have much left when I shut down for the day. That was the best way to keep the nightmares away.

That was what I wanted to do.

I also thought about going into that jail and beating Courbet within an inch of his life if I had to in order to find out where Angel Blunt was. In fact, I'd gone in there Monday night with that very thing in mind. Maggie saw me and must have guessed what I intended. Of course, that hadn't been hard to do. I had an ax handle in one hand and was pretty pent up with a full head of steam to get it done.

Monday would have been Mister Henson's birthday. I realized then that I didn't even know how old he'd been, and that had hurt bad because now I'd never know.

I was also confused because I didn't know now if I'd asked him how old he was if he'd even tell me the truth because he'd kept so much hidden. I kept tripping over his lies as I thought too much about who he had really been. That jaguar necklace at my throat was a reminder of how little I'd known about Mister Henson. I'd thought I'd known so much about him that he was boring.

Maggie turned me back from what I'd intended that night, and the only reason I'd quit on it was because I knew she would have fought me to defend her prisoner, the same man she'd regretted letting live that morning we'd killed the others.

She'd stood there in front of me and wouldn't let me pass. Finally, I'd given up and stormed out.

I didn't understand her, and I didn't think I ever would.

I was carrying out another armful of burned timbers from the funeral home to the buckboard I'd rented from the livery when Marshal Buchanan rode up.

32

"Good evening, Charlie," Marshal Buchanan said. He was tall and broad, with a wide face, long sideburns, and a handlebar mustache. He hadn't shaved much over the time he'd been gone and he was scruffy. Trail dust covered his clothes and he looked red-eyed and done in.

"Good evening, Marshal." I dumped the timbers into the back of the buckboard, which was nearly full but I was trying to make sure each load was packed as full as it could be. The mule in the traces stamped his feet restlessly. I didn't ask Marshal Buchanan the question that was uppermost in my mind.

"Mind if I light?" he asked.

"No," I said, and I knew he only had bad news to tell me. I didn't want to hear it, so I headed back into the wreckage.

Marshal Buchanan dismounted and tied his horse up at the buggy because the hitching post out front had burned as well. He pushed his hat back, sighed, and took a pair of leather gloves from his back pocket. He pulled them on as he followed me inside.

"We couldn't find Blunt, Charlie."

I stacked boards into a pile I'd carry out when it got big enough. "I figured that. If you had, somebody in town would have come down here to tell me. Probably Aiken. He's always wanting an interview."

"We followed that trail as far as we could." Marshal Buchanan started picking up timber as well and worked on a pile of his own. "I even hired a scout at Fort Davis and him ride with us. He picked up more sign than we did, but eventually the trail just petered out. The land down that way gets mighty hard, and we've been dry for a spell."

We carried our armloads to the buckboard and threw them in. The clatter of boards made the mule and the horse prick up their ears.

Fort Davis was seventy-five miles south and southeast of Pecos. I'd lived there a short time with my parents. Marshal Buchanan and the posse had gone a long way in their hunt.

"So you think Blunt is heading for Mexico?" I asked. I led the way back into the wreckage.

"Maybe," Marshal Buchanan said. "We know he's been down there before, and the Rio Grande is less than two hundred miles from Fort Stockton."

I collected more debris.

"Maggie told me what you said about the gold," the marshal said. "About Blunt thinking Mister Henson had gold stashed away somewhere. Do you think that's what he was after?"

"It's the only thing that makes sense," I said.

"You didn't mention the gold the night you were brought in."

"I'd been shot, Marshal." I faced him and didn't blink. I couldn't tell if he was accusing me of something or not. "I wasn't thinking straight." I took in a breath and let it out. "Most days, I still don't know if I'm thinking straight. Right now I'm just trying to stay busy."

"I understand. I'm just trying to make sense of things."

"Me too," I said. I carried my stack of wood to the buckboard.

The marshal was right behind me. "You don't know anything about the gold, Charlie?"

I thought about that letter I'd hidden in my rented room under a loose floorboard. The room was good, clean, like

Missus Kuáng had promised, but it would have used some work. In fact, I was working off part of my rent doing odd jobs around the building. Repairing the floor in my room hadn't come up yet.

"Marshal, does it look like Mister Henson had any gold?" Frustrated, I pointed to the burned-out husk of the building.

"No." Marshal Buchanan sighed. "No, it don't. The reason I'm asking is that I've sent word for the circuit judge. Judge Caldwell. We're holding onto Courbet for assisting with a murder and attempted murder on two counts. You and my daughter. As soon as the judge gets here, we'll convene a trial." He looked at me. "Charlie, you're the only witness there is to Mister Henson's death. You're going to have to testify if we're going to tie Mister Henson's murder to Angelo Blunt. I just want you to have your story together so you can tell it right. And not being sure of why Blunt was there at the cemetery that night could be a problem."

"Why?"

"Because the burden of the proof is on the prosecutor. Mister Murrey. If we can say for sure why Blunt rode up on you two, that would help."

I knew of Murrey, but I didn't know much about how his job worked.

"Mister Murrey has got to have all the facts," the marshal said, "and he's got to present them to the judge."

"The fact is that Angelo Blunt and his men killed Mister Henson." I was pistol-hot then. That healed wound on my head throbbed and I felt a headache coming on. I'd had a few of those since the night Mister Henson had died. "They tried to kill me too. I can testify to that. I will testify to that. Why Blunt did what he did doesn't really matter, does it? It only matters that he did it."

I was breathing hard when I finished.

"You're right, Charlie," Marshal Buchanan said softly. "That's what matters when it comes to convicting Blunt and his men of murder, but I need to find him first."

"Ask Eleanor Deno," I told him.

"I will," he promised. "Just as soon as I can find her. She's gone missing too. You had no idea she wasn't who she said she was?"

"Not until I saw her wanted poster, and I wasn't sure then till she came after me."

"Why do you think she was interested in Mister Henson?"

"They seemed to like each other." I went back to cleaning.

"Maggie said Eleanor Deno picked you up two mornings after Mister Henson's murder. Do you mind telling me what that was about?"

One thing I had to give Maggie Buchanan; she was a stickler for details.

"Eleanor Deno wanted to know about the gold Blunt was asking about," I said.

Marshal Buchanan nodded. "You can see how that's an important part of this story."

"I don't see how."

He looked at me. "For this reason, Charlie. Courbet's lawyer is going to try to throw suspicion on anyone he can. He could say you were part of the murder."

"And I shot myself? Twice?" I was ready to hit something.

"He could."

"Well, that doesn't make any sense."

"Juries like good stories," Marshal Buchanan said. "They don't always just listen for the truth." He paused. "And they won't convict a man of murder if we can't put him in that courtroom. We've got Courbet and he'll pay for his part, and for trying to kill you, but we don't have Angelo Blunt. When it comes to producing motive for the murder, which we have to have, we've potentially got a weak case. That's what Murrey told me this afternoon when I talked with him."

I stared at the ground. I had the map Mister Henson had hidden, and I wasn't going to turn it over. It wasn't about the gold. I knew I'd never see that.

It was the last thing of him that was mine alone. And I

wanted to protect Mister Henson.

I wasn't about to let his name get dragged through the mud. I would die before I stood by and allowed that. So I wasn't going to let any of that story go. I was going to hold onto it tight.

I feared it would all be wasted effort in the end because if Blunt got taken alive, or if Ellie Deno got arrested, one or both of them would reveal Mister Henson's past. I didn't know if they could prove him an outlaw, but it would get folks in Pecos talking.

So I hoped Blunt got killed and Ellie Deno got away. She hadn't hurt Mister Henson. Just lied to him. That was hurt enough, but it wasn't worth her dying over.

I hadn't told anyone about her trying to shoot me.

I figured if Blunt got taken alive, the worst case was he'd have to prove Mister Henson was really Petway. I didn't see that happening. The only thing that would have given any weight to the story Blunt and Ellie Deno told was the map that I was going to hang onto. Even that would have been just a piece of paper.

Maybe. Thinking about the trial was confusing to me. There was so much I didn't know.

"Charlie," the marshal said gently.

I only realized then that I'd been standing there for too long.

"It's getting late," he said.

I looked around at the darkening sky and knew that was true.

"Let's go get some supper," he suggested. "We can go over what you're going to tell at the trial when it's time."

33

"So this is how you tell it if Eleanor Deno gets involved in the trial," Marshal Buchanan said.

Like me, he didn't think we were shut of her yet. We were sitting at a table in Cactus Slim's, a restaurant with a menu that included Mexican fare and plenty of it. I thought I was going to shame myself because I was eating so much, but Marshal Buchanan matched me bite for bite without batting an eye.

Most of the clientele were cowboys from various nearby ranches and the restaurant served tequila. There was usually a fight in the place every week for one reason or another, and the cheap furniture and decorations Mister Roth imported from south of the Rio Grande got broken pretty often. They were cheap enough to replace, though. Mister Roth had priced out repairs with Mister Henson a couple of times, but in the end he'd always bought replacements.

"We can only guess at the relationship between Eleanor Deno and Angelo Blunt," the marshal said as he loaded another tortilla with meat and rice and beans, then topped it with jalapeno chilis, "so we can either suggest that Eleanor Deno was pulling a fast one on Blunt. Or she was marking Mister Henson as a target for Blunt."

"Why would she do that?"

"Maybe she was in trouble with Blunt over a deal

that went wrong. Maybe she told Blunt Mister Henson had more money than he did." Marshal Buchanan looked at me. "Mister Henson didn't have a lot, Charlie, but he owned that building and that land it's on. It's not worth a lot, but it's worth something."

"I know," I said. "That's why I'm clearing it out. I'm going to rebuild it. I can work for Mister Duncan at the sawmill and take my wages out in materials and time on the saws after hours to construct what I need."

Marshal Buchanan shook his head and smiled at me. "That's an ambitious project."

"It is, but Mister Henson taught me how to build. We didn't just make caskets. We worked on a lot of folks' homes and businesses."

"I guess you did." The marshal sipped his coffee. "It will still take a long time."

"I've got time," I said. "I don't have plans for going anywhere else."

"What are you going to use the building for?"

"I'm going to build a couple of rooms on the second floor. Living quarters. I don't know what I'm going to do with the lower floor yet."

"I suppose you could go into the funeral business."

I acted like I was considering that. "It was fine work, but I don't think I want to do that anymore. I could just rent the first floor out to someone who wanted shop space."

"That sounds like a fine plan, Charlie. I wish you well."

I turned my attention back to my plate and felt a little uneasy. It was the first time I'd admitted to anyone that I was thinking about the future and my part in it. I still felt guilty about that.

"I also wanted to thank you for saving Maggie," Marshal Buchanan said.

"She saved me," I pointed out. "If it hadn't been for her shooting Courbet and throwing off that whole ambush, they would have murdered me."

"But you stood by her when lead started flying." Marshal Buchanan nodded at me. "If she'd taken a stand on her own like that, it's likely they would have killed her."

"She's good at what she does, Marshal. I couldn't have done what she did."

"You killed two of those men. Maggie only killed one of them. I'd say that was doing plenty."

I hesitated, and I didn't like the idea of lying to the marshal. In fact, I thought there was a good chance I could get into plenty of trouble for it. And I'd been lying pretty regular these past few days.

"I only killed one of those men," I said. "Lavery. I shot Courbet after Maggie did, but she killed those other two men and saved my life." I told him about the trick Maggie had done using my pistol.

Marshal Buchanan grinned a little and scratched at his whiskers thoughtfully. "After Gilbride performed autopsies on them, we were wondering how that man had two bullets in him in about the same place. Sometimes that will happen, but it's still a strange thing."

"Maggie said she filed her report saying I killed him."

"She did."

"Is she going to get in any trouble?" I was worried about that now and I didn't want another burden.

"Not if we don't tell anyone." Marshal Buchanan reached for another tortilla.

I understood then that maybe shading the truth a little might not be a bad thing.

The marshal leaned back and adjusted his belt a little, letting it out. "Maggie gave you credit for killing those men, and I know why she did it. Lavery and Dockett both had bounties on their heads. Dead or alive. I'll be wiring for the rewards on them in the morning, so you'll have that money soon."

"Marshal, I don't want—"

"Charlie, I know you didn't kill those men for blood money. You were just defending yourself. And you were defending my little girl. Those men had bounties on their heads for a lot of reasons. I don't see any cause why that money can't be used to help finance your real estate empire." He smiled at me.

"Maggie should get some of the money."

Marshal Buchanan shook his head. "She can't. Not as an officer of the court, and she is that. She wanted to make sure you got the money."

I thought about that, and what she'd done that day made sense, but not the way she'd done it. I'd never seen anyone do something so cold and calculated.

Or maybe it was just her lack of any emotion at all after all the shooting.

Despite all the dead folks we'd worked on, me and Mister Henson usually got affected by the folks we dealt with. Them and their families.

That day, that incident, had kept wriggling around in the back of my mind, and it was grist for the nightmare mill in my head when I tried to sleep.

"How is Maggie?" I asked after we were quiet for a little bit.

Marshal Buchanan frowned at me. "What do you mean?"

I wanted to take the question back, knowing I should have stuck to my own business and didn't try minding someone else's. But I was worried about Maggie too. It was probably just the fact that she'd saved my life. Or it could have been that with Mister Henson gone I was looking for someone else to worry about.

"That day in the warehouse, and after," I said cautiously, "she...didn't seem to be upset about anything. She told me she'd never killed anyone before."

"She hadn't."

"She just acted so calm about...everything. Even when shooting that dead man." I shook my head. "I couldn't have done something like that. Not ever."

"A lot of folks couldn't have done the kind of work you and Mister Henson did," Marshal Buchanan pointed out. "Hardly any of them could cut a man open to fix him the way Gilbride does. I'm not talking about the knowledge of what to do to heal someone. I'm talking about opening a man up with a knife to even do it."

"I know, but those folks were already dead. And I didn't make them that way."

Marshal Buchanan was quiet for a time and I thought he was going to just ignore the question. Then he sat up and leaned toward me. "Maggie's different, Charlie. When she was a girl, all she wanted to do was be a lawman like me. She used to read law books and the newspapers, and she memorized every wanted poster that crossed my desk. Peacekeeping is in her blood, that's all."

He spoke with pride and love, and it moved me.

"I made her a deputy because that was what she wanted and she was good at it. She knows more law than any deputy I've got working for me, and she'll walk into the teeth of a problem my deputies would all think twice about."

Maggie's different.

That was the same way Gilbride had described her, and I thought about her more.

"Don't you worry about her, Charlie," Marshal Buchanan told me. "She's solid. But I'll tell you one thing."

I waited.

"She may not act like it, but she could probably benefit from having a friend who's the same age as she is."

I didn't know if I was comfortable with that in light of everything, and given the marshal's and the doctor's vague answers.

I didn't say that, though. I said, "She doesn't seem to care for me much."

"She followed you that day," her father said, and I knew I was talking to her father, not the marshal in that instant. "She killed those men protecting you. And she talks about you like I've never heard her talk about anyone. She always thought you were interesting."

"Interesting?" That seemed like such an odd word for a person to use when referring to another person.

He nodded. "Her very word. Maggie doesn't get fascinated by much outside marshal's work. But she was interested in you."

Well, you could have knocked me over with a dandelion when he told me that.

"Why?" I asked before I knew I was going to.

"You'd have to ask her."

I wasn't sure I wanted to do that. "She never said anything to me about me being interesting."

"Maggie's not a talker. You probably know that by now, but I'll tell you myownself. She's watchful. And she's always thinking. Sometimes it will be days before she comes and asks me about something that happened weeks back."

I thought that was strange. When I'd had a question for Mister Henson, I'd always asked him straight out. Otherwise I'd forget it. He was the one who put things off when we were busy, then circle back around to them at times when I'd already forgotten I'd asked.

"Something I've learned about Maggie that I'll pass on to you," Marshal Buchanan said. "Like I said, I think it would be good for her to have someone her own age to talk to about things, but you have to be patient with her. Patient. And honest. If you do that, she'll come around. If she's a mind to."

I nodded, but inside I was thinking that I didn't want her coming around.

34

Over the next week, I continued working at every odd job that came my way. They were coming fast enough that I had to postpone some and turn down others that had to be done quickly. I threw myself into the work and it didn't matter what it was. I was just single-minded purpose.

I saved my evenings for the reconstruction of Mister Henson's building. I'd finished clearing away all the burned remnants, torn down the residual supports that were charred or that I just didn't trust, and was starting on the framing. Most of the design was going to be the same, so I didn't need blueprints. I built what I had known and the construction was almost automatic.

My life was broken, twisted, and burned, but I was putting it back together. When the bounty money came in, I banked it in two accounts. One was for me and the other was for Maggie, if I ever figured out a way to get it to her.

I could take a breath because now I had a financial cushion that I hadn't expected to ever have actually. My funds, even with my work, had been getting depleted by everything I was putting into the rebuild.

During that time, I kept track of Maggie too, but I didn't go out of my way to visit. I just kept up with gossip that came my way at various job sites.

On Tuesday night, she'd busted up a fight in the Ugly

Toad. A couple of rough customers who had disembarked from the train had thought they didn't have to listen to a young, female deputy. One of them ended up having to get stitches from Gilbride to fix the ear she'd nearly torn off him. The other ended up with a broken leg.

I was betting both of them were glad to pay their disturbing the peace fines and put Pecos behind them.

***

On Thursday, I was on the second floor framing out the two bedrooms and the kitchen/living room area. I was thinking that if money got tight in the future, I could rent out one of the bedrooms too. I didn't like the idea of sharing living quarters with a stranger, but I liked the idea of losing the building over taxes or hard-to-manage upkeep even less.

I still didn't know what I was going to do with the first floor.

I was pondering that and staring up at the bones of the roof when Maggie called up to me.

"Charlie Stark."

I didn't know what to expect when I looked down at her, but I knew it definitely wasn't to see her standing there with her guns and badge on and holding a basket that looked like something Trail's End would prepare for a takeout meal.

"Good afternoon, Maggie," I said. I reached for the shirt I had hung over an overhead rafter.

It was getting on into summer now, and the days were hot. Thankfully they were long so I could get more hours in. Being able to work so much meant less time for sleeping, but I was okay with that. I was too tired to have nightmares most nights and that suited me just fine.

"Have you eaten lunch?" Maggie asked.

"No." I pulled on the shirt and buttoned it. Lunch had been on my mind, though.

"I brought food." Maggie held up the basket to prove it. The slight breeze I'd been enjoying ruffled the red and white checked cloth that covered the basket's contents.

"I see."

"Do you want to eat?"

"You came over here to bring me something to eat?" I asked. I knew that sounded impolite and I didn't want to be impolite because I didn't want to get on her bad side.

"No," she said. "I brought enough for both of us. Pa said he thought it would be a good idea if I was to check up on you and make sure you're doing all right." She looked at me, considering. "You look all right to me."

"I am," I said. "I'm all right."

"Good. You didn't answer the question."

"What question?"

"Do you want to eat?"

I considered turning her down, but I really didn't want to. From the way she was shifting her weight from foot to foot, I thought she was probably uncomfortable with the whole situation. I supposed the only reason she was there was because her pa had suggested it.

"Sure," I said. I pointed to the temporary stairs I'd built to get to the second story. The flooring I was standing on was short-term as well, but I knew it would hold us.

Maggie came up the narrow, steep stairs without a hitch, moving with an easy grace. When it came time to put in the permanent stairs, I'd build them wider.

I smelled the fried chicken in the basket before she reached the second floor.

Maggie looked around the area. "Well, you don't have a table or chairs."

Despite my nervousness and misgivings, I laughed. "Not yet, but when the time comes, I'll build them." I took the basket from her.

She looked around some more. "It looks better than it did. I've seen you working on it." She rapped one of the rafters with her knuckles. "Looks really solid."

That sounded like a compliment, but she didn't seem sure of herself.

"It is," I said, "and it will be even more solid when I finish up. But I have something we can use for a table now. Unless you have somewhere else in mind."

"No," she said. "We'll eat here. I'd planned on eating here."

35

I set up two sawhorses and put a long flooring plank across them as a makeshift table. Maggie spread out the chicken, cornbread, corn, okra, and collards. It looked like it was enough to feed four people.

"I know you eat a lot," she told me. "I hope it's enough."

"It's plenty," I said, but I wasn't sure if her thinking I ate a lot was a good thing. It definitely didn't sound flattering. I'd gotten more browned by the sun and I'd stripped off some weight, but it was weight I could stand to lose.

She'd even brought a whole rhubarb pie.

"I'm going to pay for this," I said.

"It's already paid for."

"Then let me pay you back."

"No."

I argued a little, feeling uncomfortable, but she was adamant and it felt like I was on the verge of an argument with her. That was something I didn't want, so I quit on it.

Mentioning the reward money I'd gotten didn't seem like conversation you'd have over a meal, even though I had done exactly that with her pa. So I thanked her instead.

"You're welcome," she said, and she sounded almost formal.

I took the plate and silverware she handed me and was going to wait until she'd served herself before digging in, but after I just stood there for a bit, she took my plate and filled it herself, then handed it back to me.

Since I didn't have chairs, and the makeshift table was long enough, we sat in the side-by-side window frames that looked over Second Street. A few passersby stopped and looked up at us. Then they moved on.

I knew folks were going to talk and I wasn't sure how to stop it. Then I ignored it because folks were still talking about Mister Henson and the shootout at Malpert's. I couldn't stop that either.

When she had her plate filled, as heaped as mine was, and she'd settled in the window, she said, "Tell me what you're doing here."

As I ate, I described what I was doing to the second floor. I talked longer and more than I'd thought I was going to.

"What about the first floor?" she asked. "What are you going to do with it?"

"I don't know yet."

"It seems like you should know what you're doing with the first floor before you build the second."

I laughed. "I know, but that's not how this is working out. This is my first building so I'm kind of working my way through it."

"Your real estate empire. That's what Pa says." Her lips twitched.

"Yeah," I said. "I heard about the fight at the Ugly Toad."

"It wasn't much of a fight."

"You could have gotten hurt."

"By those two?" She raised her eyebrows at me and smiled bigger than I'd ever seen her smile before.

"Yeah. Those two."

"Not on their best day," she said. "And that night was not their best day."

I pointed my fork at her bruised knuckles. "Want to explain how that happened?"

"Their faces were harder than I thought. After I figured that out, I hit them in the throat."

"And tore a guy's ear nearly off the way I heard it."

She shrugged. "He wasn't using it to listen, so I used it how I could. I got his attention and he settled right down."

I laughed at that and she joined me. A lot of the nervousness I'd been feeling slid away. Maggie was quiet and short with her conversation, but I knew she was genuine.

And she wasn't dead like most of the folks that had come into that building were.

That was nice.

Between us, we finished the pie too.

36

Another couple of weeks passed until it was time for the trial. When the date was set early in June, the nightmares weren't the only things keeping me up late at night. I worried about what the trial would bring up about Mister Henson and his past, and I worried about how it would feel to be in that witness stand in front of everybody telling my story.

I worked out my testimony with Murrey and Marshal Buchanan. Sometimes Maggie sat there in Murrey's office and listened in, but she never said anything. On some of those occasions, I got more emotional than I'd wanted to. Murrey and the marshal comforted me as best as they could, but Maggie just sat there and sipped coffee.

After Murrey pronounced me as ready as I was going to be, I thanked him and left. Maggie walked out with me and awkwardly patted me on the shoulder. Other than pulling me out of the grave, she'd never touched me before.

"You going to do just fine, Charlie," she told me. "You shouldn't be worried so much."

Then she walked back to the marshal's office.

But I still got the feeling she knew I was holding something back. Murrey and Marshal Buchanan did too, but they didn't push me on it.

No one knew where Angel Blunt was.

***

When I wasn't with Murrey and Marshal Buchanan, I worked. I got the building roofed and shingled in the evenings when it was cooler, but only just. I kept at it until I ran out of daylight or folks around me griped about the noise.

The reconstruction was coming along better than I'd hoped. Somehow I'd managed to hit a rhythm and things were happening faster. Folks were noticing and going out of their way to congratulate me and encourage me.

The fact that I had help doing the work added my determination and ability to get things done.

Maggie came over when she could, which turned out to be not as much as I would have liked. Not for the extra set of hands, but for the company. She was quiet and deliberate, so I did most of the talking and we were both okay with that. I discovered that I liked talking to her. She was easier to talk to than Mister Henson was because she didn't try to correct me. But maybe I just liked talking to her because I liked having somebody. With Mister Henson gone, there was no one.

She worked nights a lot because she wanted to. That was when there was more excitement, she'd told me.

I'd told her I was all through with excitement. She said she didn't know how she could live without it, but she smiled a little after she said it.

So she'd join me on the building if I was working on it before it got hot, or she'd join me for a few hours in the evening before she went into the marshal's office and started her time there. There was always a meal involved. Usually one of us or the other would bring something from one of the restaurants, but we sometimes just settled for sandwiches.

We'd had to set up a schedule after the day we'd both showed up with a meal. We'd managed to eat both meals because we didn't want it to go to waste, but we'd been so stuffed afterward that we didn't want to repeat the experience.

Occasionally we'd go into a restaurant if it got dark before we ate and she was not being a deputy, and sometimes we ate together even when she was. We didn't like eating in the restaurants because too many folks watched us.

Gilbride stopped by the building the night before the trial, and I knew he was there to check up on me. He was going to give testimony at the trial too. Over my wounds and his autopsy findings on Mister Henson.

He took a seat in one of the chairs I'd brought up for me and Maggie and nodded at the basket left over from the supper me and Maggie had shared about an hour earlier.

"You and Maggie seem to be getting along all right," he said.

I looked at him suspiciously, wondering if he meant anything by it.

He held up his hands in surrender and laughed. "I'm not being disparaging, Charlie. It was an honest observation."

"We are," I said, and I got another piece of lumber, put it up against the wall that separated my bedroom from the kitchen area, and marked it for cutting. Everything in that building was going to be custom fit.

"What do you think about her?"

"She's quiet," I said.

"She's still not talking much?"

"Nope."

"Do you encourage her to talk?"

"No. Why would I?"

"No reason. Just wondering." Gilbride shifted on his chair. "Her father and I are just looking out for her."

"Doctor Gilbride, me and Maggie are just friends." My face burned a little at what I realized he might have been getting at.

He shook his head. "Charlie, I'm not asking if there's any romance going on."

"Well, there isn't."

"Marshal Buchanan and I wouldn't stand in your way if there was."

I stood up, sighed in disgust, and pinned him with a hard stare. "You know, you and the marshal are starting to sound like old women sitting around matchmaking. Maybe the two of you should concentrate on getting romances of your own and getting it out of your minds."

Gilbride tugged at his shirt collar with a finger and grimaced in discomfort. Women were known to chase after him. "What I mean to say is that we're glad the two of you are friends."

"That's all it is," I said. And that was the truth of it.

"The marshal and I are glad you're friends," Gilbride said. "Maggie needs a friend."

I didn't disagree, but I knew if there was a person who didn't need anything at all, it was Maggie Buchanan.

"She talks when she wants to," I said. "And that's the way we like it."

"That's fine, Charlie." Gilbride looked at me. "What about you?"

"What about me?"

"Are you glad you have a friend?"

"I've always had friends."

"None of them you've spent as much time with as you have Maggie. You were standoffish as a kid. You hung around with Jimmy Hadley and a couple others, but you never acted like you were really close to any of them."

I hadn't been. "Mister Henson kept me busy."

"That's true. Mister Henson was concerned that since you'd lost your parents in the way you had that you might not be able to make friends."

"I didn't need them."

Gilbride nodded. "I'd noticed since we lost Mister Henson that you weren't hanging around with anyone your age. That was worrying me some."

I suddenly realized that was true. I hadn't chased after any of those casual friendships, and none of them had come around. "Most of them aren't…"I didn't know what they weren't, but I knew there was a difference.

"As autonomous as you are?" Gilbride asked.

"Maybe," I replied.

He was quiet for a moment. "I think you and Maggie have a lot in common, Charlie. I'm glad you're getting along."

After a bit, he excused himself and left. I cut a few more boards and thought about what he said, trying to figure out what had prompted the conversation, but it just made my head hurt because I was already thinking about the trial starting the next morning.

I cut the board I'd marked, fit it into place, and drove in the nails. Then I gathered my tools and headed to my rented room and hoped I could sleep.

37

The trial started bright and early the next morning, and when I walked into the impromptu courtroom in the back of Hunziker's General Store, I thought the whole town had turned out for it.

If I hadn't been a witness, and the first one called to the stand at that, I might not have gotten a seat.

Hunziker had paid me and a couple more men to move the goods in that area of his store over to Malpert's Storage for as long as court was in session. Hunziker had demanded an extra shotgun guard be set up at the warehouse, and he was.

A canvas tarp separated the back of the store from the front, and as the trial progressed, folks would step through the tarp to the front of the store to get snacks. Hunziker made a pretty penny off popcorn, licorice, and coffee during the three days court was in session.

I don't remember much about the trial. I delivered my statement to Murrey and got cross-examined by the defense attorney, Goodkind, who was a fat man in an expensive suit and was nothing like his last name. Like the marshal and Murrey had figured, Goodkind hammered my insistence that I didn't know why Angelo Blunt had ridden out to Sunflower Cemetery.

After Goodkind had gone on with that line of questioning for a bit and I was getting frustrated and ready to tear an ear from the lawyer's head to see if I could improve his hearing, Murrey stood up.

"Your Honor, I object to opposing counsel's treatment of the witness."

I'd learned there was a lot of lingo lawyers liked to throw around. They reminded me of two banty roosters posturing like they were going to fight but never actually getting to it. The folks in the courtroom loved the words and the emotions, though.

Maggie didn't seem impressed, though. She sat at the back of the court in a chair she'd brought with her and watched the tarp-covered doorway.

Judge Caldwell sat behind one of Hunziker's finest table, which was one Mister Henson and I had built for him. I thought it was fitting that it was there under the circumstances. Probably no one else in the room knew the history of the table, and I thought even Hunziker had forgotten.

The judge was a small, bald man in his seventies whose pince-nez made his gray eyes look huge, but his big, bushy mustache offset that. He wore a black jacket with a fresh flower in the lapel every morning, dark gray slacks, and usually took his boots off after he arrived. He'd keep them off until lunch, put them on again, and take them off once more when he returned from lunch till court adjourned.

In his speaking, he was short and to the point, but I got a sense of fairness about him. I thought Mister Henson would have approved of him being the judge over his murder trial, which I admit was a strange thing to even consider. But I thought about it. The lawyers argued a lot and I had nothing to do in the witness chair but think. Mostly I thought I'd rather be anywhere but there, but I needed to be there to convict Courbet.

"State your objection, Mister Murrey," the judge said. The way he said it, I got the impression he already knew what it was going to be.

"Counsel is badgering the witness," Murrey said. "We're not here to find out why Mister Courbet and his companions murdered Mister Henson in cold blood.

We're here to bring that man to justice for the heinous crimes that he has committed."

"Your Honor," Goodkind said, waving his hands around, "my client is on trial for his life. With such a precious thing hanging in the balance, surely Mister Murrey won't begrudge me the opportunity to mount a strong defense."

Courbet had been watching me the whole time I was on the witness stand. Now he was leaning forward, the chain of the manacles that bound his hands sitting on the defense table. He grinned at me and I knew he was trying to appear intimidating.

I wasn't intimidated. It was everything I could do to keep from standing up, grabbing my chair, and smashing it across his face. So, to keep myself calm, I focused on that gap in his smile that was the result of Maggie knocking that gold tooth out of his head.

"A precious thing?" Judge Caldwell adjusted himself on his chair and looked mad. "That man's life is a precious thing?"

Taking a half-step back, Goodkind suddenly looked uncertain, like it was a surprise quiz and he didn't know the answer to the question. "Yes...yes, Your Honor."

"That man is wanted for murder in other places than Pecos, Mister Goodkind. Do you intend to defend him there too?"

"If Mister Courbet so chooses, Your Honor."

"Well, I hope whoever is paying you is paying you well, Mister Goodkind, because Mister Courbet is going to keep you gainfully employed."

"Yes, Your Honor."

"Unless he's found guilty in my courtroom," Caldwell said. "Because if he is, I intend to hang him and you'll need to seek other clients."

That wiped the confident smile right off Courbet's face.

Who was paying Goodkind was a matter of rampant speculation. Aiken had been running daily special editions of the trial, along with advertisements for shopkeepers hoping to take advantage of all the folks being in town to see it for themselves. That was one of the questions that kept showing up in Aiken's editorials. He was bent on fanning the flames of any story he could throw words at

Some folks thought Angelo Blunt was footing the bill, but other folks thought Goodkind's fees were getting paid by another group of outlaws. There was even talk of him having a rich father somewhere who was paying the legal fees.

"As for this young man's testimony," Judge Caldwell said, "I'm going to direct that for a moment. With your indulgence. I think I can move things along and save us all some time. And God knows this young man has put in plenty of time in that chair being asked the same question a dozen different ways."

Goodkind looked like he was going to have an apoplectic fit, something I'd seen happen a couple times in the funeral business when Mister Henson had presented a bill. I didn't know how many times I'd heard folks say that dying shouldn't cost so much.

"Your Honor," Goodkind said with only a hint of protest. "I—"

The judge cocked an eyebrow at him and shut his water off. "Yes, Mister Goodkind?"

Goodkind seemed to sag. "Nothing, Your Honor. It is your courtroom."

"Yes," Caldwell said, "we wouldn't want to forget that, would we?"

"No, Your Honor." Goodkind looked like a stepped-on toad.

"In the interests of saving time and to get this young man out of this chair," Caldwell said, turning to me, "I only have a few questions. Are you ready, Mister Stark?"

"Yes, Your Honor," I said.

38

"Do you know why Angelo Blunt looked for you and your employer in," Caldwell glanced at his notes, but I thought the effort was to make a point that he was writing them down, not because he didn't remember, "the Sunflower Cemetery?"

"No, Your Honor." I swallowed hard but reminded myself that Marshal Buchanan thought not being wholly truthful was permissible. The only truth that mattered was Mister Henson had been murdered by Angelo Blunt and his gang of outlaws.

"Did Angelo Blunt shoot you?"

"Yes sir."

"Did Angelo Blunt shoot your employer, Mister Henson?"

"Yes sir."

"Did Angelo Blunt kill Mister Henson?"

"I didn't see Blunt shoot Mister Henson and kill him," I said. "I heard his pistol fire again, and then Mister Henson was in the grave with me. He was dead." I told it straight out, but my voice cracked and my eyes felt hot. I remembered that Maggie was sitting in the back of the courtroom as she had been every time I'd been there and I focused on that.

I wasn't alone.

"You would know that pistol firing?"

"Yes sir. Blunt had already shot Mister Henson a couple times. He shot me with it too. It was a MAS Modéle 1873. It doesn't sound like any other pistol I've ever heard."

Caldwell looked at me in surprise, but he was smiling too. "A MAS Modéle 1873? You know that for a fact?"

"Yes sir. Mister Kearney has one over at his gun shop. I identified it to him from what I remembered from that day at the sunflower. It looks very unique."

"That's good, Mister Stark, but you didn't see Blunt shoot Mister Henson that final time?"

"No sir, but I heard the pistol. Like I said, it sounds different. It's because of the eleven-millimeter cartridge the MAS Modéle 1873 uses. I'm sure Doctor Gilbride can tell you about the bullets he took out of Mister Henson."

"I'll talk to the good doctor about that in due time, Mister Stark. You've never heard that particular model fire before that night?"

"No sir. But I did after that. At Mister Kearney's gun range. I fired a pistol like the one Blunt shot Mister Henson with. They sounded the same."

Caldwell looked at me and nodded. "That'll do, Mister Stark. You're excused from the witness stand. Thank you for your time."

I got out of that chair and left the courtroom. There was nothing more I could do, and I didn't want to watch the rest of it play out.

I was afraid I'd messed up everything by not telling everything I knew about the gold and Mister Henson.

*

Maggie met me out in front of the general store.

I was taking deep breaths and trying to loosen up and clear my head.

"C'mon," she said.

"Where are we going?" I didn't know what I wanted to do. I'd thought the trial would help, but it only seemed to make things worse.

"Wick's Diner." Maggie grabbed my elbow and pulled me after her. "They've got ice cream."

39

I sat in the back of the diner across from Maggie and watched her dig into the large bowl of vanilla ice cream that sat before her. Wick's Diner only made ice cream every now and again because churning up a batch took a long time and someone had to stay at the churn to get it done. It wasn't like cooking a brisket, something you could leave and come back later too.

Wick's had put ice cream on the menu the last couple days because there were out of towners brought in by the railroad who had come for the trial. It was the biggest thing in Pecos County for a long time. While they were there, some of those folks treated themselves to meals they didn't get back at home.

"What are you thinking about?" Maggie asked.

I was watching my ice cream melt. I just didn't have the stomach for it because my guts were in knots. "The trial. What I said." What I didn't say.

"Which part?"

This was an unusual conversation because I was almost always the one to initiate conversation between us. I was never at a loss for words around Maggie. Sometimes I didn't have anything to say, but when I did have something to say, I got it said.

"The part about me not seeing Blunt shoot Mister

Henson. I'm thinking maybe that gave Courbet's attorney too much wiggle room."

"I thought you did fine. So did most of the people sitting around me. Why are you worrying about that?"

"Because…" I almost let my frustration at the situation and my performance boil over onto her, which I knew wouldn't be accepted. "Because I don't want to allow Courbet or Blunt or any of them to get off scot-free."

"Courbet is headed for a noose. There's no way he's getting out of that." Maggie ate that ice cream like we weren't talking about folks dying, like it was just casual conversation.

We had the diner mostly to ourselves because the action was all over at Hunziker's. Those that couldn't get into the courtroom were standing in the outer section of the general store. Those that couldn't get into the general store at all stood on the boardwalk outside or sat on chairs they'd brought. They were drinking tea or moonshine they'd packed in. Some folks had picnic baskets and were eating fried chicken. The trial was a public event and considered free entertainment.

"He could go free," I said. "Because I didn't see Mister Henson's murder." Once I said that, I realized that I'd seen more than I had wanted to as it was.

"He tried to murder you," Maggie said. She licked her spoon. She'd already scraped her bowl clean. "He's not going free."

"But I want him to pay for Mister Henson's murder."

Maggie looked at me. Her hair was neatly parted and pulled back into a braid that ran down her back. The collar of her dark red shirt underscored her jawline. Her dark eyes were as serious as I'd ever seen them.

"What's the worst thing that could happen if he gets off on these charges? Which he won't."

"I'll have to watch him ride off."

Maggie's lips twitched. "He wouldn't ride far."

I didn't like the cold menace in her words. "What do you mean?"

"You and me," she said, "we could ride after him and hang him ourselves."

That was tempting, but I couldn't see us doing that. Well, I couldn't see me doing that. "We can't do that."

"We've already proven we're smarter and faster than Courbet. We could do it. Folks used to hang horse thieves all the time out in the woods when they caught them."

Actually, they still did. The marshal brought a hanged man to me and Mister Henson a few months back that still had the noose around his neck. Someone had written HARSE THEF on his forehead with a knife. At the time, horses had been going missing from time to time, and that stopped after the dead man had been found. Marshal Buchanan hadn't looked too hard for the men who had hanged the man.

Frontier justice still existed in Texas.

I looked at Maggie. "We're not murderers."

"No, we're not. But if Courbet was to escape the noose here and ride out of town, somebody needs to make him pay for what he's done." She grinned. "He has a dead or alive bounty on him. We could give him the choice. Personally, I think you could use that bounty for the building of your real estate empire."

I couldn't believe what she was saying, but I knew she was serious.

"Bad men have to pay for their crimes," she told me. For a minute her eyes stared right through me, like I wasn't sitting across from her. "Bad women, too. If they don't get caught, if they don't get punished, they just go on and hurt others." Her eyes came back to me. "I'm a deputy because I want to stop that. Not everyone can stand up and defend themselves. I can do that for them. You got the building work you do, Charlie, but this is my work."

I knew she meant it. I could hear that in her voice. I couldn't help wondering if this was part of the difference Gilbride and the marshal were talking about when they talked about her.

She pointed her spoon at my ice cream. "Now, are you going to eat that or not? You're just sitting there letting it melt. Once it melts, it won't be any good to anybody."

I pushed the ice cream across the table and let her have at it.

40

The trial lasted five days. I didn't go. I didn't want to sit in that room and watch Courbet enjoy being the center of attention. I didn't want to relive that day Mister Henson died any more. I didn't keep up with the day-to-day things in Aiken's special editions like most folks did.

I worked every day because I wanted to stay busy.

I managed to get the top floor of the building finished out enough that I could put a bed in there and sleep there nights instead of continuing to rent a room that never felt comfortable to me. The outer walls were up to give me privacy I needed and I could get to the interior walls as I needed them. At the moment I liked the wide, open space of the top of the building.

The first floor was empty and without purpose, but I had the walls in place so those who were curious, and it wasn't only children, couldn't just walk in.

Work around town dried up a little while folks attended the trial, so I was able to work from sun up to sundown on my living quarters. I built a simple bed and two chairs for me and Maggie when she visited, and I was working on a proper table at the sawmill, hoping to surprise her with it in the next couple days.

I hid that map in a special hiding spot I'd constructed above my bed and I didn't look at it again. I guess I kind of buried it like Mister Henson was buried out at Sunflower Cemetery.

I knew when Gilbride offered his testimony about the autopsy and everything he'd seen, but I stayed away while that was going on. I'd already lived through all of that I wanted to, and I still couldn't completely shake it out of my head at night.

I did go when Maggie testified about pulling me and Mister Henson out of the grave that Missus Louise Mead now occupied. Everybody was silent as she told about getting me up on solid ground again.

Some of the folks in attendance told me afterward that I'd told the story better, that they could actually feel the dirt closing in on them when I was giving my testimony. Personally, I thought those folks were too imaginative for their own good and were looking for those things.

Maggie was pretty blunt with her answers, which got both lawyers agitated. She didn't worry about any of it. Just said her piece and got up as soon as they let her. They let her go pretty early.

Goodkind made a lot of accusations about Eleanor Deno not being there to defend herself, seeing as how she demonstrated what Murrey called "nefarious designs." Murrey went on to say that if Eleanor Deno showed up, he'd be glad to ask her some questions himself, but that she wasn't the one on trial. Courbet was.

By that time, Courbet wasn't in the best of moods because he'd seen which way the wind was blowing, but he still acted like he was going to be just fine when everything was settled.

Everybody knew what was coming, and it was like watching the Texas and Pacific train roll into the depot. Slow and steady, and unstoppable.

When Courbet was found guilty on Friday at two in the afternoon, no one was surprised and a lot of folks were happy.

I wasn't, and that surprised me.

They were happy that they were getting a hanging.

I didn't get Mister Henson back.

***

That evening, Maggie brought takeout from Cactus Jack's because it was her turn. We'd kind of put up a schedule for the times we were going to eat together. We didn't always do it, but we did it more often than not. I always looked forward to the meals because being around her never got old.

We were friends, good friends, and I was happy with that. No one else our age wanted to spend time with us, and we didn't miss them. Me and Maggie were pretty complete as we were.

When she arrived, I was putting the finishing touches on the table I'd built and was more than a little proud of. It still needed another couple coats of varnish, but we could use it and it looked good, and I could put those coats on as I had time.

We laid the food on the table together without talking. Sometimes we hardly spoke, but the company was always good. Then we took our seats in the chairs.

"You still don't look happy, Charlie." Maggie studied me. She sometimes did that, and I never understood what she was looking for. Every now and again I'd be afraid that I wouldn't measure up in some way that I didn't have a clue about.

That could be hard, but I ended up just trusting her and trusting that everything would be okay.

I admit that I probably didn't look happy. I still wasn't feeling happy. She'd dropped by just after the jury had come back with the verdict to let me know how it had turned out. I hadn't been happy then either. Maggie had had to go back to the marshal's office to work a shift, and I was glad to be alone to try to work out things in my head.

I hadn't been able to. It was a knot I just couldn't unravel.

"I don't think I am," I said.

She narrowed her eyes at me. "That's unusual for you not to know how you feel. You're always telling me about your feelings."

I didn't think that was the case, but I didn't argue the point. I knew I'd always talked more than Maggie did, but that was only because she barely talked at all.

"They're building the gallows in the street behind the marshal's office now," Maggie said. "Pa started in on it and other men joined in. The sawmill donated the lumber."

I'd heard all the hammering but I hadn't gone out of the building to find out what it was because I thought I knew and I didn't want to know for sure.

"The gallows will be built by Monday morning," Maggie said as she folded meat and beans into a tortilla. "Courbet will be hanged Monday morning and it will be over with." She took a bite and spoke while she chewed. "Except for finding Angelo Blunt. That's still got to be done."

"I think Blunt's gone," I said, and I felt hollow when I said it because I was afraid Blunt would escape and he'd never pay for killing Mister Henson. "He found out there was nothing here for him and he high-tailed it. Mister Henson got killed for no reason."

Maggie just watched me and sipped tea she'd brought with the meal.

"Honestly, Maggie, I don't know if I care if Blunt's ever found. He can be tried and hanged, and it still won't bring Mister Henson back."

"No," Maggie replied, "it won't. But if they try Blunt and hang him, he won't be hurting anybody else, will he?"

I shook my head.

"That's what needs to be done," Maggie said. "Whatever it takes, Blunt and the rest of his gang have to be brought to justice. They're bad men, Charlie, and they have to be stopped."

We continued eating, but we never found anything really pleasant to talk about.

***

That night I couldn't sleep very well, and when the hammering started at the gallows the next morning, I packed up my carpenter's box, buckled on my Tranter and slid my Winchester into the saddle scabbard. Then I rode the mare down to the jail.

Some of the men working on the structure noticed me arrive and stopped working to stare at me. I ignored them and tied the mare to the hitching post in front of the marshal's office. Then I hefted my carpenter's box and headed over to help the men build the gallows.

Marshal Buchanan's shirt was stained with sweat and he wore gloves with his shirt sleeves rolled up. He nodded at me as I surveyed the framing they had done to support the steps and the platform. It was a pretty good job, but I felt it needed some work.

"Good morning, Charlie," the marshal said.

"Good morning, Marshal."

"You brought your own tools."

"I did. Is there anywhere you want me to be?" I didn't want to just pick a spot and tell men they needed help.

Marshal Buchanan waved a hand around him. "Pick a spot. There's plenty to do and having a seasoned carpenter would be a good thing."

"The steps look okay," I said, "but they need more support so no one falls through them."

"We wouldn't want that. Get to it."

I put my carpenter's box down and took out a hammer, measuring string that wasn't anything fancy like the spring-loaded tape measures made by Alvin J. Fellows some of the men had, and a nail for marking measurements the way Mister Henson had done when we worked on anything. Measure twice, cut once, he'd always say.

Some of the younger men who didn't have much experience in carpentry joined me and I found myself giving directions in no time. None of them had ever built gallows. In the five years I'd been in Pecos, no one had ever been hanged.

However, the concept was simple enough and I drafted a blueprint in my head that fit with the skeleton they'd already erected. I walked them through it as they needed to know.

"Hey boy!" a raucous voice yelled. "Hey! Charlie Stark! Undertaker!"

Recognizing the voice, I turned to see Courbet standing at the jail window. He had his arms stuck through the bars and was grinning that gap-toothed grin Maggie had given him.

"Did you come down here to help build the gallows?" he taunted. "Do you think that's gonna make a man outta you?"

I didn't bother to reply because the answer was pretty obvious.

"Do you really think they're gonna hang me?" he asked.

I looked at him and all the doubts I'd had the night before just melted away. If Courbet got out, he'd kill again. That was just who he was. Maggie was right. A man like that had to be put down. He wasn't fit to live with civilized folks.

"They will," I said. "They'll hang you until you're dead. I'll help make sure this gallows will hold up when you get dropped."

He scowled at me then. "Ain't nobody gonna hang me. Angel Blunt will be back, and he'll be back for that gold too."

The gold had come up during the trial too, but Courbet didn't know why Blunt had been so sure Mister Henson had gold, so it was forgotten pretty quickly in all the violent details of the murder. There were far too many of those.

"Let him come," Marshal Buchanan told Courbet in a loud voice that carried. "We'll hang him too."

41

On Monday morning, Maggie showed up at my home at about nine o'clock. I'd caught myself referring to it as my home in casual conversation with Mister and Missus Kuáng when I went to have my laundry done, and to folks I sometimes talked to in passing along the streets. I didn't know exactly when that had happened in my mind, but it felt good. I had a place that was mine, and a life I could take pride in.

When I'd bumped into Jimmy Hadley yesterday evening after not seeing him in months, I'd realized how much I'd grown as a man compared to him. Not just in size, but in the way I thought about things. I was on my own now and the world looked different. He was still living with his pa, still carousing at the Ugly Toad since they were letting him in. I'd also noticed that the folks around us treated us differently too. They still looked at Jimmy as a kid even though he was almost a year older than me.

He'd asked me what it was like to live in the funeral building, and if I ever saw ghosts. I'd told him no. Then he asked me if Maggie was still coming around me, following me like a moonstruck calf, and didn't I think she was strange?

Well, three of Malpert's warehousemen happened to be in Wick's Diner when that conversation happened, and it took all three of them to pull me off Jimmy. I didn't even know I was going to hit him until I had a forearm shoved up under his neck and him pressed up against the nearest wall. I bruised him up some, and I scared him, but I didn't hurt him in any permanent way. At the time, I'd felt mad enough to.

Afterward, I felt bad about that. Jimmy and I had been good friends for a while. But he'd had no reason to talk about Maggie the way he had.

Maggie came along later and asked me what was going on. It had crossed my mind that she was coming to arrest me. I'd told her it was a misunderstanding and was all my fault, and that I was ready to go to jail if that was what was required.

I didn't think she believed me, but she let me off with a warning. I suspected she'd heard about what Jimmy said, but she didn't say anything about it to me.

***

I was sitting at the table and drinking coffee I'd only just made on the potbelly stove when Maggie walked in. She never bothered to knock and I'd given her a key after we hung the door at the top of the steps. Like always, she was dressed in dungarees and a shirt with her pistols belted on.

I wore one of the two black suits I had, and Missus Kuáng made sure it was clean.

"Coffee?" I asked.

She nodded, took the other china cup I'd bought from Hunziker's just last week to feel more civilized, poured a cup, and sat at the table like we sometimes did in the mornings before I went off to work wherever I was working that day.

I'd noticed no matter what time of day it was, she seemed to be awake. I didn't know when she slept other than those catnaps at night after she'd finished rattling doors around the town. She went to her house with her pa, but she didn't seem to stay there much.

"You're dressed," she said after a bit.

"I am," I admitted.

"So are you going to the hanging?"

I'd thought about that all night, tossing and turning, and ending up not getting much sleep. This morning my eyes felt like they'd been rubbed with sandpaper.

"I'm not sure," I said.

"Whatever you want to do, Charlie," she said, "I'll do it with you. We can go, or we can stay here."

"Aren't you needed down at the marshal's office to help with crowd control?"

Last night I'd noticed folks had rolled into town in wagons and set up camp wherever they could. The hanging was going to have a big audience. Folks waited in excited anticipation.

"I'm not a deputy this morning," she told me. "This morning I'm your friend."

That was the first time she'd ever called me her friend, and it surprised me. I didn't know what to say at first, so I finally just said, "Thank you."

We sipped more coffee for a minute.

"I've been trying to think about what Mister Henson would want me to do," I said. "Whether I should just stay here today and wait till all of that is over. Or if I should go and see justice done."

"This shouldn't be about what Mister Henson would want," Maggie said. "It's about what you want. Mister Henson would want you to do what you feel is right."

"What I want and what I feel is right is for Angelo Blunt to be up there hanging right beside Courbet."

"That's not going to happen unless Blunt decides to show up."

That had been part of the talk going around town, that Blunt would show up to rescue Courbet. Of course, Courbet was the one mostly saying it, although Aiken had written about the possibility of an "outlaw vengeance posse" coming to Pecos to save their "owlhoot comrade."

Marshal Buchanan had just laughed about it yesterday when I'd seen him during the time we were finishing the gallows. "Don't pay it no mind, Charlie. It's just good theater. Just a story Aiken is using to sell newspapers."

I'd said I thought so too.

But the possibility of Angelo Blunt showing up at that hanging was what prompted me to wash our coffee cups, buckle on my Tranter, pack my Winchester onto the mare, and ride to the marshal's office with Maggie at my side.

"Have you thought about it?" I asked her as we rode.

"About what?" she asked.

"Watching Courbet hang. What that's going to be like."

"Not really. I don't have anything to do with that other than to help keep the peace if the crowd becomes disorderly."

"I can't help it," I said. "Part of me feels sorry for Courbet because I know the prospect of getting walked up those steps and getting that noose hung around his neck has got to be terrifying."

"Maybe so, but it's what he's got coming for what he did." She looked at me. "You know who I feel sorry for?"

I shook my head.

"You and Mister Henson. You two were happy together. You should have had more time to be that way."

I hung onto that and hardened my heart to chase away the sympathy I had. At least for right now.

***

A sea of people surrounded the gallows when we arrived. There must have been a hundred of them at least. Men, women, and children stood or sat, waiting expectantly for the show to start.

Aiken spotted me and Maggie and started to come over, but Maggie stopped the newspaperman dead in his tracks with one cold look and he headed back where he'd come from.

Me and Maggie stood over in front of the mercantile in front of the marshal's office. I was antsy and fidgety, and I shifted often, but Maggie stood still as a statue and watched over the proceedings.

The crowd got impatient and started calling for justice

to be served. Marshal Buchanan peeked out the window a few times, but didn't come out till ten o'clock. He led Courbet, who surprised me by walking on his own while he snarled, spit, and swore at the crowd.

Four deputies, the two regular deputies and two that had been sworn in for the hanging, flanked Courbet on all sides and kept folks back from him. They carried Greener shotguns and looked like they were ready for anything.

Preacher Doolin from the First Baptist Church was presiding. He was a short man with a big gray beard and a basso voice when he spoke. Dressed all in black, he led Marshal Buchanan and Courbet up the steps that held without shaking.

I'd built those steps and I took some pride in the way they held up.

Two deputies took positions at the bottom of the stairs while the other two staggered themselves along the steps.

Preacher Doolin called everyone together and the raucous noise in the street quieted. Doolin led everybody in prayer, then he prayed for Courbet's eternal soul.

Courbet kept looking around like he was expecting someone.

I thought he'd die surprised Blunt didn't show up.

Then, when Marshal Buchanan was sliding the hangman's noose over Courbet's head, the marshal staggered back against the low railing that circled the platform and the sound of a rifle firing came a second later.

Blood blossomed on his white shirt and ran down over his black vest.

42

A plume of black powder smoke billowed out on top of Malpert's warehouse but I couldn't see the rifleman.

Me and Maggie were moving by then, looking around and pushing and shoving our way through the crowd that had only then realized they were in danger. As we fought to get to the gallows, most other folks were trying to get away from there.

I stopped being polite and bulled my way through, knocking down anyone who got in my way.

A second rifle shot cracked and Marshal Buchanan jerked back again. He was trying to get his pistol from its holster when Courbet bent a little and drove his shoulder into the marshal to knock him over the railing.

Then other rifles joined the first and bullets struck people around the gallows, opening up bloody wounds and knocking folks down. More gun smoke floated up from some of the other buildings and I guessed there was between four and six riflemen in positions over nearby rooftops.

With all the strangers in town and having to guard their prisoners, Marshal Buchanan and his deputies had stayed busy. The snipers surprised them. They'd surprised everybody.

Two of the deputies fell there at the gallows. Neither of

them had fired a shot in return.

Maggie followed me and she beat against my back with the butt of her gun. "Get to my pa!"

I continued pushing and shoving, and I finally hauled out that big Tranter, which got the attention of a lot of nearby folks and they moved out of the way fast after that.

More rifle shots claimed victims in the crowd and a bullet hit Preach Doolin in the head and threw out a spray of blood over Courbet, who was laughing maniacally and swearing at everyone.

"Hell's comin' to visit!" Courbet yelled.

When we were still fifty feet from Marshal Buchanan, who was not moving, a hue and cry rose that riders were coming. I glanced to the south and saw the dust cloud rising out there and I knew it was a lot of riders.

Astride the horses, the outlaws swept into town with Angelo Blunt leading the way. He fired his pistol into folks as his horse collided with them and sent them spinning. When that pistol fired dry, he threw it away and drew another from the sash he wore slung across his chest that supported at least three more revolvers. He continued firing as he charged toward the gallows.

By that time, me and Maggie finally reached the gallows ourselves. My heart was beating fast as a rabbit's and blood thundered in my ears. Maggie threw herself down by her pa.

I knew as soon as I laid eyes on him that Marshal Buchanan was already gone. I'd seen a few folks die from gunshots over the years I spent with Mister Henson. Either the first or second rifle bullet that had struck the marshal had gone straight through his heart.

"Pa!" Maggie screamed. It was the first time I'd heard her be emotional, and it was like nothing I'd ever heard. Her cry was ragged and as sharp as broken glass, and it cut into me bone deep.

"Your pa's dead!" Courbet shouted. He was leaning over the low gallows railing above us. Some of the marshal's blood or the preacher's had left a fine crimson mist across the outlaw's face. "An' you're gonna be next! I'm gonna—"

Growling with rage and fury, Maggie twisted on one knee and pointed her Colt at Courbet, who yelped and ducked away. Her bullet ripped splinters from the railing as it chewed through.

On the other side of the gallows, Blunt and his men kept riding for Courbet. The crowd had reached the boardwalks on both sides of the street and were throwing themselves through open doors and through windows in an effort to escape the outlaws' guns.

Chaos had come to Pecos and the immediate area boiled like hornet's nest.

Maggie shifted on her knee and took aim at Courbet again, but before she could pull the trigger, bullets from the outlaws' guns tore into the gallows' support beams, cut the air around us, and dug into the ground.

I threw myself on top of Maggie, wanting to get her out of harm's way. As soon as I had her flat on the ground, she screamed in my ear and came up with an elbow that caught my chin and dazed me for just a second.

In that time, she squirmed out from beneath me and came up throwing lead with both guns at Courbet, who was still on the gallows taking cover. Railing pales shattered and broke, hanging from nails and looking like a broken smile.

A rider barreled around the gallows and spotted Maggie standing there. He brought his pistol up and took aim, but Maggie put two bullets into his chest. Dead, he slid off the horse but his foot caught in the stirrup and the frightened animal dragged him along the street.

As though nothing was going on around her, her attention still focused on Courbet, Maggie broke open her pistols, shook out the empty brass, and started reloading.

I got to my feet because I finally remembered I needed to do that.

Another rider spurred his mount at Maggie and fired at her from the saddle.

I didn't even see the man's face to know him. I hauled that big Tranter up, centered it, and squeezed the trigger. That massive .50-cal bullet took him in the chest and emptied that saddle.

It didn't stop the horse, though, and the animal came straight at Maggie. She didn't even notice it. She was taking aim again at Courbet when the horse struck her at a full gallop and ran right over her.

She crumpled like a broken thing and lay on her back bleeding from a scalp wound where one of the horse's hooves had caught her. She was so still for a minute I thought she was dead.

Then I was at her side, my hand against her neck so I could check for a pulse. Mister Henson had taught me to do that to every person that came to the funeral home for burying. We also used a mirror to check for breath, but I didn't have that.

When I found that pulse, I almost cried. I peeled back one of her eyelids and saw that her eye was rolled back up into her head. She was unconscious, but she was alive.

All around us, folks were screaming and dying. Angel Blunt and his gang weren't there to just rescue Courbet. They were there to make a statement.

Blunt was in the midst of them, shooting everyone in sight. It didn't matter if he came upon man, woman, or child. He treated them all like they'd personally wronged him. I don't know how many folks I saw him kill, but he only paused to throw one revolver away and yank another one.

Hell had come to Pecos in the form of a blond-haired, laughing demon.

43

I gathered Maggie up and threw her over my left shoulder. I was surprised at how small and frail she felt. She'd always seemed so indestructible in the face of everything she'd gone up against. From the bar fights to the shootout in Malpert's Storage, she'd never backed down from anything and had weathered it all.

And now she was limp and small over my shoulder as I ran for the nearest alley. I kept hold of the Tranter and looked around. I didn't feel proud of the way I left folks to fend for themselves, but I had me and Maggie to look out for.

One of the snipers on the rooftops must have caught sight of me. The last few strides toward that alley, bullets danced at my heels, and one of them tore off my hat. I kept expecting to feel a bullet hit me up until I reached that alley and slung us around the corner.

I paused to take a breath because I didn't know what I was going to do next. Me and Maggie were out of the thick of it, but the alley was a brief respite at best.

"They're holdin' up the bank!" a man shouted out in the street.

When I peered around the corner, I spotted Blunt and some of his men busting down the doors to Sowers Bank & Trust. Somebody inside fired through the windows at them. I knew that because the glass in the panes fell out instead of in.

Blunt hadn't come to rescue Courbet as much as he'd come to rob the bank. That was easy to figure. With all the folks in from out of town spending money to watch the trial and now to see the hanging, businesses had been booming.

All of that money was sitting in the banks. Sowers was the largest of them. It would have the most money. On top of that, I realized that the railroad had brought in a payroll as well. Normally the Pinkertons guarded that, but they'd have a hard time getting through the crowd in the street or avoiding the snipers on the rooftops.

An outlaw on horseback rode by the alley. At first I didn't think he'd seen me, I hoped that he hadn't. But he turned that horse around and came back for me and Maggie.

I didn't know if he'd recognized Maggie as Marshal Buchanan's daughter and wanted bragging rights to Blunt or if he was just running down the two of us because we were alone and he thought us defenseless. Maggie was on my shoulder that was facing him, so he didn't see that Tranter revolver in my fist until I turned around and pointed it at him.

He tried to stop the horse, but it was too little too late.

I squeezed that trigger and that .50-caliber bullet turned him into something Ichabod Crane would hope to never meet on a lonely stretch of road.

***

I don't remember much of the run through the alleys to get to Gilbride's office. I knew the way easily, and I was paying more attention to getting me and Maggie there safe. Blunt and his men concentrated on the banks, robbing Sowers as well as Cattlemen's Bank, which was owned by the railroad baron, Jay Gould, and some of his local partners.

I also heard later Blunt and his gang got out of town quickly after that, only minutes before the Pinkertons stationed at the train depot rallied a posse and marched to Main Street to confront them.

I was only concerned about Maggie, so I didn't think about anything until Gilbride opened his door and let me in.

"I was hoping you weren't at the hanging," I said as I carried Maggie into his office.

"I try to save folks," Gilbride said. He took Maggie off my shoulder. "I'm not going to witness one get killed. Even a bad one like Courbet."

Gilbride carried Maggie to the closest table and I followed, at a loss as to what to do. No one else had reached Gilbride, but I knew they would be coming. Pecos only had three doctors and two dentists and a whole lot of people had gotten hurt just now.

"Did she get shot?" Gilbride asked.

"She got clipped by a horse's hoof," I said.

"What's happening out there?"

As he got Maggie situated, I gave Gilbride a short version of the snipers on the rooftops and Blunt's arrival shortly after the riflemen opened fire.

Gilbride got a bucket of water and some towels. Moving slow and careful, he washed away the blood covering Maggie's face and matting her hair. He touched her head and pushed on it gently.

"Doesn't feel like her skull's fractured," he said. "There could be small fractures and I'd have no way of knowing, and there's no telling what the impact has done to her brain."

That didn't sound good. In fact, it scared me even more. "Is she going to be all right?"

"She's breathing," Gilbride said. "That's always a good sign." He sighed. "As to whether she's going to be all right, we'll have to wait and see. Help me get her head up to help minimize swelling if there's any internal bleeding. That will be the real danger."

Standing on the other side of the surgical table, I helped Gilbride move Maggie. He could have managed it himself, but together we had an easier time of it and could be gentler.

"She didn't get stepped on, did she?" Gilbride felt

along Maggie's arms and legs. I knew he was checking for breaks or anything out of place.

"I don't know," I admitted. "Everything happened so fast, and I had to run for it because Blunt and his gang were shooting everybody in the street."

Gilbride peeled Maggie's shirt up enough to check her stomach. After all the bodies I'd seen working with Mister Henson, I knew he was looking for any discoloration that might be forming. Bruises blossomed on a person's stomach when there was internal bleeding, and there were a lot of blood vessels in a person's midsection.

Scars from burns and knives and I couldn't imagine what all tracked across Maggie's belly and her sides. The scars were grayed out and were years old.

"What happened to her?" I asked.

Gilbride glanced over his shoulder at me and pulled Maggie's shirt back down. "Don't you ever tell her you saw that. Do you understand?"

His voice was quiet and tense, and I knew he was mad or hurt. I wasn't sure which. For a minute, I felt just like a boy again, listening to one of my parents or the other tell me something I wasn't supposed to tell to the other. I felt guilty and threatened at the same time.

"Do you understand, Charlie?" Gilbride demanded.

I nodded. "Yeah, I understand."

"Never tell her."

Before I could reply that time, the front door to Gilbride's office crashed open and the first of the injured and dying people arrived.

44

The dead didn't actually walk in. Usually they were carried in by friends or neighbors or good Samaritans while they were still alive. Nobody wanted to admit a family member or friend was dying, the same way they didn't want to let go of that person after that person was dead. But some of those folks died shortly after their arrival, breathing their last in that room and bleeding out on the floor.

It didn't take two minutes to fill up Gilbride's office with those who had been injured. After we couldn't hold any more and they were standing outside the door, we started putting folks in the Grace Methodist Church. It was catty-corner from Gilbride's building and the preacher, Robert Wallace, had been a medical officer in the Civil War.

Wallace had experience in dealing with injured men. Folks carried many of the pews out onto the lawn in front of the church for those who were lightly wounded and dazed, but they kept some pews inside to use as medical beds for people who were more grievously injured or were dying. One condition changed into another pretty quick and without warning.

Some of the women in town had helped out as midwives, and all the mothers had given birth to their children, so they knew their way around stressful medical situations. Gilbride drafted the women who were willing to help into a nurses corps and they got up to speed just fine.

I wanted to stay with Maggie, but Gilbride told me there was nothing I could do and I'd be more of a help working with the wounded. I could tell the quick from the dead, and I was a good judge of who could be helped and who couldn't, so he put me with some of the more experienced men who'd seen battle and could make hard choices. There weren't many of us.

I hated doing that, but I did it because it was needed. And Gilbride was right. I was good at recognizing who could be helped.

Two men died in my arms and it was horrible.

One of them was a young man not much older than me who had been shot in the stomach. Gilbride and I couldn't find the gushing artery even after the doc cut him open. I had my hands in there too even though I didn't want to. Usually I'd only put my hands inside dead folks.

The other man was older and suffered from a heart attack while I was patching up a gunshot wound to his arm that wouldn't have killed him. At least, a heart attack was what Gilbride thought it was when I described what had happened later. The man was an out-of-towner and his family had been watching while I'd been trying to help him. He'd shaken and rattled, then stopped breathing and turned blue.

I hadn't been able to bring him back.

That kind of thing went on for hours, and I admit that losing that man so suddenly and unexpectedly caused me to second-guess myself several times.

In the end, Blunt and his gang had killed twenty-nine people and injured seventy-two others. The dead included Marshal Buchanan and Preacher Doolin. They headed up the list Malpert took down in his notebook.

***

Once we had the office cleaned up and everything as put to rights as we could, which had put me on the end of a bloody mop for a time, I sat in a chair at Maggie's bedside and waited for her to wake up. Gilbride said that's what we were waiting on then. Just for her to wake up.

Sitting there watching her was strange to me because I'd never seen her sleep, only catnap. I wasn't convinced she really slept. Upon reflection, I thought being unconscious was probably different than sleeping anyway.

Watching over her also felt uncomfortable because sleep, in my mind, was such a personal matter.

I did go to sleep, though, even though I tried to stay awake. Even sitting up didn't slow me down when I nodded off.

***

I woke up after midnight and Gilbride was making his rounds, checking on the two people in his office he was tending to, and to Maggie.

"You should go back to sleep, Charlie," he whispered, and he sounded bone tired.

"I don't really want to," I said. "I was dreaming, and none of it was any good." I'd woken up almost screaming and had only just caught myself in time to stop, but my heart had been beating so hard it must have been a blur.

He nodded. "Well, if you can sleep later, you should." He picked up the lantern he'd been using to get back and forth between his office and the church and started to head out.

"Doctor Gilbride," I said quietly, not wanting to disturb Maggie or the other patients, "what happened to her? I need to know."

He shook his head. "That's not my story to tell."

"She's not going to tell it. And now her pa is dead." I looked at him with desperation, and I think we both knew she would need more help after she woke up than either of us could give. "I want to understand. Is this what makes her different? This thing that someone done to her?"

Gilbride looked at me, then looked back at Maggie.

Finally, he said, "Come with me. We're not going to talk in here. Sometimes people in her condition remember conversations they hear while they're sleeping."

***

Outside, we sat on the narrow stairs. The slight chill woke me up a little more and made me wishful for a cup of coffee.

The sky was clear and shot full of stars. If there hadn't been so much blood spilled this morning, it would have been peaceful. But dark splotches stained the wood where wounded people had been carried in or walked in on their own.

"I'm not comfortable telling you this story, Charlie," Gilbride said. "Like I said, it's not mine to tell, and a physician owes a patient a certain amount of discretion. Hippocrates worked that out in Greece a long time ago. Doing no harm also means leaving a patient some privacy." He took a deep breath and let it out. Fatigue burned in him like smoldering coals, devouring him from the inside. "But after losing her father like this—" He shook his head. "God only knows what it's going to do to her. She's going to need someone. And if you're going to be a friend to her, you need to know more about what you're dealing with because you're going to be tested."

I sat and waited on him because I wasn't going to try to rush him. I knew what he had to say would have to come on its own time.

"You and Maggie have a lot in common," Gilbride said. "You'll remember that I told you that before."

"I do."

"Both of you had some bad parents, and I'm not judging. It's a fact."

"Marshal Buchanan was a good man," I said defensively.

"He was. I'm talking about Maggie's ma."

45

I hadn't expected that answer and I sat there trying to take it in.

"When Maggie was a little girl, not much more than a baby," Gilbride continued in that hollowed-out voice, "William Buchanan was a young deputy in Fort Worth. Have you ever been there?"

"No," I said.

"Well, it's a big, rough town," Gilbride said. "They call it Hell's Half-Acre, and it lives up to that name. It's filled with murderers, conmen and conwomen, and every crime you'd find between the covers of a law book. As a young man, Marshal Buchanan spent most of his time keeping the peace and enforcing the law in Fort Worth during Reconstruction. He wasn't home much. Not nearly enough to keep his young wife happy, but she had her own life. She was an actress and performed in a number of plays in theaters there."

I'd never seen a play outside of the skits put on at the local churches, so I could only imagine what that must have been like.

"From what I've heard," Gilbride continued, "Rita Buchanan was a high-strung woman. Everything had to be perfect and in its place, otherwise she would fly into fits of rage. And she liked being the center of attention. I saw photographs and playbills of her when I was down at Fort Stockton for a medical consultation four years ago. Maybe five."

He looked a little embarrassed, but he was too tired for the emotion to fully settle in. Mostly all I saw was his fatigue.

"I must confess," he said, "after Marshal Buchanan told me Maggie's story, I had to look up her mother. I hadn't meant to pry. The library there had a few Fort Worth magazines and newspapers in the archives that mentioned her. She was a remarkably beautiful woman."

"What happened to Maggie?" I asked. I wanted him to get back to the point and I knew he was deliberately avoiding it. "Why is she all scarred up like that? Who hurt her? Was it her ma?"

"I tried to understand Maggie's mother. I talked to one of the doctors in Fort Stockton that I was consulting with on another matter. He'd seen a case like this that had involved a woman like Rita Buchanan back East." Gilbride took a breath. "Rita Buchanan was sick. She didn't see anything wrong with what she was doing to her daughter. Nobody knew. Not until Marshal Buchanan realized the hell his daughter had been going through at her mother's hands when he hadn't been there."

The chill in the night suddenly grew stronger and I didn't feel like asking any more questions, but Gilbride didn't seem to be able to stop telling the story now because he kept right on.

"Missus Buchanan was jealous of the fact that her husband suddenly seemed to prefer his job over her. Marshal Buchanan told me they had some terrible arguments about his absences, and that sometimes he looked for excuses not to come home for days at a time. He figured Maggie was doing just fine with her mother. That just wasn't true and he didn't find that out till it was too late."

A couple men passed below us carrying lanterns. A night watch had been set up by Deputy Leslie Stephens, who had survived the attack at the gallows.

Gilbride licked his lips. "Marshal Buchanan said that the things he saw on a daily basis in Fort Worth at the time were bad. He didn't want to bring that kind of wretchedness home to his family, and trying to police that town took more than he could offer. He lived at that job more than he lived at home. Still, he tried to be there when he could. When he felt welcome to go home. Rita Buchanan was an emotionally abusive woman to him. She was truly a horrid person, Charlie."

"Maggie's mom gave her those scars?" My voice was dry and even I could barely hear it. I couldn't get that thought out of my mind.

Gilbride nodded. "She couldn't punish her husband for not being there when he wasn't there, so she punished his daughter. By that time, I don't think she considered Maggie to be any part of her. She was just the marshal's child, and she was vulnerable to her wrath. The damage you saw on Maggie isn't just constrained to her abdomen. She's scarred on her legs and back, too. Every place that could be covered up by a dress, her mother burned, cut, and beat. She dressed her up like a doll, all pretty and proper, to hide what she was doing. I tell you now, in my opinion, the greatest evil in this world is the betrayal of a child by a parent. No one can fix that kind of damage."

I sat there and tried to get a handle on everything I'd been told. Maybe it was because I'd never seen or heard anything like that, or maybe it was because it was coming at the end of a long, sorry day, or maybe it was because Maggie had lost her father, but I just went numb.

"Charlie?" Gilbride said.

I tried to speak and couldn't. .

"Charlie?" Gilbride put his hand on my shoulder and kneeled down in front of me on the steps. He held the lantern so the light shined into my eyes. "Can you hear me?"

"I can," I said. "I wish I hadn't asked."

"I know, but she's going to need you, Charlie. Especially now." He paused for a moment to gather his thoughts, or to steady his own emotions. "After Marshal Buchanan found out what his wife was doing to their little girl, he arrested his wife and testified against her at the trial."

"So Maggie's ma is in prison?"

"No, she's in an asylum."

"That's where they keep insane people, right?" I'd read stories about such places. In fact, Edgar Allan Poe had written on called "The System of Doctor Tar and Pro. Fether" that I had read to Mister Henson. We had agreed that it was scary and horrifying and humorous in a twisted way.

"Right. They keep the mad there. Dreadful places, Charlie. They really are." He nodded and pulled the lantern back. "The court locked Rita Buchanan up at the Texas State Lunatic Asylum. As far as I know, she's still there."

"How old was Maggie when Marshal Buchanan found out what was going on?"

"Seven. Just a little girl."

"How long did all that go on?"

"Nobody can say for sure, but my estimation of those scars told me some of them were scarred over after healing. She'd been hurt, then hurt again. I'd say she endured that kind of mistreatment for years."

"Why didn't she tell her pa?"

Gilbride hesitated, then asked me, "Mister Henson once told me under what conditions he had come to care for you. Did you ever tell anyone how bad things were at home for you?"

I thought about all the yelling, the hitting, and the times I went to bed hungry and sometimes thinking I'd die from the cold in winters. I'd never mentioned a word of it even months after Mister Henson had taken me in.

"No," I said. "Not when I was living there."

"But later? When you were living with Mister Henson? Did you tell him?"

"I trusted him. I told him some, but I didn't tell him everything." My voice broke, and I didn't know if it was because of Maggie or Marshal Buchanan or the people who had died today or Mister Henson. Some of it was probably because I felt bad for myself too. "I wanted that part of my life gone."

"Maggie...she's never had someone like Mister Henson," Gilbride said.

"Didn't she talk to Marshal Buchanan?"

"No. Never. Not one word. He even tried to talk to her about it. I watched him a few times when she was younger. She'd just sit there and listen for him to be done. Then she'd talk about something else."

"Why didn't she talk to him?"

"I think, on some level, she saw the marshal as being part of the problem."

"Did she blame him because he wasn't there?" I thought back and I was sure Maggie had never shown any resentment toward her pa. I had never seen them be as close as I had been with Mister Henson, but I hadn't seen them together much in anything other than a public setting.

"I don't know. Marshal Buchanan didn't know. She's never said." Gilbride glanced at the Methodist Church and I knew he was feeling the need to get back to his patients. "Marshal Buchanan took the job here at Pecos to provide a better home for Maggie. Someplace where things would be slow enough that he could try to get close to her." He shifted on the step where he sat. "Until today, he'd given her that home and tried to build that relationship."

"What's wrong with her? Those cuts and burns have all healed."

"Maggie has healed physically, but she cuts herself off from emotions, Charlie. She doesn't connect with people. She doesn't have friends and doesn't have much of a life outside of being a deputy. That's why Marshal Buchanan and I were hopeful about her growing and changing when she took up with you. We hoped you would open her world up somewhat." He looked at me. "That's why I asked you about it that night. Marshal Buchanan and I wanted to know if she was getting better. Looking back on that, it was unfair of us to expect that of you. I apologize."

I shrugged. "I spent time with her before that. That wasn't your call."

"I suppose not."

"Why did she start spending time with me?"

Gilbride smiled at me. "Because you're a likeable young man, Charlie. Despite everything you went through, all the sadness you experienced yourself, Mister Henson made sure you healed well enough to be your own person. I think that's why you have the feelings for Maggie that you do. You see in her the same thing that you had in you and part of you on some subconscious level wants to help her heal. I think that pulling you out of that grave that night and rescuing you affected her in ways she's probably still trying to figure out. Of course, it's possible that she had wanted to talk to you before but never had a reason. Marshal Buchanan said she'd talked about you before that night."

"She's not weak," I said. "You're wrong about that."

"You just haven't seen the weaknesses yet, Charlie. You're looking at everything based on the relationship you have with her. You've not had time to assess the relationships she has with others."

As I thought about that, I supposed he was somewhat right. "Maggie can outfight and outshoot anyone I've ever known. Mister Kearney at the gun shop told me he's never seen someone who's quicker or more accurate when it comes to pistols."

"What I'm getting at, Charlie," Gilbride said, "is that the two of you are alike and you complement each other. You've been through some of what Maggie has, and you've put it behind you. I'm hoping you can help her. I'm glad you're friends. So was Marshal Buchanan. And I'll tell you something else, when she wakes up, she's going to need a friend."

"I will be," I said. "As long as she lets me, I will be."

Gilbride clapped me on the shoulder. "You need to get some sleep if you can, and I need to go check on patients." He looked sad and he stood up like he was bearing the weight of the world. "Some of them aren't going to be with us in the morning, I'm afraid." He took up his lantern and he went.

I sat there for a short time longer, then I got up and went back to my chair. I thought I'd be awake the rest of the night, but as soon as I closed my eyes once to rest them, I was asleep.

46

When I opened my eyes again, it was almost seven o'clock and Maggie was awake and sitting on the edge of the bed. Other than looking a little pale and wearing bloodstained clothes that were covered in dust, she looked the same as always.

"Good morning," I said automatically.

"Blunt killed my pa," she told me in a flat voice.

I froze like a gopher eyeballing a diamondback and tried to figure out what to say. Most people didn't poleax you with something so grim and potentially full of trouble first thing in the morning. But this was Maggie.

Finally I nodded. "I know."

"I want to get my pa ready for burying, Charlie," she said, "and I want you to help me do that. I want it done right. With everybody that died yesterday, the undertakers in town are going to be in a rush to get it all finished. I don't want Pa to be treated like that. So I want to help."

I was only a little shocked that Maggie didn't ask me if I wanted to do that. Over the last few weeks since Mister Henson's death, I'd learned what she could be like when she had something in her head.

But I didn't like the idea of her helping prepare her father for the funeral.

Over the years I'd worked with Mister Henson, sometimes folks wanted to do that for a loved one. A final act of service, Mister Henson had called it. We'd let them help with dressing the bodies, if they were able, and only some could, but not with the embalming. Some of the chemicals were dangerous and needed to be handled carefully. A person who didn't know how to deal with them could get hurt in a hurry.

Gilbride and Mister Henson had discussed embalming one of the times I was getting stitches. Gilbride said embalming had gotten popular in the Civil War and that was where he'd learned how to do it, so soldiers' bodies could be shipped back home to their families. Mister Henson had never said when or where or how he'd learned the trade. He'd just talked about the chemicals and the techniques in the process. That was mostly what Gilbride was interested in anyway.

Now, knowing what I did, I wondered who had taught Mister Henson and why he would do it. I hadn't had much of a choice because learning undertaking had provided me a way to build a relationship with Mister Henson. I'd needed that.

"Maggie," I said, "what you're talking about would be an awfully hard thing to do."

"I watched my pa die yesterday," she said. Her voice was flat, like she was talking about it being hot outside. There was no emotion. "I don't expect this to be any harder. He's already gone."

I remembered how I'd felt after Mister Henson was dead and we were going to bury him. I had barely functioned and had hoped for the kind of numbness Maggie had.

Only now I knew her numbness was a curse. I wondered if she would ever regret not being able to feel more.

"I can do it, Charlie. I don't want anyone other than me and you to do that for Pa. He should be put away proper by people who loved him."

I couldn't argue with that even though I knew I should have. "I would ask one thing," I said. "Usually Mister Henson was there to help me. I mean, usually I helped him."

"You prepared Mister Henson for burial."

I nodded. "And I had Doc Gilbride help me do it. I'd like him to help us with your pa. If that's all right."

She thought about it for a moment, then nodded. "All right. They were friends." She got up from the bed, reached for her gun belt, and buckled it on.

"Wait," I said, standing up to follow her. "Where are you going?"

"To the marshal's office. I waited here because taking care of the burial came first. Now that that's settled, I want to know when there's a posse being readied to track down Angelo Blunt. I'm going to ride with them."

I grabbed my gun belt and hurried after her. "If a posse leaves now, how are you going to bury your pa?"

She didn't break stride. "I'll tend to the burying first. Then I'll catch up with the posse. I just need to know what they know about Blunt and what direction they'll be riding in."

47

Leslie Stephens was acting marshal, made so by a special town council meeting convened yesterday afternoon. He looked Maggie in the eye and said, "We're not going to be assembling a posse, Miss Buchanan."

I caught that right away. Miss Buchanan, not deputy. So I knew then and there things were going to go from bad to worse in a heartbeat. I glanced at the three men in the room with us. All of them wore deputies' badges, but I knew I'd seen them working on the Stephens cattle ranch. Small wonder that Stephens had no problem recruiting for the job.

Unconsciously, I stepped up beside Maggie because I had the feeling this conversation was about to go sideways and I didn't want her standing there alone.

Leslie Stephens and Maggie had never gotten along. He was young and arrogant, good-looking according to some of the women in town who'd chased after him, and he liked being in charge of things. He'd not gotten along well with the marshal. Stephens' father was on the town council and that was the reason Marshal Buchanan had gotten stuck with him because he was like a burr under a saddle.

I'd never had problems with Stephens, but I knew others who did. He liked to bully folks when he could get away with it, and he could get away with it just fine while he was wearing that badge. He didn't mind throwing an extra boot in a man's face when he was down after a drunken brawl just to get his point across. Or just out of pure meanness because the opportunity was there.

He wasn't as tall as I was, and he was lean as a fox. His dark red hair emphasized his light complexion and green eyes. He wore a Colt Single Action at his right hip and one of the new, smaller Colt M1877 Lightning Models chambered in .38 Long Colt cartridges in a shoulder holster under his left arm. Kearney's lessons had taught me a lot about guns in addition to improving my speed and accuracy.

Stephens was trying to grow a mustache to look older, but I thought it wasn't working out. He was vain enough that he went to the barber every two weeks for grooming. I was close enough to him now that his cologne filled my nostrils and I guessed that he doused himself in it.

He was only a handful of years older than me and Maggie, and I'd heard that he'd gone chasing after Maggie a couple of times but she'd pinned his ears back for him. He'd responded by letting it be known that Maggie wouldn't know a real man if she stepped on him. There was no love lost between them.

The Stephens family had one of the larger ranches outside Pecos. Martin Stephens had moved to town from Dallas to partner up with Jay Gould, the railroad man, in the railroad depot's development. Both of them planned on just getting richer. They were partners in some of the businesses in town. Martin Stephens had money and Leslie Stephens was the only son. His two older sisters had married well and brought in more profits for the family. Everyone in that household or who were employed by Martin Stephens doted on Stephens.

"What do you mean you're not assembling a posse?" Maggie asked.

Stephens showed her a half-smile and put his boots up on the desk. He looked entirely too comfortable sitting there. "Exactly what I said. The town council feels we need to get a handle on everything here in town first. Before we start stretching our limited resources." He flicked a glance at a handwritten note beside his boots. "Thirty-four people died in Blunt's attack on the town yesterday. Two of the banks got robbed."

Evidently more of Gilbride's and the other doctors' patients had died in the night.

"So you're just going to sit here while Blunt gets away?" Maggie asked. She still hadn't raised her voice, but there was an edge to her words.

Stephens scowled. "Blunt's already gotten away, Miss Buchanan. The town council wants me to stay here and train my new deputies. They don't want a repeat of what happened yesterday to ever happen again. So we're taking steps to fix that."

"You're a coward," Maggie said. "That's why you're not going."

Rage filled Stephens' face, turning his features bleak and coloring them red. He dropped his boots to the floor and leaned forward to rest his arms on the desk. "Don't say that again."

"I saw you yesterday," Maggie said. "When Pa got shot, you ducked under the gallows and headed for the marshal's office as soon as you could."

I hadn't seen that and I was impressed that Maggie had what with everything going on. Of course, she was more detail-oriented than I was.

"I went to arm myself with a rifle," Stephens grated. "A shotgun wasn't going to be of much use against men shooting from rooftops."

"You were hiding." Maggie leaned on the desk. "You were worried about your own skin while folks were out there dying. You were supposed to protect them. That was your job. That was what you swore to do when you pinned on a badge."

"There was no way to protect them!" Stephens roared. He shoved himself to his feet.

I put a hand on Maggie's arm to draw her back, but she shook me off. Stephens was only a little taller than she was.

"Blunt and his men murdered everybody they came across!" Stephens spoke so fiercely that spittle shot with every word. "Bullets hit all around me! It's a wonder I wasn't killed!"

"You hid," Maggie said.

Stephens cursed. "I've listened to all of this I've got a mind to. So you're going to leave, Miss Buchanan, and I mean right now. And just so we're clear, your services at the marshal's office are no longer needed." He crossed his arms and smiled at her. "You may have been able to wind your pa around your finger and get him to give you a badge so you could play at being a deputy, but I ain't your pa. So I'll be taking that deputy's badge now." He stuck out a hand.

I knew it was coming, and I suspect Stephens thought he did too. But we were both caught flat-footed when Maggie busted him in the face.

48

Blood spurted immediately and Stephens stumbled back, cupping his face in both hands.

One of Stephens' deputies closed on Maggie from behind and wrapped her in a bear hug. She stamped on his foot and swung her head back into his face with a crunch. After that horse had clipped her yesterday, I couldn't believe she did that. Her head had to have been sore. When the man released her, he took a step back and she whirled on him and hit him in the throat.

A second deputy moved on her too, but I stepped in front of him, grabbed him by both shoulders, and tossed him over my hip. He hit the floor hard enough to have the breath knocked out of him. He didn't appear in any hurry to get up.

Then the third deputy clubbed me behind the ear and my vision spun crazily. I dropped to one knee and managed to reach back and grab the deputy's foot. I yanked and he fell right beside me. When he tried to get up, I drove a right cross into his face that snapped his head sideways and stretched him senseless.

Swaying, I got to my feet as Maggie headed around the desk after Stephens.

He drew his Colt .45 and pointed it at her. "Stay back!"

Maggie kept walking and I went after her because I knew she wasn't going to stop. I wrapped my arms around her, managed to evade her foot trying to stamp mine, but still ended up getting my nose broken when she slung her head back. I tried to hold on but she slithered free.

Stephens cursed and eared his pistol's hammer back. Desperate, he aimed the Colt at me. "Keep coming and I'll kill Charlie!"

I froze because I didn't want to get shot and I knew if we pinned Stephens up too tight, he'd follow through on the threat.

Maggie took one more step, then she stopped. She took a breath, unpinned her badge, looked at it in her hand for a moment, and dropped it onto the desk.

After that, they arrested us.

***

I sat on the cot in the jail cell with my back against the wall and my legs crossed in front of me. I'd taken my boots off only to realize I'd been in my socks for two days now, under stressful circumstance, and I should have stopped for new ones before we'd headed over to the jail. I touched my nose gingerly to check on all the swelling.

I'd never had my nose broken before, not even with all the beatings I'd taken from my folks. They'd tended to stay away from marking my face, and I guessed that was probably a lot like Maggie's ma had treated her.

"I've never been locked up in a jail cell before," Maggie said. She was lying prone with her hands behind her head on her cot in her cell and had been so still I'd thought she was sleeping.

"I have," I reminded. I looked around. "This very cell. It hasn't changed much."

"You weren't locked up. You just slept here."

"When you're here and not sleeping in your own bed—"

"You didn't have a bed," she interrupted.

I couldn't argue with that, so I didn't. "I'm sorry you had to go through all that, Maggie. It's not fair. Maybe you can talk to the town council and get your badge back."

"So I can work with Stephens? Listen to him give me orders?" She shook her head. "No. That's not going to happen."

"Then what are you going to do?" That worried me because being a deputy had at least grounded Maggie. Now her pa and her job were gone. I'd bounced back after my losses, or at least was bouncing back. But everything she'd had in her life was gone.

"I laid here and thought about it," she said. "I've got a plan."

"What's your plan?"

"I'm sorry I got you into trouble with Stephens, Charlie. I should have come over here by myself. I was going to, but I'm glad you came with me."

That made me feel good. I'd been nursing a grudge about her breaking my nose and potentially messing up what little looks I had, but that melted away. Well, most of it melted away. Getting your nose broken hurt.

"What are you going to do, Maggie?" I asked.

When I didn't get an answer, I asked again.

Then I heard her snoring.

I sighed in frustration and tried to find a way to make myself comfortable, but I didn't have much luck. My whole face throbbed.

***

Arguing voices woke me. I was surprised I'd actually gone to sleep, and I was intrigued that anyone would argue with Stephens in the marshal's office.

He sounded pretty put out, too, but another voice rode hard over his and shut him down quick. Judge Caldwell had an orator's voice and he could call a room to attention with only a few words. I'd seen him do it at Courbet's trial.

"You will get up and let those people out, you young idiot," Caldwell said, "or I will have you up on obstruction charges so fast your head will spin."

"This is my town, Judge!" Stephens yelled. "You can't

come in here and tell me what to do!"

"You may work for the town, boy, but I run the courts in this country. I've got the power of the federal government behind me, and I'll have a United States Marshal set up shop here if you don't get up and do as I say. You can explain to your pa why there are no courts in Pecos to conduct his business in because I'll see to it that not another document in this town gets notarized."

"They attacked me, Judge."

"They probably found you annoying," Caldwell said. "I find you annoying. Now get those keys and follow me."

Boots stamped across the wooden floor and approached the cells.

I sat up and noticed that Maggie was sitting up too. She actually looked more rested than she had.

Judge Caldwell entered the room and stopped. He stared at us, then focused on me. "Stephens broke your nose?"

"No," I said. "Maggie did."

She didn't say anything when Caldwell glanced at her.

"Why would she do that?" Caldwell asked me.

"I tried to keep her from attacking Stephens." I couldn't make myself call him the marshal.

"Who broke Stephens' nose? And that of his deputy?" Caldwell asked.

"Maggie," I said.

Caldwell shook his head and glanced at Maggie again. "Well, young lady, I guess that if you get something that works for you, you should stick with it. I'd heard stories about you from your pa, God rest his soul. I think I would have liked to see you punch the new marshal."

"It could probably happen again," I said, looking at Stephens as he entered the room. "You might want to hang around a minute."

Maggie's lips twitched just a bit.

Caldwell laughed. "Don't tempt me."

Stephens glared at the judge as he walked by holding the keyring. He let me out first and handed me the keyring. "Let her out and keep her off me."

I stepped in front of Maggie and felt trepidation. "Promise me you're not going to go after Stephens when I let you out."

She looked at me. "I told you, Charlie. I have a plan. Stephens isn't part of it." She cut her eyes over my shoulder to Stephens. "He's safe enough."

Still, I hesitated a minute before I inserted that key and twisted it to unlock the cell door.

Stephens retreated and pulled one of his deputies in front of him.

Caldwell shook his head and grinned. Then he looked at us. "I heard the two of you walked straight over here from Doc Gilbride's."

"We did," I said.

"It's after noon now. One of the Johnson boys saw you in jail when he walked by. He got word to Doc Gilbride, and he sent for me. He's done a lot of testifying in my courts as I've come through, and I favor an educated man. He plays a mean game of chess, too. So I came over here to get you out."

"Thank you," I said.

"I'm also willing to bet that you haven't eaten today, and probably not since yesterday."

I thought about it and realized he was right. My nose had been hurting so much that I hadn't realized how hungry I was, but now it was in full force. "No, Your Honor, we haven't."

"Well, let's take care of that." Caldwell looked at Maggie. "I want to talk to you. I have an idea you might be interested in."

49

"What I was thinking," Judge Caldwell said to Maggie when we were settled in to breakfast at Wick's Diner, "is that you may be needing a job."

"I have a job." Maggie picked up a piece of bacon and devoured it.

Caldwell's thick eyebrows knitted. "I was given to understand that you're no longer a deputy in this town."

I was just as confused as he was.

"I'm not," Maggie said.

"Do you mind if I ask what your plans are?" the judge inquired.

"No."

"May I ask what those plans are?"

"Yes."

The judge waited, but Maggie kept eating. I'd never seen Maggie so politely reticent before.

"I think the judge would like to know what plans you have," I said.

"I don't want to talk about it," Maggie said as she cut up a biscuit smothered in gravy.

Even as well-meaning as he was trying to be, I knew the answer flummoxed Caldwell. It flummoxed me. I glanced at him and shrugged as I gave my head a shake. I wasn't inclined to move my head overmuch because my nose still hurt.

"Maybe it would be better if I told you what I had in mind," Caldwell said.

Maggie kept eating, but I was curious, so I hoped the judge wouldn't just stop there.

"I know that you did a good job as a deputy in this town," Caldwell said. "I've seen you do it, and other people have told me that you did a fine job of keeping the peace."

I ate too, because I was hungry.

"Allan Pinkerton of the Pinkerton National Detective Agency has been employing women as investigators since 1856," Caldwell said. "He took on a woman named Kate Warne who worked for him for over ten years and eventually became the head of the Lady Pinkertons, as they are sometimes called. During the Civil War, Miss Warne also became the head of the Union Intelligence Service. In that capacity, Miss Warne acquired knowledge about what the Confederacy was doing and what materials they had to do it with. You can see how I was intrigued."

"Not really," Maggie said.

"Sometimes the right man for the job is a woman," the judge said. "I believe that we will have female United States marshals in the near future. In fact, I would like to offer you an unofficial position as a female marshal."

I just stared at Caldwell, but he didn't blink.

"Unofficial?" Maggie repeated. "As in no badge?"

"That's right. At first. Like I said, I really think that will change—"

"Thank you, Judge, but no."

Caldwell sat silent for a moment. I couldn't believe it either. Any of it. Him offering Maggie such a job, and her turning it down when she'd enjoyed being a deputy so much.

I thought about talking to her, getting her to reconsider, but I realized I didn't want her to go. The offer didn't include me, and I wasn't sure if she would be all right if she went off on her own. Gilbride's words about her needing a friend still echoed in my head.

"Because you have plans," Caldwell said, and he

looked at me like I might know something he didn't.

I slowly shook my head.

"That's right," Maggie said.

"But they're plans you don't want to talk about."

"Not yet, no. And there is the fact that you're old and will die. You won't be in a position to guarantee my employment as long as I would need it."

"Old," he repeated. "And I'll die."

"Yes. My pa was old too, not nearly as old as you, but I knew he wouldn't be there for me forever either. In fact, there was—until yesterday—a chance that I might in time have to take care of him as he got older. That's why I made plans. I had just not expected to use them so quickly."

Caldwell frowned in confusion and I didn't blame him. I'd seen hints of this part of Maggie's personality, but not much of it. It wasn't pleasant, but she always told you exactly what she was thinking.

"She's blunt," I said by way of apology.

"All right," Caldwell said, "but let's talk about some other things you might not be aware of. Like the house you live in."

"It's part of the marshal's pay," Maggie said. "I'll be moving out today. Charlie and I have to prepare my pa for burying this evening. Then, after that, I'll get my things."

"Do you know where you're going to live?"

I knew then that Gilbride had talked to Caldwell and presented Maggie's problems to the judge. They had to have come up with the job offer together. Probably they'd thought it was the best option under the circumstances and Maggie would go for it.

I didn't have a clue why she didn't.

Then, when I thought I couldn't be surprised any more, she answered Caldwell's question.

"I'm going to live with Charlie."

50

"What?" I asked. Or, at least, that's what I'd tried to say. I'd been taking a sip of coffee and now wore half a mouthful. It burned when it went up my nose, and I had a coughing spell.

Maggie looked at me once I'd stopped drowning in coffee. "You have an extra room. You said you built it in case you needed to take on a roommate to help pay your expenses. I can pay."

"Maggie, men and women don't just live together," I said. "What will people think?"

"Who cares?" she asked. "And if you ask me, I think it's a shame there aren't laws that people who think about things that are none of their business should be fined. Our living arrangements are none of their business." Her dark eyes searched mine, and for a minute there was a flicker of doubt. "Unless you don't want me to live there."

"Maggie, you're welcome to live there," I said. I would not turn her away.

"There are a few changes I'd like to see happen when I do," she told me. "Some furniture and things."

"All right."

Caldwell laughed out loud and looked at me. "Looks like you're going to have your hands full, Mister Stark. It's a good thing you have so many side businesses and jobs going on."

"Charlie's got more than that," Maggie said, turning back to the judge. "He's got that whole first floor of his building that he still hasn't decided what to do with. I was thinking that your office could rent that first floor on the days you needed it. At least part of it."

"Why would I do that?" Caldwell asked with bright interest.

"Do you want to continue holding court and conducting trials at Hunziker's General Store?"

"The county courthouse is in Fort Stockton."

"You don't do business for this town down there."

"Big murder cases are held there."

"Yet you conducted Courbet's trial here."

"Sometimes the court docket gets full there."

"Do you like the arrangement at Hunziker's?"

The judge took a moment to eat a bite of his pancakes. "What kind of rent are we talking about?"

I couldn't believe I was suddenly a spectator during a business deal involving the building I owned. But I wouldn't have thought of offering the first floor as a courtroom either.

"We'll talk about that," Maggie said, "but there are other things Charlie and I want as well."

I had no clue what we wanted.

"Charlie and I will be opening a bail bonds agency, housed on that first floor as well," Maggie went on. "Just a small office to conduct our business."

"There's already a bail bondsman operating in this town."

"Noah Burns," Maggie said. "I know. I've worked with him."

"I expect he's not going to like you horning in on his business."

"Burns only provides bail to low-risk law breakers. I don't really consider them criminals. They're just people who got behind with their finances or drank too much or chose to ignore propriety."

Maggie had never demonstrated this kind of vocabulary and I was entranced watching her at work, and stunned by her vision.

"We will provide bail to true criminals," Maggie said. "In order to keep from filling jails in the area."

"And if those criminals choose not to show up to court?"

"I'll go get them." Maggie sipped her coffee. "When bail is given, the principal is regarded as delivered to the custody of his sureties. That would be Charlie and me. Their dominion, again meaning us, is a continuance of the original imprisonment. Whenever they, again, this would be Charlie and me, choose to do so, they may seize him and deliver him up in their discharge; and if that cannot be done at once, they may imprison him until it can be done. They may exercise their rights in person or by agent." She paused. "The law concerning such things goes on from there."

"Taylor versus Taintor." The judge wore a pleased smile. "That was set up to allow bounty hunters to chase down fugitives for bonding agencies."

"That's right."

"You're quite well informed, Miss Buchanan."

"Thank you. I try to be."

I wasn't as well informed and suddenly realized I needed to be, so I knew me and Maggie were going to be talking seriously when we were alone.

"So you want to establish a bail bondsman's office in my courthouse," the judge said.

"It's Charlie's building," Maggie pointed out. "It will only be your courthouse as long as you pay your rent."

"So it will."

"And he'll be happy to rent you all the space you need for your trials."

Caldwell thought about it for a moment. "I'll expect a jury box and a judge's chambers if I'm going to pay for this."

Maggie nodded. "You'll have them, but the monthly rental will be more expensive for amenities."

"We can negotiate those."

"Yes, but Charlie has a real estate empire and he plans on making a profit. He's not operating a charity."

"I suppose he isn't."

I took out a notebook and started taking notes. I didn't want to get lost.

Caldwell smiled hugely. "Is that it, Miss Buchanan? Or was there anything else?"

"I will also be employed as your bailiff when court is in session. I will get paid by the day. If I'm not there, you are free to hire someone else."

Caldwell chuckled.

"There is one last thing," Maggie said, "I notice that Mister Hunziker makes money from people getting food to eat while court is going on. Charlie will build one other small room that contains a kitchen where we can employ a small staff on court days to sell coffee, tea, and whatever he sees fit."

Caldwell waited a moment, then he asked, "Is that all, Miss Buchanan?"

"Charlie will want a signed agreement regarding this negotiation, and on days when court is not there, he will use the room as he sees fit."

"My god," Caldwell said, and his eyes twinkled, "and here I was thinking you were a waif needing help. You are an absolute pip, Miss Buchanan. I cannot wait to see what you do with all of this."

"With what Charlie does with it," Maggie amended. She turned to me. "I think you'll agree that a ten percent finder's fee for everything I've just negotiated will cover the rent for my room."

"I do," I said. I hadn't told her about her share of the bounty money yet, but it was in the back of my mind in case she went broke.

"Good," she said. "I assume you two don't have any further worries or concerns about me?"

"I don't," Caldwell said. "In fact, I'm starting to worry about young Mister Stark here. I'm thinking he may have bitten off more than he can chew by partnering up with you."

I didn't have anything either. Not about finances. But there were other worries that were taking shape. I was pretty sure Maggie hadn't told us everything she was planning.

51

When Maggie laid out plans for the courthouse again, my head was still spinning. But she sounded confident, so I decided to follow her lead and trust that things would work out. Judge Caldwell had seemed impressed.

That evening, working in Gilbride's office, me and Maggie and Gilbride embalmed Marshal Buchanan. Surprisingly, there were no tears. I hadn't expected any from Maggie, Gilbride was worn out, and I was just empty.

I'd liked Marshal Buchanan even though I hadn't really gotten to know him until lately. He'd been a good man, and he'd loved Maggie.

That night, we went and got Maggie's things from the house she'd lived in with her pa. She took his things too.

Having Maggie in my home—our¬ home, I supposed now—was strange. I missed some of the privacy I'd had, but it was good having her there too.

When I'd got up the next morning, there'd been coffee, bacon, eggs, and hashed potatoes and onion with a little jalapeno pepper. I'd never had potatoes like that before, but I liked the smell. I'd bought a few things at Hunziker's to fix for myself whenever she wasn't there, and she'd found them in the cupboard.

"This is a thank you," Maggie said when I walked into the kitchen. "Don't get used to it. I'm not planning on being a maid."

"I didn't know you could cook," I said as I sat at the table.

"Cooking is easy. It's just boring."

I dug in and the food was as good as it looked.

***

The next day, Wednesday, we went to church for the special service for all the folks that had died. Maggie left her pa's clothing for the poor.

After that, we went out to the Sunflower Cemetery and buried Marshall Buchanan. The turnout for the funeral was small, but there were thirty-three other funerals going on that day and the next, so the low attendance was understandable.

Everybody had lost somebody.

Maggie wore her pistols and stood there while me and Gilbride and Judge Caldwell and a few others said nice things about the marshal, then Preacher Wallace gave the final prayer. Me and Maggie and Gilbride filled in the grave and we all went home.

***

Over the next few days, after Judge Caldwell caught the train and moved on down the line to his next court on Thursday, I made plans to transform the first floor of the building into the courthouse, judge's chambers, Maggie's bail bonds office, and the room where we were going to have coffee and such for sale. There was even enough space left over to make a room to sequester the jury while they deliberated if it was needed.

Maggie intended to charge for that room as well.

Since I was designing the layout, I made sure Maggie got a corner office and two windows. She never said she liked the space, but I thought maybe she would.

Word got around pretty quick about what we were doing as far as construction. Judge Caldwell had mentioned it to the town council and, folks being folks, they just passed the news along.

Aiken came by and I didn't want to talk to him. Maggie pointed out that having the courthouse in the news could be good for business because other people might want to rent out the space.

I'd never built a courtroom before and was feeling pretty nervous about it, so Maggie suggested we go down to Fort Stockton and look at the new county courthouse there that had been built only last year.

We did and I had to admit it was good to get out of Pecos. The cash in the bank was holding steady because the bounty money kept me flush, and after all the shooting Blunt and his gang had done, there were a lot of repair jobs too. I worked hard every day and Maggie helped me.

Then, a week into all the renovations we were doing, Maggie left.

52

I got up to a note on the table that was short and not very informative.

Charlie—
I'll be away on business for a few days. Be safe. Keep working.
—Maggie

That was all I got. Not one word about what she was doing or where she was going.

I went over to Gilbride's and showed him the note. He was as worried as I was, but he pointed out that there was nothing we could do except wait for her to come back.

"She's a grown woman," Gilbride said.

"What do you think she's doing?" That was the question I kept asking myself.

"Whatever she wants to."

"And if she gets hurt?"

"We're just going to have to pray that she doesn't."

Well, I did me some of that too while I waited.

***

After a week passed and there was still no word, I was done with just waiting around, and I got the idea that I might know someone who knew where she went. So I headed out to the train station where the Pinkertons kept an office in the Whitman Hotel that was located across the street from the depot.

The hotel was modest and not where people with money wanted to stay because of all the noise of the train, the small stockyards, and the loading crews that worked a lot at night and early in the morning.

The small office had that sign that Allan Pinkerton was so proud of that showed an open eye surrounded by the name of the business. Pinkerton's National Detective Agency. The words "We Never Sleep" underscored the eye.

A diminutive man in a good, but cheap suit sat behind a secretarial desk in the tiny office. I would have guessed the office would have been bigger what with the detective agency being nationwide.

I sat there and fidgeted with my hat, which was another one to replace the one that had been shot off my head on what was supposed to be Courbet's hanging. I wasn't having much luck with hats.

While I sat there, I thought of Courbet and Angelo Blunt, who I figured was pretty sore he hadn't gotten his hands on that Mexican gold.

Or maybe he'd decided it wasn't real. If he'd seen the map I had, he would have changed his mind.

And killed me for it.

"Mister Stark," the secretary said.

I stood up.

"Mister Valle will see you now." He waved me to two doors at the back of the room.

Only one of the doors had Mister LAMAR VALLE written on it, so I knocked, and, when invited, went on in.

Valle's office was bigger than the one the secretary used, but not by much. He had a nice desk, a few legal books on shelves to his left, framed pictures of Allan Pinkerton, Abraham Lincoln, and General Ulysses S. Grant hanging on the wall behind him.

I thought Grant was a poor choice to be hanging in an

office in West Texas, and probably Lincoln was too. Then I realized Pinkerton himself wouldn't have been popular either.

But folks had problems they needed investigators for, I supposed, and the train needed security. Those folks would be more concerned with having someone to help them and probably not paying attention to the pictures on the wall.

Lamar Valle was in his mid to late twenties, and if he was Maggie's "friend," I was prepared to hate him. He was way too good-looking. His curly chestnut hair hung over his ears and his goatee was cut short.

I was at least four inches taller than he was when he stood to shake my hand, and I admit I took some pride in that.

"Mister Stark." He waved to the two chairs on the other side of his desk. "What can I do for you?" His accent was cultured and undeniably northern.

I sat. "I'm looking for Maggie Buchanan."

Valle frowned. "I wasn't aware that Miss Buchanan was missing."

"She not exactly missing," I said. "She left a week ago."

"She left under her own power? No one coerced her?"

"She left a note."

"What did the note say?"

"That she'd be back."

A small smile played at his lips, and I hated him a little more for that. "You know, it's very possible that when she's finished whatever she's gone to do, she will be back."

"I'm worried about her."

"I see that, Mister Stark. Did the two of you have an argument before she left?"

"No." I didn't care for him poking into my private business so casually, but I figured that was what detectives did.

"Why do you think I would know?" He seemed genuinely interested.

"Maggie worked with the Pinkertons from time to

time on law matters," I said.

"She did, but she didn't work with me. I've only talked to her a time or two."

"Then I need to talk to the person she worked with."

"That would be Mister Castor." Valle leaned forward, picked up his pen from the inkwell, and wrote a short note on a notepad. He tore the note off and handed it to me. "That's Mister Castor's address."

I took the note and felt confused. "Mister Castor doesn't work here?"

"Mister Castor," Valle said, "was once upon a time a Pinkerton agent of considerable skills. Unfortunately, he had some bad luck. But now he consults with us and makes his home in different places." He pointed to the note in my hand. "Currently, I believe, he is staying at that boarding house here in Pecos."

I thanked him for his time, asked him if I owed him anything, and he waved it away.

"Call it professional courtesy, Mister Stark. I hear you're going into the bail bonding business. I'm sure our paths will cross again. Perhaps you can do a good turn for me."

53

Missus Frederiks' boardinghouse was three blocks off Main Street and not far from the depot. Folks who stayed there were generally employed by the railroad in some capacity, but they didn't stay more than a few months.

I knew that because once me and Mister Henson had to embalm a man who'd died there so he could be shipped back to his family in Murfreesboro, Tennessee. That was the longest distance we'd ever sent a body. We never heard anything back, so I supposed the body arrived in good condition. Folks usually got hold of you if they wanted to complain.

Missus Frederiks remembered me and told me she was sorry to hear about Mister Henson. I thanked her and she went to fetch Mister Castor. After a couple minutes she returned and I thought she was going to tell me he didn't want to see me or that he was gone.

My mind immediately jumped to the possibility that he'd gone off with Maggie, and I was none too happy about that.

"Mister Castor asked me if I would show you back to his room, Charlie. If you'll follow me?"

"Yes, ma'am." I followed her and everything in the house felt small and narrow. Of course, I was to all the space in Mister Henson's—my¬—building, which was still under construction, so a lot of houses would seem small in comparison.

She stopped in front of one of the doors and knocked. "Mister Castor?"

"Show him in, Missus Frederiks." The voice boomed in the enclosed space.

Missus Frederiks looked at me and said, "Don't mind the loud voice. He's a little hard of hearing these days."

Castor harumphed and said, "Well, I heard that."

"Do forgive me, Mister Castor." Missus Frederiks grinned at me and opened the door.

I had to duck when I stepped into the room, which was small and had a low ceiling. The single bed was on one side of the room and a small desk covered in books and writing utensils was on the other.

Mister Castor sat in a wheelchair at the end of the room. Once upon a time, he had been a big man, but age and his apparent infirmity had worn him down. He was still broad-shouldered, but they sloped these days. He had an angular, withered face and a full beard that hid some of the ravages left by the years and what I suspected was a hard life. He wore a suit, but a thin blanket covered his legs.

He held a pair of military field glasses to his eyes as he stared out the window. "Aha," he said, "there it is!"

He sounded like whatever he was doing was a major accomplishment.

"I'll bring some lemonade and cookies," Missus Frederik said. "Charlie, there's a chair in the corner that Maggie favors when she comes here. Mister Castor, this is Charlie. The young man Maggie has mentioned."

"I know very well who he is, Missus Frederiks," Castor insisted. "My body may be infirm, but my mind is as agile as ever."

"Well, don't forget to talk to him. He came all this way."

"I won't forget."

I thanked her and she went away.

Castor put the field glasses on a small table beside the window, then he used his hands on the wheels to maneuver the chair around to face me. He waved to the chair

Missus Frederiks had pointed me to.

"Sit," he ordered. "If we're going to talk, I don't want to get a crick in my neck looking up at you. God knows that looking up at a normal-sized man is hard enough. You're impossible."

Feeling foolish, I sat.

"You are Charlie Stark?" he asked.

"I am."

He offered his hand and I took it.

"I am Morgan Castor." He smiled. "I have to say, it is a pleasure to meet you, young man. Maggie has told me a lot about you."

"She has?" I couldn't imagine Maggie telling anyone a lot of anything. Of course, she had surprised me at that breakfast with Judge Caldwell.

"Well," Castor leaned back in his hair and arranged the blanket more neatly over his legs, "you know Maggie. She doesn't talk a lot. So if you know her, you know to listen when she does speak."

"She's never mentioned you," I said.

"Never?" Castor looked surprised.

"Not by name. She has mentioned she had a friend in the Pinkertons."

That elicited a smile from the old man. "That would be me. I am that friend, and it is a designation I am proud to have."

"Sir," I said, "I came here looking for Maggie."

"Well, how should I know where she is?"

I was stymied and I didn't know what to do at that point. Maggie had just vanished.

I stood. "I'm sorry to have wasted your time, Mister Castor."

"Nonsense. I'm a cripple and old, so if the world doesn't come to me these days, I don't have much inter-action with it."

"I need to find Maggie."

"She went out to Sierra Blanca when she left Pecos. I can tell you that. As to where she is now, I don't know. She hasn't checked in."

I sat back down. "Why would she go to Sierra Blanca?" That little town had grown up around the Texas and Pacific Railway the same way Pecos had and was almost to the New Mexico Territory border. "And why would she check in with you?"

Castor laughed. "Because I'm a consultant in her bounty hunting business."

"What?"

"Oh, come now, Mister Stark. You're a partner in that business. She told me that you were."

"I thought we were only going to be chasing after people we had bonded out of jail who failed to show up for court."

"Well, I'm sure she'll chase those too. As for right now, she's pursuing two men wanted for the murder of a young woman, and who are believed to be in Sierra Blanca."

54

"When Maggie told me what she wanted to do a few days ago, of course I tried to talk her out of it," Castor said after I'd called him on that. "Chasing down wanted men, dangerous men, is no job for a young woman."

"We agree on that," I said.

"Especially alone." Castor narrowed his eyes at me in suspicion.

"She didn't tell me she was going," I protested. "All she left was a note."

Castor sighed. "I surmised as much when you showed up at my door. That young woman is the most hardheaded person I have ever before met. Also, Mister Aiken wrote up a nice piece in his paper about the way you saved Maggie during Angelo Blunt's attack on the town. I knew you were certainly brave enough to go with her."

I still didn't know who had seen that and given Aiken the story. Me and Maggie weren't currently on speaking terms with the newspaperman because he was selling his papers based on the hardships in our lives.

Missus Frederiks returned with the lemonade and cookies. She put the glasses on the small desk, after she moved some books around, and left the plate of cookies.

"They're chocolate chip," she said. "Fresh out of the oven." Then she left again.

"Wonderful woman," Castor commented as he reached for a cookie. "It's a shame she never remarried after her husband died. She has a real need to take care of people. But, I suppose, it's just good fortune for me. I have a wonderful housekeeper when I'm here in Pecos." He nibbled at his cookie.

"Tell me about the men in Sierra Blanca," I suggested. I was still reeling from being told Maggie was chasing after two murderers.

"Of course." Castor shuffled papers on his desk and came up with two dodgers.

I took them and looked at the sketches. Both men were older, in their forties or fifties if the sketches were close to accurate, and had lived-in faces. Leroy Upton was missing half of his right ear at the bottom, and Vince Reaves had facial tattooing, a crescent moon on one cheek and some kind of jagged lines on the other. It wasn't the kind of face you wanted for committing crimes without a mask.

"Both of those men are wanted for killing a woman named Anne Scharbauer in Big Spring, Texas," Castor told me. "They were buffalo hunters employed by the United States Army to shoot buffalo to supply meat for the soldiers. When the buffalo hunting jobs started to play out, they took to doing other things such as running whiskey to the Indians up in the Indian Territories. Reaves got the tattoos from when he'd lived with the Mohave Indians out in the Arizona Territory. Both of those men are vicious individuals."

"And you sent Maggie after them?"

"Young man," Castor said a little impatiently, "I didn't send that young woman anywhere. She went in spite of my strongest objections."

I took a deep breath and let it out. "How do you know all of this?"

"Because Maggie asked me to look into it for her and I did. She'd heard from someone in town that Upton and Reaves were in Sierra Blanca. I merely confirmed that for her."

"How did you do that?"

"What? Because I'm in this wheelchair?"

I didn't say anything.

Castor chuckled, but it wasn't all amusement. There was some indignation buried in there, and maybe some old frustration as well. "I wasn't always in this chair, Mister Stark. Once I was as young and as able as you are now. I was one of the earliest members of Allan Pinkerton's detectives. I chased criminals from Washington, DC, to Chicago, to San Francisco and a number of points between. Even now I do some piecework consulting for Allan and some of his young agents. I keep a network of contacts I built up over those years. So don't let the chair fool you. I still carry my own water."

"How did you meet Maggie?" I asked.

"I sought out the help of her father on a delicate matter here in Pecos," Castor said. "A bit of blackmail that my client didn't want to have publicly known. I didn't want to use the Pinkerton agents that were currently here because those men tend to be heavy handed, more suitable for strikebreaking, which is detestable work. When the marshal got involved in leveraging the offending letters from the blackmailer, Maggie worked with him. In fact, it was the only time I've ever seen her in a dress."

I tried to imagine that and just couldn't. Maggie as a bounty hunter I had no problem imagining, but Maggie in a dress was impossible.

I wanted to ask about that. I really did, but I was more concerned about Maggie. "Mister Castor, if you can tell me where to find those men, I'll look for Maggie there as well."

"That's very commendable, Mister Stark." Castor beamed at me. "But they'll be arriving this afternoon on the three-fifteen train."

I looked at him, and I was mad, so I was sure it showed. "I thought you said you didn't know where Maggie was."

"I did. I lied. I'm quite good at it." He laughed, then leaned forward and patted me on my knee. "I didn't know you, Mister Stark, but I do know that having you interfere in business where Maggie didn't want you was not something I was going to be part of. I value her friendship and trust far too much to endanger it."

"She told you not to tell me?"

"She did."

"Why?"

Castor thought about that for a moment. "Because, after meeting you, I think she's trying to protect some of your innocence."

"I don't understand."

"I think she feels that she has corrupted you in some manner. That she's been a bad influence. She said that since you've been friends, you've killed four men."

"Three," I said. "She lied about me killing one of them when she was the one who killed him."

"Whatever for?"

"So I could collect the bounty."

Castor laughed again. "Oh my god, of course she did." He wiped tears from his eyes, and I thought then that he had a peculiar sense of humor. I didn't see anything funny about it. "I swear, you have to love that young woman for her brashness if for nothing else. I've told Allan about her, told him he should offer her a job as one of his Lady Pinkertons. He won't, though. He looked into her a bit and decided she was too intractable."

Even after all the reading Mister Henson forced on me, I barely knew that one, but it suited Maggie to a T.

"At any rate," Castor said, "Maggie wanted to protect you."

"I don't need protecting."

"She thinks you do, so until you can convince her otherwise, you'll have to deal with her decisions."

"If she pulls something like this again," I said, "I want you to tell me."

Castor shook his head. "That's not going to happen."

"I don't want her risking her life like this."

"Let me tell you something very wise, young man. If I may. When you run across a young, independent woman like Maggie Buchanan, you never try to tell her what to do. You also don't bend to her every wish. What you do is work to become her equal. That's the only way you'll ever earn her respect."

I wanted to argue, but I knew it was true.

"I'm not a kid," I said angrily. "She can't treat me like a child."

"That's something you'll have to deal with between you and her, Mister Stark. Not me. She seems as adamant about protecting you as you are about protecting her. I can see that's going to be a problem. One which I'm not going to be a part of." Castor pulled out his watch. "In the meantime, it is almost twelve o'clock. Missus Frederiks will be along in a few minutes to ask if I want lunch. It's Thursday, so lunch will be chicken and dumplings. That is one of her best dishes. She will ask you to stay. I advise you to stay. Never turn down a free meal. We have a few hours until the train arrives from Sierra Blanca." He smiled at me. "And if you stay, I'll show you my latest sketches of birds."

"Birds?" I repeated, not sure what he was talking about.

"Yes." Castor nodded. "I've become quite the ornithologist. I'm no John Audubon, I assure you, but he and I crossed paths and he encouraged me in my hobby. He said I had a good eye for detail. Only just a few minutes ago, I saw a Chordeiles acutipennis. You probably know it as a nightjar or a nighthawk. The bird normally hunts at dawn and dusk and can catch mosquitos on the wing. Isn't that amazing?"

I searched for some way to politely escape.

Missus Frederiks knocked on the door and stuck her head in. "Mister Castor, lunch will be ready in a few minutes." She looked at me. "Charlie, there's plenty of chicken and dumplings to go around. Would you be interested in joining us?"

"You know," Castor said, "I believe I might just have that sketchbook that contains that drawing of Maggie in that dress."

He had me and he knew it. He smiled, big and broad.

"Yes, ma'am," I said. "I'd be happy to."

55

I was standing at the train depot when the three-fifteen pulled in right on time. Metal shrilled as the brakes brought the locomotive and the rolling stock to a halt.

I walked along the line of cars and looked for Maggie. A lot of people were getting off and others were getting on. Buckboards from Malpert's Storage sat lined up to transfer cargos.

"Charlie."

When I heard her call me, I tracked her voice toward the end of the train and saw her standing on the end platform of one of the boxcars. She hopped down and walked toward the middle of the car. I got there about the time the cargo handlers were running out a ramp so freight could be moved.

"I see you found Mister Castor," Maggie said.

"I did. He told me to tell you that I was smarter than I look."

Her lips twitched.

That was when I noticed her blackened left eye and split lip.

I reached for her face and she pulled her head away.

"Stop," she said, hitting me in the chest with her palm.

"What happened to you?" I asked.

"I'm still learning some things," she said. "It'll work out."

I was going to say something more, but the stench of death floated out of that boxcar and I stepped back. I put a hand over my nose and mouth. "What is that?"

"Money in the bank," Maggie announced. "All part of the plan."

She marched up into the boxcar and returned leading two horses. One of them carried a man-shaped burlap bag. The other was the mare she usually rode. It had panniers on its sides that I guessed held supplies.

"There's another one in there," she said. "Could you get it?"

It took me a minute to get moving, but I walked up the ramp and saw that there was indeed another horse with a man-shaped burlap bag waiting inside. The inside of the car stank horribly.

A big, burly cargo handler looked at me. He wore a neckerchief tied around his lower face. "Are you with her?" he asked.

"I am."

"She's crazy. She loaded these two up at Sierra Blanca, in this heat, and had us carry them to here. She says they're bounties."

"They are."

The man shook his head. "I wouldn't want to be in that business. We'll never get this stink out of this car."

"You could have told her no," I pointed out.

"Not me, brother," the man said. "The way I heard it, that hellcat walked into these guys' camp bold as you please and suggested that they turn themselves in. That's when the fighting and the shooting started. She killed one of them right out of the gate, then killed two more of their friends, who must not have been worth nothing, and finally ran down the last guy out in the woods. As far as I'm concerned, I'm not telling her no. But somebody needs to."

"Yeah," I said, taking the horse's reins, "I suppose someone should tell her no."

But it wasn't going to be me.

***

It wasn't too far to the marshal's office and we walked it without saying a word. I'd tried to talk, but Maggie wasn't having any of it. She was focused on whatever she had in mind, and I was going along with her to see if I could keep the trouble to a minimum.

Everybody in town saw us walk through with the dead men on the horses, and I knew all of them would be talking. By sundown, there would only be a few that wouldn't know about this.

Maggie had counted on that. It was all part of her plan. That was easy to see. I still didn't know everything her plan entailed, though, and leading a dead man down Main Street wasn't setting my mind at ease.

By the time she stopped at the marshal's office, Leslie Stephens was standing out on the boardwalk. He wore his guns and a Greener shotgun was leaned against the wall.

"That's far enough, Maggie," Stephens said when we were ten feet away.

Maggie stopped the horse and I stopped beside her.

"That's fine," Maggie said, taking a jackknife from her pocket and opening the blade. "You and your deputies can carry them the rest of the way."

She cut the pigging strings that held the dead man to the horse and the burlap-covered body slid off into the street. She nodded to me and I cut the ties on the one I'd led in.

Maggie walked from one man to the next and cut open the top of the burlap wide enough to expose the swollen faces that I knew would give folks nightmares for days to come.

In retrospect, dumping dead bodies on the street after Angelo Blunt and his gang had shot up the town not so long ago probably wasn't her best move, but it was effective.

No one was talking. They were all listening. Aiken stood on the boardwalk across the street and he was making notes in his notebook as fast as he could write.

"These men are Leroy Upton and Vince Reaves," Maggie said. "They're wanted—dead or alive—for the murder of a woman in Big Spring." She took papers from inside of her leather jacket and unfolded them for everyone to see the wanted posters. "They preferred dead, so here they are." She paused and looked directly at Stephens. "The bounties are fifteen hundred dollars. I want it now."

I thought that would be where things got testy, that Stephens would deny the identities of the men, or even accuse Maggie of murdering men and trying to pass them off as the outlaws.

Instead, he signed the markers confirming the men were who she said they were and gave them to her to give to the bank in the morning.

Maggie turned to the onlookers. "This is official notification that Stark and Buchanan Bail Bonds are now open. Those of you who need us, come see us. But rest assured, if you don't make your court date, we will hunt you down and bring you in."

From there, we walked home leading the horses. They were going to need baths, and I hoped someone at the livery would take care of it.

56

After we left the horses at the livery and we were upstairs, I told Maggie I'd heat up some water for her bath. I'd already lit the potbelly stove and put water in the tub in her room so that all I would have to do was add the hot water when it was ready.

I thought there might be a fight from her, either over me preparing the water or me suggesting she take a bath, and I was prepared for it because she needed to be clean again. She smelled like death herself. And I knew she would feel better for it once it was done.

But she didn't say a word. She sat in the rocking chair I'd finished for her while she was gone. I'd worked on it in the evenings, and at night when I couldn't sleep because I'd worried about her. I'd put in time, off and on, while doing other projects because I thought she would like having her own chair where she could think and maybe relax. I'd enjoyed thinking about her having that chair.

When the water was hot enough, I poured it in the tub and steam billowed up in a huge, wet cloud. Without asking, I added some bath soap that Missus Hunziker recommended after I'd asked her and made myself scarce. I hoped the soap would cut the smell of death.

While Maggie took her bath, I opened all the windows to air out the stink we'd tracked in, and thankfully it left pretty quickly, then I made dinner. I knew there was no way we could go anywhere to eat that we wouldn't be bothered or at least stared at. I figured Maggie would want to be away from a crowd. I did. Since everything had happened to Mister Henson and Marshal Buchanan, me and Maggie's lives had been pretty much on public display. I didn't care for that at all.

I was a good enough cook, and I was learning more because Maggie truly had no interest in it and we had to eat. To her, food was just something a body needed and she took no specific pleasure from it.

But I liked eating and I liked sitting across a table, just me and Maggie. We could talk or not talk and it didn't matter. Like it had been with Mister Henson.

I grilled steaks on an open flame and listened to the hiss of the grease cooking off. I boiled corn and potatoes and carrots. And I made a pan of cornbread in the oven. I'd bought a blackberry cobbler from Trail's End earlier, after talking with Castor, and brought it home before I'd gone to the train depot to meet Maggie. I still hadn't managed the trick of getting a cobbler to turn out right.

When the food was ready, I sat and waited. Then I started to worry that everything would get too cool and not be fit to eat. After that I thought maybe Maggie had passed out from being too tired and drowned in the tub with me sitting on the other side of the door.

I was about to get up when she walked from her bedroom. She wore new dungarees that looked good on her, a black shirt, and a burgundy vest that I hadn't seen before. Even though she wasn't dressed up in women's clothing, she wasn't quite as plain as she normally dressed.

And she didn't wear her guns to the table.

"I thought you'd gone to sleep," I said as she sat at the table.

"No. But I will." She used a fork to stab one of the steaks and dragged it to her plate.

"I was afraid you'd drowned."

Her lips twitched and her eyes sparkled with merriment. "I didn't drown, Charlie."

"New clothes?" I asked.

"Yes. There was a peddler on the train. He showed me some clothes. I bought a few things. Do they look okay?" She sounded a little uncertain, which wasn't like her.

"They do."

"Because I need to look professional now that we've opened the bail bonds company."

"You don't think you've scared everybody off by dropping those dead men in the street?" I poured her a cup of coffee. I'd already been drinking one.

"No." She sipped the coffee.

"You're sure?"

Her lips twitched, and the split lip made even that small expression look strange to me.

"You'll see," she said.

We ate for a time before I could say what was on my mind. "You could have gotten yourself killed going after those men."

"No."

"There were four of them."

Her eyebrows lifted. "Who did you talk to?"

"The cargo handler."

"How did he know?"

"He talked to someone who saw what happened."

She cut off a bite of steak, popped it into her mouth, and chewed. "I'm not dead, Charlie. I'm still learning some things about manhunting. Everything's going to be all right."

"No," I said. "Everything's not going to be all right. Not like this."

She looked at me, and suddenly I realized how fragile what we had, this friendship, was. Being close to anyone was hard for both of us, but it was harder for Maggie.

I hurried on so I could make myself clear. "You don't get to decide what I can do and what I can't do, Maggie. Either we're partners in whatever it is we do, or we're not."

She chewed for a minute, and I could tell she was thinking, determining where the lines were. I was afraid she was going to decide I was asking for more than she would allow.

Then she said, "We're partners."

"Good," I said, and I felt a huge knot in my chest unravel. "Because that's the only way this is going to work."

"All right."

"So that means the next time you go out for a bounty—"

"Soon," she said.

"—I'm going with you."

"You will." She pointed her fork at my plate. "You should eat. Your food's going to get cold."

I decided to leave the matter alone. I'd gotten farther with my argument than I'd thought I would. I cut into my steak.

Maggie said quietly, "It's good to be home, Charlie. Thank you for dinner."

57

As it turned out, Maggie was right about not scaring off the potential bail bonds customers.

At eight o'clock the next morning, while I was marking up boards I needed to cut to frame out the jury box, a man I hadn't met knocked on the front door. I looked at him through the dusty glass. In time there would be a foyer there and I wouldn't be able to see that door, but for now the area was clear and I had a perfect line of sight.

I was wearing overalls and a carpenter's apron with only an undershirt covering my upper body because it had gotten godawful hot. I had on work boots and work gloves as well.

The Tranter sat beside my carpenter's box within easy reach. No matter how much I tried not to think about Angelo Blunt, or the possibility of him coming back after me to find that gold, I couldn't get him out of my mind. I would glance into a window and see a reflection, catch a glimpse of sudden movement from the corner of my eye, and I'd be certain Angelo Blunt was standing right behind me.

Some days I thought there were men in town Blunt had put there to watch me, to see if I would go after that gold. Not knowing where he was or what he was thinking was hard. Men didn't quit on the notion of gold any too easy once it grabbed hold of them.

Sometimes I'd get the shakes and it would take a bit for them to pass. It had been worse before Maggie had come back home. I knew I had another pair of eyes to watch over me.

I left the Tranter where it was, wiped my hands clean on a towel, and went to answer the door.

"Are you Charlie Stark?" the man asked. He was average height and balding in the front. He had a paunch on him, but at forty or so, that was to be expected. I hoped to live long enough to have a belly on me. He was smooth shaven and smelled like he'd just gotten up from a barber's chair. His suit was nice and fitted him well.

"I'm Charlie Stark," I said.

He frowned at me. "You're young."

I was irritated enough that I almost remarked on his powers of observation, but I restrained myself. "Was there something you wanted?"

"Yes sir. My name is Nathan Forney. I'd like to hire you as my bail bondsman."

"Me?"

"Yes. You and that young woman. Your partner." Forney hooked a thumb over his shoulder. "I was over at Wick's Diner when you and she brought in those dead men yesterday. I got to thinking last night maybe you all could help me out with a problem I have."

"Are you wanted somewhere, Mister Forney?" Men would sometimes turn themselves in if they could bond out and not stay in jail till the judge came around to have a trial.

"No sir, not me. My brother-in-law got himself arrested down in Fort Stockton. He was embezzling from the shipping company where he worked. He's been in jail for a week. I've been up here doing some business with Mister Gould at the railroad. My wife sends me a message every day saying she wants her brother out of jail." He held up a telegraph sheet to prove his point.

I nodded. "You want us to help you out with that?"

"Yes sir, Mister Stark, I do. You see, I don't trust my brother-in-law not to run off the first chance he gets and leave me on the hook for his bail. I don't want that to happen. I know he robbed those people. He's done it before. When I tell him I've got you all, and I show him a copy of the paper—"

"What paper?" I asked. I hadn't been out of the Henson Building, which was what I had decided to name me and Maggie's new business and home, all morning. I was waiting for Maggie to get up so we could go get breakfast. I couldn't believe she was still asleep. Especially with me sawing boards. I was starving.

"The newspaper." Forney reached into his jacket and took out a folded tabloid that I identified immediately as the Pioneer. He unfolded the paper and showed me the front page.

In boldface type, the headline read: STARK & BUCHANAN BAIL BONDS BRINGS THEM IN DEAD OR ALIVE!

I cringed at that. And me and Maggie hadn't gotten around to thinking of a name for the business.

"Anyway," Forney continued, "this is how this will work. I can pay you to bond that sorry no-account out of jail, my wife will stop crying to me about it, and he'll know if he runs who will come and fetch him. And that will be money well spent, if you ask me."

"I don't know if we do business in Fort Stockton," I said. Maggie and I hadn't discussed all that. I didn't even know enough about bail bonds to ask questions about what we could and couldn't do.

"We do," Maggie said as she walked up carrying a package. I'd been standing too far back in the door out of the sun to see her approach until she was up on us. "Mister Castor helped me set that up last week. I knew we'd probably end up doing business with the larger cities around us. We can write bail bonds in Fort Worth too." She extended her hand to our prospective client. "Mister Forney, I'm—"

"Maggie Buchanan," Forney said with a smile. "I know who you are. I got to say, miss, you're younger and prettier than I thought you'd be."

Maggie looked good that morning. She'd cleaned the black shirt and burgundy vest and hung them up before she went to bed. Her hair was clean and tied back in a braid. She didn't smell like a dead thing anymore.

"So you can help me, Miss Buchanan?" Forney asked.

"We can," Maggie said. "Why don't you follow me back to the office and we'll sign some contracts. We can get your brother out today."

He went with her.

We had contracts?

58

After Mister Forney had gone, I looked over the contract he'd signed. Maggie was counting the money he'd left and seemed happy enough to be doing it.

"We have contracts?" I asked.

"Yes. In order to make a binding agreement, you have to have a contract."

"I don't know anything about contracts."

"I'm sure Mister Henson had them too."

I thought about that and realized that Mister Henson had had contracts. I just hadn't dealt with them.

"How did you know about them?" I asked.

"I read about them in the law books Pa had." Those books sat in her office in a box for now. The office was still under construction but at least it had a desk and chairs, and it would have bookshelves when I was finished. "Then I visited with Murrey over at his office and asked him to look over what I had drawn up. He made a couple corrections and added a few lines to protect us. After that, I had them printed by Aiken. He wrote about it in the newspaper."

"I don't read the local paper," I said. I read the papers that came from the bigger cities on the train, and even then I didn't have much time for reading because I enjoyed the woodworking and building.

"I don't know everything about the business you do at

the sawmill either, Charlie. You trade out labor for time on the saws and for materials." Maggie leaned back in her chair and put her boots on the desk.

That bothered me a little because I'd finished that desk out so it would look impressive. Having scuffmarks from boots would take away some of that.

"I also don't know how to make joints or use veneer," she said.

"I could teach you."

She looked at me and raised an eyebrow. "I could teach you contracts. Do you want to learn?"

I looked at all the print and the words that looked familiar and foreign at the same time. "Not especially."

"Okay, then how about I handle this part of the business, you handle the construction of the building, and we'll meet in the middle when it comes to the heavy lifting?"

"All right."

She lifted the package and handed it to me. "That's takeout from Wick's. Breakfast. I got up at five and decided not to wait on you this morning because I wanted to see if there was any business in the wind."

I pointed at Forney's contract. "We've got one client. That's not a bad start to a day."

"Actually, this one is our fourth contract. I talked to three other people over at Wick's who needed a bail bondsman. I've got to write up contracts and get them out to folks this morning." She cocked an eyebrow at me. "Want to come along and deal with contracts?"

I sat down at her desk and pulled up a chair, then opened the box she'd brought me. "If it's all the same to you, I'll stay here and have breakfast. Then I'll finish framing out that jury box."

Her lips twitched and she took out three more contracts from her desk drawer and pulled her notebook from her shirt pocket.

"We'll be going after a bounty in two days," she said.

"Friday?"

"Yes. I had breakfast with Mister Castor this morning.

There's a fugitive who will be in Monahans in two days."

I knew Monahans. It was a fairly new town to the north and east of us, across the Pecos River. According to the local gossip from people who'd traveled through there, the town suffered from growing pains. It had been a trail camp for cattle drives for a few years before the Texas and Pacific Railroad had laid tracks through there three years ago. Now folks were moving in, hoping to better themselves with the boom the railroad provided.

"What kind of fugitive?" I asked, and I was thinking about the story the cargo handler on the train had told me about Maggie chasing a man through the woods.

"He's a con man named Luther Green," Maggie said. "He's wanted in San Antonio, Houston, New Orleans, and Nacogdoches by some bankers and businessmen for flim-flams he's run on some of them. They gathered together and put up the bounty because they think they can get some of their money back. Me, I don't figure a man like Green is much of a saver and they're just throwing good money after bad, but I'll take the bounty."

"We'll take the bounty," I said. Rounding up Luther Green didn't sound dangerous, but I didn't want Maggie out there alone.

"All right," she said.

"How did you find Green?" I asked.

"I didn't. Mister Castor did. He has some valuable contacts in a lot of railroad towns. By the way, we're cutting him in for ten percent of every bounty he helps us find. If that's agreeable."

I nodded and took out a piece of bacon from the pile of food Maggie had brought. It was still warm and that made me happy.

***

Over the next two days, Maggie wrote a few more contracts and moved money around through the bank to cover the bonds we'd agreed to. She kept me apprised of everything, even handed me a sheet of detailed notes every evening when we sat down to supper.

We hadn't even been in business a week, didn't have a finished out office, and we were already in the black.

The only thing that made me uneasy was the prospect of going after Luther Green, the conman. He wasn't a dangerous man by any accounts, but Monahans was. Any booming Texas town carried its own menace and troubles, and you could get wrapped up in them just by being in the wrong place at the wrong time.

On Friday morning, we packed our gear, got our horses, and went down to the depot. Less than an hour later, right on time, we rode the train on down the track to Monahans.

59

I talked the whole train ride to Monahans. Maggie probably got sick of it, but she didn't say that, though I caught her drifting off as the passenger car swayed. We drank coffee, which was a chore to keep from spilling, and I studied Luther Green's wanted poster and the notes Maggie had gotten from Morgan Castor.

The Pinkerton agent had a fine hand when it came to writing, which surprised me until I remembered those bird sketches he'd showed me and how good they were.

That got me to thinking about Maggie in that dress and how different she had looked. I guessed I grew quiet about that time because Maggie looked at me and asked, "Is something wrong?"

"Just thinking," I said.

"Everything's going to be okay, Charlie."

For a minute, I had the strangest feeling that she said that more for her benefit than for mine. So, because I wanted her to be reassured too, I said, "I know."

***

Once the train arrived at our destination, we got our horses and led them down the ramp. We'd brought an extra one to bring Luther Green back on.

Then we mounted up and rode on into town. Maggie

wore dungarees and another shirt that I'd never seen before, this one a dark green like bottle glass. She also wore a fringe leather buckskin jacket that hung down over her pistols.

I'd worn one of my black suits because I'd noticed that when I was wearing one of them, folks weren't so apt to treat me like a kid. I put that suit on and I armored up with a layer of respect I didn't get even with my size.

Monahans looked like it had been slapped together. New, unfinished timber formed the buildings along Main Street. There weren't many of them yet, but they had a post office and a Western Union.

The telegraph office seemed to come to every railroad town in short order because the railroad delivered telegraph wire and poles and used the train to move building crews and repair crews along as well. The railroad always used the telegraph to communicate with their workers too, so having the telegraph was good for everybody.

They also had a general store, a marshal's office, a blacksmith's foundry, a dentist's office, a barber shop, a livery, and a single-story hotel that was adding on a second floor. There were three saloons and two sporting houses because the railroad workers had to have places to blow off steam. Boisterous piano music came from the saloons and it sounded like everyone there was have a grand old time.

As we rode along the deeply rutted road cut by heavy wagons carrying equipment and deliveries, I said, "Did you know that all of this used to have Comanches, Lipan Apache, and Mescalero Indians living here only a few years ago?"

"No, Charlie."

Maggie didn't sound too interested, but I didn't let that stop me. I knew she was listening whether she wanted to or not.

"They were," I said, "until the railroad came through. Do you know why the town is named Monahans?" I'd done some asking around while I'd been working at the sawmill. Some of those men who worked there had done business in Monahans so there was news to be had.

"No," Maggie said as she swept the street with her gaze.

I didn't think a man like Luther Green would be out on the street during the heat of the day. He'd stick to the businesses while they were open, and he'd roll through the saloons at night. I'd seen such men in Pecos a few times, and it always surprised me how much folks were willing to trust in them.

Not all folks, though. Only the greedy ones. Mister Henson had told me that a confidence man didn't fool folks as much as he allowed folks wanting something for nothing to fool themselves. I hadn't understood at first, but I'd gradually figured it out.

"They named it Monahans after the surveyor who scouted out the land for the Texas and Pacific," I said. "While he was out surveying, he realized having enough water was going to be a problem for the workers and the livestock. At that time, the railroad crews were carrying water in from Big Spring, farther east. So Monahan, that was his name, dug a well and they named it Monahans Well. Without the apostrophe. That name just passed onto the town."

"They're not very creative here, are they?"

That seemed a little harsh to me, but I supposed Maggie was distracted by thinking about Luther Green and where our quarry might be, so I didn't comment.

***

We checked in with the town marshal and let him know our business. That was Maggie's idea. She said we didn't legally have to, but since her pa had been a marshal, she wanted to be respectful.

The marshal's office looked like it had been sublet from the barbershop next door. It consisted of two rooms. The front office and a jail in the back room.

Matthew Taylor was an experienced man from the look of him, but he didn't much care for bounty hunters. He looked whipcord lean and was brown as a nut. He parted his hair in the middle and wore a gunslinger mustache. Still, for all his taciturn nature, only outdone by Maggie, he was polite enough.

"I don't know this man." Taylor handed back the dodger Maggie had given him to look at. "I haven't seen him."

"That's fine, Marshal." Maggie folded up the dodger and replaced it in her jacket. "I didn't expect you to find him for us. We'll do that, and then we'll take him with us."

"You could turn him in here," Taylor pointed out.

"We could," Maggie said, "but for now, I'm doing business through the marshal's office in Pecos."

Taylor shrugged, taking no offense. "Suit yourself."

I knew that Maggie wanted to stick it in Stephens' face. I didn't blame her, but I knew that attitude could lead to trouble. That was a talk we'd have later.

"One thing to keep in mind, Miss Buchanan," Taylor said. "I'm a one-man shop. I got my hands full with handling the fights that break out in the saloons. Usually it's just men who drink too much, cheat at cards, or decide they're interested in the same woman. We don't get much in the way of criminals or shootouts here."

"I understand, Marshal," Maggie said.

"I don't expect there to be any nonsense like what happened in Sierra Blanca."

I was impressed he'd heard, but maybe Aikens's paper made it this far out, too.

Maggie stood then and put her hat back on. "The nonsense is up to the men we go after. I'm here to bring Luther Green to justice, just like I did those men in Sierra Blanca. How hard things go depend on the men we're chasing."

Taylor frowned, not happy with the answer, but he didn't say anything else so we showed ourselves out and checked into the Silver Sands Hotel two streets over from the marshal's office.

I was going to get two rooms, but Maggie said we only needed one because we'd be watching Green in shifts once we found him.

"Why?" I asked as I unpacked my other black suit and hung it up.

"Because the people paying the bounty want their money back too, Charlie." Maggie stood at the window and looked out at the dusty street.

"I don't think they'll get it."

"I don't either, but they definitely won't get it if we don't try to find it." She turned to look at me. "And before you ask why we should care, here's why. We're getting paid a dime on the dollar for all the money we find on Green when we take him."

"All right," I said.

60

That night, we found Luther Green pretending he was new to five-card stud at a table in The Watering Hole Saloon.

I told Maggie it was probably named on account of Monahans Well.

"Why am I not surprised?" she asked sarcastically.

I could tell she was in a mood, though I didn't know why. I thought maybe it was because I'd come along with her and she was regretting that now. So I got two coffees from the bar and settled in to shut my mouth and watch Green play cards.

The confidence man favored his dodger. He was thin but had a fleshy face and full tips. He wore a derby and a good, but cheap suit like one a traveling salesman might wear. He looked like this might have been his first time out West, and he acted like it too because he kept looking around and asking questions.

The three men he was playing cards with wore dirty clothes and looked like they probably worked on the railroad or on the water supply crews. Now that Monahans had extra water, they were shipping it both ways to markets that needed it.

Green was good at what he did. He would win one hand out of every nine or ten, so it looked like he lost more than he was winning. But those hands he won were bigger. I'd caught onto that. He also bought the men a round of beer every now and again, telling them he had a generous expense account from his employer.

"He's patient," I told Maggie, leaning in close to her so my voice wouldn't carry. "He takes every other big pot, and he doesn't go into the big pots he doesn't win."

She nodded.

"What I don't understand is why he doesn't have more money in front of him. He's won more than he's showing."

"That's because he has a partner," Maggie said.

"Who?"

"The redheaded saloon girl." Maggie nodded at one of the girls working the tables. "When he hits on a big pot, he orders another beer. He gives her the extra money to hide so he won't get caught with it if those men ever catch him bottom-dealing from the deck."

I'd already caught Green bottom-dealing, and the way he would hold back cards every now and again, then pull them back out to build a winning hand when he needed to. After the next hand he won, he ordered a beer and this time I saw him slip the saloon girl the cash.

"What happens if they catch him?" I asked.

"They'll take him outside and beat him and try to get their money back."

"But he won't have it."

"That's right."

"He's willing to take a beating?"

"They're not murderers, Charlie. Just men who got roped into a game they couldn't win. If they decide they're getting cheated, they'll beat on Green. Then they'll look for their money. When they don't find it, they'll assume they were drunk and he didn't win as much as they'd thought or that he spent it buying them drinks and acting like a big-shot."

"He's willing to get beat for that money? I didn't see enough on the table for me to get beaten."

Maggie's lips twitched. "It's not just about the money for a man like Green. It's about the game."

"Poker?"

"No. Being the smartest man in the room. Men like

Green get addicted to that feeling. It doesn't matter if he's stealing thousands from a company board by selling worthless stock certificates, or if he's playing nickel poker with men who can't even read. He plays for that rush."

"How do you know all this?"

"The same way you know how bones are supposed to fit together, Charlie. I had someone teach me and I learned by observing. I watched gamblers who plied their trade in Pecos after Pa taught me what to look for."

"Why didn't you arrest them?"

"Because it's one thing to know a man's cheating, but it's another to catch him. As Murrey would point out, cheating's even harder to prove in a court of law. And to be honest, juries don't feel much sympathy for a man who's gambling away his money. Especially if he has a family that is doing without on account of it. Those men won't press charges."

We watched for a while longer, watching as the other players dropped out and were replaced with more who were bored or wanted to try their luck, then Maggie yawned and excused herself, saying she was going to bed.

"I'll find you before daybreak. When you find out where Green's staying, leave a message for me at the hotel desk and I'll come find you."

We'd already discovered Green wasn't staying at the Silver Sands Hotel like we were.

I was surprised she was leaving out so early, but I told her good night. I went and got another coffee and settled in. I was starting to decide that bounty hunting was a lot more boring than I'd been led to believe.

Then I remembered the two dead men Maggie had brought in on the train and I realized that not all bounty hunting was boring.

61

As it turned out, Luther Green didn't have a room in one of the boardinghouses as we'd thought. He was staying with the saloon girl he'd partnered with during the poker game. She had a place in a house with other saloon girls on the outside of Monahans.

I followed both of them there after they left the saloon at three in the morning and stood in the woods that ended only a few feet from the house. The dwelling was in good shape, recently built, and was already showing signs of neglect.

The saloon was still open, but most of the men who wanted to drink and play cards had gone home. Early risers came in for the steak and eggs breakfast they sold. I'd wished I could have taken an order with me because I was hungry, but I'd had no time. I did manage to get off with a cup of coffee after I paid for the mug.

Once I was sure Green was going to be at the woman's home for at least a while, I went back to the Silver Sands and left a note for Maggie, along with directions to the house, in a sealed envelope. I told the desk clerk that Maggie would be down for it when she woke up. I left him a dime tip to make sure he wouldn't forget.

Then I went back to the house where Green was.

I walked around the house as quietly as I could and hoped no one saw me. Things would have gone sideways in a hurry if someone started wondering what I was doing out there.

But no one did and I found the girl's room at the back of the house. They counted money for a time, and both of them seemed happy with the night's take. They opened a bottle of whiskey and had a couple drinks. After that they turned out the lights and I couldn't see anything else. I didn't try. I just kept watch over the front door and Green's horse, which was in a corral out back of the house.

I stood twenty feet away in the shadows under the trees and worried about Marshal Taylor finding me where I wasn't supposed to be.

***

I was almost asleep on my feet, leaning against a tree, when Maggie found me just before daybreak.

"Where are they?" she asked.

I pointed out the room.

"Go back to the hotel and get some sleep."

I wanted to argue with her, to tell her that trying to find the missing money was a waste of time, and that it would be better if we just took Green and headed back to Pecos.

I knew she wouldn't agree, though, so I went back to the hotel and passed out when my head hit the pillow. I didn't understand how watching other people do nothing for a few hours could be more tiring than working in the sawmill all day, but it was.

***

I was out longer than I'd thought I would be. I guessed with all the work and worrying I'd been doing lately, and the extra hours of going without sleep yesterday had taken more out of me than I'd expected.

I took a quick rinse and dressed in my other suit. On my way out, I turned in the suit I'd worn yesterday to get cleaned with the hotel concierge. He told me he'd have it back in my room in a few hours, and it cost more than

Mister Kuáng ever did.

Maggie's note said Green was out hoping for a poker game at the saloons, so I looked for them and found her and Green at the Wet Your Whistle Saloon.

After seeing the saloon's name, I had to admit that the town lacked a lot in imagination. But the names would probably get better as time and legends took root.

The Wet Your Whistle was a step up from The Watering Hole and offered food as well as liquor, and the whiskey was good stuff from back East instead just made from raw alcohol and burned sugar flavored with chewing tobacco. The saloon catered to workers who were just getting off shift for the evening.

I smelled frying meat and thought I was going to die of hunger.

I joined Maggie at a table in the back.

Green was on the other side of the saloon with a higher class of poker player tonight. His opponents all wore suits too and I figured they were businessmen on their way to someplace else. They could jump from the Texas & Pacific to the Southern Pacific at Sierra Blanca and continue across the New Mexico and Arizona Territories into California if they wanted.

"Is he playing the same way?" I asked.

"Different saloon girl," Maggie answered, pointing at a short brunette who was a little older than the first woman Green had partnered with, "but the same setup."

I wondered if Green would be sleeping someplace new tonight, but I guessed I would find out soon enough.

"Have you eaten?" I asked.

Her lips twitched. "Hungry?"

"I missed breakfast and lunch."

"I'll eat whatever you're having."

I went to the bar and ordered two steaks with all the fixings. Monahans was definitely a cow town. The menu tended to be limited, and I wanted something more substantial than soup or stew.

Maggie ate with me and we sat and watched Green for a few hours. Finally, she left. I went to the counter and ordered another steak. Either they made them small here or I was hungrier than I thought.

At eleven o'clock, Green started checking his pocket watch a lot. He also began winning bigger and more often, which put the other men at the table on edge. His "good luck" finally worked against him and his fellow players spouted a few surly comments.

Forty minutes later, when it became apparent tempers were flaring, Green excused himself from the game and headed out, telling them that he'd had a long day and had a lot to do the next.

I got up to follow him, but I wasn't the only one. Two of the businessmen walked outside on his heels.

Outside, they turned and followed Green into the alley. I trailed after them all and had a bad feeling about what was about to happen. The men looked like they were all done talking.

Green looked over his shoulder, saw the men, and fled into the darkness. I thought he'd had enough of a head start and that quick jump to give them a run for their money. Literally.

Instead, they caught him before he reached the end of the alley. They walloped him pretty good, but he didn't cry out for help or anything. I didn't see any knives or brass knuckles, so I was hopeful they wouldn't kill him. I let them have at him because Green had it coming for taking their money. I think he was more afraid of getting arrested than of the men beating him. After all, there was that dodger out on him.

The men took what little money Green had, kicked him a few more times, and walked off. When they'd gone, Green rolled over onto his back and laughed. He was hurting, but obviously he thought everything that had happened was just good fun. Or maybe he was thinking that those men had paid for the privilege of beating him.

I realized then that Maggie was right. All of this was a game to Green. After a few more minutes, he slowly got to his feet. He leaned against the wall and was sick for a minute, then he wiped his mouth and walked to the other end of the alley.

Silent as a ghost, I followed and stayed in the shadows.

Out on the street, a buggy waited and Green staggered for it, then took just a minute to gather himself and walked straighter. The buggy's cover was up and I couldn't see who the driver was. One of the spokes on the right wheel was missing. I tended to notice details like that.

"You're late," a woman's voice announced with some ire.

"Sorry, love," Green said as he adjusted his clothing and smoothed his hair. He'd lost his hat. "A couple of the men I played poker with decided I wasn't playing quite on the up-and-up."

"Were you?" The voice sounded agonizingly familiar.

Green laughed and flicked his hand. A pair of cards, the ace of spades and the jack of diamonds, caught the soft light coming from the sporting house near the alley mouth.

"Oh," he said, "about as fair as you and I have been playing with the bankers in Houston and San Antonio. Which is to say, not at all." He laughed again, flicked his hand, and the cards disappeared. "I'm so glad you can join me on this next venture, Ellie. I do cherish your company."

Ellie? The name threw an immediate chill into me because I figured the chances of meeting two women who might be in the same line of work was pretty small. I stepped forward, risking the light because I needed to know more about the woman in that buggy.

"There's been a change in plans," the woman said. "Something's come up and I won't be able to join you in Santa Fe as we'd discussed."

"What's come up?" Green sounded disappointed and angry.

"Another job."

"Is there something in it I might be of assistance with?"

"No. This is gunplay, Luther. Not something you'd be especially handy with."

"All right." Green took the news calmly, but he didn't

sound happy about it. Or even to trusting of the woman.

"I'd already be gone now," she went on, "if I hadn't come here for my share of the money we got on that little trick we pulled in San Antonio."

"About that," Green said, "you see, the money—"

Light reflected on the small Derringer in the gloved hand that extended from the buggy. I knew that pistol in an instant. I'd taken it away from the owner not so long ago.

She leaned out a little so she could almost touch Green's head with the stubby barrel. The light lifted her face right out of the darkness.

"Don't try that on me, Luther," Ellie Deno said in a cold, menacing voice. "I'm not one of your marks. I'll put a bullet between your eyes before I listen to this song and dance."

Green smiled, but he knew he'd pushed his game too far. His expression looked a little sickly.

A thousand things must have slid through my mind right then, but most of them centered on Mister Henson's murder and how Marshal Buchanan had been shot before he could hang Courbet. Several people might have told Angelo Blunt that Courbet had been arrested, but I was sure Ellie Deno was one of them.

And she'd been the one to bring Angelo Blunt to Pecos to kill Mister Henson.

Maggie believed that Ellie Deno might know where Angelo Blunt was, and that was good enough for me. I did too. I wanted to take her in, and since I'd filed charges against her with Marshal Buchanan for trying to shoot me if not kill me, she was wanted in Pecos to stand charges.

I reached down for that Tranter at my hip. Then I was falling forward and the ground was coming up to meet me. I didn't remember hitting the ground.

62

I thought I'd gone blind when I woke up because all I could see was black, but then I realized I was lying on my stomach in the dark alley. My head felt like someone had used a go-devil on it, only it hadn't split like firewood.

I groaned as I sat up. The world tilted crazily around me, but I managed to put my back to the wall nearest me and not throw up. I was farther back inside the alley than I'd been and it was still night, so I was hopeful I hadn't lost too much time. I tried to get to my feet and, when that didn't work, I knew I was going to have to give it a minute.

When I touched the back of my head, I felt the swelling there and my fingers came away sticky with blood. I swallowed, but that was difficult because my mouth was so dry.

At first I thought maybe Green or Ellie Deno had had a compatriot watching over them and that person had spotted me, but I was pretty sure if that was the case, I'd be dead.

Then I thought maybe I'd been robbed, only the Tranter was still at my hip and I had all the cash money on me I'd started with.

I decided I'd just been in the wrong time at the wrong place, maybe mistaken for being someone else, or had just become a target for someone who'd had a bad night. That had happened to me in Pecos before too. The guy who'd jumped me was a stranger and had apologized when he saw that I wasn't who he thought I was.

I had no other explanation for what had happened.

Using the wall, I levered myself to my feet and stood there until most of the dizziness had faded. I staggered into motion, aiming for the street where I'd seen Green meet Ellie Deno.

At the corner of the alley, I peered out.

Ellie Deno and Luther Green were gone.

***

Maggie wasn't at the Silver Sands Hotel when I got there, and there was no note. I wanted to talk to her. I wanted to tell her about Ellie Deno because we might have a chance of catching her and finding out where Angelo Blunt was. If we found Green, I thought we'd find Ellie Deno too.

Not knowing what else to do, I decided to go to the house the saloon girl shared with the other women she worked with. Green had spent the night there and might spend this one there too.

It was the only lead I had.

***

When I arrived at the woman's house outside of town, I scouted around and was relieved to see Green standing out back smoking a cigarette. The saloon girl stood beside him with her arms folded.

"Do you think Alice is prettier than me?" the woman asked.

"No, of course not," Green answered. "Nobody's prettier than you."

"Then why did you work with her tonight?" She sounded like she was pouting.

Green turned to the woman. "Do you see my face?" He stood so the light from inside the room illuminated his features. One eye was swelled almost shut and his lips were puffy.

"Yeah."

"The guys I was playing against tonight jumped me in the alley when I left." Green laughed. "I did not have a good time, Holly. Do you think if they did this to you that you could show up and work tomorrow?"

Holly hesitated. "No. Probably not."

"No, you couldn't. You'd be hurting on top of losing wages. And here's something more to think about. Those men beat me up pretty good. If they thought you, a woman, were in on stealing their money, do you think they would have just stopped at giving you a whipping?"

Holly shook her head, and I could see then that she was realizing just now what could have happened. "Probably not."

"They wouldn't have," Green said. "You're a pretty woman. They wouldn't have been able to resist. It would have gone hard on you, Holly. I worked with Alice tonight for the same reason I change everyone I work with. So the marks don't know what happened to their money. I don't want you to get hurt. Don't you see that?"

"I guess so."

"Well, you should," Green said with righteous indignation. "You should thank me for making sure you didn't get the beating I took tonight. If you think about it, part of this beating should be yours."

"You were working with Alice tonight," Holly pointed out. "That beating was partly hers. Not mine."

"Well, that's true. But look at this: I may have worked with Alice tonight, but I came home to you."

"Some of the other girls say you only come here 'cause you don't have no place else to stay, Jesse," the young woman said.

"That's simply not true, Holly," Green responded. He took another puff on his cigarette and offered it to his companion. "You know that I love you. How could what we have between us be anything but love?"

"We have a pretty good business going with your poker cheating," Holly said. "There's that. But love? Ha!"

She shook her head. "You don't think I haven't had a lot of tinhorns, cowboys, four-flushers, and peddlers telling me the same thing over the last few years?" She took the proffered cigarette and took a puff. She didn't give it back.

Green lit another cigarette. "None of them has spoken more truly than I, dear girl."

While that might have been technically true, I noticed there was no promise in his words either. What he said just sounded nice.

"If Dean finds out what we've been doing when he gets back, he'll give you worse than those men did tonight."

"I'm not afraid of him."

Holly must have been pleased enough. She slid over closer to him and said, "I'm cold."

Green put his arm around her. "What do you say we go into your room, get out my profits from tonight, and roll around in them on the bed?"

"Did you get some of the good stuff?"

Green pulled a bottle from his jacket pocket. He hadn't had it earlier, so I knew he must have gotten it after I'd been knocked out. "Right here. They tell me it's the very finest of champagnes. We'll soon know."

The woman giggled and leaned into him. They kissed and headed into the house through the back door.

Someone touched me on the arm and I jerked around, my hand already dropping for the Tranter.

Maggie's hand dropped on top of mine and she leaned in close to whisper, "Leave it. You don't need it." Her perfume was faint, but I could detect it.

I stopped reaching for the pistol, grabbed her arm, and hustled her deeper into the woods so we could talk without being overheard.

"Luther Green is working with Ellie Deno, Maggie." I spoke in a rush and I couldn't hold back. "I saw them together earlier tonight. Just a few minutes ago, I think. I'm not sure. Somebody in the alley knocked me out."

"Do you know was she doing here?" Maggie asked.

"She's been working with Green in San Antonio and Houston. She came to Monahans to collect the money he owes her for her part in all that."

"Okay, Charlie. Just calm down."

I couldn't. Excitement rattled through me. "Maybe we can find her. We know where Green is. We can look for Ellie Deno now."

"Charlie, think for just a minute." Maggie looked at me. "Let's say we find Ellie Deno. Do you think she's going to tell us where Angelo Blunt is? Does she even know where he is? You have to ask yourself that."

Maggie was right. Ellie Deno hadn't told me anything useful the last time I'd talked to her. In fact, she'd even tried to shoot me.

And I had no way of knowing if Ellie Deno even knew where Blunt and his gang were.

"It'll be okay, Charlie," Maggie said gently. "We'll get Ellie Deno and we'll get Angelo Blunt. They'll pay for the things they've done. That's all part of the plan. You've just got to be patient a little longer."

I wanted to yell at her, but I didn't. The frustration I was feeling wasn't due to her. "I don't want to be patient."

Her lips twitched. "Want and need are two different things. You might not want to be patient, but you need to be."

I pushed out a long breath and tried to relax.

She reached out and touched my forehead. Her finger came away coated in crimson. "You're bleeding."

"I got hit pretty hard," I said.

She ran her fingers over my head and found the knot. "C'mon. Let's get back to the hotel and take care of this."

"What about Green?"

She nodded back at the window on the woman's room. It was already dark inside.

"He's in for the night," Maggie said. "We'll get a good night's sleep tonight and take him tomorrow. Then we'll get home."

Resting sounded good to me because my head felt like it was splitting open, and I was ready to get back home. But I couldn't stop thinking about Ellie Deno.

"Before we pick up Green," I said, "I want to look for Ellie Deno."

"We'll do that, Charlie." Maggie took me by the arm

and led me in the direction of the hotel. "Right now, let's just take care of you."

***

At the Silver Sands Hotel, Maggie used a pitcher of warm water to clean the top of my head. While she was scrubbing—and she was none to gentle about it, more concerned about getting the cut on my head cleaned out, I supposed—a moan escaped me.

"I'm so sorry, Charlie," Maggie said. "I didn't mean to hurt you."

"I'm okay," I said, feeling a little embarrassed.

She worked a little more gently and was finally satisfied she'd done all she could to clean the wound and be certain that I was going to be all right.

"There," she said, "that's better."

She wasn't the one dealing with the constant headache, though. But I didn't mention that.

When she was finished, we went to bed, and it was awkward because we only had the one room and the one bed. I volunteered to go see if another room was available, but she told me that was foolish because only half the night was left. I'd thought I was going to have a fight on my hands, but she agreed readily enough.

I sorted the sleeping arrangements out. Maggie took the bed and I slept in the armchair in one corner of the room.

I didn't remember my head resting against the chair back, but my last thoughts were of Ellie Deno, and I dreamed of Mister Henson's murder vividly, like I hadn't done in a while. Sleep came quickly, but it wasn't restful.

63

The next morning, we searched for Ellie Deno like nothing else mattered At least, I know I spent time at it like that. We split up the town and looked in every shop, saloon, and restaurant we found.

I found the buggy the woman used at the livery. The missing wheel spoke I remembered from last night was still missing. The buggy turned out to be a rental and didn't belong to anyone.

I paid the hostler there a dollar to let me see the rental agreement the woman who had taken it had signed. Maggie's lesson about contracts had stuck with me. Like her, I supposed, I was learning about manhunting, or woman hunting in this case, on the fly.

The name on the contract was Amalie Thompson. It meant nothing to me and I supposed it was just an alias Ellie Deno was using that may or may not have been in the notes Maggie had on the woman.

For another dollar, the hostler told me he'd just let me have the contract. I paid the dollar and took the contract, then folded it and stuck it inside my jacket. I didn't know if the contract could be used against Ellie Deno later in a court of law, but I thought it might be useful to have.

That was as close as I got to Ellie Deno that day.

***

I found Maggie at a table in The Watering Hole, which was the second saloon I checked. We'd agreed to search the saloons for Green after looking for Ellie Deno because once church was over that morning, we figured he'd head back to the poker games and the sheep he could find to shear.

I went in and sat. I reached for my hat before I remembered I'd lost it somewhere in the alley outside the Wet Your Whistle last night. I decided I was having no luck with new hats. I'd kept my old one for years, ever since my head had stopped growing, and I still had it.

"I found the buggy she rented last night," I said. I took the contract from my jacket and slid it across the table.

Maggie opened it, looked at it, and handed it back. "Amalie Thompson. That's not one of her known aliases."

I didn't remember all the detail stuff like Maggie did, so I just nodded.

"If nothing else," Maggie went on, "we've found one more name we can look for her under."

"Yeah." I was still frustrated.

"Patience, Charlie. That name is one more step closer to her."

I didn't say anything because I knew it would only be a waste of breath. Maggie already knew I was upset.

We'd been so close to Ellie Deno only to lose her. And I still didn't know how that had happened. The headache I'd gotten from being smacked over the head last night had been gone this morning, and most of the swelling too. I was glad of that because it had gotten tiresome last night. Maggie had fussed over the injury again this morning and I assured her I was fine.

We took turns eating lunch at the diner next door, then settled in to watch Green play cards. The train was pulling out at 4:08 for Pecos. Maggie had already bought three tickets. We intended to be there in time to board, but only just. We wanted to cut down on the confusion when we took the confidence man into custody. Getting him quick and clean and out the door was the plan.

Green was patient again today, playing slow and building his pots gradually, letting players cycle in and out of the game so there were no big losers. He was steady and the winnings trickled in. He worked that table like it was a job, like I'd plane a piece of wood until it was the right shape.

Holly was on hand again to bleed off cash as it needed to be.

Shortly after two, the wheels came off our plan.

Three men covered in red West Texas dust walked in through the door and scoured the saloon. A bad feeling took root in the pit of my stomach and started growing.

The man in front was nearly as tall as I was and was at least fifty pounds heavier. He had a broad face and bloodshot blue eyes. At least three days' growth of dark whiskers covered his chin and made the knife scar that ran from his right cheek to his jawline stand out.

Maggie sat up a little straighter.

"What is it?" I asked, not knowing what had sparked her interest.

"That," she said in a quiet voice, "is Dean Garlow."

The name meant nothing to me and I told her that.

"He's wanted for robbing an Atchison and Denver Railway train last year. One of the men with Garlow is Kurt Erhardt. I don't know who the other one is. Erhardt is wanted for bank robberies in Chicago and Denver."

Her memory of the dodgers she'd seen continued to astound me. When I'd remarked on it, she'd pointed out I was the same way with wood, which mostly looked all the same to her, and to various joints, which were just confusion for her. We each had our gifts, I supposed.

"You're not thinking of trying to take them in are you?" That prospect made me nervous.

"It would make for a nice payday," Maggie mused.

"There are three of them, Maggie."

"I can count." A calculating gleam lit her dark eyes. "It's not always about numbers, Charlie. There's a lot of finesse to this business. It's like chess."

I didn't know she played chess. There was still so much I didn't know about her.

"Says the woman who chased two fugitives through the woods in Sierra Blanca not even a week ago," I scoffed.

"I only chased after the one." Maggie watched the new arrivals with bright interest. "I had already killed the other one. And, as you recall, I caught the one I went after."

I couldn't say anything more. Maggie had faced four men in Sierra Blanca and had only faded bruises to show for it. All of those men were dead.

"Dean!" Holly called from Green's table where she was serving him a fresh beer. Her eyes went wide and she looked like she'd been caught doing something wrong. I remembered that Dean was the name of the man she'd warned Green about. The one she was cheating on.

"Holly!" Garlow crossed the room in long strides and grabbed the woman by the arm, almost yanking her from her feet.

Holly yelled in pain. "Stop! You're hurting me, Dean!"

Men at nearby tables started clearing off, easing out of the line of fire.

I didn't realize I was getting up from my chair until Maggie clamped a hand onto my arm. I regained my good sense in that moment, until Garlow backhanded Holly and knocked her to the floor. He pulled the pistol and aimed it at Green.

I went to shake off Maggie's arm, but she was already moving. I hurried to catch up.

"Is this the man you've been cheatin' on me with, Holly?" Garlow demanded. "Don't bother denyin' it. I ran into Klara an' she told me all about this gamblin' man you took up with." He glared at Green. "If you ask me, he don't look like so much."

"No, Dean!" Holly screamed as she wiped blood from her lip. "It ain't like that!"

Garlow rolled the pistol's hammer back while Green stared up into that barrel like he was hypnotized. Then Garlow pointed the Colt at Holly. He started to say something, but by that time I had hold of his gun wrist and yanked it up.

The Colt roared in his fist and the bullet tore into the ceiling with a deafening boom.

Everyone at the nearby tables who hadn't already been moving got up then and hurried away.

Still holding onto Garlow's wrist, I wheeled around and punched him in the face hard enough to knock him backward. The Colt came away in my hand and I tightened my grip on it, not wanting him to get it back and hoping he didn't have another one hidden somewhere on him. Garlow staggered and fell to the floor, landing in a sitting position.

Behind him, Maggie stepped into one of his two companions while they were watching me and moving in my direction. She drove her boot into the side of the man's knee and I heard the bone break like a rotten branch cracking.

He screamed in pain and went down on his face. He was hanging onto his pistol and trying to get back up when Maggie rapped him over the head with one of her pistols with a dull thud. He collapsed and stayed there limp as a dishrag.

Garlow glared up at me as he wiped blood from his mouth with the back of his hand. "Boy, that's one mistake you're gonna wish you could take back." He rose to his feet and doubled his fists, then he came at me full tilt.

64

Garlow rained punches on me and drove me back through sheer strength and size. I turned most of the blows away with my forearms and my hands, which caused me to drop the Colt I'd been holding onto. Only a few punches got through, but I shook them off. Then I got his rhythm.

I'd fought a lot of boys my age when I was growing up, and I fought them when they were young men too. There'd been others in the Ugly Toad and in the alley outside of the saloon. I'd learned to fight by fighting and got an even better education from the painful mistakes I'd made. I was good in a fight, and I always had that anger in me from those bad times at home before Mister Henson started raising me.

I looked for the openings Garlow gave me, and I hammered him when they were there. He was tough, though, and he weathered a lot of the punishment I gave him.

He threw a right punch at my head and I blocked it away with my left forearm. I drove a fist into his stomach and heard his breath rush out over my shoulder in a pain-filled groan. I let up a bit to check on Maggie and he crossed with his left fist and caught me full in the face, turning my head with the force of the blow.

I reeled back, tasting blood and no longer certain which way was up for a split-second. Then Garlow stepped into my face and filled my vision. He drove another fist at my head and I barely got my arms up in time to block. I slid away from his follow-up punch, then cut back and hammered him in the jaw twice before he wheeled around and roared curses.

He picked up a chair and flung it at me, then followed it as I batted it to the side. He hit me in a flying tackle and wrapped both big arms around me. We hit the floor and I lost my breath, but I rolled to the side quickly because I knew if he got up on top of me and took control, I was finished.

When I got him flipped over, I drove punches into his face. When he covered up, I pushed off and stood, gasping for air but getting what I needed so I could still go.

Garlow coughed and sputtered as he tried to get to his feet.

I knew he didn't have enough left to keep on for long, but I was so mad at everything that had happened with Ellie Deno last night that I was ready to beat on him some more. Fighting him felt good and burned through some of that anger I had stored up since Mister Henson had been murdered. I didn't want to stop.

"C'mon!" I shouted at him. "Don't quit on me now!"

Garlow snarled oaths that bubbled out in blood on his chin and chest.

I was hurting, but I felt ten feet tall.

"Are you done?" Maggie asked quietly.

I hadn't even heard her come up.

"I'm not," I said. "I'm waiting to see if he is."

Garlow pulled a long knife from his boot and tried to get to his feet.

Maggie pointed one of her pistols at him and eared the hammer back. "Dean Garlow, the bounty on you states you're wanted dead or alive. We aim to collect that bounty whether you walk in on your own two feet or I drag you in by your boot heels. So the choice is yours."

Garlow glared at her and considered his chances. I could see him doing the calculations, thinking maybe he had one more move in him that might be fast enough. Then he dropped the knife and raised his hands.

"You're going to regret doin' this," Garlow said. "I'm gonna—"

Me and the spectators didn't get to find out what Garlow had planned because Maggie stepped up and hammered him in the temple with her gun butt. Garlow dropped on his face and groaned, dazed and talking nonsense.

I took the pigging string I'd brought for Luther Green out of my pocket and tied Garlow's hands behind his back. Then, after the big man got sense enough to stand, I helped him get to his feet.

The first man Maggie had gotten hold of was still unconscious. I tied his hands behind him too, then hauled him up over my shoulder. His broken leg swung in directions it wasn't supposed to and I knew he was going to have a bad time of it when he woke up.

The other man sat on his knees with his fingers laced behind his head where Maggie had left him. She tied him up while I kept a gun on him.

"Luther Green," Maggie said, as she stepped back from her latest prisoner.

The confidence man was headed out the back door. I'd forgotten him. I didn't know how Maggie had kept track of everything.

"If you make me chase you," Maggie said, "you will regret it."

Green halted.

"Get over here," Maggie commanded.

Meekly, Green joined our group, but he couldn't give up easily. "Miss, I promise you that no matter what you think, I am most assuredly not the man you're looking for."

"You answered to your name when I called you," Maggie pointed out.

Green thought about that for a minute, then nodded. "I concede your point. In all the excitement, I forgot myself."

"Hands," Maggie said.

He held them up and she tied them.

"Hey," a man in the crowd called out to me.

I looked at him.

"Aren't you that undertaker's kid? The one that was over in Pecos that Angelo Blunt murdered?"

"I am," I said. "I'm Charlie Stark." I chose not to correct his thinking that Mister Henson was my father. In truth, Mister Henson was the only father I had ever known.

"Of Stark and Buchanan Bail Bonds," Maggie said as she turned Green and the other men toward the saloon's front door. "If you know someone who needs bonding, let them know we're set up in Pecos and are willing to travel."

"I will," the man said. He shook his head. "The undertaker's kid is a bounty man."

"Bail bondsman," Maggie corrected.

"Yeah, that, too," the man said.

Then we walked our captives over to the marshal's office.

***

"You said you and Miss Buchanan are catching the train at four." Marshal Taylor turned the key on the cell lock and stared at the four men we'd taken prisoner who were sitting and lying inside.

The unconscious man was still out and Taylor had sent one of the crowd who had followed us over from The Watering Hole to fetch a doctor.

"We are," I said. "That reminds me. I need to go buy three more tickets."

Maggie had left to run an errand, following up on a hunch she had, she'd said.

"If you'll be okay with these men here," I told the marshal, "I'll go buy those tickets now."

"Go get them," Taylor said. "Y'all are paying rent on this jail, and me. They're not going anywhere. I'll be glad to see all y'all go." He shook his head. "The sooner y'all get out of my town, the happier I'll be. It seems y'all draw trouble like a cow pie draws flies."

***

By the time I got back from buying tickets, Maggie was sitting with the marshal in his office and drinking coffee. Taylor seemed to be in better spirits, but neither of them was saying much. Now that the show was over, most of the saloon crowd had drifted back to where they'd come from.

Maggie had a beat-up suitcase at her feet that we hadn't brought with us.

I looked at her.

She reached down and opened the suitcase, revealing stacks of greenbacks. "I estimated there's twenty-eight thousand dollars in here. Green was keeping it under the floorboards in Holly's room."

"How did you know it would be there?" I asked.

"I didn't, but where else was he going to hide it? As far as we knew, Green wasn't staying anywhere else. Folks tend to hide stuff they want to get at quick, or don't want anyone else to know about, in places that are close to them. I've had to find stuff before when I was working as a deputy."

I nodded and couldn't help thinking about Mister Henson's map hidden in my bedroom.

"There's also some banking paperwork in there," Maggie said. "The folks he cheated out of their money might be able to use to track their lost investments and make a case to get it back. We'll get ten percent of that, too, if they have any luck."

I sat down because my head was hurting and I couldn't believe we'd survived taking Garlow and the others in, and we were making a big profit off all of it to boot.

A young man with a medical bag knocked at the door.

"Doc White," Taylor said. He waved the man in and got to his feet. He picked up his key ring. "Your patient's back here. He's not awake yet, which is a good thing, I think. I need you to get him to where they can transport him because they're leaving on the train in an hour or so."

The marshal and doctor walked toward the jail in the back.

"I rented a buckboard from the livery," Maggie said.

"That's good." I hadn't thought of that and I should have. But then we'd have had two buckboards. My brain was reeling, and it wasn't just from getting hit last night and being used as a punching bag this afternoon.

"I also talked to Green about Ellie Deno," Maggie said.

The line at the ticket office had been long, and I'd had to wait because the ticket seller had been down to The Watering Hole catching up on the news. But I hadn't been gone that long. She must have talked fast.

"Did he give you anything?" I asked.

"No. Green and Ellie Deno did whatever they did together down in San Antonio and Houston, where they had to split up because not everything went according to plan. As far as Green knows, Ellie Deno hasn't seen Blunt in weeks."

Disappointed, I tried to stretch out my back, which was stiffening a little from the fight. "Do you believe him?"

"I don't know." Maggie sipped her coffee. "I know that before Green gets taken from the Pecos jail, we should have more time to talk to him."

"Then we'll do that," I said.

65

By the time we loaded our prisoners onto the train, several passengers knew who we were. At least, they knew who I was. They had gotten the story wrong, though, because they were referring to me as "the undertaker from Pecos."

"It's the suit," Maggie told me as we sat behind the seats we'd put our prisoners in. She'd borrowed handcuffs and ankle manacles from Taylor and had promised to send them back by train the next day. She'd also written down a line in her notebook about adding more manacles to our traveling kit when we went manhunting. Her lips twitched. "You might want to think about a new look."

I looked down at my black suit that was now covered in dirt and whatever had been on the floor of The Watering Hole. I'd have plenty of laundry for Missus Kuáng to tend to when we got back to Pecos.

I shook my head. "No. I'm not going to change my look." I liked the clean lines of the suit, and the fact that I had worn one similar like it when I'd worked with Mister Henson. That black suit was a way of keeping him with me.

"Well, you're going to have to have it cleaned. We have an image to present. You can look however you want when you're woodworking, but I want a more professional look when we're doing our business."

I grinned at her. "Stark and Buchanan. Bail bondsmen

and bounty hunters."

"We're not going to advertise the second part," Maggie said. "We'll pick and choose our own jobs there as we need them. Or when we want to get out of Pecos for a time. There's no reason not to make a vacation every now and again pay for itself."

I leaned back in my chair and tried to find a comfortable position. "You know, ever since we partnered up, it doesn't seem like I've had a day off."

She cocked an eyebrow. "You want a day off?"

I thought about it, then tried to think of something I'd do with a day off. I shook my head. "No. I'm not a fisherman or a hunter. I like building things, Maggie. That doesn't feel like work."

"Then, when we get back, you should concentrate on your woodworking."

I was happy at that prospect, but I wondered about her. I didn't want her riding off again by herself. There was no telling what trouble she would get into. "What are you going to do?"

"I'll manage the bonding business, of course. Write contracts. Make sure the courts get the documents they need. Go fetch the occasional lunch or dinner. And help you when you need another pair of hands."

I nodded. "That sounds good."

"I know." Maggie settled back into her seat. "The part I like most is that we're going home."

I grinned at her, but I knew how she felt, and I was glad we felt the same way. I was looking forward to spending a few days without thinking about Angelo Blunt or Ellie Deno.

***

Aiken was waiting at the marshal's office when we arrived in Pecos just after nightfall.

"I got news about the arrests in Monahans over the telegraph," the newspaperman said. He held his notebook ready. "I just want to confirm who you have with you." He glanced at the buckboard and started writing.

Maggie named our prisoners, including Raymond Coker, whom we had not known at the time we took in Green, Garlow, and Erhardt. Coker was in the newest batch of wanted posters in Taylor's office. He had robbed a train in the Indian Territories.

Maggie had found Coker in the dodges. I hadn't even thought to look. I was thinking more about Ellie Deno and how she'd disappeared so suddenly.

Stephens wasn't glad to see us either. He frowned at Maggie as we marched the fugitives inside the jail. Erhardt limped on crutches we'd paid for. Maggie had gotten a receipt for the doctor's visit and the crutches for Erhardt. She'd said it was worth a letter to the principals on the bounty to find out if we could get reimbursed for the expenses.

"This is my jail, Maggie," Stephens said. "And it's not up for you to annex as a prisoner hotel."

"You get paid for their keep," Maggie said. "You should be thanking me for bringing you business. If you don't want it, I'm sure Charlie could build a jail, too."

For a minute, I was afraid she was serious. Maybe she was. But Stephens backed down and stepped out of her way.

Aiken laughed at the exchange, but quickly stopped when Stephens glared at him.

"Get out of my jail!" Stephens roared at the newspaperman.

"Of course, Marshal," Aiken said. "Can I quote your reason for kicking me out of the marshal's office as because Stark and Buchanan Bounty Hunters filled it to capacity?"

"Do anything you please!" Stephens shouted. "Just get out!"

"Thank you, Marshal. This may be worth getting an extra edition out tomorrow." Aiken hurried through the door and he had a big smile on his face.

One of Stephens' deputies looked at me. "Ever since you two went into business, Aiken's been publishing the paper more frequently. Folks like reading what he's been writing."

That made me feel good.

After we'd gotten a receipt for the prisoners and the markers for the bank, we walked back outside.

"I'll take the buckboard back," I volunteered. "You can go on home if you want to."

Maggie pulled herself up into the buckboard. "That's all right. We'll go there together."

"Let's pick up something to eat from Cactus Slim's when we go." I took up the reins and shook them out to get the team moving. Our horses were tied to the rear and plodded along after the buckboard.

She nodded.

As we passed by Wick's, I spotted Aiken out front talking with some folks who had been passengers on the train with us. They were laughing and seemed to be in the midst of a good time.

***

It felt good to be back home at the Henson Building. As me and Maggie walked over to our home and business from the livery, I speculated on how I could mark the building's name on it.

"What are you thinking about?" Maggie asked. "It's not like you to be so quiet."

I told her what I was thinking about the building's name.

"I think it's a good idea," she said.

She was even more quiet than usual, but I suspected she was just as tired as I was.

"You took a foolish risk fighting Garlow like you did today," Maggie said as she put the key into the door lock and turned it.

"I did all right."

"You didn't have to fight him. You could have shot him."

"Shooting someone isn't my first thought when I have a problem," I said.

"You might have fewer problems if it was. Folks who know you would shoot them would think twice about doing anything that would get themselves shot in the first place."

There was something wrong with her logic, but I didn't want to get into that now.

I told her I'd think about that and reached for the lantern I'd left hanging on the wall by the door. I raised the hurricane glass, lit the candle inside, and slid the glass back down.

The golden glow of the wick flame swelling to push back some of the shadows trapped in the large room cheered me a little. Until I saw how much work remained to get everything ready for Judge Caldwell's courtroom. Then I realized I'd be able to concentrate on it steady for a few days.

Thinking about working in the sawmill, building again instead of staking out saloons and looking for bad men, cheered me too.

I was also looking forward to the Mexican food me and Maggie had brought home. My stomach was already rumbling in anticipation.

We took the stairs up to the second floor and I liked how steady and solid they felt beneath us. I'd done a good job and I knew it.

All my good cheer and happy thoughts went away the minute that golden light hit our shattered door.

66

By the time I eased the food to the floor and out of the way on the landing, Maggie had her guns in her hands. I didn't just drop the food because I didn't want it to make noise. I was so stunned by finding the broken door that I didn't think that if anyone was still inside our rooms, he would have already heard us coming up the steps. Or maybe I didn't want to go hungry.

I drew that Tranter and started forward, but Maggie was already through the door, disappearing into the darkness that waited on the other side of the doorway.

I held the lantern away from my body as I walked in behind her, thinking that if someone shot at the light they might miss me.

Moonlight filtered in through the curtained windows. Normally, the kitchen and living room always looked different during the night hours, but with papers and furniture strewn all over everything, the place didn't even look like our home.

Or maybe it was just that our private space had been invaded and I knew there was no getting back that sense of security we'd lost upon seeing the damage.

Me and Maggie made quick work of searching our rooms, but no one was there.

"Whoever did this came and went," I said. I holstered the Tranter and saw that my hands were shaking a little. It was out of anger, though, not fear.

My first thought had been that we were going to find Angelo Blunt in there. No matter where I went or what I did, Blunt haunted my thoughts. Nobody ever made me feel more vulnerable.

"Is anything missing?" Maggie asked. She struck matches and lit the other lanterns that we used in the rooms.

The extra light removed some of the emotional turmoil that was banging inside me like a rumba of agitated rattle-snakes. My knees felt weak and my breath came short. If I hadn't been scared and mad like this before, I wouldn't have known what it was that was passing through me.

"Not that I can see up here. Let me go check down-stairs. My tools are down there."

I went down and looked, but everything was there. I brought the food in too.

When I returned, Maggie was sitting at the kitchen table.

"This doesn't make any sense," Maggie said as she set the food out. "Are you sure nothing's missing?"

"I'm sure." I looked at the food, and then I thought about Mister Henson's map. "Let me go check one thing."

"All right."

I went back to my bedroom with a lantern and checked the hiding spot where I'd tucked Mister Henson's map to the gold down in Chihuahua City. I didn't know how I'd missed the broken section of wall when I'd first gone through there, but the map hadn't even crossed my mind. I'd been looking for thieves.

I checked the hollow space, but it was empty just like I knew it would be.

I slammed my fist into the wall in frustration. The noise brought Maggie and she stopped at the door.

"What's wrong?" she asked.

"Mister Henson had a map of where that Mexican gold was," I said. "That's what I found in his casket that day Courbet came to kill me. That's what Ellie Deno was hanging around Mister Henson for. She wanted to know where the gold was." I looked at the empty space. "And now it's gone."

"Charlie," Maggie said, "why don't you come to the table and sit. Get something to eat. You'll feel better."

Not knowing what else to do, feeling useless and mad and hurt, I went. I sat at the table for a long time and Maggie waited on me.

Finally, I said, "Maggie, I'm sorry. There are things I didn't tell you that I probably should have."

"It'll be all right."

"It's about Mister Henson." My voice broke. "He wasn't always Mister Henson. He used to be a man named Petway, and he wasn't a good man then. But he was a good man when I knew him."

She sat quietly and watched me.

Then I told her the story, everything I knew about Mister Henson, Angelo Blunt and his pa, and Ellie Deno. How all of them had gotten tied together over that gold that was supposed to be hidden down somewhere in Mexico City.

When I finished, I was quiet for a time. Then I looked at her, afraid of the betrayal I would see in her eyes. We'd agreed that we weren't going to lie to each other, that we would only have the truth between us because anything else would have ruined our friendship.

Instead, Maggie reached out and patted my arm. "It'll be okay, Charlie. Everything is going according to plan."

She'd said that before, and I still didn't see a plan. We were working toward something, but it seemed like every step forward we took, we slid two steps back.

She took her hand back. "You should eat. It's important to eat," she told me. "And then you should sleep because you need to be rested if you're going to work on the courthouse tomorrow."

I wiped my eyes because they were blurry. I figured it was from the long day.

We didn't talk anymore, even though I wanted to. But I was afraid of what might be said, and I was already afraid of what had just been said about what hadn't been said before.

We ate, and there was no enjoyment in it like I had looked forward to. Then, at Maggie's suggestion, we went to bed. I was afraid Maggie would be gone in the morning because I had broken her trust.

My sleep was not good. I was haunted by memories of Mister Henson and Angelo Blunt and Ellie Deno. In some of them, Mexican soldiers and outlaws chased me and I had no gun, nowhere to hide.

I looked for Maggie everywhere I went, and the thing that hurt me most was that I couldn't find her.

67

In the morning, I felt horrible. I lay in my bed because I didn't want to get up. I was afraid Maggie would be gone and I just didn't want to deal with that.

Then the smell of fresh coffee and bacon wandered in from the kitchen. My stomach grumbled.

Cautiously, I got up and dressed in dungarees and a flannel shirt. Then I opened the door to see Maggie standing at the potbelly stove. She was dressed for the day in dungarees and a dark blue shirt.

The kitchen and living room were clean, so I knew she'd been up for a while.

"Good morning," she said. "I was going to give you a few more minutes, then I was going to wake you."

"What time is it?" I asked.

"Seven-thirty." She took bacon from the frying pan and laid the pieces on a plate. "How do you want your eggs?"

"Any way you want to cook them." I was so happy she was there I didn't know what to do.

"Scrambled," she said, and reached for the eggs. "Sit down. Have some coffee. Then you've got to get to the sawmill."

"What are you going to do?" I sat.

"I," she said, "am going to the bank to take care of the bounty money, see that everything ends up where it's supposed to be, and pay the bills."

I couldn't believe she was talking so calmly. Inside, I was flailing, trying to find firm ground to anchor myself to.

"It's time to pay bills again?" I asked. That seemed real and normal.

Her lips twitched. "You need to pay attention to the calendar."

"I've been kind of busy."

"I know. Now you relax. Eat breakfast and go work. That will clear your head. Everything is going to be okay."

***

After I ate, I went down to the sawmill because I got the sense from Maggie that she wanted me out from underfoot while she took care of the things she saw needing attention.

I planed some boards for the judge's bench, getting them smooth and straight and down to the right thickness. I was going to do a good job on it. I'd taken the necessary measurements from the courthouse we'd visited in Fort Stockton.

As it turned out, Donald Bailey, the owner of the sawmill was two men short and had a big project due, so he asked me if I would help. So I did. I welcomed the hard work and put myself into it. The constant scream of the saws chewing through timber made thinking almost impossible and I welcomed that respite.

By noon I was sweaty and covered in sawdust. Bailey sent out for sandwiches from Trail's End, and me and him and the other workers sat outside in the sun and ate them.

It felt good being tired from hard labor, honest labor, and the sun felt good again. I tried to let go of the loss of Mister Henson's map. He didn't need it anymore, and I had no interest in that gold.

The only interruption in the day was when one of the hands brought in the recent edition of the Pioneer. Aiken had covered the article on me and Maggie bringing in the outlaws from Monahans in lurid prose.

In the article, I was referred to as "The Pecos Under-taker," taken from a quote Aiken had dug out of one of the men who had seen the fight in The Watering Hole.

One of the men, Brian Hitch, read the story while the others listened. I left to go back to work after I'd heard the line about me being the undertaker.

After that, all of Bailey's hands treated me a little differently and didn't talk to me, like they were afraid of me or something.

The day didn't turn out to be as relaxing as I'd thought it would be. I worked until seven because Bailey needed everybody to put in some overtime to get the order finished. After that, he marked my time in his book, told me whatever I needed when I needed it, it was mine.

He was the only one that acted the same at the end of the day.

I thought he could tell how the notoriety was affecting me because before I left, he told me, "Don't worry about it, Charlie. Give those boys a little time and they'll figure out that you're the same person you were when you came in this morning."

I told him that I hoped so, and I headed home.

***

I lit the lantern at the door, took a look around at the mess that covered the first floor, thought maybe I'd work on that tomorrow instead of going down to the sawmill, and headed upstairs.

I didn't expect supper to be on the table, either takeout or prepared, but I'd expected Maggie to be home. It was well after banking hours, but I thought maybe she'd lain down, though that wouldn't have been like her.

I lit the other lanterns in the room and chased away the darkness. Then I knocked on her door and called her name.

There was no answer, so I knocked louder, still got no response, and decided to peek into her room in case something was wrong.

I held the lantern up so I could see, figuring I was going to get bawled out for waking her. I would have been okay with that. As long as I knew everything was all right.

Her bed was neatly made and she wasn't in it.

***

I made a fried egg sandwich that I thought would hold me till Maggie got home. She still wasn't there at eleven and I took a seat in the armchair to wait for her. I was worried about her but going to look for her and not knowing where to start looking didn't make sense. So I forced myself to stay calm. Ultimately, the chair was comfortable and I was exhausted.

I slept and didn't wake up again till four in the morning. I knew something was wrong. If Maggie had come in after me, she would have awakened me and sent me to bed. She'd done that in the past.

Although I knew she hadn't come home, I had to see for myself.

The lanterns still burned around me and illuminated the rooms. I took the closest lantern and walked to Maggie's door. I knocked just to make sure, but there was no answer.

I opened the door and the bed was still made.

My heart broke when I considered the idea that the reason she wasn't there was because I hadn't told her the truth about Mister Henson and the map and the gold.

I had fractured that trust between us.

I almost wept because I felt so bad, then I caught the faint fragrance of her perfume. I took in a deep breath and I realized what had happened.

All of it fell into place. How I'd gotten knocked unconscious in Monahans and how I'd come home to find out Mister Henson's map had been taken.

I cursed myself for being so stupid.

I entered Maggie's room for the first time since I helped her move in and set up her bed. That day, I'd also presented her with the gun cabinet that hung on the wall to the right of her bed.

When I opened the cabinet, I saw that her Winchester and the Greener shotgun her pa had given her were gone.

She was hunting.

And I knew where she was going.

That fragrance had explained so much.

68

"Charlie, do you know what time it is?" Missus Frederiks stood in the doorway of her boardinghouse and looked frightened. She held her housecoat closed tight at her throat. "The folks here are hardly stirring."

I knew I looked scary. I was dressed in one of my black suits and I wore the Tranter at my hip. My Winchester hung from a sling over my shoulder. Back at the hitching post, my horse was winded from the run over here.

"Yes, ma'am, I do know what time it is," I told her, "and I'm sorry about this. But this is important, Missus Frederiks. I wouldn't be here otherwise."

My earnestness must have struck a chord in her, because she became concerned. "Is it that young woman? Maggie Buchanan? Has something happened to her?"

"Not that I know of, but I need to speak to Mister Castor."

She hesitated a moment, then stepped back and swung the door open to its fullest. "Where is she?"

"Who?" I asked, because my mind was jumping so fast, putting so many things together that I couldn't keep up with everything, much less my conversation with Missus Frederiks.

"Maggie Buchanan," Missus Frederiks said. "Where is she?"

"I don't know, ma'am. That's what I came here to see Mister Castor about." I could have said she was in Chihuahua City, because I knew that's where she'd gone.

But I didn't. I didn't want anyone else to know our business, and I knew Missus Frederiks, as well-meaning as she was, talked.

Also, I was thinking that Maggie had almost a twenty-four hour lead on me. By the time I caught the train and headed Chihuahua City, she'd be a full day ahead of me.

She could be dead a day before I got there if this went really badly.

I tried not to think about that as Missus Frederiks walked me back to Castor's room.

Before Missus Frederiks could knock, Castor opened the door and looked up at me from his wheelchair. He was already dressed and a suitcase lay in his lap, keeping company with a Sharps rifle.

"I was beginning to think you might not put it together," Castor growled. He rolled out of the room on his own, shoving on the wheels and making me get out of the way. "I thought I was going to have to do this myself."

"Do you know where Maggie is?" I asked.

"Of course I do. Who do you think helped her figure out where in Chihuahua City she needed to go?" Castor rolled past me and Missus Frederiks barely managed to stay ahead of him.

"I knew it was you."

Castor stopped in the large kitchen area and sat there looking up at me. "Don't just stand there. Missus Frederik has a buckboard out in the stable behind the house we can use to get to the train station." He looked over his shoulder at Missus Frederiks. "Missus Frederiks, we'll need the loan of the buckboard this morning."

"Of course," Missus Frederiks agreed.

"I'll see to it that you get it back this morning." Castor turned to me. "Go! The train leaves early."

***

"You knew she was going to Chihuahua City?" I asked as I drove the buckboard toward the train station. Lanterns on both sides of the buckboard bounced with the motion and cut through the night still around us.

Castor sat in the cargo area of the buckboard with his wheelchair, suitcase, and buffalo rifle. "She told me she was going."

I was going along at a pretty good clip, pushing the horses, and Castor bounced around in the back.

"When did she tell you?" I asked.

"A few weeks ago when she put this whole plan together. She'd had me looking for Ellie Deno because she thought Ellie Deno would turn up before Angelo Blunt. She was right. She's a smart one, she is. And as stubborn as any I've ever seen."

I silently agreed. "Maggie knew about the map I was hiding."

"She did. She knew about it the day you got it from Henson's casket. Not much gets by that young woman."

"She never told me," I said bitterly.

"She said you hid the map from her, so she didn't want you to know she knew." Castor shook his head. "You two have got a complicated partnership, if you ask me. You're too concerned with protecting one another to really work together."

"We'd talked about this," I said. "I thought we were over it."

"Did you tell her about the map then?"

Guilt gnawed at me and I knew everything was as much my fault as Maggie's. "No. I should have."

"Well you didn't. That's why she took matters into her own hands."

69

"She took the map to you?" I asked Castor.

"Yes. She knew I'd been down to Chihuahua City and might know my way around. I did. Those points Henson marked on that map are landmarks. The angel represents the Church of the Holy Cross. It's a big church that's over a hundred years old. That church was mostly paid for by silver mine owners after a man named Juan Antonio Trasviña y Retes deeded the land to the Catholics."

When I hit a straightaway in the road, I laid the traces across the backs of the horses and got us up to a faster speed. I almost overran the light from the lanterns, but I was working on memory of the road too.

"The pistol symbol marks the Plaza de Armas, which means Weapons Square," Castor continued, "and it was used as a parade ground by the conquistadores back when they were taking over Mexico. That was the place they retreated to if the city was attacked. The Spanish borrowed that little trick from the Romans."

"Is that where the gold is?" I was getting anxious.

"No. I'm getting to that. The angel and pistol are just two of the reference points. The third reference point, as close as I could figure, is the Mexican eagle. It's known in Spanish as águila real."

"Royal eagle." I knew the term. "That's why the bird has a crown on its head."

"Right. In this case, Henson used it to mark the building where Benito Juárez set up his temporary government while the French occupied Mexico City. The Mexicans kept part of their treasury there, and that's what Henson and his group tried to get out of there with."

Castor adjusted himself with his arms, pulling his body into a different position, but it didn't make the ride any easier.

"Where's the gold?" I asked as I steered the team onto Main Street. We rolled over the ruts as fast as we could, and I saw there were already a few people headed into Wick's Diner.

Some of them paused to look, but nobody called out.

The train depot was at the other end of town.

"According to the note written on back of the map, the gold was left in a village east of Chihuahua City," Castor said. "Only a few miles out. That was all they could do with the federales breathing down their necks while they were hiding out. They dropped it down the well in that village and covered it over with rock, would be my guess, then poisoned the water."

"The well wasn't on the map I found."

"Not a symbol, no, but the well was marked there in Spanish. Pozo de Agua de veneno. You didn't know that?"

"I don't read Spanish. That's why I couldn't read the note. I know agua means water. I didn't know what the rest of it meant."

Castor nodded. "Maggie pieced it together before she came to me and I confirmed what she was thinking. I figured out the symbols so we'd know where to look, but she knew there was a well. I just helped her figure out where it was."

"How do you know the well was poisoned?"

"Because it says so right in the name. Veneno means poison. That's one you might want to learn to read. Once Maggie and I knew what we were looking for, I contacted some historians I know in Washington, D. C. and New York. People who are starting to specialize in Mexican history. Because of all the unrest going on down there, the United States government has decided to keep an eye on things."

I slowed down as we got closer to the depot.

"It took a couple weeks before we got a reply, but one of those men I talked to told me there had been reports of a poisoned well that forced a village in that area to pull up stakes and leave because of bad water."

"How do you poison a well?" I'd never heard of such a thing.

"I suspect when we find that well," Castor said, "you'll find a bunch of chicken bones in it. The easiest way to poison a water supply is to throw in dead things, and chickens are plentiful and easy to transport. Soldiers have been doing that to poison the water sources of their enemies since war was invented."

I couldn't help thinking that was one more thing I wished I'd never learned about Mister Henson and the way he used to be.

I pulled the team to a halt in front of the small livery by the depot and set the brake. I turned to Castor. "What do you mean, when we find that well?"

"I'm going with you."

"No—"

Castor shut me up with a hand. "I'm not going to have this argument again. Maggie won it last time because she was going to go down there with or without my help. She made me promise I wouldn't tell you, and I didn't , but I had made other arrangements to deal with this. Then you showed up and I'm not turning you away. I am taking you and you are taking me because we need each other's help and Maggie is already a day ahead of us. Is that clear?"

It didn't take me long to chew that over. The train would be boarding soon.

"You don't speak the lingo well enough," Castor said. "You don't read it. You don't know anyone down there. And you don't know your way around down there."

I looked at his wheelchair.

"Yes," he said, "I know I've got some problems. I can't walk and I'm old, but that doesn't mean I'm worthless. I can shoot the ears off a mosquito with this Sharps. And a couple of my friends are going to join us on the train when we reach El Paso. Like I said, I planned for this. I've already wired ahead and they'll be waiting."

He looked at me sharply. "You've also got problems, Charlie. Your partner is down there in hostile land and planning on taking on Angelo Blunt and whoever he's got riding with him."

"What does she think she's doing?" I asked.

"She means to kill Angelo Blunt," Castor said.

"How does she expect to get out of that alive?"

Castor studied me. "I don't think she's planning on that, Charlie. That's why I need you. You're the only one I can think of who might give that young woman a reason to live."

"What do you mean?"

"I know you know she has problems." Castor looked uncomfortable. "She doesn't latch onto folks on a personal level. You're not much better, but you are. And I know you care about Maggie."

"I do."

"I'm just hoping that she cares enough about you to consider living the rest of her life. Otherwise we're going to lose her."

"She's your friend too."

Castor shook his head. "No, I'm an acquaintance. She talks business with me. Outlaws. The law. Things about policing that her pa couldn't teach her. I am a means to an end for her. Just like the way she used me to figure out that map."

"Why didn't you tell me about this?"

"Maggie didn't want me to, and I didn't want to lose what little contact with her I was maintaining. So we can both tell her honestly that you figured it out on your own. That young woman's a loose cannon. If anybody can bring her back from Old Mexico, it going to have to be you."

"You could have told me yesterday."

"So you could spend the whole day worrying?" Castor shook his head. "Nope. And then there is the promise I made. The train was already gone. It wouldn't have done any good to tell you yesterday."

"I could have gotten prepared."

"Are you ready now?" He studied me, waiting for an answer.

"Yes," I said.

"Good. Then help me into my chair and let's get on the train. I want to pick a good seat. It's going to be a long ride."

70

We took the Texas & Pacific line all the way into Sierra Blanca, then caught the Southern Pacific on into El Paso. It was a long ride, and during that time, I hashed out the rest of the details of Maggie's plan with Castor.

"She came to me with that map and an idea," Castor said as we ate dark German sausage sandwiches I'd gotten from the dining car. Getting him back and forth through the cars in the wheelchair was impossible, so we made do. "Maggie wants the man she holds responsible for her pa's death in the ground, and she knew she'd have a hard time finding him, and an even harder time catching him when he was vulnerable."

"She decided to make Angelo Blunt come to her." I'd put most of it together now, but I wanted it all nailed down.

"That's right." Castor smiled. "She's smart, Charlie. Probably too smart for her own good, if you want the truth. She'll grow into it if she lives long enough."

I was hoping that she did, that she'd still be alive when we reached Chihuahua City. "How long did she know about Mister Henson's map?"

"From the day you found it in that casket. She searched your rented room after you'd moved in there and discovered your hiding place."

I remembered Maggie telling me how she'd found Green's money in the saloon girl's room, that most folks hid things to keep them close at hand. I hadn't known at the time that she was talking about me too.

"The map was there. I checked."

"She made a copy to bring to me," Castor said. "We figured everything out from what she wrote down."

"She had you looking for Ellie Deno," I said. "We didn't go to Monahans to pick up Luther Green. She went there to find Ellie Deno."

"That's right. Maggie had asked me to find the woman. I couldn't find Ellie Deno, but I found Luther Green and I knew they had just run a flimflam down in Houston. I used my contacts to turn him up." Castor touched his nose and winked. "You're pretty sharp too, Charlie."

"I'm a day behind Maggie," I said.

"She's in a league of her own. If the two of you can figure how best to work together, you're going to be something to watch."

"Did she tell you she knocked me unconscious in an alley in Monahans?" I unconsciously touched the tender spot on my scalp.

"No." Castor didn't laugh, but I could tell he was holding it back. "How'd that happen?"

"I was following Luther Green, and he was meeting with Ellie Deno. I was about to step out and arrest her on an outstanding warrant in Pecos." I was surprised at how easily warrant rolled right out of my mouth. The legal lingo was getting easier to deal with. "Then Maggie banged me over the head with her pistol and I was out."

"You didn't mention this to her?"

"I didn't figure it out till this morning," I said. "It wasn't until I went into her room looking to see if she'd come back that I noticed her perfume. Then I remembered I'd smelled it in Monahans right before I was knocked out. What did she tell Ellie Deno?"

The sandwich in my hand had almost been forgotten. I took a bite and chewed.

"Sometimes it's hard to con a con artist," Castor said, "but if you have the right bait, it can be done. I've done it myself."

"And Maggie had the promise of that treasure map to all that Spanish gold."

Castor nodded. "She did. Gold fever is a powerful thing. Maggie knew that Ellie Deno couldn't go down to Chihuahua City by herself and get that gold. She'd have to have someone help her. Maggie figured since Ellie Deno had already been working with Angelo Blunt, the trap would work on both of them. So what she told Ellie Deno was that she'd trade the location of the map for Angelo Blunt's whereabouts. Of course, she knew Ellie Deno wouldn't give Angelo Blunt up to her."

"She didn't need her to. Once Blunt knew where the gold was, he'd come to her."

"That's right. I'm betting Maggie's going to be sitting right on top of that well somewhere, just waiting for Angelo Blunt to ride up into her sights."

"Even if she kills him, she's not going to get away. Blunt's men will kill her." I couldn't help thinking how Cornelius Crying Bear and David Asbury had tortured and killed Mister Henson. I folded the wax paper back over my sandwich and hoped I'd be able to eat it later. "Besides that, Ellie Deno could have figured Maggie was lying to her the same way she was lying."

"See? This is where Maggie excels at duplicity. She told Ellie Deno where the map was."

"So she could steal it herself," I said, understanding.

"Her, or someone she got to do her dirty work," Castor agreed. "Either way, Ellie Deno got that map. Maggie knew it had to be that map, not a copy. She felt bad about you losing it, but she thought it had to be done to better set the trap she was building."

If it worked, I felt the same way. That map wasn't a keepsake. It never had been, really. It was a dangerous secret that had almost gotten me killed more than once.

"What if Ellie Deno and Angelo Blunt aren't smart enough to decipher the map?" I asked.

"Maggie and I added to that map," Castor said. "We filled in all the missing details. Those two will know exactly where that well is. We even gave the village a name.

Pueblo de la Paloma de Luto."

It took me a minute to translate. "Village of the Mourning Dove?"

Castor nodded. "It sounds enticing, doesn't it?"

"What was the village's original name?"

He smiled and shook his head. "It probably didn't even have one, it was so small."

"There's a problem with this plan," I said.

"What's that?"

"Even with these two men you say are joining us in El Paso, that gives us five people to go up against Angelo Blunt and his gang."

"You're being generous enough to count me as a whole man, Charlie?" Castor asked.

I didn't know how to answer that, so I didn't.

"Don't go getting sentimental on me now."

"I want to get Maggie back home safe, Mister Castor. That's all I care about. When Angelo Castor attacked Pecos, he had a whole lot of men with him."

"I want her back too." Castor sighed and rubbed his face tiredly. "Maggie's plan is pretty simple, and it's devious. The question of manpower that Angelo Blunt may have comes down to this: How many of his people do you think he'd trust to take on a gold hunting expedition?"

That didn't take me long to consider. "Not many," I answered. "Just those closest to him."

Castor nodded. "That's what Maggie is betting on too. So if the four of us can get down there to her in time, we all have a chance of coming out of this."

71

The men who joined us in after we got off the train in El Paso were older than I thought they would be. I guessed they were a little younger than Castor, maybe in their late forties or early fifties.

They met us at the depot with a buckboard to transport Castor. I rode in back with him and we traveled to the hotel where we would be staying the night before saddling up for the ten to twelve day ride to Chihuahua City.

The older of the two, Wade Barlowe, was a freedman who'd come out of New Orleans. He was soft spoken and watched everything. His skin was the color of dark caramel and was spotted with darker freckles across his nose and cheeks. A blue tattoo on his neck showed the number 132 just above a scar that looked like someone had once tried to take his head off with a large, sharp blade.

He was dressed in; trail clothes that looked worn but cared for, and he packed two Colt .45s at his hips. He carried a Winchester in a scabbard over his shoulder, which he took off and stored under the seat.

When we were introduced, he shook my hand and took my measure with soft brown eyes.

"You're a big one, ain't you?" he asked.

"Yes sir," I replied.

"I hope you got some bark on you," Barlowe said. "If you don't, if you survive this little tea party, you will have."

"Yes sir."

Kyffin Gaunt was a Welshman who had left his country at a young age, hit New York, and immediately moved out West to see the land and the people dime novels had told him about. He was barely above five feet in height and was built slim. He wore a nice suit that looked a lot more elegant than my simple black one. He was a handsome man, and women watched him as he went by. His light blond hair contrasted with his sun-bronzed skin. He wore a fierce pair of sideburns and a mustache that had more red in them.

"Noswaith dda, Morgan," Gaunt greeted Castor.

I didn't recognize the words, but Castor had no problem with them.

"Good evening to you, my friend." Castor hugged Gaunt tightly as he had Wade. "I appreciate both of you coming."

"One ye mentioned the prospect of gold," Gaunt said, "I knew I had to come." He glanced at me. "The deal is, I get to keep at least as much as I can cart off, right? And take a share in any extra that we might be able to abscond with?"

Castor and I hadn't exactly talked about that, but I understood now why these men would be so willing to risk their lives.

"It's not my gold," I said. "Take what you want. I just want to make sure my friend and I get back safely."

"Ah, laddie, ye're a fine one, ye are. But can ye fight?" Gaunt tapped his head beside his left eye. "Because I noticed when I talked about getting the gold, ye had a bit of fire in yer peepers, ye did."

"I don't want my friend to get forgotten, is all," I said.

Gaunt grinned more broadly. "An' see?" he said to Castor. "There's that fire again!"

I wasn't certain I would like Kyffin Gaunt, so I didn't say anything else, and I promised myself I wouldn't let him get to me.

We had dinner at the restaurant in the hotel. Castor told his story of what was going on and what we hoped to accomplish with rescuing Maggie and dealing with Angelo Blunt.

"I've heard of Blunt," Barlowe said. "I've a few dealin's with the men he rides with, but never with Blunt."

As it turned out, Barlowe and Gaunt had been Pinkerton men for a time, but the fit wasn't a good one and they'd eventually gone their own ways. They still occasionally picked up assignments every now and again, usually arranged for by Castor, who had worked with them for years.

When Castor finished his spiel, there weren't as many questions as I'd expected. Barlowe had shrugged and said, "We know what we're after, an' who we're up against. Works for me."

"An' don't forget we get the chance to fill our pockets with gold," Gaunt said, and ordered another beer. "I like the idea of doin' this out of the goodness of our hearts an' all, but ye cannae spend goodness in a saloon."

After that, we turned in early. Everyone was tired and nervous about the next day.

***

"Lad, you really do favor those black suits," Gaunt said the next morning at breakfast.

My ears burned a little, but I didn't respond. I'd gotten to the restaurant first and been joined by Castor, then Barlowe. Gaunt was the last to come, and he looked like he was dragging. His eyes were red from drinking the previous night.

"Don't worry about Kyffin," Castor told me in an aside when we were alone. "He's a bit of a problem when he's not strictly tethered to a mission because he gets bored and doesn't like himself much. He drinks too much, gambles too much, and chases all the wrong women, but once he's on the job, there's nobody better."

"I'll take your word for it," I said. It wasn't like I had a choice.

"They're good men," Castor told me. "They've saved

my life on numerous occasions over the years. And I've saved theirs." He fell silent for a moment, then added, "When I was in a gun battle against the James gang in Killen, Alabama, in 1876, I was struck by the bullet that severed my spine and left me in the shape you see me today. Wade and Kyffin got me out of there alive when I'd given up and was waiting for the bullet that would put me out of my misery."

He sipped his coffee and I knew he was lost in the memory. I wanted to get his attention again, but I felt sorry for him and hesitated.

Then he came back to me. "Allan Pinkerton sidelined me after I lost the use of my legs, but he never forgot what a weapon this was." He tapped his forehead. "I'm devious, although Maggie has some twists and turns I haven't seen, and I have a large collection of friends and associates."

He clapped me on the shoulder. "Don't worry, Charlie. We'll find Maggie."

I'd struggled with how I was going to address the problem of Castor riding with us all day yesterday, and into the night. I hadn't found an easy way to do it, so I just hit the nail on the head.

"I don't see us getting far carrying you along in a buckboard, Mister Castor."

He laughed at me. "Nor do I. That's why Wade has made other arrangements."

72

The "other arrangements" was a harness system like I'd never seen. Wade Barlowe showed it to us in the livery after we finished breakfast.

"Back when I was a slave," Barlowe said as he showed us the saddle he'd constructed for Castor, "I was a leather worker an' was owned by a man whose son had been hurt in a fall. I made him a saddle just like this. He rode ever'where he wanted to go." He smiled at Castor. "You're gonna be surprised, Morgan. I guarantee it."

The saddle had started out as an ordinary one, but Barlowe had bolted on a stiff back that reached to just below Castor's shoulder blades. A strap ran around his chest and held him in place.

"You might get a little sore from the leather rubbin' against you for the first few days," Barlowe said, "but it'll keep you seated while we're travelin' cross-country."

"Wonderful." Castor beamed, his face lighting like a child's. He practiced riding in the livery and a handful of cowboys who'd come out to get their horses watched.

"You'll need help gettin' on an' off the horse," Barlowe said, "but other than that, you'll do fine. Those wide straps at the front of the stirrups are there to keep your feet from slidin' through."

"My god," Castor said, "I have missed this. The world just looks different from up on the back of a horse." He looked at me. "So what do you think, Charlie? We don't need a buckboard."

"An' that old man is one of the finest rifle shots ye'll ever see." Gaunt leaned against a nearby paddock and looked hungover. "When we go into this fight, we'll need him."

I still had reservations about Castor going, but I kept them to myself. I knew if I'd voiced them, I would have been arguing with all three men.

And I knew I needed help.

Maggie might need more help than we could give, and the thought of that scared me.

"That'll do," I said. I suspected they would have gone without my blessing, but they'd respected me enough to at least pretend that asking me mattered.

***

We spent the morning buying pack mules and supplies. Barlowe, Gaunt, and I had brought our horses, and Castor had picked one out from the livery remuda that was for sale.

I chafed under the delay, but I knew we had to spend the time to be properly prepared. I'd wired money to an account in an El Paso bank, and we spent it like it was on fire. I hated seeing all that money go so quickly because when Maggie and I got back to Pecos, we'd be strapped for cash for a time, especially with all the work that still needed to be done on the Henson Building.

But it needed to be done, so I did it. The money was nothing to me, but I worried that Maggie wouldn't be so cavalier about it.

Castor figured out what was bothering me and said, "Don't worry, Charlie. After we help Maggie deal with Angelo Blunt, we'll stay down there long enough to bring back some of that gold. We'll all come back flush."

I hoped so. But mostly I hoped Maggie was all right.

***

We headed out just before lunch and followed the trail Castor had laid out for us with Barlowe, who had traveled some in Mexico and knew his way down to Chihuahua and back.

I knew Maggie was out there somewhere ahead of us, and I hoped Angelo Blunt and his gang, considerably pared down from the one that had hit Pecos, were behind us.

Maggie had taken the train like we had, but Angelo couldn't have risked that. After the bank robberies in Pecos, his wanted posters were everywhere.

There was a lot of desert in that part of Mexico. The land was blistered and broken and parched. Even with the water we brought on the pack mules, and the water holes and streams that Castor and Barlowe knew about, it was a near thing some days to keep enough for the horses to drink. They went through it, and so did we.

I swear I sweated out more than I drank every day, and I didn't know a time when my suit was completely dry.

Riding eight hours a day, four in the morning and four in the afternoon with a siesta in the middle to escape the hottest part of the days, we covered almost thirty miles a day. At least, that's what Barlowe and Castor figured from their previous visits and the markers along the way.

I didn't know. I just worked at staying in the saddle. I'd never ridden so much and I was sore all over the first few days. Barlowe and Gaunt seemed to have no trouble at all, and Castor just laughed because with his paralysis he claimed he'd never be saddle sore.

73

On the evening of the second day, Gaunt pulled out one of the strangest rifles I'd ever seen. In the fading sunset, while Castor and Barlowe made our supper, Gaunt cleaned that rifle with care.

The rifle was four feet long and had a skinny barrel with a hardwood stock that led to a long, round metal butt. The S-shaped hammer made me think it was a flintlock because it was made along the same lines. The idea of a single-shot flintlock to use against Blunt and his gang didn't make sense to me. At least with Castor's Sharps rifle there was a lot of range.

Gaunt caught me staring and asked, "Do ye know what this is, Mister Stark?"

"A rifle."

He grinned mirthlessly at me. "Ah, but it is that, but it's so much more than ye think. This here's a family heirloom is what it is. Me ol' grandpap found himself a criminal over some confusion in Wales, the land where I'm from, an' he had to travel a bit. He became a professional soldier, more or less, an' he ended up in Austria fightin' the French at Austerlitz. Have ye heard of that?"

"No."

Light from the campfire played over Gaunt's rugged features and gleamed dully on the metal butt stock of the rifle. "Well, Austerlitz is also called the Battle of the Three Emperors, them bein' Napoleon Bonaparte of France, Alexander I of Russia, an' Francis II, the Holy Roman Emperor of Austria. Alexander an' Francis were workin' together, an' me grandpap was one of the rifle-men in that battle." He ran his hand over the rifle. "He carried this into that battle, an' after Napoleon whipped them, he figured he'd been gone long enough from Wales for bygones to be bygones. So he brought it back with him. It's been passed down from father to son."

Castor and Barlowe had grown quiet with the telling of the story, and I knew this wasn't just idle conversation.

"Well, me grandpap was wrong about them bygones," Gaunt continued. "He came back to Wales an' Black Tom Prendergast killed him an' took this rifle, the only thing Owain Gaunt had left behind in this world except for his wife and children. Me own da was only twelve. When he turned fifteen an' had a man's growth on him, he went huntin' Black Tom. Killed him, too, an' he took back this rifle. When I set sail for America, me pap give me this rifle an' told me it would do me well."

Gaunt's hands moved rhythmically as he polished the rifle.

"Most people that see me with it think I'm a fool for carryin' such an antique." He stood it up straight on his thigh. "They just don't know what they're lookin' at. This is a Girardoni air rifle, designed by Bartholomaus Girardoni who was from the Princely County of Tyrol. It was carried into battle by Austrians for twenty-five years, finally givin' up the ghost in 1815 after the Battle of Waterloo."

"That rifle is seventy years old?" I asked, mesmerized in spite of myself. I welcomed the distraction from wor-rying about Maggie and where she was.

"This one?" Gaunt smiled at the rifle. "Why, she's a hundred if she's a day. An' she still shoots as straight as she ever did. My grandpap called her Marwolaeth Tawel." He looked at me. "That means 'silent death' to those of ye who lack the beauty that is the Welsh tongue."

"Why did he call it that?" I asked. I'd fired muzzle

loaders before and those had all been loud.

"Because she's got the quietest voice." Gaunt stood and pulled the rifle to his shoulder. He tucked the curious metal butt stock to his shoulder, took aim, and squeezed the trigger.

What I heard sounded like a strangled cough mixed with a sneeze. The noise didn't carry far. Then, about a hundred yards away, a small branch leaped from a tree.

Gaunt fired again and again and again, for a total of twenty shots before he stopped. Every time he'd fired, a branch had fallen from the tree.

I was amazed.

"That's why the Austrian army carried these into battle," Gaunt said. "Back then, no one had a repeatin' rifle, and Henry an' Winchester have only now gotten their magazines up to fifteen. Sixteen if ye have one in the chamber. An' I don't have to deal with all the smoke from a shot. I can fire again immediately without tryin' to peer through a cloud of smoke an' not worry about havin' my position marked by smoke neither."

"He'll also have to pump that reservoir for a couple hours to get it back up to pressure," Barlowe said.

"Nitpick if ye must, Wade, but Marwolaeth Tawel has meant the different between life an' death for ye an' me before because she was so quiet an' so quick. She will again. Ye'll see."

"I'd rather reload my Winchester," Barlowe said.

"Ye can't kill quietly with one of those," Gaunt admonished, "an' sometimes that's necessary thing." He looked back at me. "They took one of these along when Lewis an' Clark explored the Louisiana Purchase. The Indians thought they were up against white men who could shoot all day, an' they thought it was magic. Marwolaeth Tawel is bringin' magic for us on this trip. Ye'll see."

I hoped he was right.

"Supper's ready," Castor announced. "If you're hungry, come get it."

Getting up reminded me of the sore muscles I had, but I wasn't going to miss a meal. After I fetched a plate, I sat and I ate and I thought of Maggie somewhere out there alone, knowing Angelo Blunt was coming, but not knowing we were.

74

Late in the morning of the ninth day, we surprised ourselves by arriving at our destination earlier than we'd thought possible. We topped a ridge and saw the scattered, tumbled down shacks that were the remnants of the place Castor had named Village of the Mourning Dove on his tricked out map Maggie had convinced Ellie Deno to steal from my bedroom a week and a half ago.

The village lay in a hollow that had given it shelter from the wind that blew across the desert and some of the harsh glare of the sun. Shadows off the ridgeline of tall hills to the east lie over the cluster of small adobe homes that had been constructed in bunches. Stunted trees, broken fences, and scrub grass that struggled to survive on the reddish crust filled the empty spaces between the houses.

Forty yards to the south, an old mine sat open with a short railway leading out of it. A couple of mine carts sat near the entrance. Farther south, hills of rock that had been dug out of the mine were partially overgrown with stubborn shrubs.

The place had been abandoned for years. For decades, if Mister Henson's story was true.

"They used to do silver mining around here," Castor said as he reined in beside me. "I turned that up in my investigation too. Those researchers Pinkerton has set up to collect press clippings found a couple stories that mentioned that from when the United States Army occupied Mexico City in 1847. Plenty of reporters covered the news for readers back in the states."

"I read about that in a history book," I said. "Mister Henson told me about the fight for the city. He talked about the Saint Patrick's Battalion, the unit that was comprised mostly of immigrants to Mexico. Germans, Irish, French, Italians. A lot of people from a lot of different countries around the world had moved here and fought against the United States Army under Winfield Scott. The Battalion lost, and after that the war ended. But Mister Henson talked about the attack on Chapultepec Castle like he was there."

"Was he?" Castor asked.

I sat there for a moment, realizing that Mister Henson, who had been a man name Petway whom I was glad I did not meet, had at one time stood in this very place.

It was all odd, and it took me away from the man I thought I'd known.

"Not that I know of," I answered. "As it turns out, there's a lot I don't know about Mister Henson."

***

We rode down into the valley looking for Maggie, but she was nowhere to be seen. I grew more worried.

"It's possible that we made better time than she did," Castor said, but I knew he was just as concerned as I was. He was just trying to mask his own feelings to put me at ease.

"She would have beaten us here," I replied. "Something's happened. We need to look for her."

Castor put a hand on my shoulder. "Look, Charlie, I know it seems bad, but you've got to trust her to get here. Something happened. Something slowed her down. If something's gone bad, we need to hope she can get here and we can help her then." He paused. "Think about it. Where in all that desert we just rode through would you start looking?"

I knew he was right, but I wanted to be mad at him. And I wanted to be mad at Maggie for running off on her own. That had been foolish. But other folks, Gilbride probably, would think what I'd done was foolish too.

"Two things you can count on when it comes to people, Charlie," Castor said. "Determination and greed. Maggie set this play into motion, and she'll be along because she intends to be here. And Angelo Blunt ain't gonna pass up on that gold in that well."

***

Once we were certain the village was unoccupied, we all gathered at the well. The mortared stone walls stood three feet tall and had a wooden windlass hoist still in place across the mouth. The opening was eight feet across, probably built wide enough to accommodate the small work force that did the digging.

A rotting stench still came from inside the well and I couldn't help but imagine how many dead chickens Petway, Salsa Jack, Simon, and the others in their group must have thrown down into the well to ruin the water. Or maybe they'd just dumped in a couple dead donkeys.

I didn't like the idea of finding out, but I knew we'd discover the truth soon enough.

We lowered a lantern into the well and saw that the water level started twenty feet down. The well walls had been reinforced with more mortared stone that reached at least to the water's surface. I wondered how deep the water was.

"They could have put that gold into the water too deep to get it back out," Gaunt said. "Or the water level could have risen." He looked unhappy at those possibilities.

"It's just as likely the water level has actually dropped and we're hitting bottom," Castor said. "Wells tend to dry up out here if they're not very deep. There's only one way to find out. We'll need to send something down."

In the scrub grass a short distance away, I found a

five-gallon wooden well bucket that was two feet tall and weighted at the end so it would sink into the water and remain upright.

We tied the bucket to the frayed rope hanging from the windlass hoist and lowered it into the water. The bucket didn't even submerge before it bottomed out with a scraping sound.

"The water's not deep," Barlowe said.

"Might have been deeper back when folks lived here," I said. "The water level might have changed, or the underground stream feeding it dried up."

"Ye can go an' think that if ye've got a mind to," Gaunt said. "As for meself, I'm gonna believe that well's chockful of gold until I see that it ain't."

I was curious myself, but not enough to volunteer to go down. With that eight-foot diameter, it reminded me too much of the mouth of an open grave, only more round. The graves me and Mister Henson had dug had measured eight feet long, three and a half feet wide, and six feet deep.

Gaunt offered to go down since he was the smallest among us. We got a new rope from our supplies and attached it to the windlass hoist, but we left the old rope in place because we didn't want to change anything for when Angelo Blunt came along.

I still believed that was going to happen. I just didn't know what had become of Maggie.

When Gaunt was ready, he took a candle down into the well with him. The candle glow reflected in the brackish, stinking water, and I didn't know how Gaunt could stand it. I was getting sick just standing topside. I couldn't imagine how bad it was down there.

A moment later, the rope went slack when Gaunt touched down.

75

"Jesus, Mary, and Joseph," Gaunt groaned from down in the well. "This smells like the inside of a slaughterhouse gut pile in Hell in August a month after every'thin's gone bad with heat and rot."

I held my hand over my nose as tears welled up in my eyes. I wasn't sure what such a slaughterhouse smelled like in the summer, but if it was anything like this, I didn't want to go to one. Ever.

"There are bones down here," Gaunt called up. He walked around on the water—well, a few inches under the water—while he explored. He picked up bones and tossed them aside. "I see chicken bones, cow bones, what may be a horse, an' there are a few human bones down here too."

Gaunt held up a human skull still dripping water between broken teeth.

"They probably killed some of those villagers to put them on the run," Gaunt said. "Then, when they come back here an' saw the poisoned well, they just up an' moved on down the road. Probably thought somebody wanted the land."

"The French Invasion was a mess," Castor commented. "Folks got scattered every whichway. What else do you see?"

"A lot of rock," Gaunt answered. "Rock that's been

worked, cut an' shaped for buildin' things. An' there's a lot of adobe mush down here to that's gonna need shovelin'. Looks to me like they gathered up rock an' tossed in pieces of houses too. If there's gold in here, she'll probably be three or four feet deep at least. I wouldn't want to go any shallower than that if I was the one doin' the burin'."

"I agree," Castor said. "Climb up out of there, Kyffin, and let's be about the rest of our business."

Gaunt took another look around. "Ye know, Morgan, I'm mighty tempted to root around in here right now, see if I can find anythin'. I'd hate to go to all this trouble, risk my life an' ever'thin', only to find out that gold's long gone."

"It's not just about the gold," I called down.

He looked up at me and the candle flame showed the mud smeared on his face. "I know, an' we'll do what we set out to do with Angelo Blunt an' his blackhearts. But, all the same, I'd like to know."

I took hold of the rope when he did and helped pull him up.

***

I'd learned a little about manhunting with Maggie, but I didn't realize how much there was left to learn until I worked with Barlowe and Gaunt and Castor. They sized up the area and figured out where Angelo Blunt and his gang would probably camp, and then they figured out where they would run during a firefight.

Because that was what was going to happen. There wasn't going to be any real attempt at an arrest. I knew Angelo Blunt would never agree to that. There was no more prison waiting for him if he was caught. Judge Caldwell would hang him for what he'd done in Pecos.

We planned on staying outside the village in the ridgeline, either to the east or the west so our prey would have the sun in their eyes. Nobody called the outlaws that, but as I watched, and helped, with the preparations we made, with all the traps we set, I knew that's what Angelo Blunt and his gang were. Prey. And we were the hunters.

After we'd finished searching out shooting covers all around the village, we also set up thick, greasy sticks of dynamite in places we thought the outlaws would run to for cover when we attacked. The obvious place was the abandoned mine. That was going to be a death trap for anyone who went in there. Gaunt had gotten his hands on the dynamite courtesy of some Mexican rebels in Ciudad Juarez.

Castor also had us set up some dynamite around the village that he could target with that Sharps. We marked the hiding places with short sticks. Even if he didn't have clear targets, he wanted to create diversions and muddy the water.

I couldn't help but marvel at the wanton destruction they prepared so callously.

Gaunt gave me two sticks of dynamite as well. "Put these in yer boots," he said. "For if ye find yerself in a bad place." He grinned. "This here is a cavalry by itsownself." He clapped me on the shoulder. "Just make sure ye don't get shot in yer feet."

I did what he told me to do, but I wasn't happy about walking around with dynamite in my boots. But I could see his point.

I watched as he put a stick of dynamite in each of his boots.

When Castor was satisfied we'd seeded our chosen battlefield as well as we could, it was almost sundown. We had a cold camp under an overhang on the ridgeline and ate jerked beef because we didn't know how far away Angelo Blunt was and didn't want anyone to spot a camp-fire.

I was worrying about Maggie when I lay down to sleep that night.

76

Three days later, Angelo Blunt and his gang rode into the Village of the Mourning Dove just before noon. I watched them through the field glasses Castor used to spot birds from his window in Missus Frederiks' boardinghouse.

He had thirty riders with him as they came down out of the ridgeline like a sidewinder, weaving back and forth along a thin trail. Ellie Deno rode beside Blunt. That part of Maggie's plan, with their number cut down because Blunt wouldn't have trusted anyone, had worked out.

I knew other things must not have worked out, either, because Maggie rode in the middle of the bunch with her hands tied behind her back. I almost got up then, but Castor laid a hand on my shoulder and held me down. He'd already seen Maggie with them and he'd known what I was going to see.

"Easy, Charlie," he said softly. "We're going to get her back, but if you want to make sure she's safe, we have to do this slow and careful. Not go running down there. That'll just get everybody killed. Probably her first of all."

I knew he was right, but it was hard watching her and knowing she was so helpless.

She was covered in dirt and her clothes were torn, but she had that rebellious set to her shoulders that told me she hadn't been broken. The men around her gave her a wide berth, but they kept her horse hemmed in and another man had the horse's reins in his hand.

When they got closer to the village, Ellie Deno spurred her horse and rode up to the well in a cloud of dust.

Angelo Blunt kept his pace and looked around.

"He's a careful one," Castor breathed in my ear. "He's thinking this might still be a setup."

Blunt was right, but he wasn't going to find out he was right until we were ready to spring the trap.

We had positioned Castor and his Sharps behind an overhang of rock on the north side of the small valley. Barlowe and Gault were to the left and right of us, holding their positions about a hundred yards from the well. They were concealed by shrubs and small trees.

Barlowe had spotted the dust the outlaws' horses raised coming in and had warned us in plenty of time to get where we needed to be. We'd set up west of the village, so the sun would be in the eyes of our enemies when it went down.

Castor was about four hundred yards from the well, and I hoped he was as good with that buffalo rifle as everyone professed him to be because those men looked awfully small from where I was lying.

My heart thumped rapidly. It was one thing to be re-acting to danger, like I had when Blunt had caught me and Mister Henson in the Sunflower Cemetery or when the attack on the town had taken place. Then it was all nerve and instinct. But it was another entirely to walk into something that was potentially as dangerous as a buzzsaw in the sawmill.

I was going to kill as many of these men as I could, and that decision didn't set easily with me.

"We'll wait till sundown," Castor whispered. "If we try to do anything now, we'll lose Maggie and maybe get killed ourselves."

I was so mad and so scared that I was trembling, but I nodded.

"By this evening, they'll be tired," Castor said. "We can use that against them. When that time comes, you can see if you can slip down there and get Maggie loose. If we can get her out of here, and us too, maybe that's where we'll draw the line."

"Gaunt won't be happy," I said.

"Wade probably won't be either, but there are more of them than we'd counted on, and we sure hadn't figured on Maggie being in their hands."

"All right," I said. I didn't have another plan, but I didn't like waiting either. I wanted Maggie out of there.

Down below, Ellie Deno had dismounted and was staring into the well. She turned back to Blunt. "It's just like she said. The well's been poisoned."

At the distance, I could barely hear her voice.

Blunt stopped his horse near the well and my hand itched for the Winchester rifle lying at my side. Today, more than ever, he looked like a blond devil. Arrogance rolled off him. After the bank robberies and attack on Pecos, he had to be thinking he was nearly invincible.

One bullet would change that.

"Even if you killed him straight out like you're thinking," Castor whispered in my ear, "they'll kill Maggie, and probably kill us too. They aren't going to leave as long as they think there's gold down in that well."

I knew that. Paralyzed as he was, with no one to help him onto his horse, Castor would be trapped right where he was until they killed him. I forced my breath out because holding it was making my chest hurt.

"All right," Blunt called as he stepped down out of the saddle. "Let's find out if there's any gold in that well."

His men dismounted too and quickly went to work like a well-oiled machine. It was obviously they'd planned this part out. Two of them set up a remuda to keep the horses in one place, tying their reins to a picket line.

One of the men stayed with Maggie, shoving her over to one of the adobe homes that had collapsed on one side. We had placed a three-stick dynamite bundle in the withered remains of the roof and covered it so that it couldn't be seen, but I knew it was there. A short length of white wood I'd taken the bark off marked its position.

The man pushed Maggie down into a sitting position with her back against the wall. Using a length of rawhide, he tied her ankles together. She stared straight ahead like nothing mattered.

Other men brought out ropes, shovels, picks, and a large piece of leather that, when tied properly, formed a bucket.

Two men climbed down into the well and set to work. Within minutes they were bringing rocks and bones and adobe mud up in that leather bucket. Water rained from the gathered sides and splashed across the dry, cracked ground.

Blunt dug a quirley out of his pocket, put it between his teeth, and lit it. When he had the quirley going good, he walked over to Maggie and squatted down in front of her.

"I have to admit, Miss Buchanan," Blunt said, "I'd almost given up on finding that gold my pa told me was out here somewhere. I didn't want to believe Miss Deno when she told me about that map you offered her for me. I didn't even want to believe it when I saw that map." He smiled. "I even had my doubts when Mister Courbet told me that was the same paper he'd seen Stark take from that casket."

Maggie didn't even bother to look at him.

"But now I've got my hopes up," Blunt said. "So, if we dig in that well and there's no gold, I promise you now I'm going to kill you slow, then cut off your head and throw it, and your body, into that well to rot."

Maggie looked up at him. "You may as well go ahead and do it now. I don't see this ending up any other way for me."

Blunt laughed and looked around to see if he had an audience. Nearly all of his men had their eyes on that well, though. All of them were waiting to see what was in there.

"You're a strange one, Miss Buchanan." Blunt stood. "So cold that it might not even be fun killing you. But I'll keep you around a little longer as a luck piece. If you hadn't run into those bandidos while you were tracking us, they might have attacked us and caught us off guard.

As it was, we were able to kill them all. And we got lucky enough to catch you in the bargain."

"Go away," Maggie said. "You're boring me."

She was cold. It was like she didn't care if she was there. I remembered Gilbride telling me that he didn't know if she was going to survive losing her father after everything her mother had done to her. If she didn't make a connection to someone, he was afraid she'd just let go.

Now she was in the perfect place to do that. And she hadn't been planning on surviving her attack on Blunt and his gang.

That hurt me and I was scared for her. And me. I didn't know who I'd be without her.

"Angel!" Courbet called. He stood next to the well, watching the men working inside it. "They've found it! They've found the gold!"

77

That announcement drew the outlaws like flies to honey. They pushed and shoved at each other to fight for space along the well.

The leather bucket came up again, and this time when it was dumped on the ground, two gold ingots spilled out across the rocks and mud too.

"It's there!" Ellie Deno shouted. She grabbed Blunt by the face and kissed him. "I told you she wouldn't lie to me if she thought I would give you up!"

"No," he said, "but she knew you would lie to her. Do you think she just accidently happened to be out here?"

Ellie Deno's joy slipped for a moment, but she turned away from Blunt and went to touch one of those gold bars and she was happy again.

Then I realized something we hadn't thought about. I whispered to Castor, "Now that they have the gold, they don't need Maggie. They'll kill her."

His face tightened and I realized he hadn't considered that possibility either. Suddenly everything we'd planned didn't make sense.

"Then we'll kill as many of them as we can and keep that from happening. You get on down there if you can, and be ready to fetch her out of there when we open the ball on this."

I eased on down the hill, drawing the attention of Barlowe and Gaunt. Castor signaled to them and they signaled back, and I figured they'd known each other long enough they had no problem communicating like that.

I got to within seventy yards of the village center. Past that point, cover got lean and I knew I wouldn't be able to escape detection even if that well started spewing gold.

The man who'd been guarding Maggie had stepped forward to watch what was going on, but he hadn't left her. With his back to her, he didn't see her hands come free, and he didn't see her get to her feet.

Instead of trying to get away, Maggie pulled the man's Bowie knife from his sheath and his pistol from his holster. He turned around in a hurry and reached for the pistol as he cried out a warning, but his hand clasped only empty air because she'd already gotten the weapon.

Maggie slashed his throat with the knife, putting an end to his yell, and eared the hammer back on that Colt as she took aim at Blunt just as the outlaw leader whirled around, reaching for that French pistol of his.

Blunt ducked and yanked Ellie Deno in front of him, so when Maggie fired, the bullet struck the woman instead of him. By then he had his pistol up and firing.

Behind me, Castor cursed and leaned into his rifle, and that Sharps roared thunder that rolled down the ridgeline.

By that time I was in motion, running for all I was worth in a ragged line down the hillside, following the line of cover I'd memorized. Bullets whizzed through the air and ricocheted from rocky outcroppings.

After her first shot, Maggie slashed the rawhide binding her ankles with her captured knife and stepped back into the wreck of a house behind her to take cover. I didn't see anyone down from Castor's first shot, and I supposed he'd shot at Blunt, who was still moving, rounding the well and using it for cover.

One of the outlaws ran toward the house Maggie had ducked into. By the time he reached the doorway, Castor's big buffalo rifle thundered again and a second later, the outlaw left his feet and hit the ground in a loose sprawl.

Maggie hadn't waited for the house to be swarmed. She'd bolted to the back and crawled up the fallen roof to launch herself out the hole there and down to the ground behind that cluster of houses. She landed on her feet and kept running, turning so that I lost sight of her in the other houses.

By then I was having to look out for myself because the outlaws had spotted me. I threw myself to the ground as a hail of bullets searched for me.

Barlowe and Gaunt were on the move too, creeping closer to the village. Gaunt had the air rifle up and he fired several times, hitting two men before they knew he was there because the rifle made very little sound and there was no smoke to give away his position.

Twenty yards from the well, the ground erupted with a loud boom! Dirt and dust rushed into the sky, and in the midst of it the broken bodies of two outlaws flew briefly before dropping to the ground.

Blunt and his gang knew what they'd run into then, and they scattered, searching for cover, trying desperately to get away from the trap now closing in on them.

An outlaw ran into the abandoned mine and took up a firing position, lining up on Barlowe, who was squatted down and duck-walking forward in a ditch that provided cover. Chunks and tufts of grass and dirt jumped up where bullets dug into the ground all around him.

On his belly, Barlowe scrambled forward while holding onto the Winchester. Then he raised himself to his knees, brought the rifle to his shoulder, fired, levered, and fired again. The outlaw's belt buckle disappeared and his shirt over his belly jumped when the second bullet struck him.

I was up and running again, trying to find Maggie in all the dust haze from the explosion that had filled the village. One outlaw sidled up to the house Maggie had scrambled into and through and started shooting at me when I was twenty yards out. I threw myself behind the low wall of wreckage that remained of a house that had stood next door.

Lying low behind the wall remnant, I was trapped and didn't have a shot at the outlaw. He kept me pinned down and a voice was screaming inside my head that if I didn't get up and move, more outlaws were going to close in on me and I'd die and be of no use to Maggie.

I couldn't shoot the man firing at me, but that spot where Gaunt had put those dynamite sticks was in plain sight thirty feet away. I pulled that Winchester up, took aim, and squeezed the trigger.

The dynamite exploded and brought the house down.

This close in, the blast rolled over me and I felt the heat and the thunder of it shaking through me. I lost part of my hearing and was nearly deaf as I levered another cartridge into the Winchester's chamber.

I pushed myself up and ran, dodging through the debris Blunt's men had dug up from the well.

Movement at the well drew my attention and I spotted one of the men who'd been doing the digging inside the well levering himself up with his pistol pointed at me. Then a round hole opened in his forehead and he fell back into the well.

I didn't look for Gaunt, but I knew he'd been the one to make that shot.

I sprinted through the wreckage of the house and toward another, desperately trying to find Maggie.

78

With my hearing mostly gone for the moment, I barely heard that sharp crack of Castor's Sharps, but an instant after that, another bundle of dynamite erupted from the ground and threw another cloud of dust into the air. It mixed with the first two and the dust was so thick I almost couldn't breathe. I didn't know if the explosion took out any of Blunt's men, but it certainly added to the confusion.

I rounded a corner and came face to face with Cornelius Crying Bear as he was reloading his pistol. I hadn't even seen him until it was too late because the dust hung so heavily in the air.

He had on another buckskin fringe shirt with the sleeves cut off. I knew it had to be another one because the one I'd previously seen him in had gotten covered in Mister Henson's blood that night and not even Mister Kuáng's laundry could have gotten that out.

I tried to bring the Winchester up and stop at the same time, but I had too much momentum built up. I stumbled forward awkwardly.

Smiling, Crying Bear dropped his pistol and grabbed my rifle barrel. He yanked on the Winchester and I fired, but the bullet whizzed right past him. Then he kicked my feet out from under me and tried to yank the rifle away.

I held on tight as I fell hard to the ground, refusing

to give up the weapon. My shoulder flared with burning pain, but I continued to hold on. We only succeeded in keeping the rifle from each other, though, because the Winchester spun free of our hands and slid away.

Crying Bear drew his Bowie knife without hesitation and sprang for me.

Then Gaunt stepped through the opening I'd just come through. He held a pistol in each hand. He must have been blinded by the dust too, because he didn't see Crying Bear until the outlaw shoved that Bowie knife into his stomach.

A surprised look filled Gaunt's face as he looked down at the knife embedded in him. He tried to bring his pistols to bear, but his hands and arms refused to work.

Crying Bear laughed as he tore the knife free. Then he stopped laughing when he saw I had that big Tranter up in my fist and pointed at his chest.

Something hit me in the side and I knew I'd been shot because blood hit the ground in front of me.

Crying Bear started to come for me, but I squeezed off a shot that hit him in the leg and staggered him. I eared the Tranter back and he spun and ran behind the house to our left.

Whoever had shot me shot again, but this time the round only pulled at my jacket. I turned and stared right at the outlaw who fired again at me from twenty feet away. His bullet burned my neck and blood trickled down.

I squeezed the trigger and that .50-caliber bullet smashed him in the chest and made him stumble backward. I fired again, just to make sure, but he was dead before he hit the ground.

As I turned to chase Crying Bear, another outlaw ran at me from the narrow alley between two houses. I threw myself at the nearest door and tore it down as I plunged inside and landed on the dirt floor. A pair of bullets chewed into the ground where I'd been standing.

Before I could push myself up, the rifleman stepped to the window on that side of the house and fired at me again. I twisted and jumped, rolling toward the back of the room.

I came up on one knee and realized the adobe walls

were old and thin. I couldn't see the man hunting me, but I knew from the angle of the rifle barrel sticking through that window where he was. I fired the Tranter's two final rounds into the wall where I thought he was.

The bullets tore through the thin barrier and the rifle barrel pulled back in a hurry.

I dumped the brass from the Tranter and didn't bother trying to keep up with it. I thumbed in fresh cartridges as quickly as I could while I got to my feet.

I was breathing hard and sticky with blood from the wound in my side. A shadow fell over the door I'd just come through and an outlaw followed it.

I raised my pistol, but before I could fire, two gunshots rang out and the man pitched forward onto his face. Gazing through the doorway, I spotted Gaunt leaning on his side with smoke curling from his pistol barrel.

"Go!" he shouted as he loaded his pistol and pushed himself up to his feet. Blood streamed down his front from his belly. "I've been cut worse than this! Go!"

I ignored him and holstered my weapon as I ran back to him.

"Ye want yer girl to get killed?" he snarled. "I told ye to go!"

I ripped a shirt off the dead man and tried to tie it around Gaunt's midsection, hoping the pressure would stanch the blood flow. The Welshman already look pale from blood loss.

Two outlaws came through the houses gunning for us while I was finishing knots in the material. Cursing, Gaunt grabbed my jacket collar and pulled me to him as he fired behind me.

One of the outlaws fell, but the other fired as fast as he could lever rounds through his rifle. Pockmarks opened on the adobe wall and crept toward us. Then the outlaw seemed to leap forward, like he'd suddenly learned how to fly, and smacked into the ground on his face.

The boom of that Sharps rifle rolled over us.

"I told ye that old man could shoot," Gaunt said. He leaned back against the adobe wall and took a ragged breath. The makeshift compress seemed to have stopped most of the blood.

Gaunt tapped me on the head with his gun barrel. "Now go on with ye. I've got all I can handle here. Ye go find Maggie. I'd like to meet her, since ever'body thinks she's worth all this trouble."

I wished him well, picked up a fallen rifle and handed it to him, then ran in the direction I'd last seen Maggie headed.

I thought I was going the right way between the houses when I found a dead outlaw in my path. I was convinced of it when I found a second and a third dead outlaw.

More gunshots rang out ahead of me and I ran faster.

A small lane led to a group of houses on a hill that sat fifty yards in back of the well. Maggie ran into what I guessed had been a barn or a stable at one time. That structure was mostly together and upright with only a few holes in the walls.

Two outlaws chased after Maggie. When she didn't turn and fire, I knew her stolen pistol was out of bullets. She was defenseless.

I ran harder, pushing myself even though my chest felt like it was on fire and my eyes were bleeding tears due to all the dust in the air. I rounded the side of the open barn entrance with the Tranter up and ready.

79

The two men heard me coming. Maggie was behind them, trapped with no place to go because that end of the barn had collapsed. They swung around with their rifles and started firing, but their bullets cut the air around me and punched through the adobe wall beside me.

I focused on them and put two rounds as quickly as I could into the center of the outlaw on the left. Before I could shoot the second man, he fired and his bullet hit me in the left shoulder and staggered me. My return shot went wild and I tried to bring the Tranter back to bear, but I knew I'd never make it.

I'd failed to save Maggie. I pointed the big .50-caliber revolver at the man and tried to hold it steady as pain screamed through my shoulder.

I saw Maggie sprint forward at the same time the outlaw did. His attention was split for just a second and I brought the Tranter to bear just as Maggie scooped the pistol from the gun belt of the man I'd just killed. Still sliding across the floor, she rolled onto her side and brought the pistol up.

I didn't know which of us fired first, but we both hit the outlaw as he was trying to shift his pistol to the new threat and run. He fell and rolled and was still.

Maggie got up and ran to me. "Charlie?" She looked at my shoulder. My arm hung limp at my side and I could barely feel my hand.

"I'm okay," I said, even though I wasn't sure if that was really the case. I reached for her with my good arm and hugged her.

She stiffened for a moment, then relaxed and hugged me back. "What are you doing here?" she asked.

"I was trying to keep you alive! I can't believe you did something so stupid!" I was hurting and mad, and I wasn't through being scared.

Gunshots still peppered the area behind us, and I knew the battle wasn't over.

"I can't believe you hit me over the head in Monah-ans!" I said. My mind wasn't working right. I should have been concentrating on staying alive, but all I could think about was how she had betrayed me and worked behind my back to almost get herself killed.

Bullets thudded into the barn wall beside me as another one struck me in the calf and knocked my leg out from under me. I went down hard, but immediately tried to get up. Maggie didn't give me time, though. She grabbed my jacket and hauled me to cover inside the barn.

More bullets punched holes through the walls and let in daylight.

"You came all this way to save me?" she demanded as she helped me to my feet.

"I came all this way to help you," I said. "We're partners, Maggie, and that has to mean something or we don't have anything. Do you understand that?"

She looked at me with cold eyes.

"Maggie," I said as I hobbled to the back of the barn where the paddocks were, "you've lost a lot. I have too. You had it bad with your ma. Your pa tried to change that."

She glared at me.

"I was trying to change it too," I said. "But I can't. I can't change it. I can't change the fact that Mister Henson wasn't always Mister Henson and that he was a bad man before he became the man I knew."

I was a little out of my head, and I hadn't talked to her

in a while, and there was all that conniving she'd done to set up her plan to bring Angelo Blunt after that gold. If I'd been in my right mind, I'd have probably realized there was a better time to have this discussion.

"Charlie, it's okay. It's going to be all right."

Together, we stumbled into one of the paddocks. The wooden railing wouldn't offer much of a defense against whoever was gunning for us, but it was all we had.

I looked at her as I reloaded the Tranter. "Did you come down here to die, Maggie?"

She looked at me for a minute then left and I thought I'd lost her again.

I could barely stand up. I knew I couldn't chase her.

Then she was back, and she carried a gun belt she had to have stripped off one of the dead outlaws in the barn with us.

"I didn't come down here to die," she told me as she reloaded her stolen pistol.

Even though she said that, I got the feeling that she was lying just a little. Either to me or to herself. But I knew it.

"I came here to kill Angelo Blunt." She strapped the gun belt on.

"You could have asked me to come with you," I said. "I would have."

"Would you have, Charlie?" she asked me. "Would you have come? Or would you have argued with me to stay?"

I didn't answer her because we both knew which of those I would have done.

"You would have tried to protect me," she said, "because that's what you do. You build things and you hope there's a better future. I just want to do what I think needs to be done."

"You left me behind," I said. "You were trying to protect me."

She growled in articulate frustration.

"Tell me you weren't trying to protect me," I challenged.

"I wasn't trying to protect you," she said.

I smiled at her. "It's too late, Maggie. I can tell when

you're lying."

She closed her eyes and leaned her head back against the paddock railing. The smell of dust and gunpowder and old manure filled the air around us.

A couple more explosions roared outside.

"Can we talk about this later?" Maggie asked.

Bullets thumped into the railings and the wall over our heads.

"Looks like we're going to have to," I said.

Peering around the corner of the paddock, my head finally clearing a little, I looked at the entrance and watched a fog of red dust roll in.

And in the middle of it, Angelo Blunt and Crying Bear led two more men into the barn. All of them had weapons in their fists.

"Charlie Stark!" Blunt yelled. "You and Miss Buchanan have become righteous thorns to me, and I mean to pluck you out!"

"You can try!" I shouted back. "But I just want you to know I've got you right where I want you!"

Blunt laughed. "You've got a mouth on you, Charlie! I'll give you that! But when it comes time, you'll be begging me to die! I just haven't decided which one of you to kill first!"

"Come on in and try!" Maggie said.

Another fusillade of bullets struck the paddock. This time some of the railings shattered. Fragments hung there, providing less and less cover.

We'd dropped down to our knees.

Angelo Blunt and his outlaws reloaded like they had all the time in the world.

Maggie started to slide out around the paddock with her pistol raised. I grabbed her arm and held her back.

"Now's our chance!" she told me.

"Wait," I said.

"Your friends aren't coming."

"We don't need them," I told her. I slipped one of the sticks of dynamite Gaunt had given me from my boot and showed it to her. It was fat and greasy and felt too light to be something so destructive. "Ten-second fuse. When I throw it, duck and cover yourself."

She nodded.

Then I took my matchbox from my jacket pocket. "When I first met you, Blunt," I said, "I was standing in a grave."

"I remember. I thought I'd left you there to stay."

Dust eddied around Angelo Blunt and his gang.

"Well, today you're standing in a grave too," I said. "And I am going to leave you there to stay."

While he was laughing and swearing at me like this was all in good fun, I lit that dynamite fuse. I counted down seconds and watched that fuse turn to ash, hoping that I had the timing right.

"Time to die," Blunt said, and he started walking toward us.

When that fuse hit the six-second mark, I wheeled around the paddock and stepped out so I could throw it with my right hand. Once it was on its way, I whipped back around the paddock wall as bullets hit the paddock again.

Peering through the railing I watched the stick of dynamite hit the straw-covered floor, bounce once, then land at Crying Bear's feet with the fuse still sparking fitfully. I hadn't been aiming for him. I'd thrown the dynamite at Blunt.

Crying Bear cursed and started to turn. The explosion hurried him on his way, spinning him through the air.

Even deafer, barely able to see through the dust and debris that was raised, I lifted that Tranter and stepped out.

Crying Bear was littered all around the barn. The other two men were dead or dying or unconscious. I didn't care which.

But that blond devil was somehow still alive. His right leg had been blown off and he was bleeding to death. I knew from all the work I'd done with Mister Henson that Blunt was a dead man. He just didn't know it yet.

He raised his pistol up to shoot and Maggie beat me to

the trigger. Her round hit Blunt in the face and punched him back onto the ground. He lay still, his one good eye left to him staring up at the collapsed barn roof.

A rider rode up to the barn entrance and came through the dust. Barlowe kept his Winchester to his shoulder as he looked around.

"You two all right?" he asked.

"We are," I said.

"Everybody dead in here that needs killin'?"

I looked at the bodies. "They're about as dead as you can make them, Mister Barlowe."

"Good." His smile looked white in his dust-covered features. "Everybody out there is dead too. Gaunt is wantin' to get at that gold in case all this gunplay draws some locals."

That surprised me. "Gaunt is still alive?" I would have sworn I was leaving a dying man."

"Gaunt is too greedy to die." Barlowe laughed. "With that gold waitin' on us in the well, he ain't gonna die anytime soon." He touched his hat. "Miss Maggie, it's a pleasure to meet you. I'm Wade Barlowe, a friend to Mister Castor and young Mister Stark there."

"It's good to meet you, Mister Barlowe."

"I'm gonna go let Morgan Castor know the two of you are still alive. He was askin'." Barlowe wheeled his mount and rode away.

Maggie and I followed, but there was a momentary pause she took that I didn't want to be there for. I knew why she did it, but I wished I hadn't seen it. There was a side to Maggie Buchanan I'd never understand completely.

EPILOGUE

We packed as much gold out of the well as we could. It was slow work because I'd been shot up and Gaunt had been knifed and shot too before it was over with. We couldn't handle any of the heavy lifting.

But Maggie and Barlowe were workhorses. They dug out a fortune, then covered what was left, and we had no idea how much was left, back over. Maybe one day we'd come back for it, and when we did, maybe it would still be there.

It didn't matter because everybody got plenty.

We stayed in Chihuahua City for a couple weeks while Gaunt and I were seen by a doctor and recovered from our wounds enough to ride. The doctor was a kind, gentle man, and he told me I was lucky with the shoulder wound because the bullet had lodged in the socket and he'd had to take it out. He told me I would have to work at it to get full use of the arm back and that it would take time.

Gaunt took longer to heal up, but when he was finally able to sit a horse, we headed north.

Fourteen days later, made slow by the gold, and by me and Gaunt feeling a little poorly, we crossed over into Texas and reached El Paso. It was good to see the Rio Grande behind us.

We said our goodbyes to Gaunt and Barlowe in El Paso, promising to see each other again to reminisce about our adventures. They also said they wanted to see the Henson Building after I'd finished it. I'd talked about it a lot and they were curious how Stark and Buchanan Bail Bonds was going to work out.

In Pecos, we put our gold in the bank and headed over to the marshal's office with the burlap bag Maggie had carried with her the whole way.

When we got to the marshal's office, Maggie carried the bag inside and set it on the desk. It stank something awful, and it was still seeping some, but I thought that was from putrefaction, not blood.

"My god," Stephens said, backing away from his desk. "What do you have in there?"

"The bounty's good dead or alive," Maggie said, "and Charlie and I are here to collect." She cut the tie holding the bag closed and burlap fell to reveal that blond devil's head she'd packed in salt to preserve.

Stephens threw up. Aikin stepped into the marshal's office and saw everything. He threw up too, but he got all the details he needed to run a special edition for the town.

***

That evening, after we were bathed and cleaner than we'd been in days, me and Maggie sat in our kitchen, at the table I'd made, and we ate takeout from Trail's End that Missus Griffin had insisted we take on the house because we'd caught and killed Angelo Blunt.

I talked about what I was going to start working on to get the first floor ready. Judge Caldwell had sent a wire asking if the courthouse was almost ready while we were gone. Maggie was going to apprise him of the situation first thing in the morning.

I talked and Maggie listened, and the sun went down. I was happy to do that every day, but I knew Maggie wouldn't be. She was driven by her demons and I knew I'd follow her wherever she took us.

That was what partners did.

IF YOU LIKED THIS, CHECK OUT THE JACK LANDERS WESTERN MYSTERY SERIES BY G. WAYNE TILMAN

INTRODUCING MODERN LAWMAN JACK LANDERS IN THIS FOUR-BOOK BOXSET!

Special Agent Jack Landers is a young Oklahoma state investigator and a Western lawman who would rather have been chasing down the Doolin-Dalton Gang in Indian Territory in the 1890's. The thirty-five-year-old lawman has several gunfights under his belt and the scars to show for it. He has dealt with tough cases and tougher crooks with no problems.

When multiple murders occur he finds himself heading a serial sex murderer task force that is statewide. Jack is divided between enforcing the law and vengeance, and things spin beyond his control—almost.
Jack has to decide between right and wrong in order to determine what to do about it…

AVILABLE NOW ON AMAZON

About the Author

Mel Odom grew up in rural Oklahoma where his family raised pigs, chickens, goats, and ducks. But he discovered a big book of Greek myths when he was in third grade that called him to fiction of all kinds: The Hardy Boys, Nancy Drew, Robert Heinlein, Andrew Norton, Doc Savage, the Shadow, Edgar Rice Burroughs, and many, many others. He dreamed of becoming a writer and one day succeeded. He's written in the fields of fantasy, science fiction, men's action adventure, suspense, mystery, romance, horror, and started writing Western novels ten years ago as an indie writer.

After blazing the trail with the Rancho Diablo books under the name Colby Jackson, Mel Odom partnered with the Wolfpack Publishing brand and helped create the GUNSLINGER series under the A.W. Hart house name.

Find more great titles by Mel Odom and Wolfpack Publishing, here: https://wolfpackpublishing.com/mel-odom/